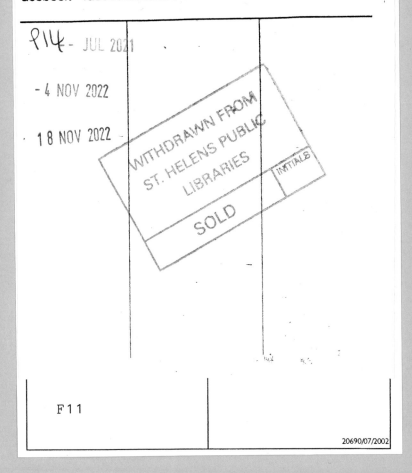

A WISE CHILD

Born at the turn of the century near the Liverpool docks, Nellie Williams endures the drudgery and ill treatment of her mother. She escapes into domestic service, but when her employer dies she is taken in and raped by Joshua Leadbetter, JP.

Nellie quickly arranges a marriage between herself and Sam Meadows and when a son is born eight months later there is doubt about his parentage. False friends fan these flames until one night after a prolonged drinking bout Sam sails for America and jumps ship.

Believing herself a widow Nellie works hard to support herself and her son. Too late she and Sam realise the depth of their love and the desperation of their plight.

A WISE CHILD

A WISE CHILD

by

Elizabeth Murphy

Magna Large Print Books
Long Preston, North Yorkshire,
England.

British Library Cataloguing in Publication Data.

Murphy, Elizabeth
A wise child.

A catalogue record for this book is
available from the British Library

ISBN 0-7505-0859-0

First published in Great Britain by Headline Book Publishing 1994

Copyright © 1994 by Elizabeth Murphy

Cover illustration by arrangement with Hodder Headline PLC.

The right of Elizabeth Murphy to be identified as the author
of this work has been asserted by her in accordance with the
Copyright, Designs and Patents Act, 1988.

Published in Large Print February, 1996 by arrangement with
Headline Book Publishing & the copyright holder.

Magna Large Print is an imprint of
Library Magna Books Ltd.
Printed and bound in Great Britain by
T.J. Press (Padstow) Ltd., Cornwall, PL28 8RW.

For Ted and all our family, with love.

ACKNOWLEDGEMENTS

I would like to thank the numerous people who have given me help and encouragement over the years, particularly Margaret Thomson Davis, Dianne Doubtfire and Mary Johnson in my early years of writing. Members of Crosby Writers' Club, and, for this book especially, Don Higham for help with seafaring research. The staff of Crosby and Bootle Libraries and, as always, my husband and all my family. My sincere thanks to all.

CHAPTER 1

Fog horns boomed eerily from the ships in the River Mersey and the November fog swirled around the tiny terraced houses close to the Liverpool docks. In the bedroom of the end house of a terrace a girl lying on the bed suddenly cried out, and an old woman turned up the wick of the oil lamp.

The light fell on the girl's white face and large terrified eyes and when the old woman bent over her she gasped, 'Oh Janey, I'm so frightened.'

'No need. It won't be long now,' Janey said, and the girl began, 'I don't mean—' but she was interrupted by the pain. She closed her eyes and clenched her teeth, pulling hard on the roller towel tied to the bedrail at the foot of the bed.

When the pain receded she opened her eyes and whispered timidly, 'I mean—it coming early. If only I was sure it was Sam's baby.'

The old woman shrugged. 'Won't make no difference, Nellie. Could be Sam's early or Leadbetter's late but who's to know? Sam hasn't got no mother or sisters to be counting up the months for him, and the other fellow doesn't know nothing about it.'

'I wish—I wish I'd told Sam about Mr Leadbetter,' Nellie murmured, and Janey said sharply, 'Now don't start that again. Keep your mouth shut, and don't spoil all I done for you.'

'I know, Janey,' Nellie said weakly. 'It *must* be Sam's though, mustn't it? It's nearly ten months since—since Mr Leadbetter did that to me.'

'Aye and only eight months since you was married to Sam,' Janey said grimly. 'And don't you forget it was me fixed that for you. You'd've been in Queer Street without me, with your ma dead and your da jumped ship in America. No bloody money coming and the state you was in an' now you're whingeing wanting open your bloody mouth to Sam. I should'a let you get took to Ann Fowler's Home for Fallen Women.'

Nellie had turned her head on the pillow, tears trickling from her eyes as the old woman ranted at her. She's talking as though she thinks the baby's Leadbetter's, Nellie thought, but she felt too weak to argue with the old woman.

The pain came again and again and with each bout she grew weaker, yet the birth seemed as far off as ever. Suddenly there was a clatter of boots on the stairs and when Janey opened the bedroom door a young boy said breathlessly, 'Mrs Nolan told me to go for the nurse and she said she'd be here in a minute. Is our Nellie all right?'

'Yes. Maggie Nolan wants to mind her own business,' Janey snapped. 'Sadie McCann can't tell me nothing for all she calls herself a midwife. Have you seen Sam?'

'He's in the Volunteer with Charlie West and some mates off an *Elder Dempster* just docked.

14

He told me to tell him when it's been born and he can come home,' the boy said. Janey thrust her face close to his. 'Don't you go for him until I tell you. D'you hear me now, Bobby?'

'All right,' Bobby muttered, trying to peer past her to see his sister, but she shut the door firmly and went back to the bed.

'Bobby says Sam's in the Volley with some mates. I'll make sure he's too fuddled to do any counting before I send for him,' she sniggered.

Nellie said nothing. She seemed to have drifted too far even to hear Janey, but the next moment there was a commotion downstairs, and a buxom midwife bounced upstairs and into the bedroom.

She seemed to take in the situation at a glance and her face grew red with anger as she examined the exhausted girl. 'Why wasn't I sent for before this?' she demanded, as she stood with one hand on Nellie's swollen stomach and the other on her pulse.

She turned away from the bed to whisper angrily to Janey, 'She's very weak. How long has she been in labour?'

'A while off and on,' Janey said evasively. 'She's so little and thin, and she hasn't been able to keep nothing down for months, that's the trouble.'

'There's something wrong,' the midwife said. 'I might have to get the doctor.' She turned back to the bed as another contraction convulsed the girl's body, and gently wiped her face. 'It's all right, Nellie love,' she soothed her. 'Don't worry. I'll look after you.'

15

Mention of the doctor seemed to have alarmed Janey and she began to sidle towards the door.

'Where are *you* going?' the midwife asked sharply.

'She doesn't need me now you're here. It's got nothing to do with me. I'm only the lodger,' Janey muttered.

'Stay where you are,' the nurse snapped. 'The doctor might want to talk to you.'

Nellie moaned weakly as another contraction began, and the midwife said in a different tone, 'Come on now, love. Don't fight the pain, Nellie. Go with it. It's a big one. *Now,* Nellie, *now,* love. Push hard, bear down *hard,* love.'

Nellie tried to obey, and as she cried out the baby's head appeared. The umbilical cord which should have been his lifeline was around his tiny neck, huge and engorged, throttling him as he was thrust into the world.

The midwife slipped her finger beneath it and with an expert flick jerked it over his head. The child emerged blue and apparently lifeless, but the midwife's care was chiefly for the mother. Janey lifted the tiny body and placed him on the cold top of the rickety washstand, pushing aside the basin and ewer, as the nurse worked swiftly with Nellie.

The midwife glanced round at the child then said urgently to Janey, 'Here, you finish clearing up,' and going to the door she yelled, 'Bobby, bring me hot water in the panmug, quick.' Swiftly she poured cold water from the ewer into the basin, then plunged the baby's body into it.

The boy stumbled upstairs with the panmug, steam rising from it, and the nurse indicated the space beside the bowl. She tested the hot water with her elbow then plunged the child's body into it then back into the cold water. Over and over again she repeated the process, only pausing at intervals to smack the tiny body.

'Don't, don't,' Nellie whimpered, but the old woman watched silently. The nurse seemed to be tiring, her movements becoming slower, then she held the child up by his heels and gave him a last hard despairing smack.

A thin reedy cry broke from the little boy and Janey exclaimed, 'Bloody hell, it's alive!'

Nellie held out her arms eagerly, but the midwife slapped the child again then laid him down on the bed and rubbed strongly at his body.

Only when the child's breathing had become regular and some pink colour had crept into his skin did she wrap him in a blanket and place him in his mother's arms.

'Isn't he lovely,' Nellie said, a smile on her tired face as she cuddled her son. She looked up at the midwife. 'Thanks, Nurse. Thanks very much,' she said fervently.

A pleased smile spread over the midwife's face as she pulled down her sleeves and buttoned her cuffs. 'Well, sometimes it works and sometimes it doesn't,' she said. 'He should be all right now, but he must be kept warm.'

A drawer had been made ready as a makeshift cradle and the midwife took the baby from Nellie. 'I'll put him in this while I have another look at you and make you comfortable,' she said, 'but then you'd better keep him in bed with you. He needs the warmth of your body.'

Janey was grumbling to herself as she pottered about collecting the soiled bedding. The nurse winked at Nellie but only said, 'Another boy! My word, 1920 has been the year for boys. I've hardly delivered any girls. Dr Wilson says it's to make up for all the lads killed on the Western Front.'

'Their poor mothers,' Nellie whispered.

'Yes, you feel for them when you've got one of your own,' the nurse agreed. She had finished examining and making Nellie comfortable and she washed her hands then lifted the baby back into the bed.

'Keep him close to you but be careful you don't overlay him,' she said. Nellie kissed the baby and the nurse said gently, 'Don't be thinking about the soldiers now. That's something you won't have to face with your lad, Nellie. That was the war to end wars.'

Nellie tried to smile, but her eyes were closed and the nurse looked at her with concern. The girl's lips were almost bloodless and there were purple shadows beneath her eyes.

The midwife tucked the bedclothes around the mother and son and said quietly, 'Don't try to feed him yet, Nellie. Just rest. I'll come back later.'

She picked up her bag and went downstairs where she met Bobby, who said eagerly, 'I heard it cry. Will it be all right now? Will our Nellie be all right?'

'Yes, as long as she's kept warm. Take the oven shelf up for the bed, Bobby, and put a brick to warm in the oven for later on. Sam's home from sea, isn't he?'

'Aye, paralytic drunk somewhere,' Janey grumbled. 'I don't know whether you done her a good turn or the child either. God knows what's in front of it.'

'It'll take its chance same as the rest of us,' the midwife said calmly. 'She'll make a good mother and Sam Meadows is a decent fellow.'

'When he's sober,' Janey said. 'But he's different in drink. Always ready for a fight.'

'That was before he married our Nellie,' Bobby said indignantly. 'When he didn't have no proper home like. He's only at the Volley now to be out of the way till the baby got born.'

'Yes, he's had a hard life and so has Nellie for that matter,' the nurse said. 'See she rests now and keep her warm. I'll be back later.'

Nellie could hear their voices clearly through the thin floorboards as she lay cuddling the baby in her arms. Thoughts of the past and the future were like a dark background to her joy in the baby as she kissed the dark down on his head and the tiny hand which lay like a starfish on her breast.

She loosened the blanket and examined him closely, hoping to see something which would clearly identify the baby as Sam's child, but she could see nothing. Surely he must be Sam's son, she thought. Surely such a lovely child could not have come from that awful attack by Leadbetter.

19

Her tears began to flow again and she turned her head restlessly on the pillow, but exhaustion overcame her and she drifted off to sleep.

She was awakened by Janey carrying a bowl of gruel.

'She's been back, bossy bitch,' she said sourly. 'Said she wouldn't wake you. You needed the rest but I'm not leaving you no longer. If you snuffed it she'd be the first to blame me for leaving you and anyhow you'll be full o' wind when you come to feed him.'

'Thanks, Janey,' Nellie said, laying the baby carefully on the pillow and taking the bowl of gruel. 'Did the nurse say I should feed him?' she said timidly.

'Get that down you first,' Janey said. 'She was carrying on about the room being cold and she's sent that oil stove.'

'Isn't she good?' Nellie exclaimed but Janey said again, 'Bossy bitch. Made up with herself.'

'But Janey, she saved his life,' Nellie protested. She drew back the blanket from the baby's face. 'Do you think he looks like Sam, Janey? He's got dark hair like him anyway.'

'That'll all rub off,' Janey said. 'He doesn't look like Sam to me. What was Leadbetter like?'

'I can't remember his face. He had a beard anyway and a big stomach with a gold chain across it.' Nellie shivered at the memory and began to weep. 'It can't be his, Janey, such a lovely baby. He *must* be Sam's. I know it's only eight months since we were married but the baby's very small. He must have come early, mustn't he?'

Janey turned away. 'Don't be too sure,' she said spitefully. 'Nine months and three weeks I make it since you come falling in here crying and whingeing about what Leadbetter done to you, and streaming with blood.'

'I don't remember much about that time,' Nellie wept.

'Well, you passed out and you took real bad,' Janey said. 'I looked after you and I done more. I got you married off to Sam quick in case you had a bun in the oven. And now you want to upset the apple cart, opening your bloody mouth to Sam when there's no need.'

Nellie wept even more bitterly. 'Has Bobby gone for Sam?' she whispered.

Janey said roughly, 'No and he's not going until I tell him. You never know. Sam might have got something said to him and he'll batter you when he gets back.'

Nellie made a sound of protest and Janey picked up the gruel bowl. 'Don't feed him now,' she said. 'Leave him asleep and you go to sleep too.'

She went downstairs and Nellie lay weeping quietly. Although she still felt exhausted sleep evaded her and her mind ranged back over the past year. In spite of her efforts to blot it out she returned to the time before her marriage to Sam when she was in service with Joshua Leadbetter JP and his wife.

Mrs Leadbetter and her children were on an extended New Year visit to relatives, and the young maid who shared Nellie's attic bedroom had been called home to a sick mother.

Nellie recalled the strangeness of going to bed alone, and then her terror on awakening to find Joshua Leadbetter standing beside her in his nightshirt, one hand clamped over her mouth and the other tearing at her nightdress.

She moaned quietly as she remembered the pain and humiliation of his attack on her, and the ferocity of his threats of gaol or worse for her if she ever complained about him.

He had finally left her, bruised and bleeding, and somehow she had managed to dress and creep out of the house. The rest was a blur until she reached this house. Her mother was recently dead and her father at sea, but Janey and Bob were still in the house and Janey had taken charge when Nellie arrived home and collapsed.

Now as she looked back on that time it all seemed like a bad dream. The days and nights of fever, the nightmares in which she had seen Leadbetter in every shadow, her longing for death. Janey had been kind, laying wet cloths on her head and giving her a concoction which brought oblivion for hours.

When she began to recover Janey had brought Sam to see her, telling her that Sam wanted to marry her. Nellie remembered him standing before her, big and awkward, twisting his cap in his hands, and saying gruffly, 'I'll look after you, Ellie.' That had been his pet name for her when they were children.

I should have told Sam about Leadbetter then, she thought, but I was too ashamed and too frightened, and I was glad to obey Janey when she told me to say nothing. I was like a sleepwalker drifting along as though everything was happening at a distance from me.

Even her wedding. She remembered nothing of it but being in a dark office and someone saying, 'Make your mark here, or can you write your name?'

Nellie thought she must have fainted because she knew nothing more until she was on the sofa in this house. She remembered that she had come out of her trancelike state enough to feel terror on her wedding night when Sam slipped into bed beside her.

Sam's lovemaking, though, had been totally different to Leadbetter's brutal assault. For such a big, clumsy man he had been surprisingly gentle and tender, soothing and coaxing her until she had timidly responded to him. 'There now, girl, that wasn't too bad, was it?' he had said when it was all over and she clung to him, weeping with relief.

Janey had questioned her next morning, wanting to know whether Sam had said anything about not being first and when she had mumbled an embarrassed denial Janey said with satisfaction, 'That was my doing. You wouldn't have healed so quick only for the way I seen to you.'

Sam had already signed on for another ship and he sailed two days later. Soon after that the vomiting began, Nellie recalled, but I was so green I didn't even know I was pregnant until Janey told me. I was so happy, too, she thought wistfully, thinking Sam would be pleased, until Janey began saying that the baby might be Leadbetter's. 'First come first served,' she had cackled.

Nellie began to weep again. What was wrong with Janey? She could be so kind, she thought, looking after me and she often saved me from a beating from Ma when I was little, but then she can be just the opposite. I can't trust her and I'm afraid of her.

Her tears falling on the baby's head woke him and he cried weakly. Nellie tried to breastfeed him then they both slept again.

She was roused by a tap on the bedroom door and Bobby whispering, 'Can I come in, Nell?' He crept over to the bed. 'Janey's been at the gin again,' he said. 'She's asleep now. Should I go for Sam?'

'Yes, quick before she wakes up,' Nellie whispered, but Bobby lingered.

'Can I see the baby?' he asked, and Nellie drew back the bedclothes to show him the child.

'Do you think he's like Sam, Bob?' she asked anxiously.

'I dunno, he's so little and Sam's so big,' Bobby said. 'His hair's like Sam's though. Black and curly. At least he's not ginger like me.'

'Janey says his hair'll rub off,' Nellie said. 'Do you think his face is like Sam's?'

The boy studied the tiny wrinkled red face. 'It's hard to tell. I think he might be like you when he smooths out, like,' he said.

'You'd better go before she wakes up,' Nellie whispered.

Bob was turning to go when they heard unsteady footsteps approaching the house, and the next moment Sam stumbled up the narrow stairs, followed by Janey.

He was a tall broad-shouldered man who seemed to fill the tiny room as he stood swaying beside the bed.

'It's a boy, Sam,' Bobby said excitedly, but Janey pushed the boy towards the door. Nellie lifted out the baby for her husband to see but he seemed to have difficulty in focusing. His face was red and his dark hair tousled as he stood like a bull in a bullring facing his tormentors, turning his head from side to side.

'Soft Sam, Soft Sam, that's what they called me, Soft Sam.'

Janey was grimacing at Nellie and shaking her head, then she pulled at Sam's arm. 'You don't want to take no notice to them lot,' she said.

Sam pulled his arm away and shouted, 'Gerrout, gerrout.'

The old woman scuttled away, and Sam rubbed his hand over his face, blinking as he tried to focus his eyes and saying, 'Ellie, Ellie,' in a bewildered voice. Nellie lay looking at him, wide eyed, too shocked by his words to speak, but Bobby had come back into the room.

Nellie was still holding the baby on top of the bedclothes, but Bobby put him back beneath them and tucked the bedclothes round Nellie.

'You've got to keep warm, Nell,' he said, then turning to Sam he said with authority, 'Come on, Sam, you're dossing with me tonight.'

Sam allowed himself to be led into the other

25

bedroom and within minutes Bobby came and said that he was asleep. Nellie still felt too stunned to speak. Why had the men in the Volley taunted Sam about the baby? Those sort of men never counted months or bothered with women's gossip, and anyway no one knew why she had come home from her last place.

Charlie West, she thought suddenly, he might talk like that but who had put the idea in his head? Again she thought of Janey. There was a side door to Janey's room which gave on to a back entry, used by Janey's moneylending clients. Charlie West, a bachelor now working ashore, was very thick with Janey and often slipped in and out of the door.

But why would Janey say anything about the situation to Charlie West? She had seemed to be trying to convince Sam that the baby was his. Confused and troubled though Nellie felt by all this, of one thing she was certain. From the moment that the nurse had placed the baby in her arms she had been sure that he was Sam's child, even though she could find no physical proof to show Janey.

Janey. I don't understand her and I'm afraid of her, she thought, but then so were most people. Not just because she was a moneylender but because she often boasted that she could cause trouble for people if she 'opened her mouth'.

And now I'm one of them with a secret for her to hold over me, but I'm not going to let it happen, Nellie vowed. Her anger because Sam had been hurt gave her courage and she decided that she would tell Sam about Leadbetter as soon as she saw him.

I've always been a coward, she thought. Afraid of Ma, of Janey, of the school board man and the other children in the street, but I've never been afraid of Sam. I've always felt safe with him. Even when he was a tough young boy, living rough and able to hold his own with street Arabs, he had been kind and gentle with her, and saved her from being hurt.

The short time she had been able to spend with him as a man had proved to her that he had not changed and that this was the true Sam. And now through me Sam's the one to be hurt, she thought, but if he knows about Leadbetter and the baby coming early he'll have an answer if anyone skits him. The nurse will back me up about the baby too. I'll ask her tomorrow, and without fail I'll tell Sam about Leadbetter too, so neither of us will have to worry about Janey or anyone else. Comforted by her decision she snuggled down with the baby and fell asleep.

Weak cries from the baby woke her some hours later. He seemed hungry and when she put him to her breast he tugged eagerly at her nipple. Nellie stiffened and curled her toes in pain, until the baby sucked in a steady rhythm, but she was relieved to see such strength in the fragile little body.

She slept again and when she woke Janey had come upstairs with a bowl of gruel.

'What about the quare feller last night, then,' she cackled. 'Wonder what he got said to him?' Nellie said nothing and Janey went on, 'He had a proper skinful. Fell out of the bed, Bobby said, and finished the night on the floor.'

Nellie still said nothing, only looked at her, and the old woman turned away.

'I'll send Bobby up with tea,' she muttered. 'I've gotta get out with me fish.'

She never even looked at the baby or asked how he was, Nellie thought, but when Bobby came up with the tea he asked if he could hold the baby.

'I helped to save him, didn't I?' he said proudly. 'Bringing the hot water up.'

'Yes. Is Sam awake?' Nellie asked anxiously. 'Janey said he was on the floor last night.'

'Yes, fell outa bed, but he's all right now. He's just put his head under the tap.'

Before he could say any more a loud knocking announced the arrival of the midwife.

'You look better this morning,' she said immediately. 'How has he been?'

Nellie eagerly told her of the strength the baby had shown when sucking and the nurse nodded approvingly.

'He'll do,' she said. 'He's perfectly formed for all he's so small. About five pounds, I'd say, but I've known smaller than him survive. But make sure you eat as much as you can so there's something there for him.'

Bobby brought up hot water and the nurse swiftly washed and changed the baby, and helped Nellie to do the same, and as she worked she talked.

'Maggie Nolan from next door is doing your washing and seeing to you during the day, isn't she? The less that dirty old faggot from downstairs has to do with you the better. I didn't want her to touch you yesterday but I had to try to save the baby.'

'I'm glad you did, Nurse,' Nellie said timidly. She took a deep breath ready to ask the nurse about the baby's early arrival, but the woman was saying urgently, 'Now listen, Nellie. Your ma was very thick with old Janey, but she's gone now and you should get rid of Janey as soon as you can.'

'But she's looked after me all these months and looked after Bobby since Ma died,' Nellie protested.

'For her own reasons, I'll bet,' the nurse said grimly. 'I'll have to go now. Remember, eat as much as you can and keep him warm—and think about what I've said about the old woman. Keep clear of her and her tricks.'

She was away, calling, 'See you tomorrow,' before Nellie had a chance to ask her about the baby, and with a slight feeling of relief she decided her questions could wait for another day.

A few minutes later Sam came upstairs and stood rather sheepishly beside the bed. He had evidently shaved and held his head under the tap as Bobby had said. His dark hair was sleeked flat but escaped into tight curls as it dried.

'You all right, Ellie?' he asked and Nellie nodded and took the baby from beneath the clothes.

'Do you want to hold him, Sam?' she asked but he backed away in alarm.

'Strewth, no, I might drop him,' he said, but when Nellie turned back the child's clothes to show Sam his feet he came close to the bed again.

'He's like a doll,' he gasped. 'Bobby told me the way the nurse brought him round, like.'

'She was awful clever the way she done it, Sam,' Nellie said. 'Dowsing him in cold water then in hot and then clouting him. I thought she might hurt him but it done the trick. I couldn't believe it when he cried out.'

'Mrs Nolan told me the old girl should've sent for her sooner,' Sam said. He bent and clumsily kissed Nellie. 'I'm sorry you had a bad time, girl,' he said but Nellie smiled happily.

'I don't care, Sam,' she said, 'as long as the baby's all right.'

Sam gently touched the baby's face with his calloused finger. 'What did the nurse say today?' he asked.

'She just said I've got to keep him warm and I've got to eat as much as I can for when I feed him.'

She blushed as she spoke but Sam only said, 'Maggie Nolan can get what you fancy, like. I've give her a few bob.'

He seemed to have forgotten the men's taunts of the previous night and Nellie devoutly hoped that he had been too drunk to register what they said, but she only said, 'Maggie hasn't seen the baby yet.'

'It was her day for the Board of Guardians,' Sam said. 'She'll be in soon.' He stretched and yawned. 'I've got to get down to the ship.'

30

'I wish you wasn't sailing so soon,' Nellie said wistfully.

'So do I, girl,' Sam said, 'but I had to sign on for the advance note. I was skint. Anyhow, I've paid the nurse and seen Maggie.'

'And left me all right too,' Nellie said. 'Have you got enough left?'

'Aye, I'm all right,' Sam said.

Nellie felt relaxed and happy chatting so easily with Sam and she began to wonder whether this was the right time to tell him about Leadbetter's attack on her. He seemed to have forgotten his doubts of the previous night, but what if talk of Leadbetter revived them?

There was another consideration too. She remembered that Janey had said that if Sam was told he might go and beat Leadbetter and find himself in trouble. Before she could decide Sam had patted her cheek and gone to the door.

'You'll be all right, girl. Maggie'll be in soon,' he said.

He went out whistling and Nellie snuggled down under the bedclothes again with the baby, not sure whether she was glad or sorry that the opportunity had passed.

Janey was out with her fish and Bobby at school but a little later the eldest child from next door, nine-year-old Susan came in. 'Me mam's still at the Guardians,' she said. 'But she told me I'd got to come in and do your dinner if she wasn't back.'

'Will you make some tea, please?' Nellie said. 'A cup for yourself as well and some jam butties for both of us.'

'Me mam might shout,' Susan said, but she was easily persuaded to eat with Nellie.

Afterwards Nellie fed the baby again then slept until she was wakened by Sam arriving home. Although his eyes seemed bloodshot he was not drunk, but his mood seemed to have changed again.

'I'm off, Ellie,' he said gruffly. 'We're off on the morning tide so I'm going aboard. I only come home for me bag.'

'Will it be a six-month trip, Sam?' Nellie said timidly. He nodded, and Nellie lifted the baby from beneath the bedclothes. 'He'll have to be christened, Sam,' she said nervously. 'What shall I call him?'

Sam raised his head and looked at her, his brown eyes like those of a beaten dog. 'Whatever you like,' he said, 'you know best about that.'

A wave of colour rushed over Nellie's face and her glance fell, but before she could speak Sam said, 'I'll have to go, Buck Madden's waiting for me. Ta-ra, then.'

He turned away and went downstairs without looking at the baby or kissing Nellie, but she jumped out of bed and called beseechingly, 'Sam, Sam.'

He came back upstairs. 'Get back into bed, girl,' he said, 'you'll catch your death.'

Desperation made her brave and she slipped her arms round his neck and reached up to kiss him.

Sam kissed her briefly, then lifted her and put her into the bed. 'Oh, God, Ellie,' he groaned, then turned away and went heavily downstairs.

Nellie took the baby in her arms and wept bitterly. If only she had told Sam the truth. Now something had happened or someone had said something which made him doubt her again, and she had lost the chance of telling him what had really happened.

I swear I'll tell him as soon as he comes home, she thought. But that was six months away and meanwhile poor Sam would have all these months with his joy in his wife and child clouded by the doubts that had been planted in his mind.

With a sudden surge of protective love, Nellie held her baby close. *He* is what matters now, she thought. I must do whatever is best for him. Nothing must hurt or harm him no matter what happens with Sam and myself. Only the baby is important. And I'm determined he'll have a better life than what me and Sam have had, she thought, kissing the child's soft cheek.

CHAPTER 2

Through the thin walls of the bedroom Nellie could hear her nextdoor neighbour, Johnny Nolan, coughing continuously but it was some time before his wife arrived. She rushed in eventually, a thin haggard woman with her face and shawl wet with the fog which still drifted about the streets.

'I'm sorry, Nell. Are you all right, girl? I've

been stuck in that place for hours. A big line of us waiting, then when I got in to the Board they wanted to know the ins and outs of Muldoon's Cat. Trying to trip me up so they can take a bit of Relief off me. Was you all right?'

'Yes, thanks, Mrs Nolan,' Nellie said shyly. 'Your Susan done me tea and jam butties.'

'And ate some herself,' Maggie Nolan said. 'I give her down the banks for taking your food after your fella's been so good to us.'

'I made her take it, honest, Mrs Nolan,' Nellie said. 'She done me a lovely cup of tea.'

'You'll have to call me Maggie if I'm going to be in and out,' Maggie said. She unwrapped the cloth she carried. 'I've brought you a soft-boiled egg beat up in a cup. Would you like a butty and a cup of tea with it?'

'Yes please—er, Maggie,' Nellie said blushing. 'Will you do enough for both of us?'

Maggie went downstairs chuckling. 'After me telling our Susan off,' she said. 'And now I'm doing the same.'

'You want to eat as much as you can, girl,' she said when she returned with the bread and butter and tea. 'A long labour's weakening and you want to keep him on the breast as long as you can. You don't want to fall too quickly for another one.'

Nellie blushed. 'Sam'll be away for six months,' she said.

She sounded sad and Maggie said cheerfully, 'He'll come home to a fine little lad then. These little babies are fighters and you can see them come on better than big fat ones.'

34

'Nurse said she's seen smaller than him survive. She said he's about five pounds,' Nellie said eagerly.

'There you are then, and she's a clever woman. She knows what she's talking about,' Maggie said. 'The old girl should have sent for her sooner. Old faggot. She could have been the death of the two of you.'

'Nurse saved the baby,' Nellie said.

'Aye, so I heard. And now you've got to get yourself strong. Sam left money with me for treats for you, to get you to eat,' Maggie said.

'I'm fine now that the baby's born,' Nellie said. 'Before that I was sick all day and every day. Couldn't keep nothing down.'

'I never seen you after you come home sick from your place,' Maggie said. 'Janey wouldn't let no one near you. I used to worry about you because I know what she is but I couldn't do nothing. I don't know how you stand her, Nell.'

'She looked after me. She was good, like,' Nellie said diffidently.

Maggie shrugged. 'I suppose no one's all bad but you wanna be careful, Nell. She'd buy and sell us before we got up in the morning. Crafty as a cartload of monkeys.'

'Nurse said I should ask her to shift,' Nellie said. 'But how can I? She came here with Ma from the Dingle when I was born and she stayed here with Bobby after Ma died and then looked after me when I was sick.'

'Only because it suited her,' Maggie said. 'That side door's handy for her moneylending,

35

and for other things too. People can slide in and out and no one any the wiser. And she had your dad's money when she looked after Bobby, and Sam's once you was married after your dad backed off his ship and his money stopped. You don't owe her nothing, Nell,' Maggie stood up. 'My mam used to say me tongue was tied in the middle and I think she was right,' she said. 'I'll leave you to get some sleep.'

She went but her words had given Nellie too much to think about for sleep to come to her. Was that the reason Janey had arranged her marriage to Sam? Because her father's pay had stopped when he deserted his ship and she wanted Sam's steady wage to replace it and keep the house going?

It seemed quite possible to Nellie and for the first time she began to wonder how Janey had persuaded Sam to marry her. I don't know why I didn't think of it before, she thought, but I was just like I was doped and doing everything she told me. But how did she fix it with Sam? I'll have to ask her.

When Janey arrived Nellie said quickly, before her courage failed, 'Janey, how did you get Sam to marry me? What did you tell him?'

Janey sniggered. 'I didn't tell him nothing about the other fella, you can bet your boots. Them fellas in the Volley were right calling him Soft Sam. He swallered everything I told him. I knew he'd come ashore and he'd be drinking in the Volley so I collared him when he'd had a few.' She sniggered again and Nellie persisted.

'But what did you tell him, Janey?' She

could smell gin on the old woman's breath and thought it might loosen Janey's tongue.

'I told him you got sent home from your place without a character because you got blamed for what another girl done. I said you'd took ill and there wasn't no money because your da had backed out in America. By the time I finished with him he thought it was his own idea to marry you.' She cackled then suddenly suspicious she thrust her face close to Nellie's. 'Wharra you asking all these questions for?' she demanded.

'I was—was just wondering,' Nellie faltered.

'Aye, good job I done it, whether you had a bun in the oven or not,' Janey muttered. 'You wouldn't have got nothing off the other fella.'

She stumped out of the room and Nellie lay thinking of what she had said. At least she answered *some* of the things I want to know, she thought, and she told me more than she realised.

Tears filled Nellie's eyes. Poor Sam. Janey had taken advantage of his good nature to trick him into marriage, she thought, and just for the sake of money. I'll make him a good wife though, she vowed, and make him glad he married me. A shadow came over her as she thought, if only I can convince him about the baby and have everything straight between us.

Maggie came in the next morning as soon as Janey had left with her fish, and Bobby for school. She brought a small bowl of broth. 'Get this down you, girl,' she said. 'It'll do you more good than gruel.'

'It smells good,' Nellie said.

'It's out of the money what Sam gave me for us,' Maggie said. 'But it didn't cost nothing hardly. I got twopenn'orth of bits from the butcher's and some barley and the kids got carrots and onions and that from the market. The stuff what gets thrown away, but when you cut the bad off there's plenty left. I made a big panful of barley broth and you should have seen them muck in.'

'Sam left me money off his advance note,' Nellie said. 'You shouldn't be bringing me your stuff.'

She thought that Johnny needed it more than she did, but she said nothing lest she offended her neighbour. She could see Maggie's pleasure in being able to give.

'I've still got the money he left me for you,' Maggie said. 'I'll get you some treat after. You've got a proper good fella, Nell.'

'I know,' Nellie said smiling.

'My kids were made up when he come to live here,' Maggie said. 'He always used to give them pennies when he seen them near the Volley whenever he was ashore.'

'Sam knows what it's like to be hungry,' Nellie said. 'When I first met him when we was kids he didn't have no home and he was living rough, like. His dad threw him out when he was only seven and he sold papers and that to live.'

'It's a wonder one of the neighbours never took him in,' Maggie said.

'He said he thought the neighbours fancied

38

there was a curse on the family. Every child after him died soon after it was born. When I met him his mam was dead. I don't know what happened to his dad. He used to be a steward on the Cunard line.'

'They must have been well off then,' Maggie said.

Nellie smiled reminiscently. 'The first time I met Sam I was carrying a bundle of washing home from the Unicorn. Some lads snatched it off me and they was throwing it to each other. I was crying. I was terrified like it would get muddy because it'd been raining. Me ma would've killed me.'

'No wonder you was frightened,' Maggie said. 'Grown men was frightened of your ma.'

Nellie nodded. 'Sam come running up. He was barefoot and ragged but he was a big lad even then and he soon got the bundle back and chased the lads. He was awful good to me. Wiped me eyes on me pinny and carried the washing till I was nearly home.'

'The only time I ever seen you was with them bundles,' Maggie said. 'Very near as big as yourself. You never played out or went to school much, did you?'

'No, me ma kept me in drudging for her,' Nellie said.

'How old was you then when Sam helped you?' Maggie asked.

'I was nine and Sam was eleven. After that he often carried the bundles for me. Sometimes the maids in the Unicorn or other places would give me a butty or a piece of cake and me and

Sam shared it. One time a milkman gave me tuppence to take a message to a maid and we got two ha'penny fish and a ha'p'orth of chips and two barmcakes.' She laughed at the memory.

'So you've known each other all that time?'

'We only met for about a year,' Nellie said. 'Then Sam got sent to the reformatory in Heswall for five years for stealing a pot of jam. After that he went to sea and I was in service.'

'So when did you meet him again?' Maggie asked.

'Not long before we was married,' Nellie said, blushing.

'Me mam wouldn't let me go in service,' Maggie said, noticing Nellie's blush and changing the subject skilfully, 'but I suppose you was glad to get away from here.'

'It was me dad fixed it up,' Nellie said. 'When I was thirteen. He'd come ashore and there was some big row, and the next thing I was in service in Jubilee Road. It was a lovely place. A sister and a brother it was, very old. Miss Agatha and Mr Ambrose. There was the cook, Mrs Hignett, and Gertrude the parlourmaid and Mrs Jones who come in to do the "rough". I got taken on to help Gertrude because she didn't want to be pensioned off, but she had arthritis terrible bad.'

'They must have been good to do that,' Maggie said.

'They was awful good to me. Mr Ambrose learned me to read and write, and Miss Agatha showed me how to sew. Mrs Hignett learned me to cook. I had to do most of the work for Gertrude but she learned me what to do an' all. I didn't know nothing when I went there.'

'Why did you leave there, then?' asked Maggie.

'They died. Miss Agatha first and then Mr Ambrose two days after. It was that Spanish flu. There wasn't no relations and a lawyer gentleman had to see to everything. Gertrude went in a nursing home and Mrs Hignett went to live with her sister. It was a terrible time. We were that upset about them dying and everything upside down.'

'And wharrabout you?' Maggie said.

'The lawyer gentleman spoke for me for a place in Newsham Park,' Nellie said. She lay back and closed her eyes, memories flooding back of the Leadbetter household.

Maggie stood up. 'I've tired you out gabbing,' she said remorsefully. 'Sadie McCann will have my life. I'll come in again after.'

Nellie opened her eyes and smiled. 'Thanks, Maggie,' she said, 'and thanks for the broth.'

'They learned you manners too,' Maggie said with a grin as she went out.

Janey arrived home in a foul mood, made worse when Nellie unwisely told her about the broth.

'So your fella give plenty to them scroungers next door. Never gave me nothing for all *I* done for you,' she snarled.

'I thought he mugged you out of his advance note,' Nellie said timidly.

'Aye, but he give more next door. I suppose he blames me now he's got his doubts about the baby,' Janey said spitefully.

Nellie jerked upright. 'But he *is* Sam's baby,' she cried. 'I know he is. That's why he's small, because he came early.'

'He's small because you never ate nothing before he was born,' Janey said. 'First babies more often come late. He's more likely Leadbetter's.'

'He's not. I *know* he's Sam's,' Nellie protested, near to tears. 'I'm going to tell Sam what Mr Leadbetter done to me, but I know he's Sam's baby.'

'Don't talk so bloody stupid,' Janey said. 'What d'you think he'd do? He'd batter you and then get shut of you.' She jerked her head at the baby. 'And *he'd* be classed as a bastard. Is that what you want? Don't be a fool, girl. Let sleeping dogs lie.'

She stumped downstairs, leaving Nellie with her mind in turmoil. Could Janey be right about the baby? *No.* All her instincts told her that Sam was her baby's father. But what if she told him about Leadbetter? Would he disbelieve her and beat her and cast her off as Janey said he would?

She knew that there was a violent side to Sam's nature and that he had often been in trouble for fighting in the years before they were married. Most important of all, dare she risk the baby being classed as illegitimate? Never, *never*, she decided passionately, holding the baby close.

Nellie spent a restless night, at one moment deciding that she must do as Janey said and say nothing, the next deciding that she knew Sam better than Janey did and that he would never hurt her or the baby. But what if he thought the baby was not his? Did he have the right to know the truth so that he could answer any taunts or should she let the whole episode with Leadbetter lie buried?

Towards dawn she decided that she could do nothing anyway until Sam came home, and fell into an uneasy sleep. The nurse was annoyed the following morning to find Nellie feverish and the baby cross and fretful.

'Has something upset you?' she demanded. 'Was it the old one?'

'I just couldn't sleep,' Nellie said evasively, but Nurse McCann was not satisfied.

'*Something*'s upset you, and you haven't been out of the house,' she said. 'Don't let that old woman bully you, Nellie, and don't take any of her concoctions either.'

'I won't, Nurse,' Nellie said meekly and the nurse nodded.

'See you don't,' she said. 'Even if you fall for another quickly—well, there's worse things than having a baby. I know she makes stuff and sells it to women who want to get rid of a baby and I've seen the damage it causes but none of them will talk. She's as slippery as an eel, but I'll get her one of these days.'

Nellie said nothing, but she remembered as a child taking coal into Janey's room and seeing her hand a small bottle to a woman, saying,

'And remember I don't know nothing about it. You never come near me.'

The woman had pulled her shawl over her head and scuttled away through the side door. Janey said nothing to Nellie, who had forgotten the incident until now.

The nurse tut-tutted as she examined the baby. 'This little fellow's upset too,' she said. 'And he can't afford any setbacks, Nellie. He's a little fighter but you'll have to do your part too. See you don't do anything to curdle your milk, and watch what you take.'

Nellie looked anxious. 'I had some barley broth yesterday,' she said, but the nurse laughed.

'That wasn't what I meant. Broth won't do you any harm. You'll have to lie flat on the ninth day and only have gruel, but apart from that you can eat most things. Are you worrying about something?' she demanded suddenly. 'About your da maybe?'

'My da?' Nellie said in surprise.

'I can see it's not that,' the nurse said.

'I never really thought about why he backed out,' Nellie confessed, 'so much has been happening.'

'It wasn't because your ma wasn't here, that's for sure,' the nurse said decidedly. 'He never came home to see her, only you and Bobby, for all she got dolled up and tried to be different while he was home.'

'I got new clothes and shoes too,' Nellie said, 'whenever Da came home.'

'Yes, and when he went, his ship hadn't passed

the Bar before they were in the pawnshop,' the nurse said. She tucked the baby in beside Nellie. 'Anyway, Nellie, your da was a decent little fellow. It's a pity he didn't drink round here or he'd have found out sooner about what went on here.'

Nellie looked bewildered and the nurse patted her shoulder.

'Never mind, love, don't worry about it,' she said. 'Who knows? He could sign on a ship again in America one day and just come walking in here. Now I'm going to give you two aspirins to bring your temperature down and I'll put a jug of water here and a cup. Try to drink as much as you can. It'll help your milk and settle the baby.'

When she had gone Nellie lay thinking about her father and when Maggie came in later she asked her about him.

'I never seen him, only once when I seen you all dressed up getting the tram with him,' Maggie said.

Nellie said with a smile. 'He used to take me out. On the Overhead Railway sometimes and he showed me where they used to live in the Dingle. You could see it from the Overhead.'

'We only come here late on in the war,' Maggie said. 'I lived with me mam in the next street till then, but Bella Edwards from number fourteen has told me a lot about youse. You had a terrible time when you was a child, didn't you?'

'I suppose I did,' Nellie said in surprise, 'but

45

I never knew nothing different so it didn't seem so bad to me.'

'Bella said your ma hated you. She said Bobby went to school and played out but you was just a little drudge. Doing the washing half the time as well as carrying it. She said your ma called herself a washerwoman but it was only a blind for how she really made her money.' She paused with the cup halfway to her mouth. 'You don't mind me talking like this, girl?'

'No, I want to know, Maggie. The nurse said some things but I don't like asking her. I never knew what was going on when I was little. I was in a dream half the time and I was always that frightened. I never spoke to no one hardly either.'

Maggie needed no further encouragement. 'Well, Bella said your da used to go on long trips but your ma always found out when he was due and she used to rig you and herself out in new clothes.'

'What about Bobby?' Nellie asked.

'Bella reckoned he had decent clothes with going to school, but you was always in rags and barefoot half the time. She said your da never went out with your ma but he used to take you out. She said nobody got to know him properly like because he didn't drink round here, and he was a bit of a gentleman. Funny when you think of your ma.'

'I wonder if that was why Ma hated me?' Nellie said thoughtfully. She recalled a time when her mother was beating her ferociously and Janey suddenly said, 'Knock it off, Harriet.

46

D'you think you'll ever see him again if she snuffs it?' The beating had stopped, but as Nellie cowered in the corner she had seen her mother's face contorted with such hatred that she had closed her eyes and tried to make herself even smaller.

'Bella said you was your da's favourite and when you was about thirteen your ma slipped up. Your da's ship had been torpedoed and he come home unexpected. You walked in barefoot and in a skimpy old frock with a big bundle, and there was murder. They could hear the row all over the street.'

'I remember it,' Nellie said. 'Not so much the row, but going off with my da. I was ashamed because I was so scruffy. He took me to this house—I think there was a minister there. I know a maid washed me in a great big bath. I'd never seen one before with hot water coming out of the taps. She put sassafras oil on my head and I slept in a bed on my own.'

'Where was it?' Maggie asked, but Nellie shook her head.

'I don't know. I was that mazed, I suppose. I know the next morning I had another bath and had me hair washed and cut, then she brought me clothes.' She blushed at the memory. 'She had to show me what to do with the stockings. Fasten them on to the suspenders on a liberty bodice.'

'And what happened then?' Maggie said eagerly.

Belatedly Nellie realised that Bella would probably hear these revelations to add to her story and she said briefly, 'I started at that good place in Jubilee Road. Johnny doesn't seem to be coughing so much today.'

'No,' Maggie said, taking the hint. 'It's the fog what makes it worse. I suppose that's why they won't give him no pension. Are you all right now, Nell? I'd better get these nappies washed through.'

After she had gone Nellie lay thinking of her childhood. Strange that until Maggie used the word hatred she had never realised that that was what her mother felt for her, but it was true. It's funny, she thought, everybody seems to know more about my family than what I do. Maggie and the nurse and this Bella, whoever she is.

Her thoughts turned to the expeditions with her father and the happy days when he was home from sea. My life wasn't *all* bad, she thought. There were those days and the year I used to see Sam. I wonder if the nurse is right and Da might come walking in one day.

With her mind diverted from her previous worries, she fell asleep smiling happily.

When she woke she remembered that she had mentioned the row to Maggie on an earlier occasion and they had gone on to talk about her first place. Maggie had not tried to probe about the row although she already knew what Bella had told her. Nellie felt that she had misjudged her neighbour, and welcomed Maggie warmly when she came in to see her.

Nellie would often have become despondent during the long days in bed if it had not been for the visits by the nurse and Maggie. In spite of her hard life Maggie Nolan had an irrepressible cheerfulness, and always hoped for better times to come. She called several times each day to help Nellie and always managed to make her laugh with thumbnail sketches of their neighbours or anecdotes of her children.

'I don't know any of the neighbours,' Nellie said wistfully one day, 'even the ones who were here when I was a kid.'

'You'll soon get to know them when you're on your feet again,' Maggie said cheerfully. 'They're not a bad lot.' She laughed. 'We all jangle about each other but we pull together. We haven't got much, none of us, but nobody wouldn't see you short if they had anything to give you.'

'Janey doesn't seem to mix, like,' Nellie said cautiously.

'No, but you'll be made welcome,' Maggie said. She hesitated. 'You know, the way you got knocked about, people would've stood up for you, Nell, only they were that frightened of Janey and your ma. They nearly all owe Janey.'

'But they won't think I'm tarred with the same brush,' Nellie said.

Maggie laughed again. 'Anything but, girl. They're just sorry they couldn't do nothing for you when you was little. That fella in the bottom house that beats his wife and kids—nobody never buys him a drink even when they know he's skint, and they won't take a drink off him neither. Oh, there's ways

49

of making people like that know what we think about them. Fellas that go too far.'

Sometimes Maggie talked about her own childhood, when she lived in the next street. 'We never had much money because me dad was a docker but we was happy,' she said. 'Mam had five lads but she always wanted a girl so she was made up when I was born. They all spoiled me, the lads as well as Mam and Dad.'

'Do your brothers live near?' Nellie asked and then was sorry when Maggie's smile faded.

'There's only one left,' she said with a sigh. 'Four of them got killed in the war. Three in one week, our Richard and our Billy and our Walter. They all joined up together, see.'

'Mr Ambrose in my first place—he said brothers shouldn't be sent into action together. So many lads from the same family get killed in the same battle,' Nellie said.

'It very near killed me mam,' Maggie said. 'I lived with her and me youngest brother, our Henry, because Johnny was in the army. He got wounded in 1916, and our Freddie died of wounds that year.'

'You had a bad time,' Nellie said sympathetically. 'Is that why Johnny's chest is bad?'

'Johnny reckons there was gas trapped in some of the trenches although the gas attacks was over,' Maggie said. 'But I think it's because he was laying in water in a hole for hours after he was wounded in the leg. Anyhow he got sent back to England although they kept him in the army, and that's why they won't give him no pension.' She laughed. 'I wouldn't never have had so many kids if he'd got kept in France, but he could get home on leave like from England.'

'You must have been glad he was safe,' Nellie said.

'Oh aye, and we really got on our feet then. Living with me mam, I could save. Johnny's allotment wasn't much but it was regular and Mam minded the kids while I went out cleaning.'

'When did you come to live next door?' Nellie asked.

'Near the end of the war when Mam died and our Henry went in the army. I got a nice little home round me but then when Johnny came home he couldn't get work and I lost me cleaning job, so in no time all me nice bits were in the pawnshop. Still, plenty worse off than me,' Maggie said cheerfully.

The Nurse McCann paid her last visit to Nellie on the day that she allowed her downstairs for the first time. She approved Nellie's arrangements for keeping the baby warm, but wrinkled her nose distastefully at the smell of rotten fish that pervaded the room.

'Have you done anything about getting rid of that old woman?' she demanded.

Nellie shook her head. She was ashamed to say that she was afraid to tell Janey to go, so she murmured nervously, 'I can't, Nurse. She was good to me.'

The nurse snorted. 'So you told me,' she said.

'Now I've warned you, Nellie, not to take her concoctions and don't let her bully you, but don't borrow from her and get into her clutches whatever you do. There's too many round here that'll never be free of her. If they borrow a pound she gives them eighteen shillings and makes them take two shillings' worth of her stinking fish to make up the pound. Then they're paying it off for ever.'

Nellie said nothing and the nurse went on, 'You know your ma worked with her, beating up anyone who couldn't pay, but now she's gone Janey's got someone else to terrify these poor souls. It makes my blood boil.'

'I never knew—about Ma, I mean,' Nellie whispered. She realised that she was not surprised by the midwife's words, as she recalled her mother, tall and rangy, more like a man than a woman. A man's cap was always skewered to her sandy hair and she wore her sleeves rolled up, a sacking apron and men's heavy boots laced with string. She had a loud and raucous voice, frequently raised in anger.

The nurse's voice broke into her thoughts. 'Yes, love, Harriet was the bully for Janey. I've seen people after she'd beaten and kicked them half to death, but no one would ever talk. Dr Wilson tried for years to get them behind bars but they were too crafty.'

Nellie flushed and bent her head and the nurse said briskly, 'No need for you to feel ashamed, Nellie. I know you often felt the weight of your ma's hand and her boots yourself.

I'm just warning you not to get into Janey's clutches. I know you'll have to wait eight weeks for Sam's allotment to come through, but you can get tick at the corner shop. Mrs Deakin knows you'll have money coming.'

'I'll be all right. Sam left me money,' Nellie said.

'That's good. He's a decent fellow and you're a good girl, Nellie, although you got all the spirit knocked out of you when you were a child, and now you've got a lovely baby. Stand up to that old woman and do what's best for all of you. If you won't tell her to go, try and find somewhere else to live.'

'But what about Bobby?' Nellie said.

'Take him with you, but if you can't, don't worry about Bobby. Everything slides off him like water off a duck's back. He'll be working soon anyway and making his own life.'

'You know a lot about people round here, Nurse,' Nellie said with a shy smile.

'I know *everything* about people round here,' the nurse said emphatically, 'but I don't gossip. I speak my mind though and some people don't like it, but that's my way.'

'I'm very grateful for the way you looked after me,' Nellie said blushing, 'and for—for what you've told me like about Janey. Most of all for the way you saved the baby.'

'Aye, well, like I said at the time, sometimes it works and sometimes it doesn't,' the nurse said but she looked pleased.

After some thought Nellie had decided to name the baby Thomas, after her father, and

Nurse McCann agreed to be his godmother. Bobby was a very proud godfather. The baby continued to thrive and Nellie soon regained her strength.

CHAPTER 3

The months until Sam's return passed quickly for Nellie. As the weather improved and she grew stronger she ventured out, at first only as far as the corner shop with Maggie beside her to give her support and then further and further afield.

Fear of what her neighbours might think about her baby's early arrival made her afraid to leave the house at first but Maggie came one day and announced that she would walk to the corner shop with her.

'It's not doing the baby and you no good, being stuck in the house all day with that stink of rotten fish. I know Bobby does your messages but what about when he starts work?' she said.

They set off, Nellie keeping close to her friend and glancing about her timidly. She had left her coat behind in her headlong flight from Leadbetter's house but most of her neighbours wore shawls so she wore her mother's shawl with the baby wrapped snugly within it.

Many of the neighbours were at their doors,

and when one asked to see the baby the others clustered round.

'God luv him, hasn't he come on? Your Bobby said he was like a fourpenny rabbit born,' said Bella Edwards. She was a hugely fat woman who had borne ten children, seven of whom survived.

'Nurse McCann saved his life,' Nellie said shyly, and there was a chorus of praise from the women for the nurse.

'Proper clever she is. Better than the doctor half the time and not just with babies,' said another woman, 'the way she can tell you what's wrong with the kids and what to do for them.'

Bella's huge body shook as she laughed. 'Mind you, she doesn't put any bones in it. She tells you right out what she thinks of you,' she said.

'Come on, Nell. Nurse'll have me life if you catch cold,' Maggie said. 'Her first time out,' she explained to the women.

To a chorus of 'Watch yourself, girl,' and 'He's a lovely lad,' Nellie and Maggie walked on to the shop. The fact that what she had dreaded had been in reality so easy and pleasant gave Nellie courage and a determination to confront her problems in future.

Her resolve was soon tested. She knew that Charlie West was often in and out of Janey's side door but one day he swaggered down the street and knocked on the street door of the house. When Nellie opened the door he pushed past her into the kitchen without a word.

He was a small man with a narrow foxy face and black hair parted in the centre and sleeked back close to his skull. An ex-seaman now working ashore and a bachelor, he lived nearby with his mother who doted on him.

He ran his eyes over Nellie and then slipped his arm round her waist. 'Nice little figure you've got since you dropped your bundle, Nellie,' he said offensively.

Nellie tried to twist away from him, her face scarlet, but he held her firmly.

'What are you worrying about?' he said. 'Sam won't mind. Soft Sam. He'll believe anything you tell him, won't he?'

Anger gave Nellie strength and she gave him a push which sent him staggering against the table. 'Keep your hands off me,' she said. 'And don't you call my husband names. He's worth ten of you.'

Surprise kept him silent for a moment then he laughed unpleasantly. 'What about this wonderchild then?' he began but Nellie stepped forward and hit him across the face with all her strength.

'Why you—' he began but Janey had opened the door into the parlour. She said viciously to him, 'Button your lip and come in here.'

Charlie put his hand to his face and scowled at Nellie, his face dark with anger, but he obeyed Janey and went into the parlour.

Nellie snatched up the baby and flung her shawl round both of them. She was shaking as she knocked at Maggie's door and after a glance at her face Maggie drew her in and said urgently, 'What's up, girl? The baby—?'

Nellie shook her head then shook it again, unable to speak as Maggie asked, 'Sam?'

Maggie's youngest children sat on a sack before the fireless grate and the room was bare and cold, but Johnny Nolan stood up from the dilapidated armchair for Nellie to sit down, and Maggie slipped a comforting arm around her.

'That Charlie West,' Nellie said with a sob. 'Putting his arm round me and saying things about Sam.' She wiped her eyes. 'I smacked his face,' she admitted.

'Good for you!' Maggie cried. 'I hope you hurt him.'

'I give him a shock, I think,' Nellie said. 'Janey called him into the parlour, so I run in to you.'

'I'm glad you did,' Maggie said. 'Did he come through from her parlour? I know he's always in and out there.'

'No, he pushed in when I opened the door,' Nellie said. 'I'll be more careful next time.'

'There's fellas like that,' Johnny said, 'take advantage, like, a woman on her own.'

'But Nellie's not on her own,' Maggie cried. 'Sam'd beat the living daylights outa that little runt if he knew. Tell him you'll tell Sam if he tries it again. That'll frighten the life outa him. Mind you, that Charlie West only tries it on with women to cause trouble, but he'd run a mile if they took him on. He's as queer as a nine-bob note.'

Nellie began to smile and Maggie said heartily, 'That's more like it, girl, and now you've started

57

it try giving Janey a belt if she annoys you.'

Nellie stood up. 'Thanks, Mag,' she said, 'and Johnny,' smiling timidly at him. 'I was just that upset.'

'Aye, well, don't get upset over that little toad. He won't bother you no more probably after you've clouted him like that,' Maggie said.

'I hope so,' said Nellie but she thought uneasily of the look on Charlie West's face and wondered how he would take his revenge. 'Will you come in for a cup of tea in the morning, Mag? Bring the kids. I miss our talks.'

Maggie agreed, and Nellie went back to her own house but all was quiet there. She sat by the fire nursing the baby and thinking of the bareness and coldness of the house next door, yet there was a warmth of feeling there.

She looked round her own kitchen wondering what she could do to make it more comfortable for Sam to return to. Bobby had started work with a building firm as a 'can lad' with hopes of being apprenticed to a tradesman when he was sixteen, and when he came home Nellie discussed her plans with him.

'These houses aren't no good, Nell,' he said. 'The fellas at work said that when I said where I lived. They said they was built on a marsh; that's why they're so damp and the floorboards are rotten. And the cockroaches and bugs and that.'

'Well, we can't pull them down and we can't get nowhere else so we'll just have to do the best we can,' Nellie said sharply.

Bobby laughed. 'You haven't half changed,

58

Nell,' he said. 'You was always frightened of your own shadow, Mrs Deakin at the shop said. And the way you was before Tommy was born, like you was half dead.'

'Aye, well, I've got to be more hard faced now for Tommy's sake,' Nellie said. 'Ask the fellas at work the best way to shift the cockroaches and bugs, Bob.'

Her plans for the house helped to push the thought of Charlie West to the back of Nellie's mind and she slept soundly. Maggie came in the following morning with her two youngest children, Walter who was two years old and Richie who was four.

'I've missed you coming in since I was up, Mag,' Nellie said, smiling at the children.

'I didn't like to be running in and out. It was different when I was looking after you, like,' Maggie said.

'Gosh, you're dafter than me even,' said Nellie.

Nellie had a good fire burning and she had cut a plateful of bread and jam and made tea. The children sat wide eyed gazing at the flames and devouring the bread and jam, and Maggie broke a piece from her own slice and gave it to Richie.

'Don't give him yours, Mag. There's plenty more,' Nellie said standing up to cut more bread.'

'I worry about him,' Maggie said with a sigh. 'I took him to the dispensary yesterday and the doctor said he had rickets. Said he needed better food but what can I do? We're only just keeping alive as it is. Johnny got two half days on the docks last week but they only take the Relief off us so we're no better off.'

Richie had stood by Maggie's chair and she said anxiously, 'Do you think he looks more bandy, Nell?'

'No, I think kids' legs are all bandy when they're little,' Nellie said. 'They'll straighten out when he grows up.'

Maggie looked unconvinced. 'I'd kill for a job,' she said, 'but there's nothing. All the jobs are took. Step washing and cleaning, taking in washing, everything's took. Johnny's got no pull at the docks, no family, like, there, and he hasn't got no money to give backhanders. I'm getting desperate.'

'Never mind, Mag, things'll get better,' Nellie comforted her. 'You know you're welcome to anything we've got.'

'I don't like putting on good nature,' Maggie said, lifting the corner of her apron to dry her eyes, 'you and Sam have helped us already.'

'And look what you've done for me,' said Nellie.

'We didn't have no fire when you came in yesterday,' Maggie said, 'but we do usually. The kids get wood from the back of the market and coal off the sidings, like.'

'You're welcome to coal from our coalplace any time, Mag,' Nellie said. 'I'd rather see it going on your fire than on Janey's.'

'But then she pays for it in her rent,' Maggie said.

'Rent! What rent? She never lets on about

60

rent and I don't like to ask her,' Nellie said.

'And here's me thinking you were getting more tough,' Maggie exclaimed. 'You're too soft for your own good, Nell.'

Nellie smiled. 'I know,' she said, 'but I'm getting better, aren't I? Our Bobby said last night I was.'

Maggie smiled too. 'You've still got a long way to go though, girl,' she said. She stood up and drew her shawl round her shoulders then went to Tommy's makeshift cot, where he lay waving his arms and legs and gurgling to himself. 'God luv him, he's as good as gold, isn't he?' she said. 'We never hear a sound out of him in the night.'

'Yes, he sleeps right through,' Nellie said proudly.

'Sam'll be made up when he comes home, the size of him now,' Maggie said.

She turned to her children but Nellie said quickly, 'Can they stay for a bit, Mag? Our Bobby's home at one today, being Saturday. He'd be made up if they had their dinner with him.'

Maggie's face grew red. 'I'm sorry for moaning like that,' she said. 'We don't do so bad really.'

'You weren't moaning,' Nellie protested. 'Not like me last night.'

'I suppose he'd gone, Charlie West?' Maggie asked and when Nellie nodded she went on, 'It makes me mad. Johnny tries so hard and the likes of West leaves the sea and walks right in to a job. Mind you, we know how he did it.'

'How?' Nellie asked.

'Because he's a "bum boy" and the fella that took him on was another one like himself. They stick together.'

'I'm thick,' Nellie confessed. 'I never knew about fellas like that.'

'There's a few round here, but some of them can't help themselves, like. They're to be pitied,' Maggie said. She began to laugh. 'That's one thing no one can't say about Johnny Nolan, anyway, that he's a bum boy.'

She went out smiling, and Nellie gave the little boys string and wood to play with. She had a stone jar full of cheese toasting in the oven and when Bobby came home she toasted thick slices of bread and spread the cheese on it.

Bobby had brought home a blowlamp and a bottle of Lysol and as he cut the toast into strips for Richie and Nellie helped Walter, he told her excitedly about the advice his workmates had given him.

'They told me to go over the walls with the blowlamp to kill the bugs and to wash the bedframes and the floors with the Lysol. The boss said I can have some cement to fill the holes round the fireplace to keep the cockroaches out too.'

After the children had eaten their fill of the toasted cheese, followed by broken biscuits and tea, Nellie took them home by the back entry.

Bobby had received his first week's wages of six shillings and proudly handed four of them to Nellie, so before taking the children home she went to the corner shop. She then wrapped some tea and a tin of condensed milk, a loaf and a jar of jam, and took them next door.

The children carried a bag of broken biscuits paid for by Bobby to share with their brothers and sister.

'I've brought you these, Mag,' Nellie said. ' A mug out of Bobby's first week's wages.' Before Maggie could speak she went on quickly, 'When all your kids are working you can do the same for me.'

Tears had filled Maggie's eyes as she looked at the groceries but she blinked them away and protested, 'But Nellie, girl, you need that money.'

'No I don't, Mag. Sam's allotment has come through and all so I'm really on Easy Street.' She laughed. 'Don't tell Bobby though. He thinks he's keeping the house.'

While Maggie recovered her composure Nellie rattled on about the plans that she and Bobby had for the house.

'The fellas at work have told him what to do and lent him a blowlamp. They've give him some Lysol an' all and the boss is going to give him something to fill up the holes and keep the cockroaches out. The Keatings powder is no use. There's too many of them.'

Johnny Nolan came in the yard door and Nellie said hastily, 'I'd better get back in case Bobby starts without me and burns the house down.'

Maggie put her hand on Nellie's arm. 'You're a good girl,' she said huskily, 'and a good neighbour.'

Bobby was already upstairs when Nellie returned, tearing the mouldy wallpaper from the walls of his bedroom. Nellie looked in dismay at the exposed laths where the plaster had come away with the wallpaper.

'You won't be able to use the blowlamp, Bob,' she said. 'It was only the paper holding it together.'

'I'll be careful,' Bobby promised, blithely ripping off the rest of the wallpaper. 'The laths are too damp to take fire,' and he proved to be right.

His workmates had advised Bobby to use whitewash on the walls instead of wallpaper as a deterrent to the bugs but Nellie looked doubtfully at the walls. 'Do you think we'd better have paper to cover up the holes?' she asked but her brother said decisively, 'No, whitewash. Never mind the holes.'

Johnny Nolan showed them how to mix the whitewash and before nightfall Bobby had whitewashed his bedroom walls and Nellie had scrubbed his bedframe and floor with Lysol.

'And now the bugs can bugger off,' Bobby announced, when they came downstairs and Nellie made supper.

Janey was sitting by the fire and she sneered. 'The proper big fella now, aren't yer. I hope that's the end of it.'

'No. I'm doing Nellie's room next and then the kitchen. I'll do your parlour if you like,' Bobby said, flushed with success.

Janey thrust her face close to his. 'You keep outa my parlour, d'ya hear? I don't want no one

64

rooting round in there.' She turned to Nellie. 'You an' all. Keep outa my room.'

Nellie said nothing, but Bobby said cheekily, 'Wharrabout your fire? You want us in to light your fire, don't you?'

'Yes, while I'm in to watch what you're up to,' Janey said. She snatched up her mug of cocoa and stumped into her own room.

Bobby and Nellie looked at each other. 'I should have said if we can't go in there she can't come in here,' Nellie said, 'but I never think what to say till it's too late.'

'You should tell her though, Nell. Ma never cooked meals for her. You're too soft.' Suddenly he grinned. 'Mind you, Ma never cooked for anyone. We all just seen to ourselves.'

'I wouldn't mind cooking for her if she'd eat it in the parlour,' Nellie said quietly. 'I don't want her eating with us when Sam comes home.'

'No. For one thing she stinks,' Bobby said, and Nellie looked warningly at the parlour door.

They did Nellie's room the following day. Although the paper was mouldy in patches it came away without the plaster and Bobby was able to use the blowlamp thoroughly and then to whitewash the walls.

Nellie washed the floors and the bedframe with Lysol and stood looking wistfully at the ancient flock mattress. 'I wish I could buy a new mattress, Bob,' she said.

'You could get one weekly from Cookson's now you've got my wages,' Bobby said.

Nellie's eyes lit up but then she said

doubtfully, 'But what would Sam say? He mightn't like me going into debt.'

'If you paid a shilling a week you'd have it paid off by the time Sam got home,' Bobby said. Nellie was easily persuaded and she was amazed at the ease with which the hire purchase was arranged when she showed proof of Sam's allotment and told the man of Bobby's job.

'As soon as I've paid this off I'll get you a proper mattress, Bob,' she promised her brother.

Bobby's mattress consisted of two sacks stuffed with straw, but he said airily, 'Don't worry about me, Nell, I'd sleep on a clothes line, and the straw doesn't harbour the bugs so much.'

It was a joy to Nellie to find a friend and ally in her brother as they grew to know each other. Bobby had always spent as much time as possible away from the house, and Nellie had seen little of him when they were children, and rarely seen him on her days off from service.

He was an open, extrovert boy with many friends, and he was very proud of the part he played in saving the baby's life. The affection he poured out on her and on Tommy warmed and delighted Nellie.

She was surprised when he suddenly said as they worked together on the kitchen walls, 'It's funny. I never really knew you before, Nell. It's the gear being like this, isn't it?'

'Yes it is. But I never seen much of you till now. You was never in the house, was you?'

Bobby laughed. 'No wonder, was it? I could never make out why you come home on your

66

day off though,' he said.

'I was a fool,' Nellie said ruefully. 'Me first day off, the cook, Mrs Hignett, give me a ham shank and some fruit cake for me to bring home so I thought I had to come here. Once Ma saw the food that was it. I had to come every week and she had jobs lined up for me and all, right up to me going back. I hated me days off.'

'Why didn't you go off somewhere and eat the stuff?' Bobby asked.

'I tried that one day when it was just fairy cakes but Ma went up to the house creating. Made out she was worried about me. Miss Agatha said I owed a duty to my mother and I shouldn't have worried her, so I had to come home after that in case she came again.'

'Didn't you tell them what she was like?' said Bobby.

'No, I was too upset because Miss Agatha was vexed with me. I tried to tell Mrs Hignett but she said I should respect my mother because she was my mother and my home was my home no matter what it was like. They didn't have no idea and I suppose Ma made herself look respectable.'

'She was crafty like that,' Bobby agreed.

They decided to wallpaper the kitchen and Maggie helped them.

'You don't want to be stretching too much while you're breast feeding,' she told Nellie, and set her to trim the edging from the rolls of wallpaper while she and Bobby papered the walls.

Bobby filled in all the holes round the

67

fireplace with mortar then Nellie scrubbed the floor with Lysol and when it was thoroughly dry they laid the linoleum which Nellie had bought.

Janey was annoyed by the disruption caused by the cleaning and raged at them before retiring to her own room while they worked.

'We've found a way to get rid of her, anyhow,' Bobby joked to Nellie, but she knew that the relief was only temporary. She had still not managed to pluck up courage to tell Janey that she must have her meals in her own room.

Each week Nellie managed to buy something to improve the house. In the market she bought gingham for curtains and brightly coloured bale ends of cloth for cushion covers for the chairs for a few pence. She also went frequently to the mug market and bought bargains in dishes.

Bobby was able to get flour bags for her from a friend, and she unpicked and washed them and made tea towels and a tablecloth from them.

Nellie was working on the tablecloth after the evening meal when Bobby had gone out, and Janey was crouching in the chair Nellie thought of as Sam's, smoking a clay pipe and glaring malevolently at her as she embroidered the corners of the tablecloth.

'You daft mare,' Janey sneered. 'All this for a fella what went barefoot and no arse in his trousers until he got put away for stealing. He won't have seen no tablecloths in the reformatory.'

Nellie's face grew red but she stitched on

doggedly. 'Sam had a good home until his mother died,' she said. 'You told me that yourself.'

Janey sniggered. 'Aye, and his father scarpered. I could tell you something about that too.'

Nellie was determined not to rise to the old woman's goading and said nothing, but Janey went on, 'Why d'you think the neighbours wouldn't have nothing to do with him? I know more about his family than what he does himself.'

Anger gave Nellie courage. 'What do you know?' she demanded.

'If I told you you'd be as wise as what I am,' Janey said. 'But you're not the only one in this house with a secret.' Janey sniggered gleefully.

Nellie was silent as she stitched carefully and after a moment Janey said spitefully, 'Cat got your tongue? He'll think he's come to the wrong house and when he looks in the bassinet he'll be sure.'

Fortunately at that moment there was a discreet knock on the side door, and Janey went into the parlour. Nellie's hands were trembling and she put away the tablecloth and picked up the baby.

His dark hair had rubbed off as Janey had predicted and the new hair that was growing was fair. He was still small for his age but looked healthy, with bright blue eyes and a ready smile. Sometimes Nellie fancied that his expression was like Sam's. Certainly there was nothing about him to remind her of the ape-like Leadbetter.

The next night Janey arrived just after Bobby when Nellie was preparing to serve the meal. It was spare ribs and cabbage and Nellie tried to avoid watching the old woman's dirty fingers tearing at the ribs or listen to her sucking the bones.

'You turned out a good cook, any road,' Janey said when the meal was finished. 'I suppose they learned you when you was in service.'

It was an olive branch, Nellie realised, and she accepted it and smiled at the old woman, although she despised herself for doing so. 'They learned me everything in me first place,' she said.

It was not only Janey's dirty habits which annoyed and worried Nellie. She often dropped hints about the baby while Bobby was present but he was oblivious to them, engrossed in his comic or his own plans. Nellie could ignore them too, but she was worried when Janey tried to involve Maggie.

When Maggie spoke about Tommy's birth weight, Janey broke in. 'Aye and he'd have been smaller still if she hadn't gone over her time.' Nellie blushed but Maggie ignored the old woman and later she said that she thought Janey was going soft in the head.

'She'll finish up like poor Mrs Drew over the road,' she said, referring to a woman suffering from senile dementia who was cared for by her daughter, Gertie.

Another day, when Maggie had been singing to the baby, Janey leaned over him later and began to sing, 'Joshua, Joshua, what a naughty boy you are.'

Maggie stepped behind her and put her finger to her head significantly and Nellie was able to smile and ask about Maggie's children.

When Sam was due home Nellie's neighbours advised her to go with the other women to meet the ship.

'Make sure you get some of his pay-off before it all goes over the bar of the Volley,' they said. 'You could go down with Buck Madden's wife.'

Nellie smiled at them but privately determined that she would wait for Sam at home.

The day before he arrived she had an upsetting encounter with Charlie West. As she turned the corner of a road he was coming the other way and they came face to face for the first time since she had slapped his face. He barred her way.

'Well, well, the woman herself,' he sneered.

'Get out of my way. You'd better watch yourself,' Nellie said quickly. 'Sam'll be home tomorrow.'

Charlie West laughed unpleasantly and pulled open Nellie's shawl. 'He's got a shock coming, hasn't he? Fair-haired blue-eyed lad and Sam as black as your hat. It's not me he'll be belting.'

Nellie clutched Tommy to her and tried again to pass West but he stepped in front of her.

'Let me pass,' she said angrily. 'You don't know what you're talking about.'

'It's you stopping me,' he said. 'Man mad, you are. Sam's going to have his work cut out keeping an eye on you.'

Nellie's arms were occupied with the baby but she lashed out with her foot and caught him on the shin. As he staggered and howled with rage and pain she slipped past him and fled down the road with his shout of, 'You wait, you bitch. I'll get you for that,' following her.

She ran through back entries and passageways until she reached her back gate and rushed through it to sit down on an upturned dolly tub, breathless and shaking.

She knew she had made an enemy of Charlie West but how much harm could he do to her? How much had Janey told him so that he could tell Sam lies mixed with truth which Sam might believe?

Should she tell Sam what had happened with Leadbetter or should she bury the episode? Back and forth in her mind the familiar arguments raged. She was quite sure that the baby was Sam's child but could she convince Sam? She recalled the day Sam had left and his words about the child's name: 'You know best about that.'

A letter had arrived from Sam after several weeks which had eased her mind although he only wrote,

Dear wife,
I hope this finds you well as it leaves me at present, also Bobby, Janey and the baby. It is very hot here. I hope to see you soon.
    Yours faithfully
    Samuel Meadows

Nellie wrote in return telling him that she had called the baby Thomas after her father, and Nurse McCann and Bobby were his godparents. Also that she and Bobby were cleaning the house.

Now as she thought fondly of Sam and remembered his kindness to her when they were children she decided to tell him the whole story, but then she thought of her hurried marriage and the early arrival of the baby and how these facts could be twisted.

She knew that Sam had a violent temper at times. Would he cast her off and refuse to recognise Tommy as his son, so making him illegitimate?

There were many children in the neighbourhood born out of wedlock and absorbed into their mothers' large families, but Nellie recalled seeing a child running down the entry in tears, pursued by other children shouting, 'Bastard, bastard. You haven't got no father.'

Back and forth the arguments raged in her mind and later she could only sit, sick at heart, nursing the baby and sipping a cup of tea while Bobby and Janey ate the meal she had prepared.

'Aren't you going to have nothing, Nell?' Bobby asked anxiously. 'You don't want to be bad for Sam coming home.'

The baby was fractious too and after his meal Bobby walked about with him trying to soothe him. 'Maybe you're both too excited about Sam coming,' he said, and to the baby, 'Are you going to see your dad tomorrow, young fella me lad?'

'Tee hee, it's a wise child that knows its own father,' Janey cackled.

Nellie leaned back in her chair closing her eyes and made no reply, and Bobby took the baby into the back yard. After Janey had gone to her own room, Nellie made herself eat a slice of bread and butter and drink a cup of cocoa then, after settling the baby, she went to bed.

Worn out by her worries she slept immediately, but woke at about three o'clock in the morning, feeling calm and refreshed. The May morning was mild, but a fresh salty wind cleared the narrow streets of the noxious smells which usually hung there.

Tommy slept peacefully, lying on his back with his arms flung above his head, and Nellie leaned over him consumed with maternal love, so innocent and vulnerable in sleep.

She recalled the day that Sam had left, when she had decided that the baby was more important than anyone. Now that Tommy had become a real person to her she felt this even more strongly. All her doubts were resolved. From now on everything she said and did would be guided by what was best for her son.

Janey, Charlie West, even Sam if necessary— she would fight anyone who threatened Tommy in any way. No one will ever hurt him while I'm alive, she vowed, then feeling strong and confident, she slept again.

CHAPTER 4

The following day Nellie set to work as soon as Janey had left with her fishbasket, and Bobby for work. By the time that Sam arrived in the late afternoon the wind had dropped and rain was falling heavily, but the kitchen was warm and welcoming.

A bright fire burned in a shining grate and the new cushions were in the wooden armchair with a packet of Woodbines and a box of Swan Vestas on the arm of the chair. Nellie had laid the table with the new tablecloth and dishes, and a savoury smell of hotpot filled the air.

The baby, now sleeping in his cot, wore a romper suit that Nellie had knitted, and she had made a flowered wraparound pinafore for herself. Her face was pink with excitement and tendrils of her brown hair had escaped from her bun and curled round her face.

She had been too busy to be nervous but when she peeped out of the door and saw Sam striding down the street, his seabag on his shoulder, she retreated behind the table suddenly apprehensive.

Sam stepped in and dropped his bag at his feet, then stood tongue tied and ill at ease, looking at Nellie. Neither spoke for a moment or moved towards each other, then Nellie said timidly, 'Hello, Sam.'

He smiled at her, his teeth a flash of white in his brown weatherbeaten face. 'Hello, Ellie. You all right, girl?' he said. Rain had soaked his coat and his dark hair lay in wet rings over his head.

He glanced round and Nellie said quickly, 'Tommy's asleep, Sam.'

Sam looked startled and it was clear that for the moment he had forgotten the baby, but he moved to the cot and looked in. Nellie drew back the blanket covering the sleeping child and Sam whistled soundlessly.

'He hasn't half grown,' he said. 'Looks real healthy too.'

Nellie felt weak with relief. Sam had evidently forgotten or intended to ignore the doubts planted in his mind by his false friends, which had clouded the baby's birth and made their parting so unhappy.

'Sam, you're drenched,' she exclaimed, timidly touching his wet coat.

'Aye. Cats and dogs out there,' he said cheerfully. He took off his coat and sat down in the armchair leaning back and stretching out his legs to the fire with a sigh of pleasure.

'God, this is the gear,' he said. 'Woodies and Vestas too.'

'You look thinner, Sam,' Nellie said shyly. 'What was the trip like?'

'Lousy,' said Sam. 'I took real bad when we was only five days out. Like as if I was on fire and me neck all swelled up. I couldn't swaller nothing, only water, and that hurt me throat. I was like something out of a sideshow for a few days but then the swelling went down but me throat was still sore.'

'What was it, Sam?' Nellie asked.

'I dunno. One of the lads said his kid had mumps and he looked like me, but that's a kids' thing, isn't it?'

'Yes, a few round here have had it. A little lad in Marsh Lane died of it,' Nellie said. 'I'm terrified of Tommy getting anything like that.'

'Don't worry, girl, he looks healthy enough to me,' Sam said. He looked at Nellie as she bent over the oven.

'Are you keeping all right yourself, Ellie? Looking after yourself, like?'

Nellie blushed. 'Yes, Sam,' she said. 'Maggie Nolan's been a real good friend to me and our Bobby's been the gear. We done all through the house together.'

She closed the oven door and Sam sniffed the air. 'Something smells good,' he said.

'It's a hotpot,' Nellie said. 'It's ready now. Should I put yours out, Sam?'

'Ooh yes. I'm starving. Haven't had nothing since me breakfast,' Sam said. 'You look as if you could do with feeding up and all, girl.'

He devoured the meal with obvious enjoyment and Nellie refilled his plate as soon as it was empty.

'They learned you to cook good in your place, girl, didn't they?' he said. 'But you must've had a talent for it like to do as good as this. Real tasty it is.'

'That's what I liked best,' Nellie said shyly, 'helping the cook.'

77

Sam glanced at the embroidered tablecloth and the new dishes and round the bright warm room. 'They learned you more than cooking, Ellie,' he said. 'You told me about this in the letter but it's different seeing it. You write good letters too, Ellie.'

'You write a good hand yourself, Sam,' she said. 'I suppose they learned you to write copperplate at Heswall.'

'Pity they never learned us what to say. Took me half an hour to write six lines,' Sam said, laughing.

'Mr Ambrose in me first place learned me to read and write,' Nellie said. 'I never hardly went to school.'

Sam's smile faded. 'Mr Ambrose? Was he the son?' he asked.

'No, there wasn't no son,' Nellie said. 'Just Mr Ambrose and Miss Agatha. They was a brother and sister—very old.'

'Why didn't *she* learn you?' Sam said gruffly.

'She learned me to sew but he used to be a teacher in some posh school where all the lads lived in, like.' She pretended not to see Sam's scowl but she felt flattered that he seemed jealous of her employer. She was not to know then that that first small cloud would become one that would overshadow most of her life.

The baby woke and Nellie went to lift him from the cot and the moment passed. She came to sit near to Sam and he held his finger out to the baby. Tommy seized it and dragged it towards his mouth and Sam laughed.

'Bit of a cannibal, isn't he?' he said but Nellie

told him that the child put everything in his mouth.

'All his black hair come off like Janey said, and this fair hair's grew now,' she said, then with a flash of inspiration she added, 'I hope he doesn't go ginger like Ma.'

'As long as he doesn't turn out like your ma no other way,' Sam said with a grin.

They were sitting at either side of the fire, Sam in his armchair and Nellie opposite him nursing the baby when they heard Janey coming up the back yard. There was the sound of her fishbasket being dumped in the lean-to then she came in the kitchen, taking the roll from her head on which she carried the basket.

Sam had lit a Woodbine and was leaning back in the chair with his legs stretched out and a mug of tea on the hob beside him. At the sight of his obvious contentment Janey scowled even more ferociously, but she said nothing to him. She glared at Nellie. 'You didn't wait for me and Bobby, then?'

'The hotpot's in the oven,' Nellie said. She hesitated, wondering whether she dared suggest serving Janey's meal in the parlour, but at that moment Bobby came in. The warmth of his welcome to Sam offset Janey's surliness as he eagerly asked Sam about his voyage. By the time Sam had answered and Nellie had lifted the hotpot from the oven the opportunity had passed. Janey was sitting at the table with Bobby waiting to be served.

'What d'you think of the kitchen, Sam?' Bobby asked. 'Me and Nellie done it. We done the bedrooms an' all. The fellas in work let me lend a blowlamp and the boss give me some Lysol and mortar.'

'It looks the gear,' Sam said.

Bobby went on, 'I got flour bags for Nellie off me mate for this tablecloth and she got the dishes outa me wages, d'ya like the dishes, Sam?'

'Yes. I liked what was on them an' all,' Sam said with a grin.

'Jumping outa your bloody latitude,' Janey sneered. 'Aping your betters and none of youse ever been anything but scruffs.'

They were all silent with amazement for a moment then Bobby said cheerfully, 'Aye, but we're coming up in the world. Oilcloth on the floor *and* a tablecloth.'

Sam grinned and Janey glared at him.

'I seen some of your mates going in the Volley,' she said. 'And a gang with them expecting to be mugged an' all. You'll be getting the name for a skinflint skulking in the house keeping your money in your pocket.'

Sam stood up and snatched his cap and coat from the door, his face red with anger.

'That's something no one can't ever say about *me*,' he shouted. 'I've always stood me wack and everyone knows it.'

He lunged over to the door and Nellie swiftly followed him, and stood on the step plucking at his sleeve.

'Don't take any notice, Sam,' she said, 'I think she's going funny in the head.'

She looked up at him beseechingly and Sam's

anger seemed to cool. 'All right, girl,' he said, 'but I'd be going down to the Volley to mug the lads anyway.' He suddenly bent and kissed her cheek. 'Don't worry, Ellie,' he said and swung away down the street.

Janey had come behind Nellie, too late to hear her words but in time to see Sam's kiss, and Gertie Drew who had been sitting on her doorstep across the street came over to Nellie. Gertie was an emotional girl, forever saying that she had come over faint, or shedding ready tears like the heroines in the novelettes she read.

'Oh, Nellie,' she gushed, 'I seen your husband kiss you. I think it's so romantic when the fella's come home from sea. It makes me want to cry.'

Janey pushed Nellie aside. 'Cry then,' she said viciously, 'the more you cry the less you'll pee. You need a bloody man yourself.' She turned back into the house, leaving the two girls speechless.

Gertie was the first to recover. 'The old cow. No wonder everyone round here hates her,' she said.

Nellie whispered soothingly, 'Take no notice. She's in a twist because she was out when Sam come home. She hates to miss anything.'

Gertie tossed her head. 'I'm not worried about the likes of her,' she said loudly, then flounced back across the street.

Nellie felt unable even to look at the old woman when she went back into the kitchen, but Janey seemed to have recovered from her ill humour.

81

'I told her, didn't I?' she cackled. 'Stupid mare. God help her soft sense.'

Nellie was too angry to reply. Janey had not only deliberately spoiled Sam's first evening at home, but she had treated Gertie with cruelty, even though she knew the circumstances of Gertie's life.

Foolish though Gertie seemed, her histrionics and her novelettes were a way of escape from an intolerable life. She worked long hours in a toy factory, and hurried home in her lunch break and again at night to feed and clean her senile mother. Gertie had to deal with the havoc created by her mother while she was locked in the house in Gertie's absence, and often she read the novelettes while sitting up with her mother after a particularly violent spell.

Bobby went out and Janey returned to her parlour. Nellie fed the baby then carried him upstairs where she had taken the cot.

'You can't come in the bed tonight, love,' she whispered as she tucked him in, 'your daddy's home,' but the child was already asleep. Nellie stood looking round the room and pressing her hand on the mattress. I wonder will Sam notice the mattress, she thought blushing.

Downstairs she found it hard to settle down to darning and she was alarmed when Bobby came in and said that he had seen Charlie West going into the Volunteer.

'Mrs Hancock said, "There's Charlie going in with his latch lifter. It's the only drink he'll buy all night." Scrounger. He's got a cheek, hasn't he, Nell, when he's working ashore?'

Nellie agreed but she became more and more alarmed as the night wore on, and she wondered what was happening in the Volunteer. It was nearly eleven o'clock when she heard voices in the street, including Sam's, and the next moment he came in.

'I've just very near carried Johnny Nolan home, legless,' he said laughing.

'Drunk,' Nellie exclaimed. 'But Johnny never drinks.'

'I seen him when I was going in the Volley and took him in with me,' Sam explained.

'He'll be worse because he's not used to it,' Nellie said. 'He'll have a bad head in the morning.'

'He had a good time tonight though, any road,' Sam said. 'Drowned his sorrows.'

Nellie waited nervously for Sam to mention Charlie West, or to hear of taunts that had been made, but Sam said nothing more about the company in the Volunteer. He ate the bread and cheese Nellie provided then sluiced his head and face at the sink, while Nellie banked down the fire with wet slack.

The baby still slept and Nellie undressed modestly with her back turned to Sam, but once in bed she went swiftly and naturally into his arms.

'God, girl, there's nothing of you,' Sam exclaimed as his hands moved over her body. 'I'm very near afraid to touch you in case you break.'

'Don't worry. I'm thin but I'm strong,' Nellie whispered pressing close to him.

Sam kissed her hungrily and they made love gently yet passionately. For a while they slept then woke to make love again.

'I'll miss you when you go back, Sam,' Nellie whispered, but Sam laughed and hugged her.

'We won't worry about that yet,' he said, 'I've only just come home.' He stretched and yawned. 'God, I'd forgotten how comfortable it is to sleep in a bed.'

Nellie smiled. 'It's a new mattress, Sam,' she said. 'I thought we'd have a better chance of getting rid of the bugs and that with a new one, and be more comfortable.'

'Where'd you get the money?' Sam demanded. 'You never borrowed off the old girl, did you?'

'No, I paid a shilling a week off it at Cookson's,' Nellie said. 'The nurse told me never to borry off old Janey. It was Bobby told me about getting it from Cookson's.'

'How did *he* know?' asked Sam yawning, and before she answered he was asleep again.

Nellie was up early to attend to the baby and make breakfast for Bobby and tea for Janey, but Sam slept all morning.

After a meal of bacon and egg and black pudding Sam went out to the 'Pool to see his mates and then to drink at the Volunteer. Before leaving he put a generous portion of his pay-off on the table.

'That all right for you, Ellie?' he asked.

'It's fine, Sam, but have you kept enough for yourself?'

'Oh, aye, plenty,' he said bending over the cot.

Tommy reached up and seized his hair, and Nellie had to disentangle the child's hands.

'By God, he takes after your ma all right. She always had her hands in someone's hair,' Sam joked and went out laughing.

Sam's day followed the pattern of most seafarers when they were ashore and Nellie accepted it as normal. Sleep until midday, a meal then a drinking session or a visit to the 'Pool to see mates, another meal and another drinking session at night.

It was traditional that when men were paid off after a voyage and were flush with money they treated everyone in their local for as long as the money lasted.

When the money had gone they in their turn would be treated by others temporarily affluent. All that was required was a 'latch lifter', a few coppers for a pint or even a glass of beer to protect dignity and provide a reason for being in the public house and available for being treated.

Although Sam drank heavily he never seemed to Nellie as drunk as on the night of Tommy's birth, and he was never belligerent. Nothing was ever said of any taunts or any reference to Charlie West. Nellie could only surmise thankfully that the subject of Sam's marriage had been superseded by newer topics and West had been afraid to carry out his threats.

As the days passed Sam's afternoon sessions grew shorter. After his midday meal he began to nurse the baby, gingerly at first but with increasing confidence, and Tommy responded to him, crowing with delight when his father approached his cot.

'Eh, they know their own,' Maggie said one day when she had called to see Nellie. 'He's usually that shy with everyone, isn't he, Nell?'

Seeing Sam's pleased smile Nellie was sure that he now had no doubt that Tommy was his child, and she wondered how he had been convinced.

On Fridays Janey was busy with her fish and her moneylending and was always late home. Bobby went out immediately after his meal and Sam and Nellie sat in peace, Sam lying back in his chair smoking and watching Nellie knitting a jacket for the baby.

'You've made this place real homey, girl,' he said suddenly. 'I've come into harbour here all right.'

Nellie blushed. 'Bobby helped me,' she said. 'And Maggie helped with the papering. Bobby got me the flour bags for the tablecloth and tea towels too.'

'He's a good lad,' Sam said and Nellie eagerly agreed.

'I'm made up because we've got real close, like. I never knew him properly before, but we're real mates now,' Nellie said.

'I'm glad he's here to stick up for you,' Sam said. 'I don't trust that one,' jerking his head at the parlour door.

Sam smoked for a while in silence then he said gruffly, 'George Adams what's on my watch. He goes to the market on Saturday nights when he's ashore with his missus. Do you want to go tomorrow night?'

'With you? Oh yes, Sam,' Nellie said. 'Does George Adams live near here?'

'Sydney Street,' Sam said. 'He's older than me, like. He's got five kids but he's a real good mate. Always reading. Buck calls him the Professor but he got Buck reading a book when we was homeward bound, so he had to stop calling him Professor. It was only a laugh though.'

Janey came home a little later and Sam went out to the Volunteer. Nellie wondered whether he would stay at home more if Janey stayed in the parlour, although Janey's attitude to Sam had changed. She seemed anxious to be on good terms with him, but Bobby had told Nellie the reason for this. Sam had given Janey money for gin on several occasions.

On Saturday Nellie washed her hair and braided it carefully before putting it up in a bun. She had washed and ironed her blouse although it would scarcely be seen under her shawl, and dressed Tommy in his best clothes. Later when she walked down the street with the baby tucked in her shawl, her purse plump with money in one hand and her other hand through Sam's arm, she felt as though she was floating on air with happiness.

The market was crowded and they failed to see George Adams and his wife but they enjoyed themselves. Nellie bought meat and bacon when it was auctioned off cheaply and Sam bought oranges and sweets, then took her to a china stall.

'Pick out something for yourself, Ellie,' he said. 'I didn't bring you nothing. Never thought of it till I seen George with things for his wife and nippers.'

'It doesn't matter, Sam. You give me plenty from your pay-off,' Nellie protested.

'That's different. George keeps a bit extra by, because he says you can get stuff cheap in foreign parts. Different too.'

'You pick something, then,' Nellie said, and Sam chose a vase covered in swags of pink and blue flowers for Nellie and for Tommy a mug with 'Baby' picked out on it in gold.

Nellie's happiness would have been complete if Sam had not shown so many signs of jealousy. He scowled and pulled her away from stalls where the men stallholders joked with her.

'The men don't mean no harm, Sam,' Nellie protested. 'It's just their patter, like. They can see I'm with me husband and baby.'

'You was leading him on. Smiling at him,' Sam shouted at her, after jerking her away from one of the stalls.

Nellie looked nervously at his angry face and said timidly, 'I wasn't, Sam, honest,' and after that Sam seemed more reasonable.

In spite of his earlier outbursts Nellie enjoyed the outing, and looked forward to showing her present to Bobby and Maggie. She hoped that Sam would stay at home for the rest of the evening but when they reached the house Janey was sitting in the kitchen.

Sam put the parcels on the table and went out again. 'Just going for a pint,' he told Nellie.

'Wharrave you got there?' Janey asked, and Nellie proudly displayed her vase from Sam and the baby's mug.

'You've properly fell on your feet, haven't you?' the old woman said. 'I done you a good turn all right when I got you fixed up with Sam.'

Nellie had to acknowledge that she had cause to be grateful to Janey, whatever her motives had been, and she said warmly, 'Sam bought these oranges and sweets, too, Janey. Will you have some of them?'

The old woman agreed and carried her booty into her own room.

When Sam stepped out of the door he was about to walk up towards the Volunteer as usual, but on an impulse he turned and walked the other way towards Seaforth. He felt that he wanted to be alone to sort out his confused thoughts and feelings.

At first the streets he walked through were narrow, crowded with children playing and mothers gossiping at their doors, but gradually the surroundings changed. After the terminus of the Overhead Railway he walked along a wide road with tramlines running along the centre, with a narrow footpath edged with hawthorn trees. A few carts and pony traps and an occasional motor car passed as Sam walked along, his wide shoulders brushing against the hawthorn flowers and releasing their sweetness, but he was unaware of his surroundings.

Why had he been so narky with Ellie? She'd been so happy, made up to be out with him, and with the bits he'd bought her. He'd been made up himself too, he could hardly believe it. Him, Sam Meadows, walking along with a pretty little wife on his arm and a kid anyone would be proud of, and money in his pocket.

Then he had to go and spoil it all shouting at Ellie. He felt disgusted with himself when he thought of the frightened look on her face, and remembered when he had first seen her look like that.

When she was a skinny little girl with bare feet and a tattered frock, crying because lads had taken her ma's washing. But then he was the one who had taken the frightened look away by getting the washing back for her, and chasing the lads.

He walked more slowly as he thought of those days. Carrying the washing for her and sitting in the corner by the shippon sharing the bits of food people gave her. The time when he had done well with his paper and bought a Wet Nella for each of them. The square heavy cakes made of breadcrumbs doused in treacle were very filling and Ellie had said, 'Oh Sam, I feel real full,' when she finished it. She sounded surprised. Not often she felt like that, poor kid, Sam thought now.

He'd meant to treat her often and look after her but then he'd seen that jar of jam outside a shop, ruby red with the light shining through it. He'd snatched it up—couldn't help it somehow—then run right into Dusty Miller the scuffer.

That was it. Five years in the reform school

at Heswall, then when he was fifteen signed on a ship—no choice. His first ship torpedoed too and three days in an open boat.

Sam had reached a field where an old white horse came to the fence to blow in his face. He stroked it and rested for a while and when he set off again he thought again about Ellie. Ellie! The way she whispered her name to him that first day he'd thought that was what she'd said, and she let him go on calling her that, too shy to tell him it should be Nellie.

She was so different to any other girl, he thought. All the kids he knew were tough—had to be—and Ellie had had a worse life than most of them yet somehow it never toughened her up. Maybe because she was kept indoors as a drudge and a punchbag for that old cow, her ma, or maybe she'd just had all the spirit knocked out of her. And now she was his wife and it was up to him to look after her.

He walked more slowly as he tried to remember the night when old Janey had waylaid him outside the Volunteer. I was half fuddled, he thought, didn't know what she was on about at first. She nattered on about Nellie being ill and getting turned off from her place because of what another girl done, and her ma dead and her da backed off, then she come right out with it.

Something about if Nellie was married to me she'd be safe, or she might marry a fella who'd knock her about or even finish on the streets. It was all too quick for me and I was in a daze, like, Sam thought, but when I seen Ellie and she looked that lost and ill I just hunkered down in front of her and told her I'd look after her.

And now I'm frightening the life out of her with me bloody temper. It wasn't like that at first. The old girl seen to everything then I had to go back but when I got the letter saying that Ellie was expecting I was made up. I thought I was a hell of a fellow, he recalled, and the fellows all pulled my leg. 'Didn't take you long, wack. Two nights,' Buck Madden said and another fellow said Sam'd finish up like Albert Snell with twenty-two kids. All good natured though.

He was nearer the mouth of the Mersey now and the air was salty and fresh. He turned back his face, darkening as he remembered the far from good-natured skitting at the Volley on the night the baby was born. He'd been half cut but not too drunk to know that they were making out he'd been tricked into marrying Ellie. Even hinting the kid wasn't his. Calling him Soft Sam.

I should've battered the lot of them, he thought. But maybe the landlord had seen that coming. He'd been bundled out quick enough by him and his two hefty barmen.

Good job he'd been with Buck and George Adams on his next trip. Two good mates. George had told him babies often came early, two of his did, and they were small like Tommy, but they were healthy lads now. Buck told him them lot in the Volley were just trying to start a fight, and he was right.

Tommy was his kid all right. Look at the way he took to him right away. Like Maggie

Nolan said, kids know their own. He's not like me to look at, Sam thought, but it's just as well. A roughneck like me. He's more like Nellie, in nature anyway, although he's fair and her hair's brown. His spirits rose as he thought about the baby and the softness of the child's body in his arms.

He remembered something else old Janey had said the night she waylaid him. That he'd be getting a good wife and a home to come back to. That was right anyway although he didn't trust that scheming old mare. Yet perhaps she was trying to do him and Ellie a good turn, getting them fixed up together. A home for him and someone to look after Ellie. The old one liked manipulating people.

Yet there was *something,* he told himself. Something he couldn't pin down. The way Ellie would look away from him, couldn't look at him straight, and the way she seemed afraid to cross the old girl. I don't like being kept in the dark, Sam thought angrily, but then he thought that he was sure Ellie wouldn't trick him. Yet why did she look so guilty sometimes?

Sam realised that he was nearly home, yet his thoughts seemed as muddled as ever. The only thing is, he decided, I'll just have to watch me bloody temper, as he recalled the events in the market. He went into the house.

Nellie was sitting darning a sock but she stood up immediately and began to prepare his supper. The vase stood in pride of place on the dresser.

'I didn't go to the Volley,' Sam said. 'Went

for a walk instead. Hasn't half give me an appetite.'

'Where did you go?' asked Nellie.

'I struck up past Seaforth. Past the Liver Hotel,' Sam said. 'You want to take Tommy that way sometimes, girl. Get him away from the smells round here.'

'I will, Sam,' Nellie said meekly.

Later when they were in bed Sam gently stroked her face.

'I give you a fright tonight, Ellie, didn't I? Shouting at you in the market.'

Nellie said nothing, and Sam kissed her and held her close.

'It's just me bloody temper, girl,' he said in a muffled voice. 'It gets the better of me, but I'll watch it from now on.'

'I don't want nothing to do with anyone but you, Sam,' Nellie whispered, 'I feel safe with you.'

There were no more incidents before Sam sailed the following Thursday, and it seemed that his demon of jealousy had been cured.

CHAPTER 5

Nellie was sure that Sam's passionate lovemaking would result in another pregnancy for her, and she was disappointed when her period arrived as usual after he left. She hoped that it was because she was still breastfeeding Tommy, and Maggie agreed with her.

'Some people say it doesn't work for them but it always worked for me. As soon as one child was weaned I'd fall for another one. Some women round here keep babies on the breast until they're a couple of years old, just to get a spell before the next,' she said. 'Anyway, you don't want to be dragged down with too many kids, Nellie.'

'No, but I'd like one or two more,' Nellie said. 'So I could still keep Tommy nice and well fed, yet I could enjoy looking forward to a baby instead of being like I was before he was born.'

She stopped, fearing that she had said too much, but Maggie only said, 'You're bound to have a spell now anyway. Sam's away for about a year, isn't he?'

Yes. Tommy'll be eighteen months old before he sees him again. I don't half miss him, Maggie,' said Nellie with a sigh.

'Aye you've got a real good man there, Nell. He might seem rough but he's got a heart of gold. He's got real feeling for people and especially for poor kids. And he's not so rough now either. Doesn't get in fights like he used to.'

'He's got different mates now. Buck Madden and a fellow named George Adams,' Nellie said. 'He sounds a real nice fellow.'

Maggie was a happy woman now. Through a friend Johnny had obtained a job in a stables as an odd-job man with a steady wage. Johnny's health had improved with the better weather and the work was not too heavy for him. It was temporary but there was a possibility that it could become permanent, and it gave Maggie a welcome respite from her dreaded visits to the 'Parish' and regular money for housekeeping.

The hot weather had a less welcome effect in that it encouraged the vermin which swarmed in most of the houses. Even Nellie and Bob had to resume their battle against them, and the situation was much worse in most of the houses.

The women of the street spent most of the evenings at their doors and Maggie and Nellie often joined the group which gathered round Bella Edwards' step.

'We're druv out be the creatures,' Bella declared dramatically. 'I tell yiz I dread going to bed. Between the bugs and me old man I don't get a wink of sleep.'

Bella was a huge shapeless woman, and one of the other women surveyed her. 'Worn away to a shadder, aren't you, girl?' she said, amid laughter.

Like Bella, many of the women had had ten children or more and seemed to accept their constant childbearing philosophically.

'Must be something they put in the beer at the Volley,' Bella joked.

Bella's married daughter Katy lived opposite to her mother and Nellie became friendly with her.

Katy Rimmer was a quiet girl totally unlike her mother. She had three children and she told Nellie that she was determined to have no more than four, and her husband agreed with her.

'I made up me mind long before I got married,' Katy said. 'You know our Wally was walking down past them posh houses in Trinity Road one day and a scuffer chased him. Said people didn't want the likes of him near them.'

'But he wasn't doing no harm just walking down the road,' Nellie said indignantly.

'Well, you know me mam doesn't bother. Wally was dirty, like, and barefoot and his jersey and kecks were all raggety. Wally didn't care, at least he said he didn't, but I thought then that wasn't going to happen to my kids if I had any. They'd never be chased because they was scruffy. I'd keep them clean and tidy.'

'And no one will ever chase mine either,' Nellie declared.

'It's easier for us, like, because we've both got good husbands,' Katy said. 'Peter's different to the fellows round here, like your Sam. They're proper men, like, nothing sissy about them but they've got a bit of feeling for other people. A bit of consideration,' and Nellie agreed.

'I suppose some of the women lose heart,' she said, 'with everything against them.'

Most families in the street lived a hand-to-mouth existence, only surviving by pawning everything possible on Monday hoping to reclaim it on Saturday. Many of the men could only obtain casual work on the docks. This often meant only one or two half days of work, even though the men had stood in the

'Pen' twice each day hoping to be picked out by the foreman.

The wives of men at sea were often in desperate straits when the allotment left to them was held up. It was almost impossible for women to obtain work.

In spite of this the women tried to keep each other's spirits up and women like Bella could always raise a laugh. They all helped each other and shared what they had. 'We'd go under if we didn't,' they said. 'It's the poor what helps the poor. Nobody else cares a brass farthing for us.'

The children, though mainly ragged and ill fed, were happy enough, never having known anything different. The girls played hopscotch or games with cherry stones, and swung on ropes tied to the lamp-posts, or played skipping. Sometimes two of the mothers on opposite sides of the narrow street turned a long rope for the girls to skip in. Often the girls were joined by some of the younger women who screeched with laughter as they bumped into each other in the crowded rope, or their dilapidated boots flew off.

The boys lived in a world of their own, running along the back-yard walls, playing kick the can or football with rolled-up newspapers and fishing down grids for coins. Often they hung around the docks, clinging to the backs of wagons to fill a cap with brown sugar from a burst sack or carob beans, known as 'locusts', to chew, until a shout of 'Whip behind' made them scatter.

Nellie found Katy a kindred spirit, as they were both determined that their children should have a better life.

'Me mam thinks I'm daft because I'm learning my kids manners,' Katy said. 'To say please and thank you and that.'

'I'm going to teach Tommy all that,' Nellie said. 'I feel ashamed now when I think the way I was when I went to me first place. I didn't know nothing. I'd never sat at a table or used a knife and fork or cleaned me teeth or nothing. The cook Mrs Hignett said I didn't know no more than a Hottentot one day.'

'It wasn't your fault,' Katy said.

'She didn't mean it nasty,' Nellie said. 'They was all very good to me. Learned me what to do about everything, not just the work, and Mr Ambrose and Miss Agatha learned me to sew and read and write.'

'You must've been in good service,' Katy said. 'My first place I went as a general maid, and they didn't know much more than what I did meself. He had a shop and they'd got on a bit, like. I had to do everything and I got worked half to death for five bob a week. Me next place was better but I left there to get married.'

They both borrowed novelettes from Gertie Drew although Katy had less time for reading than Nellie. Nellie had become friendly with Gertie, who was only five years older than her, and often joined her when Gertie sat on her doorstep in the evening. Mrs Drew's bed was in the kitchen, and from the front door Gertie could watch her mother as she slept.

When winter came Nellie went into the Drews' kitchen to talk to Gertie while her mother slept. She was shocked at first by the bareness of the room but Gertie said quietly, 'Me poor mam breaks everything when she has a spell on her. She can't help it, doesn't know she's doing it, but it's no use having much here.'

'You're a good daughter, Gertie,' Nellie said impulsively, but Gertie shook her head.

'I've got to look after Mam,' she said. 'She was a real good mother to me always and after me da died we were all in all to each other.'

Nellie was slightly embarrassed by Gertie's sentimental speech but she respected her loving and uncomplaining care of her mother. Sometimes when she wrote to Sam after reading Gertie's novelettes, she was tempted to draw on them for a romantic message to Sam, but her courage always failed.

She felt that Sam might think she was silly, especially as Sam's letters were still only the stereotyped six lines.

Nellie was gradually becoming more self-confident in some ways although still shy and timid with strangers. She had made up her mind to defy Charlie West and not allow him to upset her, but several times when she saw him approaching she fled down another street. On one occasion she passed a group of men on a street corner, not realising until too late that West was among them. He pushed forward.

'Hello, Nellie, how's business?' he said putting his arm round her shoulders.

100

Tommy had been toddling beside Nellie, but she snatched him up in her arms, jerking away from West, and hurried away, her face burning as she heard jeering laughter from the men. She was shaking when she reached home and told Maggie about it.

'Hard-faced little sod,' Maggie said indignantly. 'What was he talking about?'

'I don't know,' Nellie wept, 'except all them fellas laughed.'

'Don't let it upset you, girl,' Maggie said. 'I know that gang. Hardknocks and ne'er-do-wells the lot of them. Anyway, you tell Sam about them. It won't be long till he's home, will it?'

'Just over a month,' Nellie said.

'Then you tell him, Nell. He'll soon sort that lot out,' Maggie said.

Nellie nodded but the more she thought of the incident the more she wondered whether she would be wise to tell Sam. She remembered his anger in the market. Would he believe that she had done nothing to encourage Charlie West?

She said nothing to Janey but she was sure that the old woman knew something about it from the hints she dropped. Janey had been surly and spiteful since Sam had gone back to sea and Nellie wondered whether it was because Sam had not mugged her from his advance note, or whether it was because he had shown such affection for Tommy.

'The quare fella's very sure the lad's his,' she said one day. 'He might get a nasty shock one of these days. What's bred in the bone will come out in the flesh.'

'Tommy *is* Sam's child. I know he is,' Nellie exclaimed. The attack was so sudden that her eyes filled with tears although she had been determined not to respond to any of Janey's hints about Tommy's parentage.

'Youse two are well matched anyhow,' Janey jeered. 'A whingeing little mare like you and Sam, the big soft ha'porth. He swallered everything I told him.'

Nellie sat with her head bent, saying nothing, and Janey seemed to lose interest. She returned to the subject several times though during the following weeks and Nellie found it hard to ignore her taunts, especially when she spoke of seeing Leadbetter's fair-haired children.

The spring days were warm and Nellie tried to obey Sam by taking Tommy into purer air away from the smells from the gasworks and tannery and the match factory but she was nervous away from her own neighbourhood.

If she saw a policeman she was afraid she might be turned away as Katy's brother had been, and if she passed well-dressed people she thought that they looked disparagingly at her.

She was happier when on several occasions Katy and her children joined her and Tommy and they went to Seaforth Sands. It was a popular spot for the people of Bootle, not too far from home and on sunny days the sands were crowded. A man with a 'Stop Me and Buy One' tricycle did a roaring trade in ice-cream.

Tommy was at first nervous of the sand and shrank from contact with it but the other children encouraged him and soon he was playing as happily as they with it.

'He'll have to get more tough if he plays out in the street,' Katy remarked.

'Yes, but I don't want him to get *too* tough,' Nellie said. 'I don't know why all fellas have to be tough anyway.'

'It's expected,' Katy said. 'Look at Peter. He's fine when he's on his own with me but if anyone else is there he has to be the tough fella, the big boss ordering me round, like.'

Nellie nodded. 'It's just the way they are,' she said. 'The way Sam nursed and cuddled Tommy in the house, but when he was out where his mates could see him he didn't take no notice of him.'

'I saw a motto on a calendar once,' Katy said. ' "Don't expect more from people than they are able to give." I think it means the way Peter and Sam are, if you know what I mean.'

'They can't help it, like,' Nellie said.

'The way they was brought up,' said Katy, 'but this is where we've got a chance with our kids, Nell. We can bring them up different.'

'Sam brought himself up really,' Nellie said. 'He got turned out to fend for himself when he was seven. His mam died and his dad disappeared.'

'He's done well, then. To turn out the way he has,' Katy said.

'He got sent to the reformatory at Heswall when he was eleven,' Nellie said. 'At least it was better than the *Akbar*.'

'The *Akbar*,' Katy exclaimed. 'Me Nin's brother got sent there for three years when it was the old training ship in the river. Very near killed him, she said. Mind you, that was ages ago, about thirty years.'

'They learned Sam to read and write at Heswall,' Nellie said. 'With living rough, like, he'd never been to school.'

'It's a wonder the school board man never got after him,' Katy said. 'I used to be terrified of that fella because me mam was always keeping us home to mind the other kids. I don't know how your mam got away with keeping you off all the time.'

'I remember him coming one time and Ma carrying on at him, but then Janey went out to him and he never came no more,' Nellie said. She laughed bitterly. 'Ma was saying I was too delicate to go to school and I was in the middle of a big wash, just putting sheets through the mangle.'

'I wonder what Janey said to him?' Katy said, but Nellie had not heard her comments although she now wondered about them.

Later, after the evening meal, which had been Janey's favourite tripe and onions, Nellie diffidently asked the old woman how she had dealt with the school board man.

Janey sniggered. 'Your ma was bellowing at him but he was used to that. I just told him I'd report him for acting dirty with kids if he didn't leave us alone. He was gobbling there like a turkey cock, red in the face, saying he'd never heard such a thing, and he'd have the law on me. He changed his tune though when I said I'd get half a dozen women to swear he'd interfered with their kids.'

'But he seemed so respectable,' Nellie exclaimed. 'Did he really do that?'

'Nah,' Janey cackled. 'But he knew the women'd do what I told them. He was blustering there for a while but he knew he was beat. I told him: mud sticks and people'd say there was no smoke without fire. He never come near us again anyhow.'

She laughed happily, pleased with herself, but Nellie looked at her with horror. No wonder people were afraid of the evil old woman, she thought. And she knows something about me that I want to keep hidden and something about Sam's family that it would hurt him to know. She slept little that night.

Nellie knew that Janey was annoyed that she was making friends in the street, and one day when Katy called while Janey was there, to arrange an outing, the old woman said suddenly, 'Why don't you go to Newsham Park where you was in service, Nellie? Mr Leadbetter, wasn't it? I heard he lost his son and daughter with scarlet fever.'

'There's a terrible lot of that about,' Katy said in alarm. 'Me mam's heard the fever hospital's full and three kids have died from round here.'

Janey ignored her and fixed glittering eyes on Nellie. 'Your boss has got no son now,' she said. 'I heard he was looking for any born the wrong side of the blanket.'

'That's got nothing to do with me,' Nellie said faintly.

Fortunately Katy was too concerned with the danger to her children to pay attention to Janey, but later when she was alone Nellie thought long and hard about her problem.

She was not sure whether Janey's comments about the Leadbetters were true but in any case it was clear that the old woman was not going to let the matter rest. I'll have to tell Sam in case he hears it from someone else, Nellie thought, but she quailed at the thought. If only Sam was not so jealous.

Nellie talked often to Tommy about her father and what they would do when Sam came home. The child was still small for his age but he was healthy with bright eyes and clear skin. Nellie bought a tablet of Pears soap and bathed him every night, but even that annoyed Janey.

'You're laying up trouble for yourself,' she jeered. 'Sam won't believe he's his when he sees you trying to make a gentleman outa him. Pears soap, for God's sake.'

Nellie made no reply. She believed that Tommy would be less likely to fall victim to the diseases which were common in the neighbourhood if he was kept clean so she continued to bath him and dress him in clean clothes and to ensure that his food was not contaminated.

Tommy was nearly eighteen months old when Sam returned and he was delighted with the child. Nellie again waited at home for him. She had dressed Tommy carefully and waited at the door for Sam and as soon as she saw him approaching she said to the child, 'Here's your dad, Tommy.'

The child toddled to meet him and Sam dropped his bag and swung his son up into his arms. 'By God you've grown, young fella,' he exclaimed, grinning broadly, 'walking an' all.'

He picked up his bag again and still carrying Tommy walked into the house and kissed Nellie.

'This looks real homey,' he exclaimed looking round the room which Nellie had again carefully prepared for his homecoming. 'I've been thinking about coming back to this.'

Nellie was pink with pleasure. 'The wallpaper got mouldy but me and Bobby done it again,' she said. 'I got the sofa from the pawnshop and done it up. I thought you might have docked last night, Sam.'

'We was supposed to but there was a hold-up. Them bloody dockers were trying to warp us in before midnight though, but luckily we couldn't tie up till nearly six o'clock.'

'I thought the sooner the better,' Nellie said. 'Luckily I didn't tell Tommy just in case. He's been like a hen on a griddle this morning.'

Sam smiled proudly and sat down with the child on his knee. 'I would've been glad to get in early last night. It's them dockers,' he explained. 'If they can warp us in even one minute to midnight we don't get no pay for today even though we don't come ashore for bloody hours.' He stopped abruptly. 'Eh, I'll have to watch me language, won't I? Don't want him coming out with swear words.'

'He'll be a while yet,' Nellie said laughing. 'Although he can say Bobby now and Mag.'

'Can't he say Sam?' he said.

Nellie looked surprised. 'He says Dada and Mama and baba,' she said, 'he's been saying them for ages.'

Tommy was jumping up and down on his father's knee and Sam hugged him. 'Your da's thick, lad,' he said laughing. Tommy pulled at his father's ears and chuckled with pleasure and Sam said suddenly, 'He doesn't half smell nice, Ellie.'

'I bath him every night and I bought Pears soap for him,' Nellie admitted. 'I think it'll keep him healthy but Janey thinks I'm daft.'

'Don't take no notice to *her*, girl,' Sam said. 'She doesn't know what soap and water's for.'

Sam seemed reluctant to part with the child even to eat the bacon and sausage that Nellie fried for him, and after the meal he lay down on the sofa with Tommy in his arms. Both fell asleep and Nellie crept about, careful not to disturb them.

She wondered whether Sam had intended to go to the Volunteer but when he woke he seemed content to play with Tommy in the back yard, teaching him to kick a ball and hoisting him up onto his shoulders.

Good job *I'm* not the jealous sort, Nellie thought. He's hardly looked at me, but still, I'm made up he's making such a fuss of Tommy. Shows he can't have any doubts.

She cooked spare ribs and cabbage for the

evening meal on the gas ring which one of Bobby's workmates had fixed up for them in the scullery. 'It makes all the difference,' she told Sam. 'I don't have to have a fire every day for cooking.'

'Who done it?' Sam asked suspiciously, but Nellie was prepared for the question.

'Some old fellow who works with Bobby,' she said carelessly. 'Bobby and me put together for the half crown he wanted for it.'

She was determined to treat Sam's jealous remarks casually as she felt that tears and protests would only make him more suspicious. It seemed an inauspicious time to tell him about Charlie West and Nellie decided to wait until Sam had been at home for a while.

Now he was still in a good humour, sniffing the air and declaring that the food smelled good. 'The grub was terrible on this voyage,' he said. 'A Chinese cook doped to the eyeballs half the time and the galley lads were dirty little scows. Never used to bother me but you've spoiled me, Ellie.'

Nellie smiled. 'I like everything clean,' she said. 'The cook in me first place was real particular. Everything had to be spotless. I think it's safer for Tommy if everything's clean and so far touch wood he hasn't had none of the illness that the other kids have had.'

Sam now unpacked his bag and proudly produced the presents he had brought home. There was a gaily coloured drum with fringe hanging from it for the baby, and for Nellie a gaudy scarf and two heavily decorated jars which released a musky fragrance when the lids were removed. For Bobby he had brought a tiny shrunken head. He told Nellie it was a fake when she showed signs of revulsion but later he told Bobby that it was real. 'Don't tell your sister though because she'd go mad,' he whispered to Bobby who was delighted with the gift.

Nellie decided to give one of the jars to Janey and asked Sam to give it to her.

'It'll take more than this to cover the smell of her fish,' he joked, but he seemed too happy to refuse anything.

Nellie had made her plans some weeks earlier for serving Janey's meal in the parlour. She had bought a tin tray in the penny bazaar and now she laid it with a bottle of stout and a glass and a plate of bread.

Fortunately Bobby arrived home before Janey and Nellie served the meal for him and Sam and put Janey's portion between two plates. As soon as she heard Janey come into her room Nellie put the plates on the tray then, after knocking on the parlour door, carried it in.

Janey was fumbling in the fishwife's pocket she wore beneath her apron and she looked up angrily. 'What do *you* want?' she snarled.

'I've brought your dinner, Janey,' Nellie said. Her voice was calm although she was trembling as she put the tray on the table. 'It's cooler in here. I'll make a cup of tea for you when you're ready.'

While Janey was still stricken dumb with surprise she escaped to the kitchen, shutting the door firmly behind her. She sank into a chair by the table and Bobby clapped her on the back. 'Great stuff, Nell,' he said. 'You did it at last.'

Sam looked from one to the other in amazement. 'What's going on?' he demanded. 'And what about your grub, Ellie?'

'I'll get it in a minute,' Nellie said breathlessly, and Bobby explained to Sam that Nellie had been trying to pluck up courage to make Janey eat in her own room.

'I have to let her come here in the winter, like, until her fire burns up,' Nellie said, 'but she doesn't need a fire now.'

'You shouldn't even be cooking for her, be rights,' Bobby said. 'It's not as if she's family.'

Nellie nervously signed to him to speak quietly, but Sam said firmly, 'You done right, girl. You don't want that dirty old scow near Tommy.'

There was no sound from the parlour and Nellie waited nervously for Janey to appear, but when she did she said nothing. She sat down by the table and Nellie placed a mug of tea before her, but then just as Nellie relaxed, feeling that all had gone well, Janey suddenly said, 'I told you, didn't I, about that fella you worked for? Joshua something. I heard he'd lost his son and now he's looking for some of his by-blows to take the lad's place.'

'Yes you told us,' Nellie managed to say quietly. 'With scarlet fever. Katy said the fever hospital was full.' Her hands were trembling and she was sure that Sam could not fail to hear the tremor in her voice and the malice in Janey's.

He was sitting in his chair with Tommy standing between his knees, but he only said in alarm, 'Scarlet fever? The hospital's full, you say. It's that bad round here?'

'Katy said it is,' Nellie said. 'But the whooping cough was bad last winter and Tommy didn't catch it.'

'He must be strong and healthy then,' Sam said. He made no reference to Janey's remarks and Nellie hoped that he had decided to ignore the old woman. She hoped too that he had decided that he could trust her and that during this time ashore she could tell him all that she had concealed from him.

CHAPTER 6

Maggie had hinted that Sam might be more demanding in bed after their long separation, and Nellie found that this was true. Sam made love with a passion and urgency which aroused strange feelings in her, and she found it difficult to resist the urge to abandon herself to them.

'Was I too rough, girl?' he asked her when they lay exhausted.

'No, Sam,' Nellie said meekly. She was alarmed by the strength of the tide of passion which had risen in her. She had responded timidly to Sam on other occasions but she had never felt quite like this. Am I a bad woman?

she asked herself in dismay. Mrs Hignett had told her that only bad women let their feelings run away with them when they were out with a young man. Not that I was ever out with a boy, Nellie thought.

Once she had heard a recently married niece complaining tearfully to the cook.

'It's a man's nature, Elsie,' Mrs Hignett had said. 'I've heard the mistress in me last place told her daughters before they were married it was their duty to lie back and submit to their husbands. That's what marriage is about. You've made your bed and you must lie on it.'

I wish I knew more, Nellie thought. She had never been able to make friends in the street or in school who might have enlightened her when she was a child, because she spent so much time as her mother's drudge. She thought of asking Maggie, but although a good neighbour Maggie could be very indiscreet. I wouldn't want no one to know I was so daft, thought Nellie.

In the novelettes it was always the other woman who experienced 'unwomanly feelings' for the hero, and the heroine was always as pure as driven snow. I'd get no sense out of Gertie, Nellie thought, and I wouldn't like to ask Katy. A married woman with a baby having to ask questions like that!

Bella never encouraged dirty talk among the women who gathered by her step, and the respectable women if they spoke of what they called 'that side' of marriage did so with impatience or resignation to the demands made on them by their husbands. Nellie had never heard anyone say that they felt as she did, and she remembered her feelings with guilt.

'I don't bother with them foreign women when we're in port, Ellie,' Sam said suddenly. 'When I was only a little lad me mam was always telling me to keep away from bad women in ports if I went to sea, and I suppose it stuck in me mind. I don't fancy other men's leavings anyhow.'

Nellie said nothing. What would Sam say if he knew how she felt? That she almost *enjoyed* it. He'd think she was one of them bad women his mam had talked about.

Sam spent most mornings in bed then after a meal he would take Tommy to the corner shop for sweets or play with him in the back yard. He bought a brightly coloured ball for the child and never tired of teaching him to play football with it. The rest of the day and evening Sam spent in the Volunteer, 'mugging' men to drinks as was customary and expected from returning seafarers.

Maggie had secured a cleaning job for two mornings a week, and Nellie looked after her two youngest children while she was out.

'We can't go wrong these days,' Maggie said gleefully. 'I'm making the most of it while it lasts.'

Maggie thought that Sam might object to Nellie caring for the children while he was at home but Nellie assured her that it made no difference.

'He's always in bed while they're here in the

morning and even if he gets up he doesn't mind. I think he really likes kids.'

'Yes, he's a good man,' Maggie said. 'I know he still sups every night but he never gets falling drunk, does he, or in any fights. Did you ever tell him about Charlie West?'

'No, I thought I'd better not,' Nellie said, and she was surprised when Maggie said, 'No, better not with him being so jealous, like, but Charlie's lying low now, isn't he?'

And I thought no one knew the way Sam is, Nellie thought. You can't keep nothing to yourself round here.

She never accompanied Sam to the Volunteer, but stayed at home as most of the women did, so she was rarely seen out with Sam. At home he was still like the boy she had known as a child, kind and considerate with her and a doting father to Tommy, who always welcomed him with delight.

He was a good friend to Bobby and the young boy obviously admired him. Sam discussed Bob's job and his workmates with him and gave him good advice about avoiding bad company—which might have benefited Sam himself.

Nellie continued to serve Janey's meal in her own room, and the old woman seemed to have accepted the situation. She sometimes grumbled at Sam when he was nursing Tommy or playing games with him.

'You're too soft with that lad. You'll have him spoilt.' One day she said jeeringly, 'Soft Sam. You're as soft as butter with him.'

115

Nellie held her breath and Sam half rose to his feet with an exclamation of anger, but fortunately the baby said, 'Sam Sam.'

Janey took advantage of the distraction to slip into her own room and Nellie said quickly, 'No, Tommy. Say Dad, Dad, love.'

'He's real quick, isn't he?' Sam said admiringly and the moment of danger passed.

Janey took the first opportunity to make her peace with Sam by praising the child.

Nellie wondered whether Sam would suggest a visit to the market on Saturday night, but instead he told her that they were invited to a party.

'George Adams is having a hooley on Saturday night,' he said. 'And he's asked us.'

'A hooley?' Nellie said. 'Who'd be there, Sam?'

'Buck Madden and his missus and George's brother Albert and his wife. Some of Rose's relations and other people. It'll be a good do.'

Nellie looked apprehensive. 'I won't know anyone, Sam,' she said and Sam laughed.

'You'll know me, girl,' he teased her, 'and anyhow you'll probably know plenty of the women there. You know Buck an' all. He said they're always good do's at the Adams'.'

Nellie prepared carefully for the party, putting the finishing touches to a blouse she had made and on the day washing her hair and pinning it carefully into a neat bun on the nape of her neck. Sam wore a suit he had bought on a trip to America and Nellie felt proud as they walked to the Adams house, though nervous at the prospect of meeting new people.

She would have preferred to leave the baby with Maggie but Janey had been affronted when it was suggested.

'He should be here in his own place,' she said, 'not sleeping with all those kids,' and Sam backed her. He was morbidly afraid that Tommy would be infected with a disease by other children.

In the end Nellie had compromised with a makeshift bed for the child on the sofa. She thought that if he was upstairs Janey might not hear him if he woke and cried.

The Adams house was already crowded when Nellie and Sam arrived, but Rose Adams took Nellie under her wing and introduced her to the other women. Sam went to join the men in the kitchen where a barrel of ale had been provided.

Nellie was overcome with shyness and could scarcely speak at first, but when she felt able to look around the parlour she discovered that she had met several of the women and knew others by sight, so gradually she recovered from her shyness. Buck Madden's wife came to sit beside her and soon Nellie was laughing at her droll comments.

A rough red wine known locally as Red Biddy had been provided as well as the ale and port wine, for the women, and everyone quickly became merry. One of the men came into the parlour and the other men drifted after him, including Sam.

'All right, girl?' he said quietly to Nellie and

when she nodded happily he joined a group of men near by.

Presently Rose Adams drew Nellie and Mrs Madden out to the kitchen with her to pile plates with thick sandwiches of corned beef or egg. Other women carried round the sandwiches and plates of spare ribs.

Many more men had arrived bringing with them large bottles of overproof rum.

'Pinched from the docks, probably,' Rose Adams whispered to Nellie. 'I never asked all this lot and I'm sure George didn't.'

'These fellas can smell a do,' Jessie Madden said.

'Well, as long as they behave themselves,' Rose said tolerantly.

Everywhere was crowded now but someone found Nellie a seat just inside the parlour door. She could see Sam in the corner with the same group of men and he seemed to be enjoying himself.

Nellie was enjoying herself too. It was all new and strange to her, but she was pleased to be accepted by the other women and made so welcome by Rose. All went well until a woman asked Nellie how many children she had.

'Only one so far,' Nellie said shyly. A woman who knew her broke in. 'She keeps him lovely an' all, don't you, girl? He's a credit to you.'

More men were crowding in from the lobby and one of them, named Jed Jones, said jeeringly, 'Aye, Pears soap, no less, I got told, as if he was gentleman's son. You'll have to try it on Sam, girl. See if you can get him to match.'

118

The next moment Sam had pushed through the crowd and gripped the man's shirt, pulling him close. Their faces were only inches apart as Sam snarled, 'Wharra you getting at? Spit it out.'

'No offence, Sam, no offence,' the man stuttered. 'Just agreeing with the women, like—a bit of a joke.'

'Aye, well save your jokes for your own mates,' Sam said. 'Keep your tongue off my wife and child.'

Sam had slackened his grip on the man and George Adams unobtrusively slipped between them. 'Ale in the kitchen, lads,' he said, and Jed Jones scuttled thankfully away.

'You can't do right for doing wrong with some people, lad,' Rose Adams said to Sam. 'If you neglect your children they talk about you, and if you keep them nice they still talk. Have another sandwich, Sam.'

Nellie was trembling with shock and fear. She wondered whether Jed Jones was one of the men who had been in the Volunteer on the night of Tommy's birth or one of those who had been with Charlie West on the street corner. She was relieved when Sam took the sandwich and crouched down beside her chair to eat it.

'All right, girl?' he asked.

Nellie managed to smile at him and say quietly, 'Isn't Mrs Adams nice?'

'George is a good mate too,' Sam said.

Neither of them mentioned the incident which had just happened although both were disturbed by it.

Nellie was even more disturbed a little later when Sam had rejoined his friends and she had carried plates to the kitchen with Rose. Among the group with Jed Jones was Charlie West and he raised his glass mockingly to Nellie.

She ignored him and rushed into the scullery with the plates but he followed her.

'Hello, Nell,' he said in a caressing voice. 'You're looking very nice tonight.'

Nellie blushed and kept her head bent and Jessie Madden said warningly, 'Beat it, Charlie. Don't be trying to cause trouble.'

Charlie laughed. 'Aye, I believe Sam's in good form tonight,' he said, 'but he can't object to me praising his wife.'

In a low voice he said to Nellie, 'I won't say nothing to praise the child because there's a bit of a doubt there, isn't there?'

Nellie looked at him as though mesmerised like a rabbit with a stoat and said nothing.

Charlie said even more quietly, 'Sam won't mind, will he? Soft Sam.'

Jessie came beside Nellie again. 'Are you still here?' she exclaimed to West. 'Beat it or we'll make you wash them plates.' He laughed and turned away and Jessie said, 'What was he saying to you, girl? A proper troublemaker, that feller.'

'Maggie Nolan says he's a pansy,' Nellie said, not answering the question.

Jessie was easily diverted. 'She's right,' she said, 'but he's always trying to make up to women to hide it, like.' She laughed. 'I should've offered to kiss him. That would've got rid of him quicker than the thought of washing dishes.'

Rose Adams paused beside them. 'Is something up?' she asked.

Jessie said, 'Only that bloody Charlie West trying to make up to Nellie. I shifted him.'

'Is *he* here?' Rose exclaimed. 'Now I know *he's* just pushed in because me and George can't stand him. I haven't seen him.'

'You wouldn't. He's such a bloody little runt,' Jessie said.

Nellie still felt uneasy when they all went back to the parlour where a man was reciting 'If' amid laughter as he forgot the lines and had to be prompted by his wife, interspersed with comments like 'You daft fool' from the woman and 'You nagging cow' from the man.

'I got learned that at school,' Buck said. 'I don't remember them words in it though.'

It was all good humoured and the man was followed by others who sang or recited.

Nellie was again sitting near the door and Sam had moved to lean against the wall. She was beginning to relax and forget Charlie West when suddenly he pushed through from the lobby followed by some of his cronies who shouted, 'Come on, Charlie. Give us a song.'

Nellie peeped at Sam but he was still smiling and she remembered that he knew nothing of what had happened while he was at sea.

Charlie West stepped into the centre of the room and began to sing 'Roses of Picardy', holding his glass aloft and looking soulfully round the company as he sang. To some it might have appeared just chance that he looked

121

directly at Nellie as he sang the line, 'But never a rose like you', but Nellie gasped and Sam started forward.

His way was unobtrusively barred by George Adams and at a nod from George, his brother, a big burly man, interrupted Charlie.

'Eh, enough of that soppy stuff,' he shouted drunkenly, lurching to the centre of the room and pushing Charlie into a group by the window as far as possible from Sam, 'let's have a proper song. "Blow the Man Down".'

He began to roar out the verse and the guests joined in the chorus, holding glasses aloft and swaying from side to side. Unseen by most of them Sam grabbed Nellie's arm and pulled her out into the lobby. 'Get your shawl. We're going,' he snapped.

Nellie snatched up her shawl and managed to fling it around her before she was pulled out of the front door and along the street. Sam strode along, gripping her arm, his face dark with anger, and Nellie had almost to run to keep up with him.

'Sam, you're hurting me. My hair's coming down. Stop,' she pleaded, but Sam was oblivious to her protests. His grasp on her arm never relaxed nor the speed with which he strode along, and Nellie was breathless and dishevelled, and grateful for the darkness which hid her distress. Sam never spoke although Nellie sobbed, 'Sam, Sam,' as she was pulled along.

When they reached Johnson Street Sam thrust Nellie before him into the house, then both stood aghast.

Janey lolled insensible in Sam's chair, an empty gin bottle on the floor beside her and Tommy lay on the floor sobbing—hoarse, hiccupping, hopeless sobs which showed that he had cried for hours.

Nellie snatched her arm from Sam's grasp and flew to the baby. She snatched him up. 'Look at his face,' she cried. Two long scratches furrowed his cheek, which was red and inflamed, and his clothes were soaked.

The meek and sobbing wife was instantly transformed into a fury. 'You gave her that gin,' she yelled at Sam. 'That's why she wanted him here. Have you got wood between the ears or what?'

'It was just for minding him, like,' Sam mumbled. He had approached to look at the child but Nellie was holding Tom close as she pushed past Sam and snatched a napkin from a string over the fireplace and dry clothes from a drawer.

She cuddled and soothed the baby, but her fury increased when she sat down to change his clothes and found that there were more scratches on his tender skin from an open napkin pin, and red marks as though from slaps.

'What's she been doing to him?' she said with a controlled fury more powerful than a shout. 'Get her out of here. Out of my sight or I'll kill her.'

Sam obediently hauled the old woman to her feet, turning his head aside as he was assaulted by her foul breath, and half dragged, half carried her into the parlour.

When he returned Nellie was taking a tin of Vaseline from a cupboard, still cradling the child in her arms. He was calm now, only hiccupping occasionally and clinging to his mother. Nellie sat down again without looking or speaking to Sam and he sat down in the corner of the kitchen while she soothed the scratches with Vaseline and dressed the child in his dry vest and nightgown.

'There was an open pin in her neckshawl,' Sam volunteered at last. 'She must have been trying to nurse him like and it scratched him.'

'Lucky that was all she did,' Nellie said grimly. 'She could've fell him in the fire the way she was.' She had the baby over her shoulder now with his head snuggled into her neck as she gently rubbed his back and crooned to him.

Sam tentatively came forward and crouched by Nellie's knee. 'All right, Tommy lad?' he said quietly to the baby.

He looked so miserable that Nellie relented and lifted the child round to sit on her knee facing his father.

'Dada,' Tommy said and began to sob again but he soon stopped when Nellie cuddled him and Sam gently stroked his head.

Later when the child was settled in his cot and they were undressing for bed Sam noticed the bruises on Nellie's arm where he had gripped her.

'Did I do them, girl?' he asked in dismay.

Nellie nodded. 'And I lost all me hairpins an' all,' she said.

124

'I never meant to hurt you, Ellie,' Sam said humbly. 'It's just me bloody temper runs away with me.'

'It nearly did a couple of times tonight,' Nellie said with newfound courage.

Sam scowled. 'I didn't expect to see them lot at the do,' he said.

Nellie said quickly, 'They only pushed in, Rose said. They weren't asked.'

'That little runt Charlie West,' Sam said. 'I'll swing for him one of these days.'

'Maggie says he's a bum boy,' Nellie said hoping to make Sam laugh. 'She says he makes up to women but he'd run a mile if they took any notice.'

'I don't know about that,' Sam growled. 'I think he likes it both ways. Does he make up to you?'

For a moment Nellie hesitated. It was a perfect opportunity to tell Sam about West, but she thought of Charlie's hints about the baby, and his involvement with Janey, and of Sam's unreasonable jealousy, and only said, 'No, Sam. He's thick with Janey but he goes in and out her side door.'

Sam said nothing but he had noticed her hesitation. Later in bed he made love as passionately and urgently as he had done on his first night at home but Nellie felt too drained by the emotions of the evening to be aroused by him.

She lay awake for a while wondering why Sam was so bitter about Charlie West. Had he been the ringleader when Sam was taunted on

125

the night of Tommy's birth and the one to call him Soft Sam?

What had Janey told West about their marriage? She had certainly said something that allowed West to drop hints to her and to taunt Sam. Perhaps about how clever she had been in arranging the marriage.

Surely Janey had not told West anything about Leadbetter? Oh God, I wish we could go right away from here, miles away, she thought despairingly. Just me and Sam and the baby and Bobby, but she knew it was a hopeless wish.

The next morning she was able to conceal the bruises on her arm, but the scratches were very noticeable on the baby's face. Sam was still asleep when Nellie carried the child downstairs, but Bobby and Janey were in the kitchen, Janey drinking tea and Bobby eating bread and jam.

He came immediately to look at the child. 'Wharrave you done to your face, lad?' he exclaimed.

'He scratched it on a pin in Janey's neckshawl,' Nellie said, looking resentfully at the old woman.

'No, he never,' Janey exclaimed. 'Crying little get. Don't ask me to mind him no more. Never stopped whingeing.'

Nellie drew in her breath in outrage but before she could speak, Janey had gone into the parlour, banging the door.

'It was *her*,' Nellie whispered to her brother. 'Sam found the pin open in her neckshawl and she'd hit Tommy an' all. I could've killed her.'

'She had him in the parlour when I come in,' Bobby said. 'Said she didn't want Maggie nosing in because he was crying. She couldn't hear him in there.'

'Did you see him? Was he all right then?' Nellie asked.

'I just went to bed,' Bobby confessed. 'I'm sorry, Nell. I thought he was asleep.'

'It's not your fault, lad. It's mine—and Sam's,' she added angrily. 'It was him wanted Janey to look after him and gave her gin an' all. Paralytic she was.'

Her anger with Sam flared up afresh and she scarcely looked at him or spoke to him when he eventually came downstairs. Tommy was playing on the rag rug and Sam lifted him into his arms.

'Them marks don't look so bad this morning, do they?' he said.

'Bad enough,' Nellie said grimly, banging his breakfast on the table.

'Is your arm all right, girl?' Sam asked.

'I'm not worried about me arm,' Nellie exclaimed. 'It's leaving me child to be knocked about be that dirty old crow.'

Sam hurriedly shovelled down his bacon and egg and escaped without speaking further. I don't know what's come over her, he thought. That carry-on last night and the way she is now. I didn't know she had it in her. Always thought she was that quiet and frightened like. Maybe there's a lot I don't know about her.

He had reached the Volunteer and he shrugged his thoughts aside and went in. George Adams and Buck were already there.

'Bringing the empties back,' George said and Buck greeted Sam cheerfully.

'A good do, wasn't it, Sam?'

'It was,' Sam agreed. 'You and your missus went to a lot of trouble, George.' He felt ashamed when he reflected that George had twice narrowly saved him from getting into a fight.

'Sorry I lost me rag, like, a coupla times, George,' he muttered.

'That's all right, lad,' George said. 'Me and our Albert got rid of that lot. I don't mind anyone pushing in, like, as long as they behave themselves but them lot were just looking for trouble.'

'One of them fellas, named Jones—me dad sailed with his father years ago,' Buck said. 'He was a trimmer like me dad and one time when they was on the old *Maury* Jones was caught stealing from his mates.'

'From his *mates*!' George exclaimed.

'Aye. You know they only took a few singlets and pants and that aboard—didn't have much to take anyhow—and they caught this fella stealing from their lockers. Me dad said the men fixed him for it, said he musta been glad to get ashore at the end of the trip and he left the sea after that. Lived near us but to the day he died dad wouldn't look on the same side of the street he was on. Stealing from mates. You can't get no lower than that. No wonder the son's no good.'

Sam felt with shame that Buck was talking

to ease any awkwardness, and he said gruffly to George. 'I didn't behave no better than them, though. And dragging the wife home early an' all.'

'Don't worry about it, lad,' George said.

Buck said, 'Jessie was made up with your wife, Sam. Thought she was a proper nice quiet girl.'

George agreed. 'Rose said the same. I think she's calling round to see her today. I hope she enjoyed the do while she was there.'

'Oh yes, she did. So did I,' Sam said. He felt uncomfortably that his friends thought that he had treated Ellie badly, and after buying them another drink he left.

He walked down to the dock road and walked along trying to let all the activity distract him from the gloomy suspicion that he had made a fool of himself at the party.

A timber ship was unloading and the smell of the wood reminded him of young Bobby. He should make a good joiner. Really likes the smell of the wood and handling it and he'll have a trade at the end, he thought. I'll have to try to fix something like that for Tom. I don't want him to go to sea, but there's plenty of time yet.

He thought again about the previous evening and the scratches on the baby's face. It's a wonder I never went for the old one, but Ellie properly took the wind outa me sails. I didn't think she had it in her to get mad like that.

He smiled as he remembered Buck describing her as a nice quiet girl. He should've seen her in the kitchen. Like a tiger. He wouldn't've knew her.

Sam's smile faded. Do I really know her at all, he thought, a familiar doubt clouding his mind. I was real fond of her when we was kids and I'd often thought about her after, but I didn't *know* her. Never seen her again until Janey waylaid me that day. We just picked up where we left off and the next thing we was married and then I was off back to sea. She's straight though, I'm sure she is—or else she's a bloody good actress. He tried to dismiss his doubts.

Sam was glad to be hailed by an old shipmate who was talking to the policeman at the dock gates, and he went over to them.

'How do, Sam?' the man said. 'Swalleed the anchor or are you just on leave?'

'Came ashore last week,' Sam said. 'I heard you was on the docks now, Syd.'

'Aye, me eldest lad was getting a bit wild, like. Thought I'd better come home to keep an eye on him.'

'The sea's no life for a married man,' the policeman said. 'Not if he's got kids. Otherwise he might be glad to get away.'

They all smiled. 'I've been married since I last saw you, Syd,' Sam said. 'I've got a nipper too. Eighteen months, walking and talking too.'

'It's more when they're older you need to be there,' Syd said. 'I took a chance but I was lucky. Me da-in-law is a foreman so I got picked out.'

'Being in the Lodge was a help too,' the policeman said with a grin.

'The Paddys do it an' all,' Syd said defensively. 'Look after their own, like.'

Sam soon said goodbye and walked away. If I left the sea how would I go on, he wondered. Syd had fell on his feet but most fellows he knew who were dockers were bloody desperate, but he could always get a ship. I'd like to see Tommy growing up but I won't have to be keeping him out of trouble like Syd's lad, not for years yet anyhow. The thought that he could also keep an eye on Ellie slipped into his mind but he thrust it away.

Nellie rapidly cleared away and washed up Sam's breakfast dishes, then sat down taking Tommy on her knee and cuddling him. He showed no sign of distress now but Nellie felt that she could never atone for leaving him at the mercy of old Janey.

A little later Mrs Adams called on the pretext of bringing some leftovers from the party—spare ribs and boiled bacon and some port wine and rum. 'We always get too much in for a do,' she said. 'Although mind you it might all have gone if George and his brother hadn't threw out some of the gang that pushed in. I wouldn't have minded if they'd behaved themselves, but they kept trying to cause trouble.'

She admired Tommy but said nothing about the scratches on his face until Nellie spoke about them.

'We left him with old Janey from the parlour,' Nellie said. 'She was drunk when we got back here. Sam said she had an open pin in her neckshawl.'

'Poor little lamb,' Rose Adams said.

'He was breaking his heart crying. Must have been crying for ages,' Nellie said, indignation rising afresh in her.

'Just as well you left a bit early then,' Rose said diplomatically. 'Although I was sorry to see you go.'

Nellie blushed. 'Sam got annoyed with that Charlie West,' she said in a low voice.

'He's a nasty piece of work,' Rose said. 'We wouldn't have invited him but once they're there—' She shrugged. 'You don't like to be nasty.'

She looked up at the tin clock on the mantelpiece. 'I must go,' she said. She had been nursing Tommy and she kissed him and handed him to Nellie. 'He's a lovely child. A credit to you, Nellie.'

'He was very small born,' Nellie said blushing. 'But he's come on fine since and he hasn't had no illness so far.' The child stood on her knee and slipped his arm round her neck. He wore a blue romper suit which matched the colour of his eyes, his skin was clear and Nellie had combed his fair hair into a coxcomb.

Rose sighed. 'When you look at him and think of the way some kids are round here,' she said. 'Mind you, God help them, it all gets too much for some of the women. It's all they can do to get the kids enough food to keep them alive, never mind decent clothes. We're lucky with steady money, Nellie, little though it is.'

'I know,' Nellie said eagerly, 'and Sam's very good to me, gave me a lot of his pay-off and brought presents for us, like.'

'Yes, he's a good lad,' Rose agreed. She looked round the room. 'He's a lucky lad an' all. You've made a nice home for him to come back to, love.'

'Our Bobby helped me. He's working for Meldrum's. Going to be a joiner,' Nellie said.

'That's a good trade for a lad. Well, *any* trade is,' said Rose. 'Any job is hard to find. I worry because my eldest lad leaves school next year.' She picked up her shawl and moved to the door.

'I'm sorry about coming away early like, last night,' Nellie said impulsively. 'It was just—'

'I know,' Rose said. 'Sam lets them fellas annoy him. Don't worry, love. It'll soon sort itself out. Takes time to settle into a marriage, you know.'

'I wouldn't ever give Sam no cause,' Nellie murmured, nervously twisting her apron string.

'I know you wouldn't, and so does Sam really. He's just a bit quick tempered, like, but he thinks the world of you,' Rose said. 'Mind you, fellas! They rather be hung, drawn and quartered than tell you.'

She left and Nellie went back into the house smiling. What a nice woman Rose Adams was, and so tactful. I'm sure she called to see if I was all right, after the way Sam rushed me away, Nellie thought. And she pretended not to notice the scratches on Tommy's cheek until I said how they happened. A thought struck her. I hope she didn't think Sam would do anything like that, but she dismissed the idea.

Sam returned a little later and Nellie told him of the visit by Mrs Adams. She had recovered from her unusual anger of the morning, but they were cautious with each other. Both felt that they had learned a lot about each other since the previous day.

CHAPTER 7

Sam had signed on again and left a few days later. The night before he left when he made love to Nellie she felt again an almost irresistible urge to cling to him and let herself be swept along on the tide of his passion.

She managed to resist but she wondered whether Sam had been aware of how she felt when later as they lay half asleep he said suddenly, 'Remember when me and Buck was going aboard just after Tommy was born? You jumped outa bed and called me back. Put your arms round me neck.'

Nellie blushed. 'I'm sorry, Sam,' she murmured. 'I don't know what came over me.'

Sam laughed. 'Don't be sorry, girl,' he said. 'I was made up. Pity me and Buck had to get off right away.'

It seemed a good moment for Nellie to talk about her feelings but as she hesitated, trying to find the right words, Sam said proudly, 'When you think of Tommy then, like a fourpenny rabbit, and the way he is now. A real strong lad.

You take good care of him now, Ellie. Don't let him play out in the street while there's all this fever about.'

'I won't, Sam,' Nellie said meekly.

'Let him play in the back yard or take him out yourself. Did you take him up Seaforth way like I told you?'

'Yes, I told you in the letter, Sam. Me and Katy took the kids to Seaforth Sands.'

'It'd suit me better if you took him out be yourself,' Sam said masterfully. 'Don't take no chances of him getting nothing off other kids.'

'I won't, Sam,' Nellie said. She said nothing about her strange desires. The moment had passed.

After Sam had left Nellie took the baby into her bed again for company. She missed the warmth of Sam's body and the pleasant sensation of lying safe in his arms. Tommy seemed to miss his father too and looked up hopefully when Bobby came home.

'It's only me, lad,' Bobby said sadly.

One day when Janey had been unusually friendly, Nellie spoke about her brother to her.

'Bob misses Sam,' she said. 'In a way it was almost like having me da back for Bob when Sam told him tales about his voyages.'

Janey sniggered, 'Your da never had much to do with Bobby,' she said. 'Why should he?'

Nellie could smell gin on the old woman and felt that it would be wiser to say no more about her father.

She still wondered why he had backed off at such a time. With his mother dead Bobby needed him more, and on his rare visits home her father had always taken her out on her day off. He nearly always made long trips, sometimes of two years, but always she was sure of his affection when he returned.

Janey was not deterred by her silence. 'He he,' she cackled. 'It's a wise child that knows his own father. Sam's not the first in this house to be taken for a mug. He he!'

Nellie looked at her with dislike. She's always hinting, she thought, making out she knows something about everyone. She was determined not to rise to old Janey's bait. The old woman took a swig from a gin bottle Nellie now saw beside her chair.

'Harriet always dolled herself up for your da but he turned his nose up at her,' the old woman chuckled. 'He just made it too plain one time and she got mad. Took up with a Norwegian sailor. Lars—what a bloody name. And there was Bobby. Your da had gone on a China run so we passed him off all right. Your old feller was as daft as Sam. Mugs both of them.'

She suddenly slipped down in her chair and the bottle slipped from her hand. She snored loudly and Nellie looked at her with distaste but she knew that she would have to take Janey to bed.

She held her breath to avoid breathing in the fumes from the old woman and managed to drag her to the parlour, and drop her on her frowsty bed. She took off Janey's boots but otherwise left her fully clothed and covered her with the filthy blankets, suspecting that this was how she usually slept.

Nellie was disturbed by the tale and looked curiously at Bob when he came in. He was a tall, thin boy with a snub nose and a wide mouth and dark red hair. His open friendly face and his wide smile were very attractive and Bobby was popular with everybody.

Janey's trying to make out he's not my brother, Nellie thought, but I don't believe her. She could see many inconsistencies in the story the more she thought about it.

The next morning Janey said abruptly, 'What was you going on about last night? Trying to make out Bobby's a by-blow. Do you want to get him out or sump'n'?'

'*Me!*' Nellie gasped. 'It was you, Janey, who was talking about a Norwegian seaman and all that.'

'Was I, girl?' Janey said smoothly. 'I'd had a drop too much and you know what they say—when the wine's in, the wit's out.'

'Good job I didn't believe you, then,' Nellie said.

'You didn't say nothing to Bobby?' said Janey.

Nellie shook her head. She wondered whether the old woman's mind was failing. Drink had never affected her like this, and the secrets she often hinted about were never divulged. She kept them as a threat or a weapon.

Nellie greeted Bobby with extra affection when he came home from work and piled his plate with the rabbit stew she had made.

'Ar ay, Nell, you haven't left nothing for yourself,' he protested.

'Yes I have, and old Janey's got hers,' Nellie said. 'You need more, Bob. You're a growing lad.'

He *was* growing, she thought. He had been tall and bony like her mother and now he was filling out. He wasn't never like her in character, thank God, Nellie thought, but now he doesn't even look like her. Even his hair isn't gingery like hers any more.

There was a strong bond of affection between them which was very important to Nellie. With Bobby she could discuss old Janey freely, and wonder what went on in the parlour when Janey shot the bolt inside the door and they could hear voices and clinking noises.

'She's up to no good,' Bobby declared. 'We don't know who's sloping in and out that side door,' and Nellie agreed.

By common consent they said nothing about these activities to the neighbours or to Janey herself.

Sam was only away for six months but during this time Nellie had an experience well known to seafarers' wives. Sam's allotment to her was held up and for six weeks Nellie had only the few shillings each week from Bobby and eleven shillings she had managed to keep from Sam's pay-off to keep four of them.

She eked it out as sparingly as possible but the day came when she was without a penny in her purse or food in the house. Janey had offered a loan but Nellie refused.

'The blooming cheek,' she said later to Bobby. 'She never cracks on about rent or paying for her food and then she has the nerve to offer me a loan.'

'If she gave you what *she* owes you we'd be all right,' Bobby said. 'You could get tick off Bessy, you know, Nell.' Nellie remembered that the nurse had given this advice too and timidly asked at the corner shop.

'Of course,' the proprietor Bessy Deakin said. 'I know I can trust you, Nellie. I wonder if some of those top fellas would like it if their wives were left without money?'

Nellie received the same sympathetic response from the butcher and the milkman also but she had to nerve herself to ask them for credit.

George Adams' money had also been held up and Mrs Adams told Nellie that there was no disgrace in asking for 'tick' in these circumstances.

'I've had to do it a few times,' she said, 'but people know who they can trust. We're lucky we're able to do it, Nellie. Many a family round here would've starved without their neighbours when their money's been held up.'

Nellie had become very friendly with Rose Adams. She was a kind and motherly woman who did much to give Nellie more confidence in herself, and Nellie felt that she could turn to her for advice and help.

She had avoided Katy and Gertie while she was in difficulties, afraid that a casual remark would reveal her straits, but she still saw Maggie every day. She had managed to conceal her lack

139

of money for a while but when Maggie realised the situation she was furious.

'The way you and Sam helped us and then to shut us out when you've got a bad patch. I thought we was friends, Nellie.'

She was genuinely upset and Nellie tried to make amends.

'I would've said, Mag, honest, but we haven't gone hungry. I've got tick off Bessy and the butcher,' Nellie said.

Maggie went on. 'To think you was worried like that and never let on. And the money Sam's give us and the way you've helped me out and fed our Richie when I was hairless about him.'

'Maggie, I know things are better for you, like, but I know you've never got nothing to spare,' Nellie said, but that made matters worse.

'We're not bloody destitute,' Maggie said, her face red. 'Not so bad off we can't help a neighbour—or maybe you don't want help from the likes of us. We're not good enough.'

Nellie burst into tears and immediately Maggie changed. She threw her arms round Nellie and hugged her.

'There there, don't cry, girl,' she said. 'I was just that hurt when we'd been good friends. It's all right, Nell.'

The quarrel was quickly made up but Nellie realised that she must be more careful in future. Maggie had feelings too and could be easily hurt because of all she had endured. Nevertheless life was good now for Maggie, her only worry Richie's bowed legs.

'We was at rock bottom before he was born,' Maggie told Nellie. 'Many a day I never broke me fast and then when he was born me milk wasn't no good to him. It was Gertie's ma what saved him. That was before she went funny in the head. She used to slip me a tin of conny onny to feed him, and I'll never forget her for it. Poor woman. She doesn't deserve what's happened to her.'

Johnny Nolan looked a different man now as he walked to and from his job and not only because of his improved food. He walked with his head up full of confidence.

'The boss told him his job's safe,' Maggie said. 'Unless he's laid up for weeks in the winter he'll keep him on. His own lad was gassed and wounded but he died.' Maggie still had her two mornings' cleaning which brought in six shillings a week, and she often received scraps of food or a piece of soap. 'It's not Pears but it'll do us,' she joked.

Maggie was outraged when she discovered that Janey paid nothing towards the cost of the rent and food. 'And she never let on even though she knew your money was held up?' she exclaimed. 'The miserable cow. She's rolling but she'd skin a flea for its hide.'

'She was narked because I wouldn't take a loan off her,' Nellie explained. 'Nurse McCann told me not to and our Bob said I could get tick.'

'I'm glad you had the sense, girl,' Maggie said forcefully. 'There's plenty round here rue the day they ever got in her clutches.'

'That's what the nurse said,' Nellie agreed.

Nellie had also become closer to Gertie. Mrs Drew had been slightly better and sometimes she joined Gertie as she sat on the doorstep, and even walked out with her daughter, Gertie's arm firmly linked in her mother's arm.

The improvement was only temporary, and one night Nellie heard sounds of screams and breaking furniture from across the road. She asked Bobby to watch over the baby and hurried across. The noises had ceased but Nellie knocked gently on the window then asked through the door, 'Are you all right, Gertie? Can I help?'

Gertie opened the door, looking dishevelled. 'It's all right, Nell. Mam had a bad turn but she's all right now. Will you help me to settle her?'

Nellie concealed her amazement at the state of the house and helped Gertie to lift her mother, who was slumped in the corner of the room, and settle her in the bed in the kitchen.

Mrs Drew was breathing stertorously and Nellie looked at her doubtfully. 'Should she have the doctor, Gert?' she asked.

'Yes, but I'll tidy up a bit first,' Gertie said. 'I don't mind you seeing the mess, Nell, but I don't want anyone else to. Mam was always so proud and dignified.'

The leg of a small table by the window had been broken and dishes had cascaded from it to the floor and broken and the mirror above the fireplace had been shattered.

In the back kitchen the chaos was even more.

A solid wooden chair was the only whole piece of furniture and it lay among the ruins of the stone sink. A cupboard door had been wrenched off and the contents swept to the floor.

'Mam's enormously strong when this trouble's on her,' Gertie said. 'I'll just clear the kitchen and shut the door on this and get the doctor. I'll send Jessie's lad for him.'

While the neighbour's lad went for the doctor, Gertie and Nellie swept up the broken dishes and put the shattered mirror in the back kitchen, but first they attended to Mrs Drew. They had simply lifted her on to the bed and covered her with a blanket to warm her, but now Gertie brought down a clean nightgown and sheets from upstairs.

Together they removed the sick woman's nightdress which hung in shreds, and replaced it with the fresh nightgown, while Gertie spoke soothingly to her mother.

'Don't worry, Mam. We're just making you comfortable. Everything's all right, Mam.'

Nellie felt her eyes fill with tears as Gertie lovingly kissed her mother and the older woman tried to smile. Her mouth seemed twisted and when the doctor came he told them that she had suffered a stroke.

'Nothing much you can do, Gertie,' he said. 'Just keep her warm. You've got a feeding cup, haven't you?' Gertie nodded and he said, 'Try her with a drop of milk. She may not be able to tell you if she's thirsty but don't worry about food at present.' He patted Gertie's arm. 'You've been a jewel of a daughter. Done

143

everything possible for her.'

Gertie went to the door with the doctor but after he left she dashed into the back kitchen. Nellie sat down beside the sick woman, smiling at her and wondering why Gertie had not returned to her, but when she heard muffled sobs from the back kitchen she understood.

A little later Gertie came to the bedside, red eyed but composed.

'Thanks, Nell,' she said. 'I'll be all right now.'

'I'll help you with the back kitchen,' Nellie said. 'But first I'll go over to our house and make a cup of tea.'

Before Gertie could protest she left the house and returned shortly bearing a tray with a teapot full of tea, cups and saucers and two slices of bread and butter.

'Mrs Hignett, the cook in me first place, told me you should have hot tea and a slice of bread or cake after a shock,' she said, and Gertie admitted later that she felt much better for it.

'I just got upset the way the doctor spoke,' she said. 'As though this was the end for Mam.'

'It'd be very hard for you if it was, Gert,' Nellie said gently, 'more so because you've been looking after her for so long and had so much to do for her, but maybe for your poor mam?'

Gertie's lips quivered but she said nothing and Nellie left her with her mother and tried to clear up the back kitchen.

Gertie came to help and when they had done all they could Nellie went thankfully home to bed. Gertie promised to lie beside her mother and sleep, and send a message to the factory that she would not be at work.

The next morning Nellie went across to Gertie's house as soon as she saw the curtains drawn back, to find that Mrs Drew's condition was unchanged. Gertie said that she had been able to give her mother some milk from a feeding cup with difficulty but that she had slept for the rest of the time.

'I don't know what to do,' she said. 'I'll have to work to keep us. One thing, my poor mam will be easier to look after now.'

'Has the doctor been back?' Nellie asked.

'No, and I don't want him,' Gertie said. 'I've sent for my cousin to come. He'll repair the back kitchen window and get me a new sink so no one knows what Mam was like last night. He's a good fellow. He won't say anything.'

'It's nothing to be ashamed of,' Nellie exclaimed. 'Your mam didn't know what she was doing.'

'Yes, but if the doctor seen it he might try to put her away, like,' Gertie said. 'One time when she'd had a spell I made the mistake of bringing a doctor in. A stranger, not Dr Wilson, and he brought a fella with a strait-jacket for her, but I wouldn't let them take her. They couldn't do nothing because she never went out so she couldn't be no danger to anyone.'

Nellie impulsively hugged Gertie. 'What a lot of worry you've had, Gertie love,' she said, but Gertie shook her head.

'These last few years, like,' she said. 'But even then we had our good times, me and Mam. Times when she was just her old self and we could have a laugh together. That's why I couldn't let them put her away, Nell. What if she had a good spell and realised where she was and that I'd let them do it?'

Nellie offered help and another neighbour, Jessie, who knew only that Mrs Drew had had a stroke, offered to sit with her while Gertie worked but in the event their help was not needed. In the small hours of the morning Mrs Drew suffered another and fatal stroke.

After the funeral Nellie often went to sit with Gertie in the evening. The cousin had taken down Mrs Drew's bed and brought down from the bedrooms the sofa and oddments of furniture and ornaments which had been put up there for safety.

'I'll take a lodger later on,' Gertie said. 'But I'll have to give myself a few months first.'

Nellie agreed. She was surprised to find Gertie so sensible about her loss. She had expected her to be very emotional and inconsolable but she seemed to have quietly decided that death was the kindest way for her mother to avoid further suffering.

The neighbours were all very sympathetic.

'Your mam thought the sun, moon and stars shone outa you, girl, when you was little,' Bella said. 'Nothing was too good for you. She was a good mother and when she needed it you was a good daughter to her. You haven't got nothing to blame yourself for and there's not many can say that when they lose someone.'

Nellie was still very friendly with Bella's daughter Katy but they had spent less time together, partly because Nellie was with Gertie and partly because Katy's eldest child Amy had started school. Katy went back and forth with her to the school four times a day in spite of her mother's jeers.

'Me mam thinks I'm coddling her,' she told Nellie.

'I don't see why,' Nellie said. 'I'll take Tommy when he starts school.'

'Ma thinks I should let Amy go with the big girls from the street,' Katy said. 'But I remember when I first started school. Our Sophie used to run off with her mates as soon as we got out of the street and I was terrified. Didn't know what to do when I got to school and how to get home when I came out. Everything's going to be easier for my kids than it was for me, as much as I can make it anyhow.'

Nellie felt very close to Katy in their views and wondered whether she could ask her for advice about the problem of her response to Sam, but it was Rose Adams who made it easy for her to discuss it.

Nellie had confided that she was disappointed that again her period had arrived which meant that she had not conceived.

147

'I was really hopeful because Tommy's been weaned for so long,' she said.

They were sitting by the fire in Rose's kitchen on a grey and overcast day which made the room dim and confidences easier.

'Perhaps you're *too* anxious,' Rose said gently. 'I knew a woman in Wordsworth Street who was desperate for a child, and when she gave up hope and adopted one, she started with her own within months. She'd been married twelve years too.'

'I was so sure this time though,' Nellie said. 'Sam—you know—being away so long.' She stopped, blushing, but Rose seemed to understand.

'Aye, Sam is like George. They don't go with the foreign women. I used to think that was why I started every time George went back nearly. I've had three miscarriages, you know.'

'So you've started eight times,' Nellie said. 'I don't know what's wrong with me.'

'Give yourself time, love,' Rose said. 'Sam thinks the world of you, you know, Nellie.'

'I do of Sam,' Nellie murmured shyly.

'But do you tell him?' Rose asked. 'He's a real good lad, but he's never had much affection. Knocked from pillar to post when he was a child then a hard life in that reformatory and then at sea. You should make a fuss of him, let him know that he's loved, Nell.'

Nellie nerved herself. 'I feel sometimes, I want to be more like he is like when he's very—when we're in bed like...' Rose said nothing and

148

Nellie plunged on. 'Mrs Hignett, she told me only bad girls let their feelings run away with them, like.'

'But she was talking about girls who aren't married, surely?' Rose exclaimed.

'Yes, I suppose so,' Nellie said. 'She said when a girl is with a young man.'

'Well, she was right to warn you to watch your feelings then, Nellie, because of the risk to yourself, but I'm sure she didn't mean when you was married, girl.'

'But—but I've heard other people,' Nellie said, her cheeks burning, 'nobody seems to—to like it and get excited, like.'

'Well, I do,' Rose said roundly, 'and so do other people but they won't admit it. That's because they moan about fellas giving them babies and they don't want to admit they're half to blame.'

Nellie was silent with amazement and Rose said cheerfully, 'So you give Sam a nice surprise when he comes home, girl. Let your feelings run away with you.'

Nellie blushed and smiled and no more was said on the subject, but Nellie felt even more fond of Rose. She was so nice, she thought, didn't make me feel a fool, like. I wish I'd had a mother like her.

Nellie was very relieved when her money came through and she was able to pay her debts. The experience had shaken her and she determined to put away a few pennies and not to buy anything but absolute necessities. No more dishes from the mug market or material for clothes for the baby or herself.

Sam's money would have been sufficient to keep herself and Tommy but it also had to stretch to feed Bobby and old Janey. Bobby was now indentured so his small wage as a can lad was reduced even further.

Nellie had to help him out with clothing, usually from Cazneu Street market, which she altered and washed, and by knitting jerseys for him, often from wool unravelled from secondhand jumpers.

She always tried to provide a hot meal when he and Janey returned from work, but it was difficult to provide sufficient. Bobby, as a growing lad, had a huge appetite, and Janey watched his plate jealously and complained if her serving was less. Nellie was determined that Tommy should have an adequate amount but often her own share of the food was very small. She told herself that she needed little as she was so small and slight, but she often resented Janey's greed.

Janey was again having her meals with the family since Sam left, but there were still mysterious sounds from Janey's parlour on the occasions when she retired there and shot home the bolts on the inside of the door. There were often raised voices too, either on these occasions or when Janey was visited by her moneylender clients, but Nellie tried to ignore them.

She had decided to be more like her brother Bobby, who sailed through life apparently without a care in the world.

CHAPTER 8

Nellie looked forward eagerly to Sam's return for several reasons. She crushed down the thought of the advice from Rose during the day but at night she let her mind dwell on the prospect of Sam's lovemaking with a mixture of nervousness and longing.

She wondered too whether this time she would conceive again. If she could have another child who resembled Tommy surely it would convince Sam that Tom was his child. Not that he ever openly doubted it. His affection for the boy never wavered, but Nellie was sure that some lingering doubt, although unacknowledged and unrecognised, was at the root of his distrust and jealousy.

Perhaps this time, especially if she showed Sam how much she cared for him, his time ashore would pass without any jealous scenes. She thought of Rose's words about Sam's need for affection and resolved to show him how much she and Bobby and the baby had longed for his return.

Nellie met Buck Madden's wife shortly before the ship was due.

'Won't be long now before they're home,' Jessie Maddox said. 'Mind you, I don't know why we should be excited about it. The fellas spend more time in the Volley than what they do with us.'

'Sam played with Tommy in the back yard most afternoons,' Nellie said shyly. 'At least he did the last time he was home. Teaching him to kick the ball, like.'

'Must want him to be a footballer,' Jessie said. 'I think the novelty's wore off with Buck and our kids.'

'Perhaps it'll have wore off with Sam this time,' Nellie suggested, but Jessie laughed.

'I don't think so,' she said. 'He's got the fellas' ears wore out about how marvellous young Tommy is. And then Buck and our eldest lad have never got on, and me other three are girls.'

'I'd love a little girl,' Nellie said wistfully.

'Plenty of time yet for you, girl,' Jessie said. 'Be glad you've had a bit of a break. I've lost two. A lad of three and another lad at six weeks. James and Matthew, on top of the four what lived.'

'How could you bear it? Losing them, I mean,' exclaimed Nellie thinking of her own little boy.

'You've *got* to bear it, girl. Just get on with it because you've got the others to see to, but you never really get over it. Never forget them,' Jessie said. 'My poor mam only reared three out of nine and me dad wasn't no comfort to her. All he cared about was the drink. Mind you, Buck did his best for me but they can go back to sea with their mates and put it out of mind, like.'

Nellie found that several seafarers' wives felt that their return was a mixed blessing.

'I dread him coming home in one way,' a neighbour said. 'You get enough of his pay-off from him to settle the debts and redeem the things out of pawn, and the rest goes over the bar, mugging his mates.'

Another woman agreed. 'He's in bed all morning then afternoon and night he's in the Volley. I don't get no allotment while he's home either.'

'But you've still got to keep them while they're home,' the first woman said. 'And they want better food than what us and the kids have while they're away. Then when the pay-off's finished they're scrounging off us for ale money. I'm glad to see him home but I'm always glad to see the back of him when he goes. The allotment's not much but you get it every month.'

'Aye, except when it's held up,' another woman said, laughing.

Nellie hesitated. She was unwilling to seem to boast yet she felt that it was unfair to Sam not to say that he behaved differently with money. She compromised by saying only, 'Mine was held up this trip.'

'Aye, that often happens,' the first woman said. 'Mind you, it's not the fella's fault. It gets stopped off their money regular but we don't get it on time.'

Nellie felt even more loving towards Sam after these conversations and she worked hard to prepare a welcoming home for him.

Sam arrived with gifts as usual. A silky shawl for Nellie, toys for Tommy and a clasp knife for Bobby.

'I'll give the old one money for gin,' he told Nellie then grinned. 'We won't be leaving Tommy with her, will we?'

He was delighted to see how much Tommy had grown. The child was shy at first, but when the toys were produced he was soon chattering to his father, and afterwards monopolised his attention for the first few hours.

Bobby and Janey returned and Nellie served the meal, taking Janey's into the parlour.

The old woman made no protest, pleased with the money Sam had given her for gin. Bobby was delighted with his clasp knife and immediately began to carve one of the pieces of wood he brought home for the fire.

'Come and get your dinner. Never mind that,' Nellie commanded.

'Getting proper bossy, our Nellie,' Bobby said to Sam. 'Remember when she wouldn't say boo to a goose?'

Sam looked from Bobby to Nellie. 'Aye, I see what you mean, lad,' he said. 'She's not as quiet as she looks.'

There was silence for a moment broken by Tommy shouting, 'More bread.'

Sam was about to give bread to him but Nellie put her hand over his. 'More bread what, Tommy?' she asked.

'More bread, please,' the child said smiling at his mother.

'That's a good lad,' Nellie praised him.

Sam exclaimed, 'Listen to that, and he's not three yet.'

'I'm learning him manners,' Nellie said. 'You

know Katy Rimmer, Bella's married daughter, well, I've got friendly, like, with her. She's got three kids and she's learning them all to say please and thank you and that. Their Amy's started school and the teacher said she was a nice polite child.'

'That's a good idea,' Sam said approvingly. 'But you don't have to get no ideas from anyone else, Ellie. You got learned manners.'

'Not here,' Nellie said grimly. 'I often think about the cook saying I didn't know no more than a Hottentot when I went to me first place. No one's never going to say that about Tommy, not if I can help it. Mind you, I wouldn't have started learning him so young, only for Katy.'

As they sat with cups of tea after the meal Sam said suddenly, 'There's something I've got to tell you, Ellie.' Bobby stood up to go but Sam said, 'Hang on a minute, lad. This concerns you an' all. It's about your da.'

'About Da?' Bobby echoed sitting down again.

'You know we was talking about him last time I was home, Ellie? Well, it turned out a fella on our gang was a shipmate of your da's. Was in New Orleans with him on his last voyage. He said your da never backed off. He thinks he was murdered.'

'Murdered!' Nellie and Bobby exclaimed in unison.

'Aye. He said they was walking down this place and they seen an old black woman carrying a big basket. She was limping along and your da went to take the basket off her

155

and carry it. To cut a long story short a gang of white men came round them. This fella Bert said he seen your da getting dragged off.'

'Didn't he help him?' Nellie said indignantly.

'He couldn't have done no good. He said they was holding him back, but I think he just run for his life. But he said they had murder in mind all right and there was a big gang of them. He got back to the ship and he fell in with a fella from their fo'c'sle who told him to keep his mouth shut.'

'So he never reported it?' Bobby said.

'No, Bert said this fella told him if it got to the bridge—to the officers, like—they'd have to make a fuss. Get the British Consul and that. He said it might hold up the ship or Bert might get left behind to answer questions, and God knows what would happen to him.'

'But he might have saved Da,' Nellie exclaimed.

Sam shook his head. 'No, girl. I know what it's like in them parts. They do what they like. Your da would be murdered right off and his body'd be buried somewhere. Plenty of places round there for a body to be hid and the scuffers there wouldn't worry too much about looking for it an' all.'

'But Bert could have said something when he got home. At least we'd have knew about Da,' Bobby said.

'I said that to him,' Sam agreed. 'But he had his own troubles when he got back. His lad had been torpedoed near the end of the war and adrift in an open boat nine days. Picked up

156

and taken to Australia, and to hospital. Then he was sent home. When Bert got back the lad was dead and buried. Died on the way home.'

'Poor fellow,' Nellie said. 'He wouldn't be thinking about nothing else at a time like that.'

'He said then he heard your ma was dead so he didn't bother no more,' Sam said.

They all sat in silence then Nellie said with a sigh, 'Well, at least we know now. We won't be thinking he might walk in any time.'

'I'm sorry Da's dead,' Bobby said, 'but I'm glad he didn't just back off and leave us,' and Nellie agreed.

She began to prepare the child for bed and Sam and Bobby went out together, Sam to go to the Volunteer and Bobby with his friends to a boxing club.

Nellie's thoughts were all of her father and she bathed and dressed the child in his nightclothes. Her father would never see his grandson. She remembered his kindness to her when he was home from sea, and wept for him.

When Sam returned, Nellie began to look forward to going to bed with a mixture of excitement and nervousness as she remembered the advice Rose had given to her.

When they were in bed Sam at first held her in his arms gently stroking her hair.

'Are you upset about your da, girl?' he asked quietly.

'In one way, but in another, like Bob said, I'm glad to know,' Nellie said. 'At least he got killed trying to do a good turn, not just in a fight.'

'I didn't know whether to tell you or not,' Sam said. 'But I thought you'd want to know, like.'

'It always bothered me that Da backed off just at that time,' Nellie said. 'Y'know, me ma just dead and Bobby still only a kid, and he knew I'd miss him. I know he never really had much time for Ma so he wouldn't have gone because she died. I'm glad he couldn't help not coming home.'

'I think that feller Bert felt better when he'd spilled it out to me,' Sam said. 'I said we wouldn't say nothing to no one else about it.'

'We should've told Bobby that,' Nellie said in alarm. 'You know the way he talks to everyone.'

'Not to no one who could cause trouble,' Sam said.

His mouth came down on hers and as he caressed her she gave herself up to the strong tide of passion which rose in them and swept them to a climax.

'I love you, Sam,' she whispered and drew his head down to hers.

He held her close and kissed her, his lips almost bruising hers. 'I love you too, Ellie,' he whispered, kissing her eyes and her throat.

They lay quietly for a while, Nellie in Sam's arms with her arms about his neck and her head on his shoulder.

'By God,' Sam said at length. 'No wonder they say you can't fathom women. You're full of surprises, Ellie.'

He began to kiss her again and as Nellie

responded to him he made love to her with a passion and urgency that frightened her.

'Oh God, Ellie, oh God,' he gasped as she clung to him trembling. 'I'm sorry, girl. I'm like a bloody madman.'

'No Sam, it's me,' Nellie said. She hid her face in his neck, suddenly shy. 'Are you shocked, Sam?' she whispered.

He stroked her hair. 'No, girl, just surprised, like.' He smiled. 'I didn't think you had it in you.'

They lay spent with emotion until Sam said suddenly, 'But why now, Ellie? You was never like that before.'

Nellie thought he might be vexed if he knew that she had discussed it with Rose so she said only, 'It's just with listening to other women talking about their husbands, like. Made me think what a good husband you are, Sam.'

'But what do they talk about?' Sam asked.

'About when the husbands come home. None of them are as good to their wives as what you are, Sam. Even Buck Madden.'

Sam drew back his head and looked at her. 'Buck! There's nothing wrong with Buck. Has his missus been saying different?'

'No, it's just that he doesn't take an interest in his kids as much as what you do in Tommy,' Nellie said.

'He's a real good father,' Sam said indignantly, 'And a good husband and a real good mate.'

'It was just she said that the novelty's wore off a bit with their kids,' Nellie said hastily. 'It's all new to us with Tommy.'

Sam smiled but he was still indignant on Buck's behalf. 'Fancy Jessie Madden calling Buck though. She wants to be married to some fellas I know. She'd value Buck all right then.'

'No, honestly, Sam, we was only talking about the way you play with Tommy and talk to him and she said the novelty wears off. She wasn't calling him. Did you know she lost two children?'

'Aye, I remember how cut up Buck was,' Sam said.

'It was other women, really, talking about the way their husbands drank nearly all their pay-off and never came home hardly,' Nellie said. 'Made me realise how good you are.' She reached up and kissed him again.

'They done me a good turn, then,' Sam said, kissing her and holding her close.

Long after Nellie fell asleep Sam lay awake. No wonder fellas said you never knew where you were with women, he thought. Ellie was certainly a bundle of surprises. Where was the timid frightened little girl he thought he had married? She was still shy and timid in some ways but in others—!

He thought of the night of the Adams' party and the way she had been transformed when they returned home. Mind you, that was just like a tigress with her cubs. Mother's instinct, he thought. But tonight! I wouldn't never have thought she had it in her. Never would have believed she could be like that. I hope nobody's been tutoring her, he thought grimly. I'll bloody soon cure them if they have. But the next moment he felt ashamed of his doubts.

Ellie was straight, he was sure of it. He thought of the reason she had given him for being so loving and smiled. Other women's talk. But Buck Madden's wife talking about him too.

Buck was the best fellow ever trod shoe leather. Been a good mate of his for years. That woman doesn't know when she's well off. Then he remembered what Buck had told him about his son. Giving him cheek and his wife sticking up for the lad. Putting Buck in the wrong.

And Syd had left the sea because of trouble with his eldest lad. I'll never have nothing like that with Tommy, he thought. Ellie won't go against me and she'll bring Tommy up proper while I'm away. Learn him manners an' all. Me and Tommy'll always be good mates. He was smiling when he fell asleep.

Sam's time ashore passed happily, the days spent taking out his son or drinking with his mates, and the nights in passionate lovemaking with his wife. Nellie tried to show Sam all the affection of which Rose thought he had been starved, and Sam said several times how much he appreciated the comfortable home she had made.

Sam sometimes gave Nellie orders about her care of Tommy and she always accepted them meekly and submissively, but this was the tradition of the neighbourhood, and Sam, although masterful, never bullied his wife.

On Saturday they went to the market and met Rose and George Adams there. Rose was leading her youngest child, a boy of seven, by the hand, and Nellie held Tommy's hand as he toddled beside her. The two men walked behind them and although Sam watched Nellie jealously he could see nothing to which he could take exception.

Nellie had not seen Rose since the men returned from sea, and although Rose asked no questions Nellie whispered shyly, 'I took your advice, Rose.'

'Good. Sam looks happy anyway,' was all that Rose said but she smiled warmly at Nellie.

The crush in the market was growing and Sam lifted Tommy in his arms. 'There y'are, lad. You can see a bit more now.'

Tommy wound his arms round Sam's neck and kissed him unselfconsciously and Sam beamed with pride.

Nellie had seen both Charlie West and Jed Jones in the distance while Sam was away but managed to avoid them, but by an unlucky chance as she and Sam returned from the market they met West at the corner of the street.

He pretended to look guilty, darting nervous glances at Nellie and Sam. 'Oh oh, I didn't know you was home Sam,' he said with a nervous titter.

'Is that why you're hanging round here?' Sam demanded, and put Tommy down to stand beside him. 'What's your game?'

'Nothing, nothing, Sam,' West stuttered,

darting away down the side entry. Sam made to go after him but the child was gripping his leg. They went into the house and immediately Sam began to shout at Nellie.

'What's your game? What's your fancy man doing hanging round here? Thought I was away. So that's what goes on when I turn me back.'

He loomed menacingly over Nellie and she began to cry.

'He's just a troublemaker. I've never seen him except in the distance and I've always dodged him.'

'Dodged him? What's going on between you?' Sam shouted.

'Nothing, Sam, nothing,' Nellie wept. 'He's just a troublemaker,' but it was only when Tommy, sensing the quarrel, began to cry loudly that Sam calmed down.

Nellie tried to convince him that West had just put on an act to cause trouble between them. 'I hate the fellow,' she said. 'He'll be laughing now especially if he thinks he's made us fall out. Laughing up his sleeve.'

Sam muttered that West would laugh the other side of his face when he caught him, but he remained sulky and suspicious. When they went to bed he turned his back on Nellie, and hurt and angry she turned away from him.

The next morning they scarcely spoke. Sam slept until midday and then ate bacon and eggs in silence before picking up his cap and walking out without a word.

As it was Sunday Bobby was at home and

he looked at Nellie in surprise. 'Sam got a bad head?' he enquired.

'He's got *something* bad,' she said grimly. She cleared away the meal, clashing the dishes together loudly, then wiped Tommy's face.

'If anyone asks, we're going over to Gertie's,' she announced. 'We might go out somewhere.' As Janey always went off early on Sundays on her mysterious errands it was clear that Nellie meant Sam, but Bobby prudently said nothing.

She whisked the child over to Gertie's house and Gertie ushered them into the kitchen which was now comfortably furnished, and gave Tommy a picture book to look at.

She made tea for herself and Nellie. 'Everything all right, Nell?' she asked.

Nellie hesitated then decided to confide in Gertie. She was not a gossip.

'I'm so mad,' she said in a low voice. 'We had a lovely night at the market last night. We met Rose and George Adams with their youngest and everything was the gear. Then when we got home we met Charlie West almost outside the door and you should have seen the act he put on, Gert. Pretended to look guilty and said he didn't know Sam was home. As if he'd been coming to see me on the sly.'

'I hate that fellow,' Gertie said. 'He thinks he's the answer to the maiden's prayer. If he only knew what people think about him.'

'He's a born troublemaker,' Nellie said.

She felt her eyes fill with tears and Tommy

164

looked up apprehensively. Gertie quickly distracted his attention by bringing out more books while Nellie blew her nose and composed herself.

She smiled at Tommy and said to Gertie, 'Do you want me to help you in the back kitchen?'

'Oh yes, if you don't mind,' leading the way while Nellie murmured to her, 'Little pitchers.' In the back kitchen they were able to speak more freely.

'Honestly, Gertie, the way Charlie West went on he nearly convinced me, and Sam was raging. If Tommy hadn't been hanging on to his leg he'd have run after that little runt and battered him.'

'Don't worry. He'd have made sure of a hidey hole before he tried it on with Sam,' Gertie said. 'What makes fellas like that tick, I wonder? And then I suppose you and Sam fell out?'

Nellie nodded miserably. 'I don't know why he takes notice of fellas like that. He carried on about it last night and then this morning he ate his breakfast and walked out without a word,' she said.

'He'll get over it,' Gertie comforted her. 'Once he has time to cool down and think about it. But that little runt West! Someone *should* batter him. Do him the world of good.'

'I'm sure he wouldn't have tried it on last night if Sam hadn't been carrying Tom,' Nellie said.

'Never mind, Nell, at least you haven't got a black eye to show for it,' Gertie reassured her.

'No, that's one thing about Sam. It's only words,' Nellie said, managing to smile.

Tommy appeared in the doorway and Gertie said briskly, 'I'll tell you what. Why don't we go to Derby Park? It's a lovely day and what's sauce for the goose is sauce for the gander, I say.'

Nellie agreed but said that she could not be out too long as she would have to be back to prepare the meal.

They spent some happy hours in the park and Nellie had to admit that she felt much better when they returned. The change of scene and Gertie's company put the quarrel with Sam in perspective.

She was preparing the meal when Sam returned looking sheepish, but Tommy prattled to him about their outing.

'You went out, then?' Sam asked.

'Yes, with Gertie to Derby Park,' Nellie said briefly. She was tempted to quote Gertie's remark about the goose and the gander but her courage failed.

She served the meal in silence, putting Janey's portion between two plates as she had not returned, but Bobby talked about what had happened at the boxing club, and Tommy chattered about a dog he had seen at the park and ice-cream which Gertie had bought him.

Nellie bustled about when the meal was over, leaving Sam to sit alone with his cup of tea and cigarette. Bobby squatted on the floor carving a little dog for Tommy from a piece of wood.

Sam admired it. 'You done that real good,

lad,' he said, 'you must have a knack for it.'

'Mr Bushell says I have,' Bobby said, colouring with pleasure. 'He said they might send me to this house they're doing up in Yorkshire.'

'You never told me nothing about that,' Nellie exclaimed.

'It was only yesterday morning. I was just showing off with me clasp knife,' Bobby said laughing. 'He might have forgot tomorrow.'

'That's real good, that dog,' Sam said. 'See this, Ellie? Very nearly barking at us.' Nellie came beside Sam's chair to admire the carving, and after that they spoke freely to each other, although a tiny residue of doubt remained in Sam's mind and a sense of grievance in Nellie's.

Sam was due to leave in two days' time, and that night they made love again but with more restraint than earlier in Sam's leave. They forgot their differences for Sam's last day and spent a happy time with Sam only going to the Volunteer quite late for a farewell drink with old friends.

'I hope I've started with another baby,' Nellie whispered to him as they said goodbye in the kitchen the following day.

'Well, if you haven't it'll give Tommy a bit longer to have all the attention,' Sam said laughing.

At least *he* won't be disappointed if I haven't, Nellie thought as she stood at the door with Tommy, ready to wave goodbye to Sam as he turned the corner.

CHAPTER 9

Nellie was again disappointed in her hope for another baby, and the same happened after every trip for the following years.

Every leave followed the same pattern. Sam would arrive home bearing gifts and full of good intentions but always at some time during his time ashore there would be a scene provoked by his jealousy. Anything, no matter how trivial, could be the cause.

Nellie's timid protests would be drowned by Sam's shouts, but although he often raised his fist as he towered over her, red with temper, he never actually struck her. Tommy's distress at these scenes could always bring them quickly to an end.

The rest of his time at home was always very happy and their ardent lovemaking revived Nellie's hopes for another child, but they were always dashed when her period arrived as usual after he left.

For Sam, Tommy seemed sufficient to fulfil all his aspirations, and his pride and joy in the child unlimited. He took the boy out every day while he was ashore, walking proudly past people in the street with Tommy holding his hand.

Nellie wondered sometimes whether it was an act of defiance towards those who had taunted him, but at others she was sure it was simple delight in the child and pride in the affection between them. On Saturday nights the three of them went to the market where Nellie bought meat that was auctioned off cheaply and Sam bought sweets and fruit and more gifts.

They were happy outings but sometimes marred by a jealous outburst from Sam, when he accused Nellie of flirting with the stallholders or of deliberately becoming separated from him by the crowds. As soon as Tommy showed any sign of distress Sam calmed down immediately.

While Sam was away Nellie's life was quite full. She had become even more friendly with Gertie and sometimes Maggie looked after Tommy while Nellie and Gertie went to the cinema. He was quite happy playing with Maggie's children and, when his mother returned, hearing the story of the film in detail. Sometimes he made up little stories himself with different endings to the films.

Nellie still wore her mother's shawl, a black knitted one with a deep fringe, but Gertie wore a coat for work as some of the younger girls did. For their outings to the local cinema Gertie always wore her mother's shawl. Nellie appreciated her tact in doing so.

One night as they queued outside the cinema a girl came to speak to Nellie. 'Do you remember me, Nell? Lily. I worked with you at that house in Newsham Park. Leadbetters' house.'

'Lily!' Nellie exclaimed but could say no more as memories overwhelmed her.

'My poor mam died that time when I went

home because she was sick, y'know,' Lily said. 'I never went back there because I had to stay home to look after me dad and the little ones.'

'I'm sorry, Lily, about your mam, I mean,' Nellie managed to say. 'Er—this is Gertie. I worked with Lily,' she said to Gertie.

'And *didn't* we work in that place!' Lily exclaimed. 'But listen, Nell. When I went back for me things and to tell them about Mam the cook said you'd just walked out, but you know what it was like trying to talk to her. She was as deaf as a post. Did you have a row?'

'I was just fed up,' Nellie muttered, 'and I was sick.'

'She give me the coat you left there. I would've brought it to your house, honest, only I didn't know where you lived,' said Lily. 'I let our Maisie wear it when she started work.'

'It's all right,' Nellie said. 'I'd grown out of it anyhow.' To change the subject she added quickly, 'I'm married now, Lily. Got a little lad.'

'Are you?' Lily said. 'I'm courting, but we can't get married until I've got the kids off me hands. I don't want me dad bringing a stepmother into them.'

'How old is the youngest?' asked Gertie.

'A lad six then there's two girls, eight and eleven, and two working.'

'You'll have a long time to wait then, won't you?' Gertie said sympathetically.

'We don't mind. Give us time to save up. We want to start proper, me and Joe,' Lily said.

Nellie was grateful to be able to stand silently while they talked, and try to recover from the shock of the meeting. Fortunately the queue began to move, and Lily dashed back to rejoin her sister further back. There was no time to make arrangements to meet again but Nellie was not sorry.

She visited Rose Adams frequently and was visited by her, and Maggie remained a staunch friend. Nellie spent a lot of time with Katy, and sometimes the two girls went to town together to look at the shops, although they rarely bought anything there.

When Nellie shopped alone she always stayed in her own neighbourhood. She was secure and confident among people she knew well but still shy and timid with strangers.

Janey still hinted about secrets she could tell about Sam's family and about discreditable episodes in Nellie's mother's past, and gave veiled hints about Leadbetter, but Nellie ignored her. She felt strong and capable of handling the old woman while she had Bobby to back her up.

Bobby was very highly regarded by his employers and liked by all who knew him. The gift for carving which he had shown led to him being sent to work in Yorkshire at the end of 1924 when he was seventeen years old.

Mr Meldrum's partner and brother, Mr Orlando Meldrum, was based there in charge of a contract to restore an old house and a church. Bobby was still serving his time but had shown such skill that he was allowed to carve panels and pew ends.

The firm arranged for him to lodge with an old couple in a cottage in the village and he was very happy there.

'They couldn't treat me better if I was their son,' he wrote to Nellie. 'And you should see the meals. I'm getting fed like a fighting cock.'

Nellie was pleased and proud at her brother's promotion but sadly missed his cheerful and supportive company in the house. She was relieved though that he was making a new life for himself away from the area.

Unemployment was growing and life was becoming increasingly desperate for the people of the neighbourhood. Even the boys of Bobby's age who had managed to find a job had now been cast off in favour of boys leaving school who would work for less.

'I told him I'd work for the same five shillings if he'd only keep me on,' one of Bobby's friends told Nellie. 'But he said what if I started courting? I'd be wanting more money or leaving, so he was taking a school leaver on he could keep for a few years. "And then be sacked like me," I said, and he just laughed and said it was the way of the world.'

'And you can't get nothing else?' Nellie said sympathetically.

'No, I get turned away everywhere,' the boy said. 'Me dad's in the same boat. After all they got promised when they was in the trenches. Sometimes I feel like drowning meself.'

Nellie thought of this conversation whenever she felt miserable because she was missing

Bobby, and counted her blessings.

Several times during these years Sam's allotment was held up but Nellie was more prepared for the situation now. She asked for credit at the corner shop and from the butcher and the milkman and they gave it without hesitation, knowing that she would repay as soon as possible.

Although she was granted credit so readily Nellie still felt humiliated at having to ask for it. If only I had a little job like Maggie's, she often thought, but such jobs were hard to find.

Married women were not employed in the local factories, just as in jobs like teaching or clerical work. No matter how poor, men saw themselves as breadwinners and would have felt disgraced if their wives worked in a regular job. 'Her feller mustn't be able to keep her,' was disparagingly said of a skilled glovemaker who was allowed to stay in work by her employer after marriage.

It was permissible for the women to find a 'little job' cleaning or hawking without loss of face but Nellie could find no way of earning a little extra.

It was through Rose Adams that she eventually found a job. Rose cooked dinners for teachers at a nearby school and one of them told her of a daily cleaning job in a large house in Balliol Road. It was not far in distance from Nellie's home, although a world away socially.

It was only after Nellie had secured the job that she began to worry how Sam would feel about it. Would his pride be hurt? Would he think she wanted to be independent?

Rose reassured her. 'George will make him see the sense of having a bit extra for when the money's held up,' she said. 'Tell Sam you want to buy bits for the house so he'll know he's still keeping you.'

Maggie was now working for three mornings a week and her youngest child was at school, so Nellie could leave Tommy with Katy without offending her neighbour.

Nellie enjoyed the job. There were two elderly maids and a cook living in, and two daily women were employed. The older daily woman, Mrs Taggart, did the scrubbing and rough cleaning and Nellie was expected to help wherever she was needed, sometimes helping the cook or waiting on table for a luncheon party, or acting as ladies' maid for the young ladies of the family.

She was deft and capable and always willing, although the cook and Mrs Taggart told her that she was being exploited. 'They're saving the cost of a scullery maid and another parlourmaid on top of what you do for them girls,' the cook said.

Mrs Taggart told her she was too soft. 'It's the willing horse that gets all the work,' she said. 'They're putting on good nature.'

'I don't mind,' Nellie said. 'Only I think it's me should be doing the rough scrubbing, like. You was here first.'

'Jeez, girl, I'd run a mile if I got told to do them things you do,' Mrs Taggart said. 'I'm all right with me scrubbing.'

Nellie enjoyed using the lavish amounts of

food when she helped the cook, and handling the damask tablecloths and napkins, and the beautiful glass and china and silver cutlery. Her employers showed their appreciation of her willing help by giving her small gifts of food or clothes in addition to her wages. She had no worry about Tommy if she was asked to stay late as he was very happy with Katy and her children.

One day Nellie served a luncheon party unaided, as both maids were ill, and afterwards her employer, Mrs Duncan, called her into her eldest daughter's bedroom.

'You did very well today, Ellen,' she said graciously. 'Miss Lydia has no further use for this coat. Would you like it?'

'Yes please, ma'am,' Nellie said eagerly. The coat was of dark blue velour and she carried it home joyfully and tried it on first to show Katy, who admired it, and then to show Maggie and Janey.

'It's lovely, Nell. Real good quality. You look a treat,' Maggie said. However, Janey said sourly, 'What's the quare feller going to say? He'll think you're trying to get off with a fella. Only the young girls wear coats.'

'He won't,' Maggie said indignantly. 'Sam's got more sense. Why, if I got a coat like that I'd wear it and I'm no young girl.'

But Nellie's pleasure in the coat was ruined. Although she told Janey that she was sure Sam would like the coat, a small seed of doubt had been planted in her mind about it. She put the coat away carefully, deciding that she would keep it until Sam came home and wear her shawl meanwhile.

Maggie told her that Janey was not out all day as she used to be and while she was at home she was in Nellie's kitchen with a big fire burning.

'You can see it as you pass the winda,' Maggie said. 'Half way up the chimney.'

'I know,' Nellie said with a sigh. 'It's two steps forward and one back trying to save while I'm keeping her.'

'You're too soft, girl. You should ask her for rent and keep,' Maggie said forcefully, but Nellie shrugged.

'I can't, Mag, not after all this time. But if she'd just show some consideration. I went to give Tom a jam butty while I got the tea ready and there was a little heel of loaf. She's ate it all.'

In spite of old Janey's wastefulness Nellie managed to buy new clothes and boots for Tommy and to make the house more comfortable for Sam.

Just before the child's fifth birthday Sam came home again, loaded with gifts as usual and full of good intentions to have a troublefree time ashore. Tommy had grown a sturdy little boy in spite of his unpromising start, with large blue eyes and curly hair that was now more brown than fair, and the same shy manner as his mother. He had been looking forward to Sam's return, as he had promised before he left to take Tommy on a trip on the Overhead Railway when he returned.

It was too late on the day of Sam's homecoming for the promised trip, but when Sam said goodnight to the child he told him that they would set off early the next day for the Overhead.

'He looks that much older every time I see him,' Sam said later to Nellie.

'I suppose you notice it more after not seeing him for a bit,' Nellie said. 'He misses you more than ever now Bobby's not here. I wish you was working ashore, Sam.'

'So do I, girl, but what's the use? No work to be had,' said Sam. 'How's Bob going on?'

'The gear,' Nellie said eagerly. 'He says he never saw such food.'

'He's fell on his feet, then?' Sam said. 'What about the job?'

'He loves it. They let him do carving and all that even though he's not out of his time,' Nellie said. 'And it isn't only the good food where he lives. He's with an old couple and they couldn't do no more for him if he was their own son, Bob says. The only drawback is he misses his mates and me and Tommy.'

'I'll bet you miss him an' all, girl?' Sam said, and Nellie nodded, looking tearful.

'Still, it's the best thing could've happened for Bobby,' Sam encouraged her. 'You've got to think of that, Ellie.'

Nellie nodded, trying to smile.

Sam went to the Volunteer later but only for a couple of hours, and the next morning he was up early as he had promised. Nellie dressed Tommy and stood at the door watching proudly as they walked down the street together, Sam tall and well built walking with his sailor's roll and the little boy trotting beside him wearing his new gansey and boots.

Tommy felt proud too as he walked along, holding his father's hand and looking down from time to time at his new boots. They turned into the general shop on the corner of the street to buy sweets, and Mrs Deakin who owned the shop remarked on his new attire.

'You're a lucky lad, Tommy,' she told him. 'You've got a good dad who looks after you and your mam. Youse don't want for nothing.'

Sam shuffled his feet. 'I've been lucky,' he said. 'I've always got a ship handy, like. Nellie'd like me to work ashore but the sea's all I know.'

'You're better off as you are, lad,' Mrs Deakin said, 'things is terrible round here and getting worse. Who'd have thought it? We got told we'd had a good life after the war, but here it is, 1925, and things are worser than ever.'

'Aye, homes fit for heroes,' Sam said bitterly, 'that's what we got told. It's bad on the docks, I know, and the miners' wages is being cut, some feller told me.'

'Yes, God help them,' Mrs Deakin said dolefully as she weighed out the sweets. 'Working a full week underground and the wages that bad their families are very near starving. People are getting desperate. There'll be trouble, I'm sure.'

'Aye, they'll be pushing fellas too far,' Sam agreed.

'There's more on the Parish than ever round here and the poor kids only skin and bone,' said Mrs Deakin. 'No, you stick to the sea while you can get a ship, lad.'

Tommy pondered on the woman's words as they climbed the steps and rode on the Overhead Railway, but his father spoke only of the ships they saw. It was an enjoyable day for both of them. Tommy was excited by the sight of the ships in dock and those in the River Mersey, especially when Sam pointed out ships on which he had sailed, and Sam enjoyed the boy's delight and his comments on all he saw.

When they had returned home and were eating the rabbit stew prepared by Nellie, Tommy said suddenly, 'Why are the kids skin and bone, Dad? What does it mean?' Nellie looked up in surprise and Sam said quietly, 'We went for sweets to the corner and she was going on about the way things was round here.'

To Tommy he said, 'She meant the kids was thin because they don't get good dinners like your mam does for you.'

'Mrs Deakin said I was a lucky boy, Mam,' Tommy said. 'She said I'd got a good dad.'

'And so you have, lad,' Nellie said, smiling at Sam.

'You've gorra good mam an' all,' Sam said gruffly. 'I tell you what, Tom. I reckon your mam shoulda come with us today to see the ships.'

Tommy held his spoon above his plate while he considered the idea then he said, 'But who'd do the rabbit stew?'

His parents laughed but Sam said, 'Right. That settles it. Tomorrow we'll go again and your mam will come with us. And before you start—we'll fetch fish and chips in for our tea tomorrow.'

Nellie blushed with pleasure and impulsively leaned over and kissed Sam, and although he bent his head over his plate and muttered, 'Hold on there, girl,' it was clear that he was pleased.

Nellie began to make plans, and when she took Tommy up to bed she brought down the coat to show Sam. 'Mrs Duncan gave it to me weeks ago when I done some extra work,' she said. 'I haven't wore it—didn't think I ever could, like, but I could wear it tomorrow, couldn't I?'

Sam looked doubtful. 'She should've give you an extra couple of bob for the extra work, never mind her cast-offs,' he said.

'But this is worth more than a couple of bob,' Nellie said. 'It's hardly wore and feel the weight of it, Sam.'

Sam fingered the material. 'Real good stuff in it, all right,' he agreed.

Nellie changed the subject and quietly put the coat away but the next morning when she had dressed Tommy in his new clothes and combed his hair, she brought down the coat and put it on.

'Gosh, you look posh, Mam,' the child exclaimed and when Sam laughed he turned to him and said quickly, 'You look posh an' all, Dad.'

'Do I?' Sam laughed. 'I couldn't tell you how long I've had this here suit. Got it in Hong Kong years ago. An American suit it was called because of the pleats, but it's kept good with me only wearing it ashore.'

Impulsively Nellie went to Tommy and hugged him, 'You look the poshest of all in your new boots and gansey,' she said. Her heart was full of love for the child. How sensitive he was, she thought fondly. How quick to praise Sam too in case he felt left out. Nothing must ever hurt him, she thought passionately.

Sam ruffled Tommy's hair. 'Well, seeing we're all so posh, we'd better go out and let people see us, hadn't we?' he said.

He said nothing about the coat when they were in the house but later as they took their seats on the train he said quietly, 'The lad's right, Ellie. You do look posh. Suits you, that blue colour.'

Nellie smiled with delight. She had felt strange at first wearing the coat instead of wrapping her shawl around her, and selfconscious as she walked down the street with Sam, but she was surprised at how quickly she became used to it.

They had corner seats on the train and Tommy sat on Sam's knee, his arm around his father's neck as Sam told him the details of the ships which filled the long line of docks, and pointed out others which stood out in the river.

Nellie sat opposite to them, glancing out of the window occasionally as the train passed

181

the docks, but most of the time watching her husband and son.

If only they could always be as happy as they were now. That their lives were not overshadowed by Sam's jealousy and suspicion. Was it something in Sam's nature that caused the scenes or was it because he sensed in some way that she had deceived him?

She had determined to bury the memory of Leadbetter for ever, but now she thought—what if I had told Sam? Would it have made his jealousy worse or would it have meant that he trusted me completely so that there was no need for jealousy? If only I knew. Although it was too late to tell him now. Better to let sleeping dogs lie, as Janey says.

They had a happy day and carried parcels of chips and fish home for their meal. Nellie kept Janey's portion warm and carried it through as soon as she heard the old woman return.

Janey eyed her malevolently. 'I could've done with something more warming,' she grumbled. 'I'm feeling the cold these days.'

'We went out for the day,' Nellie said, too happy to be intimidated by the old woman. 'Me and Sam and Tommy. On the Overhead then to the Cast Iron shore. I wore me new coat.'

'And I suppose the quare feller walked behind you watching was you giving any fellers the eye?' Janey said, but Nellie faced her with confidence.

'No, he never,' she said quietly. 'He said I looked posh and the colour suited me.'

Janey cackled derisively but she said no more,

intent on the food, and Nellie escaped into the kitchen.

At least she didn't mention Leadbetter, she thought. Maybe she's given it up as a bad job now she knows she can't make me cry about it. Bob's right. It's better to stand up to her.

On Sunday Nellie wore the coat again when she and Sam took Tommy on the ferryboat to New Brighton. The pier head was crowded and Nellie clung to Sam's arm as he carried Tommy on his shoulders down the steeply sloping floating roadway on to the landing stage.

'The tide must be out,' Sam said, but when Tommy exclaimed he said quickly, 'It's all right, lad. It'll soon be in again. I only meant that's why the roadway's sloping,' and Tommy clasped his hands round his father's forehead, reassured.

There was already a crowd waiting to board the ferryboat which was just arriving. From his vantage point Tommy had a good view as the boat bumped against the landing stage and was tied up. The sun was shining and the crowd was in a happy mood.

Tommy squealed with excitement as the gangway was released and fell with a clatter on to the landing stage and passengers began to pour off the ferry. Soon others began to embark and two burly ferrymen in navy jerseys and caps stood at either side of the gangway ready to draw it up again.

Tommy's joy was complete when one of the men waved to him. 'Dad, Dad, the man waved to me,' he shouted and people turned to smile at the excited child.

Sam's face was red with pride and pleasure and Nellie whispered to him, 'He's a different lad when you're home, Sam. He's too quiet sometimes but just listen to him now.'

Sam took care to walk up the gangway on the side nearest to the man who had waved to Tommy and the man solemnly shook the child's hand.

'Welcome aboard, mate,' he said, then to Sam, 'You've got a fine lad there, wack.'

When the ferryboat cast off and made her way upriver they went on deck and Tommy asked so many questions about the shipping they passed that Nellie said laughingly, 'Give your dad a bit of peace, Tom love.'

'No, he's all right. Them's good questions,' Sam said, still glowing with pride after the ferryman's remark.

When they arrived at New Brighton Sam bought ice-creams which they ate walking along the promenade, and a bucket and spade for Tommy. Later, when the tide was right, Sam paid for a deckchair on the sands for Nellie, where she sat with the shoes and socks while Sam and Tommy paddled, and then they came back to her and built an enormous sandcastle, complete with turrets and moat.

Nellie watched them happily, aware that Sam was enjoying himself as much as the child. He never had nothing like this when he was a kid, she thought, and neither did I, but Tommy's having a better childhood than what we did. And he'll have a better life too, she thought fiercely. I'll see that he does.

Later they walked along to Perch Rock. The wind had become more chill and Nellie turned up the collar of her coat, but Sam and Tommy seemed oblivious to it as they crouched over the pools left by the receding tide.

'Look at the little fishes and crabs,' Tommy exclaimed. 'Can I take some home in my bucket, Dad?' but Sam told him it would be cruel.

'They'd only die in the back yard, lad,' he said. 'They belong here,' and the child nodded trustingly.

He fell asleep on the homeward-bound ferryboat, and Sam carried him off the boat and on to the tramcar which took them near home, where he woke up.

It was a happy day and Nellie was surprised at the details of it which Tommy could remember, when he spoke wistfully about it in later years.

CHAPTER 10

Sam's time ashore was the happiest since their marriage yet before he left they had the most serious quarrel they had ever had.

Although Sam went to the Volunteer every night and sometimes returned slightly drunk, he was never aggressive until this night. He was late, and as he stood supporting himself on the door jamb Nellie could see blood on his cheek from a cut lip, and blood on his knuckles.

'Have you been fighting, Sam?' she asked nervously.

'Aye, battered him. Shoulda killed him,' he said thickly.

He swayed and Nellie said, 'Sit down, Sam,' but he went on.

'Bert—Bert bloody Hagan.'

Nellie felt a stab of fear. Bert Hagan was one of those who had taunted Sam on the night of Tommy's birth.

'Called me, me—called me Soft Sam the Mira—Miracle Man,' Sam muttered. 'And him—the bloody little runt.'

Charlie West, Nellie thought, aghast. Sam closed his eyes and swayed and Nellie went towards him.

'Sam,' she began, but before she could say any more he swung his arm out wildly. It caught her and sent her staggering back off balance to fall and strike her head on the corner of the dresser. Blood poured from a deep cut on the side of her head.

Janey darted in from the parlour and her screams brought Tommy running downstairs, white faced with terror. He flung himself down beside Nellie. 'Mam, Mam,' he cried as she lay unconscious. 'Oh, is she dead, Janey?'

'Very near,' she said, looking malevolently at Sam who stood saying, 'Ellie, oh God, Ellie,' over and over again.

Sam approached to bend over Nellie but Janey pushed him away.

'Give her some air,' she commanded.

Shock had sobered Sam and he said humbly,

'Oh God, is she all right? Jeez, I never meant it. What can I do?'

'You and your bloody temper. You'll swing for it one of these days,' the old woman said. 'Get her some brandy and I'll try to bring her round.'

He hurried out and Tommy said in a trembling voice, 'Is Mam going to die, Janey?'

'No, lad. She'll be all right in a minute,' she said. She tittered, plainly enjoying her moment of power over Sam. 'Won't do him no harm to get a fright. Knocked the stuffing outa him, hasn't it? Fetch me a wet cloth, lad.'

Nellie's eyes were opening when Sam returned and he lifted her gently on to the sofa. Janey removed the cloth from the cut and the blood flowed afresh.

'That needs stitches, girl,' Janey said, but Nellie said weakly, 'Oh no. I don't want to go to the hospital.'

'Try a drop of the brandy,' Sam urged, alarmed by her white face, but she said that she would prefer a cup of tea.

She closed her eyes, holding the cloth over the wound, but blood still trickled from beneath it and Sam said anxiously, 'I think you'd better go to the hospital, Ellie.'

He was sitting in the corner to keep out of Janey's way as she bustled about making tea, with his arm round Tommy who was leaning against his knee. When Nellie opened her eyes they were both gazing at her fearfully and she tried to smile.

'All right, I'll go in a minute, Sam,' she said.

'Come here, Tom.' She hugged him and told him she was all right. 'Go back to bed, son,' she said gently, 'you're freezing. I won't be long at the hospital. Stitches only take a minute.'

He went obediently and when the tea was finished Sam took her shawl from behind the door. 'We'd better go now, girl,' he said.

Nellie held the shawl closely over her head to keep the cloth in place and clung to Sam's arm as they walked to the hospital.

They waited for a long time in the hospital's casualty department, sitting on hard benches, and Nellie leaned against Sam, thankful for the support of his arm.

'I'm sorry, Ellie,' he whispered, and she squeezed his arm without replying.

She felt no bitterness towards him, only sorrow that the secret lay, like a maggot in an apple, eating away at their happiness. If only she dared to tell Sam, but the longer time went on the harder it became to explain to him, and the stronger the arguments against telling him.

Would Sam believe her if she told him now after all this time? Would he think he had been tricked into marriage and that she was a willing party to it? How can I expect him to understand when I don't understand myself how I could let Janey arrange all that and even keep quiet when she told me to. I must have been drugged or out of my mind, Nellie thought.

She leaned her head on Sam's shoulder and tears of misery and despair trickled down her face.

Poor Sam. He was a good man. Whatever

188

his doubts he never left her short of money or turned against Tommy in any way and she respected him for that.

When she was finally called to a cubicle the doctor only glanced at the cut. 'Clean it up, Nurse,' he said brusquely. 'Needs a stitch.'

Nellie felt sick and frightened, and humiliated by the contemptuous attitude of the nurse and doctor, neither of whom had spoken to her.

The nurse cut away some of Nellie's hair and swabbed the cut. 'Ready now, Doctor,' she said.

The doctor spoke to Nellie for the first time as he picked up the needle, 'Fell against a door, I suppose,' he sneered, 'that's the usual story.'

The nurse laughed and he turned to her. 'God, these people. Animals behave better.' Nellie felt too ill and humiliated to protest and he inserted two stitches with little concern for the pain he was causing.

She clenched her teeth and managed to refrain from crying out and something about her passivity seemed to strike the doctor. He produced a small torch and shone it into each of her eyes in turn then said brusquely, 'Admit her, Nurse. Some concussion.'

Nellie was struggling to her feet, drawing her shawl around her, and the sense of his words failed to penetrate her mind until the nurse hustled her into another room.

'Is it finished? Can I go home?' Nellie asked timidly. The nurse said impatiently, 'Didn't you hear Doctor? You're to be admitted.'

189

'But—but me husband's waiting for me,' Nellie faltered.

'He'll be told. Sit there and wait for the porter,' the nurse said, bustling away.

Nellie sat on a hard chair waiting for what seemed hours before the porter appeared with a wheelchair.

'Sit in here, love,' he said and Nellie's eyes filled with tears at the first kindness she had been shown.

'Now now, missus, no waterworks,' the man said cheerfully. 'You'll be all right, love.' He wheeled her rapidly to a large ward with rows of beds close together down each side and a small table in the centre of the ward where a nurse sat.

Nellie was taken to a bed halfway down the ward and given a calico nightdress to wear, then the nurse came to her and whispered, 'Let's see your feet.' She glanced at them and said, 'You're clean enough. If Sister asks say you've had a bath. Get into bed.'

She went away and Nellie crept between the icy sheets, trembling with cold and fear. Moans and cries came from the closely packed beds and an occasional scream of pain from a bed near the door.

Nellie was unable to sleep and her mind was full of a confused jumble of thoughts. Fear of what was to happen to her, worry about the row with Sam and what had been said to him at the Volunteer, familiar feelings of guilt because she had deceived him.

She thought of Tommy's frightened face and

grieved that he had been so worried. Poor little lad. He was so sensitive and he loved both her and Sam. Suddenly she was shaken with anger and her mind cleared.

These rows had to stop for Tommy's sake. There was no need for them. She gave Sam no cause for his unreasonable jealousy. Just the opposite. How many times had Charlie West tried to make up to her and been refused?

I'm always blaming myself because of the way we got married and because I didn't tell him what Leadbetter done to me, but none of that was my fault. It was Janey what tricked *me* into getting married just as much as she tricked Sam, but in the end she done us both a good turn. I've got a good husband and a home and Sam's got a good home to come back to and we've both got our Tommy, best of all.

Engrossed in her thoughts she had not realised that the night sister was in the ward until she arrived beside the bed with the nurse.

'Admitted overnight for observation, Sister,' the nurse said. 'Suspected concussion.' The sister shone her torch on Nellie and moved on without speaking.

The word 'overnight' had cheered Nellie although she was uncertain what was meant by concussion.

I'm going to stop blaming myself for these rows, she thought. It didn't make no difference to Sam what Leadbetter done to me and Janey only made out the baby might be his to have a hold over me. I know now she'll never tell Sam, because she fixed up the wedding to have

191

Sam's money coming in so she could stay dug in her parlour, so she's not going to risk that.

I *knew* from when Tommy was born he was Sam's and Sam must know it too or he wouldn't dote on him the way he does, so why does he listen to them fellers in the Volley who are only looking for a fight?

I'm going to have it out with Sam, for Tommy's sake, she thought. Her mind dwelt fondly on her little son. He was all that mattered now. At last she fell asleep.

The doctor who came the following morning was an older man with a less brusque manner than the casualty doctor but like him he spoke only to the nurse.

'Discharge her,' he said briefly and after he left the ward the nurse pulled a screen across and dumped Nellie's clothes on her bed.

'Get dressed,' she said. 'Leave the nightdress on the bed and wait by Sister's office.'

The screen only covered the side of the bed nearest the door and Nellie dressed, fumbling with buttons and laces and conscious of many eyes watching her.

She waited nervously outside the office until a nurse went in leaving the door open and spoke to the sister. They both looked at Nellie then the sister handed a slip of paper to the nurse.

'Nonsense,' Nellie heard her say in a loud hectoring voice. 'It's a way of life for these women, getting knocked about by their men.'

Nellie's face burned and she longed for the courage to confront the woman, but the next moment the nurse came out and thrust the paper into Nellie's hand.

'Give that to the porter on your way out,' she said, and swept away.

Nellie walked out as quickly as she could, her eyes stinging with tears of humiliation, so agitated that she was halfway down the street before she remembered the paper she should have given to the porter. I'm not going back, she thought, even if they send a policeman after me.

She was shaking when she reached home, and Sam took her shawl and helped her to a chair.

'You shouldn't have come home on your own, girl,' he said. 'You shoulda sent a lad for me.'

'I didn't think,' she said. 'I was that glad to get away. Where's Tommy?'

'That Katy one come for him,' Janey said. 'Wanted to know what was going on, I suppose. It'll be a nice bit of jangle for the lot of them.'

Nellie bent her head and Sam said quickly, 'I'll make that tea if you want to get off with your fish, Janey.'

'No, I'll have to lose the day,' she said in a whining voice. 'I'll have to lay down. I never closed me eyes last night and when I seen you walking down the street at five o'clock I thought she'd snuffed it.'

'Five o'clock!' Nellie exclaimed. 'Where was you till then?'

'At the hospital,' Sam said. 'I think they forgot about me, like, then some fellers was brought in; a sling broke on the docks. I was there ages after that. I couldn't find no one then a porter told me you was kept in.'

Nellie said nothing until Janey had gone into the parlour then she turned to Sam and burst into tears.

He put his arms round her and said anxiously, 'Does it feel bad, girl?'

'No, it's not that,' Nellie said. Suddenly all her anguish and humiliation at the contempt shown her boiled up. 'It's the way they treat us. Like we had no feelings. As if we wasn't human beings like them. And to leave you there worrying all the time. They treat us like dirt.'

'I know, girl,' Sam said grimly. 'I've had it all me life. It gets me that bloody mad because we can't do nothing about it.'

He stood up and began to stride about the kitchen. 'We've got to take it from the likes of them but by God, Ellie, I won't take it from me own class. I'm not having *them* putting me down and I'll fight any man that tries it, by God I will.'

'It's Tommy *I'm* thinking about,' Nellie challenged him.

Sam said quickly, 'And so am I, girl.'

'He's never going to be treated like this, I'm determined,' Nellie said. 'I'm going to get him away from here. He's going to have a better life than what we've had and no one is ever going to treat him bad. He'll get respect all his life, I'll see that he does.'

Her face was red and her eyes glittering and Sam went to her in alarm.

'All right, all right, girl, don't get worked up,'

194

he said. 'Lay down for a bit. Why did they keep you in?'

'Concussion, they called it,' Nellie said, allowing herself to be settled on the sofa and her shawl spread over her. 'I'm sorry, Sam. It just makes me so mad.'

'I know, girl,' he soothed her. 'Don't worry about our Tommy. I've got me plans too. Between us he'll be living like a rajah.'

Janey had returned to the kitchen when Katy brought Tommy later. 'He was like a hen on a griddle until he seen you,' she explained. 'But he can come back to ours while you have a rest.'

'It's all right, thanks, Katy,' Nellie said, hugging Tommy. 'I'm all right now and he can stay with me.' She saw Katy looking at the dressing on her head and said, 'I fell and cut me head on the corner of the dresser and they kept me in case I had concussion.'

'And did you?' asked Katy.

'I couldn't have had. They let me out,' Nellie said.

Katy said only, 'You wanna be careful. Send Tom up to me any time you like, Nell.' She left and Nellie held Tommy close to her and kissed him.

'You've got that lad soft, kissing and cuddling him,' Janey sneered, but Nellie ignored her. Sam had gone into the yard and Janey went on, 'Took the starch outa him, didn't it? Might learn him to watch his bloody temper.'

Nellie looked at her umsmilingly. 'It was an accident, Janey,' she said. 'You know as well as I do Sam wouldn't hurt me deliberately.' She

195

felt the child relax against her arm and she said to him quietly, 'Your poor dad got a shock and so did you, son, but I'm all right now.'

Tommy smiled at her and hugged her.

Nellie dozed all morning, but later she insisted on getting up and cooking the meal. Janey had been whining again about missing her day with her fish but Sam gave her money and she went out.

Nellie was still determined to have it out with Sam about his jealousy before her courage failed and her opportunity came when Tommy was in bed and Janey had shot home the bolts inside her parlour door. Sam was sitting opposite to Nellie beside the fire watching her turn the heel of a sock.

'Aren't you going out, Sam?' she asked, and he shook his head.

'No. I'll give the Volley a miss tonight. Catch up on me sleep,' he said yawning widely.

It's now or never, Nellie thought. She laid her knitting down on her knee and leaned forward. 'Sam, I've got to talk to you. These rows—they're upsetting Tommy. We've got to stop, Sam.'

'I said I'm sorry,' Sam muttered. 'Didn't mean to belt you last night.'

Nellie was trembling but determined. 'I know, but why, Sam? Why don't you trust me? Why do you listen to them fellers?' Sam shuffled his feet and made to stand up but Nellie put her hand on his knee. 'Sam, we've got to sort it out, lad. We can't go on—a row every time you come home. I wouldn't do nothing behind your back, lad. I don't want no one but you.'

Her face was white and her huge eyes were fixed pleadingly on Sam. He twisted about in his chair and ran his hand through his hair. 'You've gorrit wrong, girl,' he said gruffly. 'It's just me bloody temper, like.'

Nellie could see beads of sweat on his forehead but she persisted.

'Tell me, Sam. Why?' She gripped her knitting until her knuckles were white and her other hand tightened on Sam's knee. She took a deep breath. 'Is it because Janey fixed up our wedding?'

Sam squirmed uneasily and looked away from her. 'Forget it, girl. I won't start no more rows,' he said, but Nellie was implacable.

'I want to have this out once and for all, Sam,' she said. 'Is it because we got married in a hurry, like? Is that what them fellers go on about?'

'I suppose so,' he mumbled.

'She done it for her own ends, Sam,' Nellie said. 'But we shouldn't have let her. It was just I was sick and you were fuddled with the drink, like, weren't you? What did she say to you, Sam?'

'I don't remember,' he mumbled. 'Something about you being sick and your da's money stopped. And she said I'd have a home to come back to.'

'Well, that was true,' Nellie said, apparently unheard by Sam.

He sat looking down at the floor, his hands clasped loosely between his knees. 'I can't

197

remember no more,' he said. 'I was just that addled with the ale and it was a shock like when she waylaid me.'

Nellie began to cry. Evidently she had been wrong to think that Sam felt everything had turned out well. Evidently he still felt he had been tricked and regretted his marriage. All the other things she had meant to discuss, the night of Tommy's birth, Charlie West, Sam's jealousy, fled from her mind.

She said wildly, 'I'm sorry you was tricked but I was tricked too. You don't have to keep to it. You can be like you was single again. I don't want nothing from you. I can work to keep me and Tommy and we won't bother you no more.' She wept bitterly and Sam jumped to his feet open mouthed with shock.

'Ellie, Ellie, what's the matter, girl? Have you gone barmy or sump'n'?'

He crouched down and attempted to put his arms round her but she shouted, 'Get off, you don't want me,' and gave him a vigorous push which sent him sprawling on the floor on his back.

The sight of him lying there, his mouth open and his eyes wide with amazement, was too much for Nellie and she began to laugh hysterically.

Sam scrambled to his feet but he was afraid to touch her and instead banged on the back of the firegrate. Maggie hurried in in alarm, and Sam told her he thought Nellie had gone off her head. 'Must be the cut or the bang she got on the dresser,' he said. 'I don't know what's best to do, like.'

Nellie was still laughing, although more quietly, and Maggie put her arms round her. 'You're all right, girl,' she soothed her.

Nellie wiped her eyes. 'I'm sorry,' she said. 'It was just seeing him laying there on his back.'

She began to laugh again but Maggie looked alarmed when Sam said, 'She pushed me over.'

Seeing Maggie's face, Sam explained. 'I was just croodling down like and she pushed me. Caught me off balance. I'm worried about her head.'

'There's nothing wrong with me head,' Nellie said loudly. 'I was trying to talk to him and I got ratty then he fell over and I laughed. That's all. I've got a splitting headache now. I'm going to bed.'

'That's a good idea,' Sam said, relieved, and Maggie agreed.

'I'll come up with you, Nell,' she said. 'See you in to bed, but you could do with a cup of tea first.'

Nellie allowed herself to be given tea and aspirins and tucked into bed, but later when her headache had gone she lay thinking how her plans had gone awry. In the imaginary conversation with Sam when she was planning the confrontation Sam had made all the replies she wanted, but when it came to the real thing he had not played the part she had planned for him.

I didn't sort out any of the things I wanted

to and all I found out was what I didn't want to know, she thought ruefully—that Sam was addled with drink when he agreed to marry me. It's no use. I'll just have to hope Sam stops the rows for Tommy's sake, or I really will break up with him. Tommy must come first. But she wept at the thought.

Sam had been thinking things over too, although he was unaware of all that Nellie meant to discuss. Nellie's words about taking Tommy away had struck him like a bolt from the blue. In spite of the occasional rows, he had always considered that they were a happy family, and had boasted to his shipmates about his wife and son.

Yet Nellie seemed to think he wanted to be single again. Or was it that she wanted to be rid of him? Charlie West had hinted as much in the Volley. Not that he believed that little runt, he told himself, but why had Nellie come out with that? Maybe it had been in her mind and the knock on the head had made her talk more freely. Yet she had started off by saying she never wanted no one but him.

Sam felt bewildered. I feel as though I've had a knock on me own bloody head, he thought. And Nellie seemed to be making out she'd been tricked into getting married by Janey too. God, what a mess, he thought. But no one wasn't ever going to separate him and Tommy, by God they weren't.

The calm way she came out with it about splitting up. Fellers never split with their wives

200

except like Dusty Miller because his wife was on the game. Parading round Lime Street as large as life when Dusty got home unexpected. I'd better talk to Ellie, knock this idea on the head right away, Sam thought.

Sam and Buck and George Adams had all signed on the *Mauretania,* due to sail two days later, and the night before he left Sam said as he slipped into bed, 'Tomorrow night I'll be on the *Maury.* I'm worried about leaving you, girl, after the knock on the head.'

'There's nothing wrong with me head, Sam, only the cut,' Nellie said. 'And that's healing up.'

'But all that wild talk, like, the other night,' Sam said. 'You never meant that, surely, about keeping Tommy to yourself—splitting up, like.'

'I just don't want him upset no more with the rows,' Nellie said. 'I don't know why I said that about splitting up because it'd break his heart. He's that fond of both of us.'

'It was the knock on the head,' Sam said. 'And all that talk about when we was married.'

Nellie waited for him to say that he was glad he married but he said no more and she thought angrily, if he's sorry he got tricked into it, well so did I and maybe I'm sorry too.

She knew in her heart that it was not true but hurt pride made her say, 'Janey tricked both of us but Tommy shouldn't suffer because we was daft. What's done is done but none of it's his fault.'

201

Sam's pride was hurt too at Nellie's apparent assumption that they both regretted their marriage and he turned over, only saying, 'Yes, and don't forget you're a married woman when I've gone, neither.'

They both lay awake and Sam could hear Nellie crying into the pillow but he kept his back firmly turned against her.

Finally he could stand it no more and he turned to her, 'God, girl, stop it. What are you crying for, Ellie?' He put his arms round her and she sobbed into his shoulder.

'I wanted to sort things out, to stop the rows and I've only made things worse. Now I know as you're sorry you got married.'

'I never said that,' Sam protested.

'As good as,' Nellie said. 'When you said you was addled with drink.'

'Ay, when the old one tackled me,' Sam said. 'But not when we got married. You seemed more drunk than me that day.'

'I think she was giving me drugs to make me better,' Nellie said.

'And you was the one that come right out and said you was sorry—that we was daft,' Sam said.

'Only because I thought you were sorry,' Nellie said and Sam rolled up his eyes.

'Women!' he said. 'No wonder they say you can never fathom them. I tell you what, Ellie, Janey's the real mystery. Why did she want us married?'

'Maggie told me,' Nellie said. 'Me da's money had stopped and she wanted regular pay coming

202

into the house. It suited her to stay in the parlour.'

'Well, by God!' Sam exclaimed. 'Now I've heard everything. Anyway, girl, we're wasting time. I'm off tomorrow.'

He tightened his arms round her and Nellie raised her lips for his kiss.

'Oh Sam, if only you didn't have to go,' she whispered, then the tide of passion overwhelmed them.

'Are you still sorry we got married?' Sam teased as they lay, spent, in each other's arms.

Nellie clung to him and kissed him passionately. 'There's your answer, lad,' she whispered.

'And there's yours,' Sam said, kissing her eyes and her lips and her breast. 'Oh Ellie girl, I wish I wasn't going tomorrow.'

The next day Buck Madden called for him and waited while Sam said goodbye to his wife and son.

'Go to the hospital and get them stitches out soon,' Sam said gruffly and Nellie looked alarmed.

'I don't want to go back there, Sam,' she said. 'I'll go to the chemist.'

But Sam said masterfully, 'You go to the hospital and get it done proper, d'you hear?'

Tommy put his arm round his mother's waist and looked defiantly at Sam but Nellie only said meekly, 'Yes, Sam.'

Sam picked up his bag. 'Right then, ta-ra, girl.'

He rubbed his hand over Tommy's head but

the boy burrowed his head into his mother and only muttered, 'Ta-ra,' when Sam said, 'Ta-ra then, son.'

Nellie found it very hard to part with Sam and was annoyed that Buck had not left them alone to say goodbye, and Tommy was upset when his father had gone.

'I'll be a big school lad when me dad comes home,' he said.

'Yes and big school lads don't cry,' Nellie said. 'I'll write and tell him you didn't cry when he went.'

Tommy said thoughtfully, 'He might have wanted me to cry,' and Nellie was amazed by the child's perception.

She found that her neighbours knew all about Sam's fight with Bert Hagan.

'My feller said he'd never seen a fight like that for a long while,' Jessie said. 'Then he come home and battered you.'

'He never done nothing to me,' Nellie snapped. 'Only fell against me and I cut me head on the dresser.'

Jessie tossed her head. 'His bloody bad temper must be catching,' she said, flouncing off.

Later when Nellie wrote a carefully edited version of the conversation to Sam, she found herself smiling, and included Jessie's remark about her catching Sam's ill temper, thinking that it would give Sam a laugh.

On Monday morning Nellie left Tommy playing in the street with Katy's children and as she walked to the shop, fell in with Bella who was on her way to the pawnshop. She was hung about with numerous bags and bundles and Nellie offered to carry some for her.

'Thanks, girl. I must be getting past it. I'm blowing for tugs, my feller says,' panted Bella.

She seemed to breathe more easily when Nellie had taken some of the bundles and they walked along slowly.

'I see Sam's gone on the *Maury*,' Bella said. 'Anyway he's with good mates now, girl. Not like them lot he was with just after you was married. My feller said they was saying all sorts to Sam in the Volley, trying to start a fight.'

'They did too,' Nellie said. 'Sam battered some fellow called Hagan.'

'Him, was it?' Bella said. 'There's been bad blood there since they was in the same fo'c'sle, that time I was talking about. Before your lad was born. Trouble on shipboard and then when they was ashore in Valparaiso. Sam knocked two of them out.'

'I think Charlie West was there as well,' Nellie said.

'I wouldn't be surprised,' Bella said, 'nasty bit of work that feller, girl. Always stirring up trouble but he'd run a mile if anyone went to belt him.'

They paused on the corner while Bella eased her back and redistributed her bundles, and Nellie said quietly, 'Sam was staggering when he come in that night, and he caught me off balance. I cut me head on the dresser but it was an accident. I got told Janey was saying different but she's a liar.'

'Aye, and another troublemaker,' Bella said

205

comfortably. 'But I suppose you can't get rid of her. Does she see to you when you get caught, like?'

'What do you mean?' Nellie asked.

She so obviously had not understood that Bella said immediately, 'I must've got it wrong, girl. With you only having the one, like, I thought the old one must be dosing you.'

Nellie blushed furiously. 'I wouldn't take it,' she exclaimed. 'I'd love another baby, Bella. A little girl or another lad for company for Tommy. It just hasn't happened.'

'Fancy that,' Bella said. 'My fella only had to hang his kecks on the bedrail and I was off again.'

'Maggie said it might be because I had a bad time with Tommy,' Nellie said.

'Could be, girl, but it done you a good turn. You don't want to get dragged down be strings of kids, specially with your feller away at sea all the time,' said Bella. 'There's plenty round here wish they only had the one, believe me.' They started off again and when they reached the pawnshop Bella took the bundles from Nellie.

'You're a good girl,' she said. 'Don't worry. I'll put the word round about your head, and about the old girl an' all.' She leaned closer to Nellie. 'Try to get shut of her though, girl, or get away yourself. There's trouble brewing in that quarter.'

Leaving Bella in the shop, Nellie walked along deep in thought. She felt that she had learned a lot from Bella and she was pleased that she had been able to tell Bella the true facts. She had no doubt that everyone in the neighbourhood would soon be informed, and although she disliked the idea of everyone knowing her business, at least it would be the truth.

She thought of Bella's words about Janey dosing her to get rid of babies. Fancy people thinking that. You could have knocked me down with a feather, she thought, and the way I've been hoping for another baby.

And that was why those fellows were saying things to Sam. Because of some trouble at sea. They're like spiteful old women, she thought.

When she heard someone say, 'Hello, Nell,' she was so preoccupied that she smiled automatically until she realised it was Charlie West.

She dived into the nearest shop, which was a greengrocer's, and waited until he grew tired of hanging about before she emerged. I'll clout him with me cauliflower if he's still there, she vowed, but he had gone.

Later she told Maggie about it. 'And I would have done it and all,' she declared. 'Clouted him, I mean.'

Maggie laughed. 'I think you would too,' she said. 'I'll tell you what, Nell, you're not half different to the quiet little girl you used to be. Remember when you used to run home away from him crying?'

'Yes, I'm a real hard knock now,' Nellie said, and was amazed when Maggie laughed until she cried.

CHAPTER 11

Tommy was five years old in November and started school in January 1926. Nellie took him to school and went to bring him home for the first few days, then he went with Katy's eldest girl, Amy.

He was still shy and timid and Nellie worried that he would be bullied but Katy reassured her.

'Our Amy'll look after him,' she said. 'And with all me brothers and sisters living round here there's plenty of their kids to stick up for him.'

The first few days were foggy and cold and Nellie dressed Tom in his best jersey and trousers with warm socks and new boots on his feet. He wore a thick coat and a woollen scarf which Nellie wrapped round his neck, crossed on his chest and under his armpits, then fastened at the back with a large safety pin.

He stood out among the children in the playground, most of whom were poorly dressed in hand-me-down jerseys and coats with broken or patched boots or plimsolls, or in police clothes.

It might have gone hard for Tom at first without the protection of Bella's grandchildren, but soon he disarmed some of those who resented him, by his innocent friendliness and his willingness to share the bread and jam his mother gave him for playtime.

On the days that Nellie worked Tommy had his dinner with Katy's children, and the money that Nellie paid her was a help to Katy.

Her husband Peter had broken his leg in a fall down a ship's hold so times were hard for Katy. She was lucky in that she had her mother Bella living across the street and numerous members of her own family and Peter's living near by, all of whom helped her.

'I don't like taking it though,' she confided to Nellie. 'It's all right with me own family but Peter's Aunt Mary Anne makes it sound like charity. She takes all the good out of anything she gives me. Always a speech with it or making out it was Peter's own fault.'

'But everyone takes turns with the bad times and the good times,' Nellie said. 'Look at the Nolans. Maggie was out of her mind a few years ago trying to keep them all fed and worrying about Richie's legs and look at them now. Times will come good again for you too, Katy.'

It was true that life was good for the Nolans now. Maggie still had three mornings a week cleaning and Johnny had held on to his job in spite of bouts of bronchitis in bad weather. The eldest girl Susan was now working in Carroll's tobacco works and earning seven shillings and sixpence a week and Josie was due to leave school at midsummer. Years of good food had cured Richie's rickets and now his legs were only slightly bowed.

Not all of Nellie's neighbours were so

fortunate. A family named Doyle lived in the bottom half of the house next to Bella's—father, mother and six children. The father worked for one of the many local firms who employed and fired men on a daily basis and as there were always more men than jobs it was an even more precarious life than that of a dock worker.

The mother was a bedraggled woman with a bad squint and the children sickly so Nellie was not surprised to hear that the youngest child had died. She met Mrs Doyle and sympathised with her and asked when the funeral would be, thinking that she could offer to mind the other children if she was not working.

'Not till Monday,' Mrs Doyle said, wiping her eyes. 'His suit's in. I can't redeem it, like, till Saturday.'

Nellie was lost for words but later she wondered whether she should have offered to lend the money to get the suit out of pawn.

Maggie advised against it. 'You'd only hurt her feelings,' she said. 'And the funeral's fixed up now anyhow.'

Nellie lay awake for some time that night, counting her blessings, and the following day she prepared Janey's favourite meal of tripe and onions.

'Me favourite,' Janey exclaimed as Nellie heaped the food on her plate.

'Yes, well, you done me a good turn getting me married to Sam,' Nellie said. 'We've never gone short.'

Janey looked at her suspiciously but said nothing.

Sam too spent many sleepless hours lying in his bunk thinking of the last few days of his leave. Of Nellie lying on the floor with blood pouring from the cut on her head and Tommy's terrorstricken cry, 'Is me mam dead, Janey?'

He thought of Tommy and the way the child had shrunk away from him when he put his arm round him to comfort him, while Nellie lay on the sofa. The boy had stood rigid and unyielding within his arm until Nellie had smiled at both of them and called Tommy to her.

With bitter self-disgust Sam thought of how he must appear to his son. A bully who had nearly killed his mother. No matter that Nellie's life had never been in danger. Sam felt that Tommy would never trust him again.

He remembered the day he had left when Buck Madden had called for him. Nellie had tried to arrange her hair to cover the dressing but Buck had said right away, 'How's your head, Mrs M?' and Nellie said it was almost better.

Sam always groaned to himself when he thought of what happened next. I had to talk sense into her when she was saying about going to the chemist for them stitches, he thought. All I said was, 'Go to the hospital and get it done proper, d'yer hear?'

It's the way all the fellers talk to women. I couldn't talk like that when we're on our own with Buck there. He'd think I was a right bloody cissie, but the way Tommy put his arms round her and glared at me. As if I was going to clout her or sump'n' and he'd fight me—me own son!

211

Give Ellie her due, she laughed it off, thought Sam, but it give me the shock of me life.

For once he was sorry when the ship docked, wondering what sort of welcome was waiting for him. He walked slowly up the street, his seabag on his shoulder, but Ellie must have seen him pass the window. The next minute she had the door open and she was shouting, 'Tommy, Tommy, quick, your dad's here.'

Relief flooded through Sam as he stepped inside the house and flung his seabag down then put his arms round Nellie.

Tommy came running downstairs and Sam raised his head. 'Hello there, lad,' he said and Tommy put his arms round him butting his head against Sam's chest.

'You're not half growing,' Sam said, 'Nearly as tall as your mam.' He looked round the room. All the usual careful preparations had been made for him, even the Woodies and the Vespas. So Ellie didn't hold nothing against him and neither did Tommy by the looks of things.

Sam sat down in his chair and Tommy sat on the stool beside him. 'Did you see any flying fish, Dad?' he asked eagerly.

Sam shook his head. 'Not this trip, lad. It was the Atlantic run this time. I'll tell you about it after.'

Nellie bent over him to put a mug of tea beside him and he saw the scar on her head. 'Is your head better, girl?' he asked diffidently.

'Yes. I went to the chemist, Sam, and he give me a note to take to the hospital to get the stitches out,' Nellie said.

Sam shook his head. 'So you had your own way, girl.'

'I was that frightened of going to the hospital,' Nellie said defensively, 'but Mr Doyle was awful nice. He gives me this note. The doctor read it out to the nurse. I wrote it down so I could tell you what it said.'

She took a slip of paper from behind the clock and read aloud. ' "Mrs Meadows is nervous about returning for the removal of stitches as in her confused state she lost the slip of paper she was given on discharge. I have assured her that she will be treated with consideration." '

She replaced the paper. 'Wasn't that lovely? I wish I could talk like that, but d'you know what the doctor said to the nurse? Pompous ass!'

Sam drank some tea then lit a Woodbine and lay back in the chair stretching out his long legs. 'By God, this is the life, girl,' he said.

The next few hours were so pleasant and happy, as Tommy told him about school and Sam talked of incidents on the voyage, that he began to feel sorry that he had worried so much while he was away.

Even when Janey came in she only said, 'You're back, then?' She lingered while Nellie took her meal through to the parlour and Sam pulled out some coins from his pocket.

'Get yourself a drink, Ma,' he said.

Janey cast a lightning glance over the money in her hand and smiled with satisfaction before she nodded to him and stumped off into the parlour.

It was only later that Sam realised that Tommy had not forgotten or forgiven. When he said easily to the boy, 'I'll see you into bed before I go to the Volley, lad,' Tommy went to where Nellie sat knitting and put his arm round her shoulders.

'I'll stay up with me mam until you come back,' he said defiantly.

Sam felt his face burning with anger and he opened his mouth to yell at the boy and clenched his fist, but Nellie said quickly, 'Oh no you don't, Tommy. Don't be trying it on just because your dad's home and you're a big school lad now.'

Sam saw the way the boy looked at his mother, his eyes wide with hurt surprise at being misunderstood, but Nellie ignored him and turned to Sam.

'He's getting proper independent, like, since he started school. Mind you, he needs to stand up for himself with some of them hard knocks there.'

Sam knew that she was talking to bridge the awkward moment but he was unable to speak. The lad wanted to stay up to protect his mam from him, Sam. It should have been funny—the size of the lad compared to him—but Sam could see no humour in it. Instead he was bitterly hurt at the injustice of it.

Some women round here get battered every Saturday night, he thought, and in between times too. I never meant to knock Ellie down and I done all I could, took her to the hospital an' all and yet I'm getting treated like this.

Nellie stood up and thrust her needles into her knitting. 'Just for that *I'll* take you to bed tonight. Teach you not to try it on, m'lad.'

Sam stood up too, and took his jacket and cap from behind the door. 'I'll gerroff,' he muttered, and went out.

Buck Madden and many of Sam's shipmates were in the Volunteer and a pint was put into his hand as soon as he entered. 'Get that down yer, lad,' Buck said cheerfully. 'Good ale this. Better than the horse's piss we got in New York.'

Sam's spirits rose. This was the place to be. I'm getting like a bloody old woman, he thought, worrying over moods and sulks. He drained his glass and called for a round. He thought of the days before he was married when life was simple. Anybody annoyed him he just belted them, had a good straight fight, then had a pint together when it was over.

None of this brooding over this and that. I should've give the lad a good hiding, he decided, and maybe give Nellie a belt now and again to show her who's boss.

More pints had appeared before Sam and he had been drinking them rapidly as he pondered. Someone struck up a song and Sam joined in, now swaying slightly and bawling out the song with his eyes closed.

A barman appeared by their group. 'All right, lads. Keep it down,' he said. 'Snowy and another copper are in the back.'

The other men stopped singing but Sam continued until Buck pulled at his arm. 'Stow it, Sam,' he said urgently, 'don't want to get

215

us barred out the first night home.'

Other men added pleas for him to stop and Sam's voice trailed away. 'It's the women,' he confided to Buck, 'used to be simple, like, know wharra mean.'

'Aye, I know, Sam,' Buck said soothingly. 'Never mind, lad, we can gerraway from them in here.'

One of the other men joked. 'You haven't half got a drouth on you tonight, Sam. The way you lowered them pints. What did she give you for your tea, salt fish?'

Sam thrust his face near to the man menacingly. 'What's it gorra do with you?' he said and the man looked indignant.

'Only a bloody joke, for God's sake. What the 'ell's wrong with you?'

Fortunately at that moment George Adams came in. 'Only come for the last one,' he said. 'Me youngest lad's not well so I stayed in.' A pint was pushed into his hand but as soon as possible Buck drew him aside.

'I don't know what the 'ell's wrong with Sam tonight,' he said. 'He's in a right funny mood. Looking for a fight.'

'He's been in a queer mood all the trip,' George said. 'Something on his mind. I'll try and talk to him.'

'Hope his wife hasn't got mixed up with the old one in her parlour,' Buck said. 'The missus said the jacks have been sniffing round there. Might be trouble.'

George dismissed the idea. 'No, Nellie doesn't have nothing to do with her, only cooking her

216

food, like,' he said. 'And the coppers know it. Rose was only saying tonight how happy Nellie is with her job and the lad doing well at school. Must be something else with Sam.'

The barman called time and Sam's two friends walked home with him. He was too drunk by this time for any conversation and once indoors he slumped down on the sofa and began to snore loudly. Nellie was unable to rouse him and finally went to bed, hoping that he would wake at some time and come to bed.

Earlier when she had taken Tommy to bed she had said nothing until the boy was in his nightshirt and she was tucking him into bed, although she knew that he was feeling hurt and misunderstood. She kissed him. 'Goodnight, son,' she said. 'I know why you wanted to stay up but there won't be no more accidents. Your poor dad's still upset over the last one so we'll have to make him happy while he's at home, won't we?'

Tommy flung his arms round her neck. 'Oh, Mam,' was all he said and Nellie hugged him silently. As she pulled the bedclothes up round him he said, 'I'll ask Miss if I can make a boat for me dad like the one I made for you,' and Nellie kissed him again.

'Go to sleep now, lad,' she said and went downstairs.

She was not dismayed at Sam's drunkenness when he returned, as George had said to her, 'First night home. Strong ale in the Volley, girl. I've only had one because I stayed home for Timmy.'

When she woke the next morning Sam was lying beside her, deeply asleep, and she crept downstairs.

It was nearly time for Tommy to return for his midday break when Sam woke, but he was up and dressed and shaved when the boy came home.

'Tommy's got to go back after dinner, y'know, Sam,' Nellie said timidly, thinking that he expected to take the boy out, but Sam smiled.

'I know, girl,' he said. 'Just thought I'd tidy meself up a bit before he come home, like.'

Tommy proudly announced that Miss said his work was the best and he had been given two pear drops as a reward. 'I saved them for you,' he announced. 'One each.'

He pulled them from his pocket and presented one to Sam and one to Nellie. Both sweets had collected fluff from his pocket and Tommy said doubtfully, 'I only had one suck of them.'

Nellie and Sam assured him that the fluff didn't matter and that they would enjoy the sweets after their dinner. 'You're a good lad,' Nellie said. 'Both for getting the sweets and keeping them for us,' and Sam heartily agreed.

'Pity we can't go out, lad,' he said, 'but I'll take you on the Overhead again on Saturday.'

After Tommy had gone to school Buck Madden called again. 'Didn't think I'd see you up after the skinful you had last night,' he said.

'I don't remember much about it,' Sam said.

'The way you lowered them first pints,' Buck laughed. 'One of the lads said you must have give him salt fish, Mrs M.'

'No, spare ribs and cabbage,' Nellie said. 'And it wasn't salty.'

'You had a right cob on an' all,' Buck said to Sam.

Sam was surprised. 'I don't remember having no cob on,' he said, but Buck assured him that he had wanted to fight. 'Good job George come in,' he said. 'Just for the last pint, because his lad wasn't well.'

'I'll have to go and see Rose. See if I can help,' Nellie said.

'Tell George we're in the alehouse now,' Buck said, and as they went out she heard him telling Sam more incidents from the night before.

He's a good mate, Nellie thought, but he's always putting his foot in it. She wondered why Sam had had a cob on the previous night. Surely it wasn't because of what had happened before Tommy went to bed? Sam seemed to have forgotten it now anyway.

She found Rose and George very relieved because the boy's temperature had come down and he was sleeping peacefully.

'Mr Doyle the chemist gave George a good bottle for him,' Rose explained. 'Seemed to bring the fever down right away. He's a proper clever man. Only failed his last examination or he'd have been a doctor.'

Timmy was so much better by Saturday that Rose was able to leave him with her eldest daughter while she and George went as usual to the market. There they met Sam and Nellie with Tommy and stopped to talk.

Tommy told them excitedly that he had been on the Overhead Railway with his father and described the ships they had seen.

'He's coming out of his shell, isn't he?' Rose said, when Tommy had gone to buy candy floss. 'He thinks he's the man of the house when you're away, Sam. Ready to defend Nellie against anyone.'

'Aye, even me,' Sam said grimly. 'Squared up to me when I come home.' He wanted to recall the words as soon as they were spoken but Rose only laughed.

'Well, he had to show you what he could do, didn't he?' she said. 'Show you Nellie was in good hands.'

They all laughed and Nellie thought, God bless Rose. She always knows the right thing to say. Sam too seemed to appreciate Rose's tact and he made no jealous outbursts while they were out, though Nellie felt that at times he had to struggle to restrain himself.

They made their usual purchases of meat and fruit, and Sam bought Nellie a gaudy brooch with the word Mother on it and some marbles for Tommy.

George bought a monkey on a stick to amuse Timmy and later when he was showing the toy to Timmy and making him smile Rose remarked that Sam was a good man.

'Aye, he's got a good heart,' George said. 'But he gets the black dog on him sometimes. Broods too much. He looks a tough feller but he worries over things.'

'I thought tonight he seemed cut about Tommy squaring up to him,' Rose said. 'Y'know, George, we always think Tommy's nature comes from Nellie but I think there's a lot of Sam in him too.'

'Yes, Sam's more thin skinned than you think from looking at him,' George said. 'A real good mate though.'

At the same time Nellie and Sam were discussing Rose.

'George's wife is a nice woman,' Sam said. 'D'you see much of her when we're away?'

'Yes, I often go there or she calls here,' Nellie said. 'She's got a sort of motherly way with her. You feel you can ask her anything.' She blushed as she spoke, remembering what she *had* asked Rose. 'George is a good man too, isn't he? They seem happy, like. He's never jealous of her.'

She spoke without thinking but Sam said sharply, 'Aye, but she looks *married.*'

'How do you mean? She's always tidy and she looks healthy, like,' Nellie said.

'I don't mean she looks dragged down like some of the women round here,' Sam said. 'But she looks sort of settled. You look like a little girl in your mam's shawl.'

'I do wear me mam's shawl,' Nellie said. 'But I'm not a little girl—well, I'm not very tall, like, but I don't look like a *little girl.*'

Sam laughed and drew her on to his knee. 'You might think you don't, girl,' he said, 'but that's got said be other people too. That

221

you look too much of a kid to be a married woman, like.'

'I can't help being small,' Nellie said indignantly, 'but I *feel* like a married woman and a mam too. People talk daft.'

She seemed close to tears and Sam changed the subject by asking about her job.

'Mrs Duncan was a bit narked because I said I wouldn't be in while you was home,' Nellie said. 'Mrs Taggart the cleaner said it was because she thinks the likes of us shouldn't put our husbands before her lousy job. She's a case, Mrs Taggart.'

Mrs Taggart and the cook had said much more which Nellie had no intention of telling Sam because she knew he already had reservations about her job.

She thought that Sam would return to drinking in the afternoon now that Tommy was at school but unless Buck Madden called for him, Sam seemed content to sit talking to her as she ironed or prepared the meal. Sometimes he went with her to the shops in Great Homer Street, and one occasion they went to the pier head and took the ferry to Seacombe.

Nellie enjoyed the outings but she told Sam that she felt guilty about going on the ferry while Tommy was stuck in school, but they were always home before he returned.

'We'll all go on Sunday, girl,' Sam said, and on the Sunday they did more.

They went on the ferry to Seacombe then took a train to Chester. Nellie wore her coat for this outing and was glad that she did, as they moved among the well-dressed crowds, but on other occasions she wore her shawl. She was determined that Sam should have no cause for jealousy, but for this time ashore, at least, Sam seemed to have conquered his demon. Nellie felt though that it only lay dormant and that some tiny core of doubt could rouse it again and cause another jealous outburst from Sam.

The confrontation between Tommy and Sam seemed to be forgotten by both of them and they grew closer every day. The streets through which Tommy walked to school were always full of people going about their business and Tommy seemed to enjoy the walk to school as much as school itself.

'We seen men with big shovels on their shoulders and women with buckets and scrubbing brushes. Amy said they were going to clean the ships and we seen brown men with hats one on top of the other piled on their heads,' he told his father.

'Aye, they're lascars off the ships,' Sam said. 'Them men come from a very hot country, Tom, that's why they're brown. The sun shines all the time there.'

'We seen Henry Nolan an' all but Amy said we hadn't got to talk to him because he was keeping douse for the bookie's runner up the jigger,' Tom said.

Sam and Nellie looked at each other and Nellie said severely, 'Amy was only making that up. Don't you never say that to anyone or you'll get Henry into trouble, do you hear? It's like one of the stories you make up, lad, so don't say no more about it.'

Tommy said, 'No, Mam,' in a subdued voice but later after Sam took him to bed, he came downstairs smiling.

'I see what you mean about Tom making up tales, girl,' he said. 'You shoulda heard what he's been going on about. A big long story about coal heavers and ships' cleaning women and a shipwreck. I was sorry when it finished.'

Nellie laughed. 'I know,' she said. 'If I go to the pictures with Gertie he always wants me to tell him the story when I get back then he makes up a different ending, like.'

'He's not half clever—there's no two ways about that,' Sam said proudly. 'And he's getting a better start than what we had, too.'

One of Bobby's infrequent letters had arrived by the late post and Sam picked it up again and laughed. 'I tell you what, Ellie, I think Tom can write better even now than what Bobby can.'

Nellie flushed. 'Our Bob wasn't never good at school learning, like, but he could do arithmetic, and look at the good job he's got now. And he got away from round here an' all.'

'He's done well for himself,' Sam agreed. 'I hope he gets home before I sail so I can see him again.'

Bobby had written that he was to be transferred back to the Liverpool works for a special job, but it was postponed and in the meantime Sam signed on for a timber ship bound for Canada.

'Got to take a ship when you can get it,' he told Nellie and she agreed, although Tommy

224

was upset at parting from his father.

'I won't be away long, lad,' Sam told him. 'And you have some more yarns for me and I'll try to think of some for you when I get back.'

Nellie soon found that some people were jealous of Sam's quick 'turn round'. She was in a group by Bella's step when a neighbour, Maud Jenkins, said spitefully, 'I see your fella got a ship very quick. He must be well in with somebody or good with his backhanders.'

'Sam doesn't give backhanders,' Nellie said. 'He got the ship because he's a good seaman.'

'Are you making out my fella isn't?' Maud screeched, but Bella's voice boomed out.

'Stow it. Stands to reason Sam gets more ships being big. If the fellers are waving their books the boss can see Sam head and shoulders over other fellers.'

'Especially your Bert, Maud,' another woman sniggered. 'With his duck's disease. His arse rubs 'is footprints out.'

Maud's face was red with temper and she thrust it close to Nellie. 'Think you're smart, don't you?' she sneered. 'And one kid. You must be clever with a crochet hook an' all.'

'Crochet hook?' Nellie stammered. 'What's a crochet hook got to do with it?' but again Bella intervened.

'Don't talk so bloody daft, Maud,' she said. 'You can see the girl doesn't know what yer on about. If she wanted to get rid she wouldn't need no crochet hook, living on the same floor as old Janey, *as you well know.*'

Maud was silenced but an older woman said quietly to Nellie, 'You wanna be careful with them concoctions, girl. God knows what the old girl puts in them but we've seen the damage they can do, haven't we?' she appealed to the other women and everyone agreed.

'There's worse things than having a baby,' someone said.

'But I *want* another baby,' Nellie said, feeling bewildered and near to tears. 'I wouldn't take nothing off Janey anyhow. Nurse McCann told me not to.'

Maggie came over and joined the group. 'That's right. Nellie's been dying for another for company for Tommy,' she said, 'but I think the old girl's to blame for her not having no more. Sump'n' went wrong when Tommy was born because she left Nellie in labour too long. If I hadn't sent their Bobby for the nurse Tommy wouldn't be here and Nellie mightn't be neither.'

'That's right. The nurse saved his life,' Nellie said, and several women began to praise the midwife.

'You wanna go and see her, girl,' Bella advised, 'she might put you right. Or go and see Dr Wilson. You've got the money now with yer little job.'

'Aye, much gets more,' Maud muttered, but she could see that the tide of opinion was against her and she soon withdrew into her own house.

Later Nellie and Maggie walked back together to their houses and Nellie said eagerly, 'I never even thought of that—me long labour, I mean, stopping me having another. Do you think the nurse could help me, Mag?'

'She's a clever woman,' Maggie said. 'I believe she's not too well. Would you go to Dr Wilson?'

'I wouldn't like,' Nellie said. 'Not to a man over something like this. I'll go and see Nurse McCann though.'

The following morning she washed thoroughly and changed her underclothes before setting off to see the nurse. Nurse McCann lived in a small house near Marsh Lane with her sister, also unmarried, and it was the sister who opened the door.

'My sister's not well. Nurse Watson's taking her calls,' she said abruptly, preparing to close the door, but desperation made Nellie fluent as she explained why she had called.

She was admitted and taken upstairs after the sister had explained to the nurse, but Nellie was horrified at the change in the once big hearty woman. Nurse McCann seemed to have shrunk and even her voice was now threadlike, but her eyes were bright with intelligence and interest as Nellie explained why she had come.

'I can't examine you, girl,' she said ruefully, 'but I think you should see Dr Wilson. It might be that your womb is tilted slightly, making it more difficult to conceive.'

Nellie had brought a photograph of Tommy which she had intended to send to Sam. 'You saved his life, Nurse,' she said shyly. 'He's a real good boy and his teacher says he's very clever. That was taken last week.'

Nurse McCann's eyes filled with tears as she gazed at the photograph. 'Can I keep this, Nellie?' she asked.

Nellie said eagerly, 'Of course, Nurse. He wouldn't've been here if it wasn't for you.'

'Thanks, girl,' the nurse said. She propped the photograph on the table beside her. 'At least I've got something to show for my life,' she said, then with a flash of her old spirit, 'And go and see Dr Wilson. Never mind you don't like going to a man. Royalty have men doctors to attend them and what's good enough for them is good enough for us.'

Nellie was smiling when she left the house, but she felt sad as she walked home. It wasn't fair for a woman who was needed so much to die young, she thought. Would she ever pluck up courage to see Dr Wilson? she wondered. Some day perhaps—but not yet.

CHAPTER 12

Bobby had only made brief visits on Sunday afternoons but now he was back at the Liverpool works for two weeks. All the neighbours were amazed at the change in his appearance. He was now nineteen years old and tall and broad shouldered with bright eyes and a tanned face.

'You look the picture of health, lad,' Maggie said when he came out of Nellie's door with her.

Bobby said cheerfully, 'No wonder. The air's great up there and I've been living like a lord. You should see my bedroom and the food! All lovely and fresh and plenty of it—as much as I can eat.'

'You've fell on your feet, then,' Maggie said with a sigh.

Bobby looked round the grimy street, at the shabby women at the doors and the ragged children playing in the gutters. The polluted air was filled with unpleasant smells from the matchworks, the tannery and the fertiliser factory, and from the various cargoes being unloaded at the docks.

'I'd forgot it was so bad,' he admitted. 'Our Nellie does her best to keep the house nice, but out here! The house is always stinking with Janey's fish too.'

Maggie wrapped her arms in her apron and tossed her head. 'Mind you, there's worse places than this,' she said. 'At least we all stick together and help each other out, and the kids don't mind because they've never known no different. It never bothered you when you lived here.'

'I know,' Bobby admitted, 'but now I've seen different I'd like to get you and Tommy away from it, Nell.'

Nellie could see that Maggie was offended and she said lightly, 'I say the same meself when them cats are yowling round the house after the fish but I suppose I'll go outa here feet first.'

'Jeez, girl, I hope it's many a long day till that happens,' Maggie exclaimed. 'No more than for meself. Mind you, I suppose Janey will see the two of us out.'

'Yes, I think she's pickled in gin,' Nellie said and went off laughing with her brother.

It was a treat for Nellie to have Bobby home again and to be able to talk freely to him. She could talk about Sam's jealousy to him, knowing that her brother's admiration for Sam meant that he would not misunderstand, and they could say anything at all to each other about the old woman in the parlour.

Bobby often talked about the cottage and the old couple he lodged with. 'You should see them, Nell. Neither of them are tall and they're that fat they're as broad as they're long, very near, and no wonder. You never saw anything like the food, Nell. When I think of the way everyone round here is always scatting and scraping to get enough to eat, it doesn't seem right somehow. What we eat in a week'd keep this street for a month.'

'They must be well off then,' Nellie said.

'They don't think so. Well, they don't say, like, but Mr Handley only works for a farmer. But they grow all their vegetables, and fruit for pies and they keep chickens and a pig. Sometimes we have rabbit pie.'

'It sounds lovely,' Nellie said wistfully. 'Don't you ever feel outa place there, Bob?'

'No, I get on fine with everyone,' Bob said.

He hesitated and Nellie said mischievously, 'Any nice girls there?'

It was all that Bob needed and, blushing and stammering at first, he told her all about his

230

girlfriend, Margaret, always known as Meg.

'She's lovely, Nell,' Bobby said proudly, 'and real clever. She cycles into the little town, Sudely, every day to work in an office. I go to church with the Handleys and Margaret sings in the choir there. That's how I met her.'

'You'll have to bring her home for me to meet her,' Nellie said and Bobby agreed although he looked doubtful.

All too soon the job was finished and Bobby left for Yorkshire. He seemed eager to get back there but Nellie missed him a great deal, and Tommy said it was nearly as bad as when his dad went. 'Although that's worser,' he said quickly 'When me dad goes.'

While Bobby was home Nellie served Janey's meal in the parlour making the excuse that there was not room for four at the table, but as soon as he left Janey returned to eating with Nellie and Tommy.

To see the old woman's dirty fingers among the food disgusted Nellie and she found the smell that rose from the old woman equally nauseating. I don't know whether she's getting even dirtier or I'm noticing it more, she thought, but I can't stand her much longer.

She was alarmed too because Janey's mood seemed to have changed yet again and she made constant references to Leadbetter.

'I wonder what Sam'd say if he knew why you come home in such a hurry,' she said once. 'And got me to fix up for you to marry him an' all.'

'That's a lie and you know it,' Nellie said

231

hotly. 'It was you fixed it up and I told Sam why too.'

'A likely story,' the old woman sneered. 'You wouldn't be here to tell the tale if you done that. He'd 'a murdered you. Why should I want youse married anyhow?'

'Because my dad's money was stopped and you wanted Sam's allotment coming in,' Nellie said, too angry to be cautious, but Janey shot her such a venomous look that she recoiled.

'Don't get clever with me, you stupid mare,' the old woman hissed, thrusting her face close to Nellie's. 'You could be praying he was Leadbetter's if I opened me mouth.' She turned away but Nellie gripped her arm.

'What do you mean? Tell me what you mean, Janey,' she begged, but Janey only sniggered spitefully.

'Wait and see. What's bred in the bone'll come out in the flesh. Just wait and see.'

She went into her parlour still sniggering and although Nellie asked her several times during the following days what she meant, she would only say, 'Wait and see.' Finally Nellie stopped asking and decided to put the old woman's remarks down to vindictiveness and not allow herself to worry about them. She could manage this during the day, but often she lay awake at night worrying. There was no one she could confide in.

Gertie Drew had now taken lodgers, an elderly woman with a daughter who had a twisted spine and a club foot. In spite of her disabilities it was the daughter, Letty, who provided for them as an outworker for a tailoring firm.

'Mind you, she must be stronger than she looks,' Gertie told Nellie. 'She's got the sewing machine on the go morning noon and night, and she does all the cooking and washing as far as I can see.'

'What does her mother do?' Nellie asked.

'Bugger all,' Gertie said frankly. 'She's never in. Always wandering about. I think she might have gypsy blood be the look of her, that swarthy skin and her black eyes and hair. Wouldn't it be romantic if she was really a gypsy, Nell?'

'I seen her in Trinity Road one day,' Nellie said, 'and in Derby Park another day when I took Tommy, but Letty wasn't with her.'

'No, she hardly ever goes out,' Gertie said. 'Mind you, I'm not complaining. They're real good lodgers. Quiet and pleasant and regular with the rent.'

It was assumed that the mother, Mrs Gilligan, was a widow but Bella soon corrected Nellie when she spoke of the widow in Gertie's house.

'Widder woman me foot,' Bella said. 'She's got a husband alive and well. Went off to live over the brush with a woman in Keats Street, then they went off to live somewhere near Spellow Lane. Mrs Gilligan's supposed to be able to tell the future but she never foretold that. Him clearing off with the other one.'

Her huge bulk quivered like a jelly as she laughed and Nellie was sorry that she had been the cause of Mrs Gilligan's secret being aired.

233

Nellie had become a great favourite with Bella and was often invited to sit beside her on her step. It was a mixed blessing, Nellie found.

It signalled that she was under Bella's protection and warned off people, like Maud, but often Nellie was in a dilemma, wanting to get on with her work at home but unable to leave without offending Bella.

Nellie had little spare time now that her hours had been increased at the house in Balliol Road. One of the elderly maids, Jane, had collapsed and been taken to Bootle Hospital. Mrs Duncan had not taken on a temporary replacement for her although she still entertained as much as ever, but expected Nellie to do the work in the few extra hours that she paid her for.

Often she was kept so late that Tommy had to be put to bed by Katy or Maggie, or kept up long past his bedtime, but Nellie made no complaint. She thought that by working extra hours she was safeguarding Jane's job until she was ready to return, but the cook and Mrs Taggart told her that she was mistaken.

'I seen Jane last night,' the cook said. 'She'll never be able to work no more and she was heartbroken. She hasn't got no family so it'll be the Kirkdale Homes for her, God help her.'

'But won't Mrs Duncan—?' Nellie began but the two women laughed derisively.

'Not her,' Mrs Taggart said. 'No, girl. She's full of funny tricks but that's not one of them.'

'But in my first place I was taken on to help Gertrude because she was crippled with arthritis

234

but she didn't want to give up work. Then when Mr Ambrose and Miss Agatha died they left it in the Will that Gertrude was to go in a nursing home.'

'There's not many like that, girl,' the cook said. 'Proper toffs. These lot are Johnny-come-latelys. Beggars on horseback. Don't know how to behave.'

'You let the missus know you can't do everything and you can't go working late on account of your little lad,' Mrs Taggart said. 'Tell them girls you can't run after them and be parlourmaid as well.'

'And kitchenmaid and assistant cook or whatever you're supposed to be down here,' the cook broke in. 'And all for charwomen's wages. Stand up to her, girl. She won't sack you, no fear. Bragging to her posh pals as if she's gorra big staff.'

Indignation on Jane's behalf helped Nellie to ignore the bells ringing for her as they all worked frantically to prepare the dinner. She had taken off her kitchen apron and smoothed her hair and was taking a tray of silver into the dining room when one of the daughters stormed downstairs.

'I'm going to complain to my mother,' she said furiously, 'My sister and I have been ringing for you for twenty minutes.'

'I'm sorry, miss. I've only got one pair of hands,' Nellie said, and the girl stormed upstairs.

Even when Mrs Duncan sent for her Nellie stood her ground although she was quaking inwardly. Think about Jane, she told herself.

'I'm very disappointed in you, Ellen,' Mrs Duncan said severely. 'Miss Alexandra tells me that you not only failed to answer her bell, but you were impertinent when she spoke to you.'

'I said I only had one pair of hands and it's true, ma'am,' Nellie said.

'Jane's illness has come at a most inconvenient time, Ellen, but we must all pull our weight in these circumstances. I've arranged for the charwoman to come back for an hour to help with the washing up and she can help cook. Agnes must help in the dining room and you must go immediately to assist my daughters with their hair and their clothes,' Mrs Duncan said.

She turned away as though the matter was closed but Nellie said in a quavering voice, 'I'm willing to do my best until Jane comes back.'

She hoped that the cook had misunderstood and Mrs Duncan would tell her that Jane's job was safe, but she only said graciously, 'We'll say no more about it. Go to Miss Lydia and Miss Alexandra at once.'

Nellie went to the kitchen and repeated what had been said before she went to the bedroom shared by the daughters. No money spared on these two, she thought, looking round the luxurious room, yet poor Jane!

'Ow, you're hurting me,' Lydia yelled as Nellie dragged the brush through her hair.

'Sorry, miss,' Nellie said indifferently. She was determined not to hurry as she usually did, or to be tactful about dividing her time equally between the quarrelsome sisters. Soon Alexandra was complaining that Nellie was spending too much time on her sister and too little on her.

'I'm not going to be ready in time,' she stormed. 'Do my hair at once.'

Nellie laid down the brush and Lydia thrust it back into her hand, screaming at her sister.

By the time that Nellie went downstairs both girls had shed tears of temper and were not speaking to each other.

'Common as muck, the pair of them,' the cook said. 'You can't make a silk purse out of a sow's ear, girl.'

'It was Alexandra clatted on me to her mother,' Nellie said. 'I made sure her hair looked a mess at the back.'

'You're learning, Nell,' the cook said approvingly. 'The missus has kept out of the way tonight but she'll have to see me tomorrow. She's got another dinner party planned for Saturday and I'm going to have it out with her. Tell her straight.'

'If I could get another place cleaning I'd leave,' Nellie said. 'But they're few and far between, aren't they?' She sighed. 'I can't go on like this though. Not being there for Tommy when he comes home. I thought I'd fallen on me feet with five mornings' cleaning.'

As she spoke she was rapidly preparing devils on horseback savouries, then putting the finishing touches to an apple Charlotte.

'I won't half miss you if you go,' the cook said, 'but I don't blame you. You've been put on long enough here. Why don't you try for a cook's job?'

Nellie shook her head. 'No, I couldn't live in and anyway I'm all right helping, but I'd be no good on me own.'

'You don't know what you can do till you try. You want to think a bit more of yourself, girl,' the cook said.

By the time the dinner party was over they were all exhausted and Nellie hesitated looking at the mountain of washing up. 'I feel mean going off and leaving this,' she said, but Mrs Taggart told her to go.

'Don't you worry, girl,' she said, 'I won't break me back over it. I'll take me time and I'll make sure she pays me for every minute I'm here. When I think of that poor dear laying in the workhouse!'

Tommy was still awake when Nellie reached home, anxious to show her a tooth that had come out, and he clung to his mother. 'I thought you was never coming, Mam,' he said, and Nellie was even more determined to change her job as soon as possible.

Before she found another job some changes at the Duncan house made her decide to stay there. A girl came from an orphanage to train as parlourmaid and Nellie was free to spend more time in the kitchen. Both of the daughters had their hair bobbed and were told by their mother that they must help each other and not call on Nellie.

Nellie had made it clear that she was unable to stay on in the evening except for special occasions, and as she found later the cook had threatened to leave unless she had help from

Nellie with the elaborate menus planned by Mrs Duncan. Although gradually Nellie slipped back to working wherever she was needed in the house she stayed on. Always she dreaded change and preferred to be in a familiar place.

Summer was nearly over and Bobby had still not brought Meg to see Nellie, but instead Nellie and Tommy had been invited to the Handleys' cottage. She dressed Tommy carefully and wore her blue coat and a matching felt hat.

'You don't half look smart, Nell,' Bobby exclaimed when she stepped off the train, holding Tommy's hand. Meg was with Bobby and he explained that she too had been invited to tea.

Meg was a thin girl with dark eyes and dark curly hair, and a friendly manner. Nellie liked her immediately. They walked from the station and Tommy was enchanted by the wildflowers which grew beside the lane and the birds which hopped fearlessly in the hedgerows.

'This air is lovely,' Nellie said. 'Breathe in, Tommy lad.'

As they walked along Meg told her that she was an only child and her mother had died when Meg was seven years old. 'There's only me and me dad now,' she said. 'He works in flour mill.'

They were all warmly welcomed by Mr and Mrs Handley and Nellie and Meg were sent to lay their coats on Bobby's bed and tidy themselves. Nellie looked round the room at the rose-patterned wallpaper and the big soft bed covered by a white quilt. There was an old-fashioned chest of drawers and a clothes cupboard and the air scented with newmown hay flowed through the open window.

Nellie sat down on a cane chair. 'Eh Meg, no wonder our Bob thought he was in heaven when he come here,' she said. 'We miss him, me and Tommy, but I hope he doesn't never get sent back to Liverpool to work.'

'The Handleys think the world of him and so does me dad,' Meg said. 'He's a Liverpool man himself.'

'Your dad is?' Nellie said in surprise, and Meg explained that her father had been stationed near Sudely during the war and decided to move there from Liverpool.

There was much laughter as they all squeezed round the table in the parlour of the cottage. 'Good thing as lasses are thin and the little lad too,' Mr Handley said.

'Eh, if they favoured me and thee, dad, we'd not fit,' Mrs Handley said.

Tommy was silent with amazement at the amount of food provided. The big York ham which Mr Handley carved to supplement the chicken already on their plates, the crisp salad and whole hard-boiled eggs, the plate tarts filled with damsons, gooseberries and apples, and the parkin and fruit cake.

'Eh, tha mun eat up, lad,' Mrs Handley said jovially. 'Tha'll not match thy uncle else.'

'No wonder our Bob's grown so big and healthy,' Nellie said to Mrs Handley, as Bobby passed up his plate for yet more ham and the old lady looked at him fondly.

'I do like to see a lad relish his food,' she said, 'he's a real good lad, is Bob.'

Nellie wondered why she was not taken to see Meg's father but it was only when Meg and Bob were seeing them off at the station that Bob said, 'Next time you'll have to meet Meg's dad, Nell. It was better to spend all the time with the Handleys today.'

Meg blushed and looked tearful but Nellie pretended to notice nothing and only said, 'That'll be nice. Oh, it's been a lovely day, Bob. I'm made up you're so comfortable here. The Handleys are lovely.' She kissed Meg warmly and invited her to come to Liverpool with Bob any time, but she felt sure that there was some reason why she had not met Meg's father.

Mrs Handley had given Nellie a straw bag before they left and as soon as the train started to move she and Tommy unpacked it excitedly.

As well as the pasties there was a cold cooked chicken wrapped in a cloth, a dozen fresh eggs in a box filled with sawdust, some ham wrapped in muslin, a large piece of parkin and a jar of bottled damsons. There was also a crusty loaf and a bowl of yellow butter.

'That's because I said I liked the bread and butter best of all,' Tommy said, jumping about with excitement. 'Oh, I *wish* my dad was home, Mam.'

'So do I, lad,' Nellie said. 'He wouldn't half enjoy this stuff. I'm going to hide some of it from Janey, Tom. It'd be wasted on her.'

Nellie boiled three of the eggs for breakfast the following morning but she waited until Janey had eaten her egg and left before she produced the homemade bread and butter. 'I'm not being sly, lad,' she told Tommy. 'She wouldn't understand that Mrs Handley meant the bread and butter for you.'

'And it'd be wasted on Janey,' Tommy said, and joined in when Nellie laughed heartily. The bread and butter was the only part of the gift that Nellie kept entirely for Tom and herself. Gertie was delighted with a couple of fresh eggs and a piece of parkin, and the chicken and ham was shared between Nellie, Maggie and Katy. Maggie and Katy also had two eggs each and some parkin, and the chicken legs were reserved for Peter Rimmer.

Katy had confided to Nellie the previous week that she was worried about Peter. 'He doesn't seem to be picking up his strength,' she said. 'You know, if I could get better food for him I'm sure he'd get better. Just when you need it most it's hardest to get it though.'

'I know,' Nellie said. 'Your mam was telling us about poor Mrs Burgess at the top end. Three of her girls have got TB, and some new doctor at the dispensary told her they need cream and eggs and meat. How does he think she can get them when she's on the Parish? Like your mam said, he only made it worse for the poor woman.'

'I suppose I shouldn't be moaning,' Katy said. 'At least I've got me mam and the family to help me out, although they're all struggling themselves. And Peter doesn't need the food to save his life, like, but some good grub would make all the difference in the world for him. I wish I could win the Irish Sweep.'

'Have you ever had a ticket?' Nellie asked and when Katy shook her head she said, 'Neither have I, so I don't think we've got much chance.'

Remembering that conversation now, Nellie was doubly pleased to be able to help her friend.

'Honest to God, Nell, it was great to see Peter mucking in to them chicken legs,' Katy said. 'He's been real down in the dumps but the treat really bucked him up. I done the eggs for him too to build him up, like.'

Nellie had again boiled three eggs for breakfast on the second morning, and she and Tommy had enjoyed their eggs but Janey said sourly that hers tasted no different to a shop egg. Nellie decided that she need feel no qualms about leaving Janey out of the largesse. It was true that good food was wasted on the old woman.

CHAPTER 13

Tommy was seven years old in November and Nellie decided that her visit to Dr Wilson could not be put off any longer. She felt that it was unfair to Tommy to neglect any chance of providing a brother or sister for him, and also she longed for another child.

She had seen Dr Wilson in the area but she had never visited him as a patient and she trembled with nervousness when she was admitted to the surgery and tried to explain her errand. He soon put her at ease by talking about her father and telling her that Tommy resembled him.

'I didn't know you knew me dad, doctor,' Nellie said. 'He wasn't home that much.'

The doctor smiled at her. 'He came to me to arrange something for you when you were thirteen, Nellie. We fixed up for you to go to Agatha and Ambrose D'Arcy because they were old friends of mine. You were happy there, I think.'

'Oh yes, Doctor,' Nellie said fervently. 'They were so good to me. Miss Agatha learned me to sew and Mr Ambrose learned me to read and write. I was brokenhearted when they died.'

'Yes, it was very sad. Now tell me why you are here, Nellie,' Dr Wilson said.

Nellie explained and the doctor asked her numerous questions, and then examined her, talking about Tommy as he did so, so that she was not embarrassed. After she dressed he told her that she had nothing to worry about.

'Nurse said my womb might be tilted because I was in labour so long with Tommy,' Nellie said timidly.

'So that's what you've been worrying about?' Dr Wilson said. 'You're all right, Nellie. Nothing to affect your health. Just be thankful you've been spared having hordes of children to make

244

you old before your time.'

He smiled at her and Nellie said, 'But why, Doctor? Me and Sam—'

She stopped, too embarrassed to go on, but the doctor said heartily, 'Nothing to stop you and Sam having normal relations, Nellie.'

'But another baby. For Tommy's sake. Company, like,' Nellie stammered.

'No, he'll do much better as an only one,' the doctor said decidedly. 'Far too many children born in this neighbourhood already, and every fresh mouth to feed means less for the others. Sam's proved himself. You've got one child, so be satisfied, Nellie.'

He came round his desk and ushered Nellie to the door. 'You've got nothing to worry about. You're a healthy girl,' he said before calling for his next patient. Nellie paid her one and sixpence before being shown out of the side door of the house, and walked away, thinking that she had made a mess of the interview.

Going through all that and the money and all and I'm no wiser, she thought. He didn't know what I was on about. Thought I was worrying about what Nurse told me. The thought of the nurse made her decide to visit Nurse McCann again while she was respectably dressed in her coat and her best hat. She bought a bunch of flowers but when she arrived at the house she was told that the nurse was too ill for visitors, so could only leave a message and the flowers.

For the rest of the day Nellie was too busy to think about her visit to the surgery, but when she lay in bed at night she went over the doctor's words in her mind. He's got a bee in his bonnet about big families, she thought. That's why he thinks it's better for Tom to be an only one.

She recalled the doctor's words that she and Sam could have normal relations, feeling hot with embarrassment yet thinking scornfully that she and Sam didn't need telling that. Dr Wilson's very nice, she thought, but them sort of people just don't understand us. Saying Sam had proved himself, as though that was the way people like us talk. He wouldn't say that about his own posh friends.

Yet he was a good man. Fancy him fixing up with me dad about me first place. And he thinks Tommy looks like me dad too. She lay for a while thinking about her father with love before slipping into sleep.

The next day she bought a pig's trotter on the way home from work and took it to Katy's house for Peter.

'They just come out steaming in Daly's and I thought Peter might fancy it,' she said.

'He will, Nell,' Katy said. 'He loves a pig's foot. He's gone out on some crutches the hospital lent him. Made up, he is, to get out again.'

Nellie told Katy about her visit to the doctor. 'I think I wasted me time and me money,' she said ruefully. 'He didn't seem to know what I was getting at. Thought I was worried about meself because of what the nurse said. I just couldn't say the right things to explain.'

'Never mind, it's over now,' Katy consoled her. 'It's been hanging over you, thinking you should go, and now you've been and it's done with. He didn't say you couldn't have no more either.'

'No. He said I was a healthy girl,' Nellie said. 'Said I should be thankful I hadn't got hordes of children. I think he's got a bee in his bonnet about big families.'

'I don't know him,' Katy said. 'You know people round here only call a doctor when they're on their last, but he goes to a woman in Drinkwater Street. She was in service with Dixon's the greengrocer's until she was married and she still goes back to do washing and mending. Mrs Dixon sends Dr Wilson to her every time she has a baby. She's got six and he was carrying on shocking with her husband.'

'Six isn't many,' Nellie said. 'A woman in Scotland Road reared twenty in two rooms. Mind you, I wouldn't fancy that.'

'I wouldn't blame you,' Katy exclaimed. 'Like me ma says, there's medium in all things. Four's my limit. I'm determined.'

Nellie was again thinking of her visit to the doctor when she left Katy's house and walked home. As she neared her door she was suddenly struck by a thought which made her stop dead, then stumble into her own house.

She dropped into a chair by the table and sat with her clenched fist pressed against her mouth as she recalled the doctor's words, 'Sam has proved himself.' He meant that Sam had proved he could make a baby because of Tommy.

But what if Tommy was not Sam's child? Could that be the reason they had not had any more children? But he *must* be Sam's, she thought frantically. From the minute I held him in my arms I felt that, but another small voice suggested that perhaps she had *wanted* to believe it.

Why, why were there no more babies? The doctor said she was a healthy girl. He must have thought it might be Sam's fault but then because of Tommy he said that about Sam proving himself.

Nellie sat hunched in the chair, her eyes closed, feeling as though she would go mad as thoughts beat round in her brain like trapped birds.

Tommy arrived home from school and looked at her in alarm. 'What's up, Mam? Are you sick?' he asked anxiously. Nellie stared at him, desperate to see some resemblance to Sam but she could see nothing. He was the model of her father but there was nothing of Sam in him.

'Go out and play. I'm going to lay down. Gotta headache,' she said, stumbling upstairs to lie on her bed. Oh God, that can't be the reason, she thought. He hasn't got nothing of Leadbetter about him either, but unbidden, the memory of Leadbetter's children came to her. They were fair too but that was because of their mother being fair.

Had the same thing happened with her? Was Tom the result of that awful night, but showed no likeness to his father, like Leadbetter's other children?

Unable to bear her thoughts she jumped up and walked about the room. I can't believe

Tommy belongs to that fellow, she thought. Look at the way he took to Sam right away and Maggie said they know their own. He *must* be Sam's son.

And yet why haven't we had any more? She flung herself on the bed again, burying her head in the pillow, trying to shut out the images which rose in her mind. She was unaware of time passing and she was surprised when she heard Janey's voice downstairs, talking to Tommy.

She forced herself to go downstairs. 'I've got a terrible head,' she said. 'Couldn't hardly lift it from the pillow.' She opened her purse and gave Tommy money to get fish and chips for Janey and himself, then went back to bed.

What can I do? What can I do? she said over and over to herself. If only Nurse wasn't so ill. I could tell her the truth, tell her everything and she'd tell me what to do. And she wouldn't say nothing to nobody else, but I can't trust anyone else like that.

If only I'd talked to Nurse when Tommy was born, but I was just that frightened, she thought. Frightened that Janey would shout at me if I didn't do as she said and keep me mouth shut. It's her. She's the cause of it all. I'll get rid of her, Nellie thought wildly.

Could I tell Dr Wilson? she wondered. Get him to make some excuse to send for Sam and then see if Tommy could be Sam's child? But the doctor would get it all out of me about Mr Leadbetter and that might cause more trouble. He might say it was his duty to see Leadbetter and he might get me sent to gaol like he said.

Or if Sam found out about Leadbetter he might go and batter him and get locked up for it. Maybe Janey was right when she said the likes of us don't stand no chance against the likes of Leadbetter.

A little later Tommy came up. 'Auntie Katy's putting me to bed,' he said. 'Is your head better, Mam?'

'Yes it is,' she lied. 'Goodnight, son.' She kissed him and held him away from her looking searchingly at him. Oh God, give me a sign, she prayed silently, but she could see no likeness to Sam in the child. Except in his nature, she thought, worrying about my headache. She remembered Leadbetter's selfish spoilt children. There was no feeling for others in *them*.

Worn out by emotions she fell asleep and when she woke the thought came to her that nothing had changed. Sam knew nothing of her visit to the doctor and he and Tommy still loved each other as father and son, untroubled by any doubts. But then she thought, is that true?

Sam had never wavered in his affection for Tommy, but was there no doubt at all in his mind that Tommy was his son? Why was he so jealous, seeming unable to trust her? Even though he thinks he doesn't take no notice to them troublemakers, Nellie thought, some bit of what they say might stay in his mind.

Unable to bear her thoughts any longer she went downstairs and made herself a cup of tea, and as she sat sipping it another thought occurred to her. The doctor had said she was healthy but he didn't know about the bad time she had before Tommy was born.

Perhaps it was because of the drugs Janey had given her that she was unable to have more children. She remembered her neighbour saying, 'God knows what she puts in them concoctions or the damage they do.' Although the stuff Janey had given her was not the same as the concoctions to get rid of a baby, it might have been just as harmful in a different way. Thank God it never harmed Tommy, Nellie thought, although it might have done me some damage.

She felt as though a weight had been lifted from her. I don't know what come over me getting worked up like that, she thought, but I'll never do it again. I *know* that Tommy is Sam's son. I'll stop moithering about another baby an' all, and be thankful I've got a lovely lad like Tommy, too, she decided.

Nellie had wondered whether Bobby was too ashamed of his home to bring Meg there so she was pleased to receive a letter from him asking if he could bring Meg to tea on the following Sunday. She wrote back immediately, saying how welcome they would be.

She always kept the house as neat as possible but now she went in for an orgy of cleaning which enraged Janey.

'I never seen anything like it,' she declared, 'you'd think the Queen was coming.'

'Bobby's girl is more important to me than the Queen,' Nellie retorted.

By the time Sunday arrived she was exhausted

but satisfied that the house was as nice as she could make it, and that the smell of lavender furniture polish would mask that of Janey's fish.

There had been a dinner party at the Duncans' the previous night and Nellie had helped the cook and waited on table, although Mrs Taggart had come for the washing up. Before Nellie left for home the cook had slipped a bag to her. 'Put that under your shawl, girl,' she said. 'She's got a cheek. Half a crown for all you done tonight. I've put the Charlotte mould and the makings of an apple Charlotte in it. Don't see why your visitors can't have the same as this lot.'

Nellie was delighted. 'All the apple Charlottes I've made, Cook, and I've never tasted it. None of it never comes down from the dining room.'

'I know, but you will now,' the cook said with a wink. 'I've put the remains of the leg of lamb in too. I'll tell her a dog run off with it. Just be sure you bring the mould back.'

Nellie was relieved that Janey had gone off on one of her mysterious errands when Meg and Bob arrived. It was a bitterly cold day and Nellie had a big fire burning and the kettle boiling for an immediate cup of tea.

'This is nice,' Meg said, looking round the room, 'lovely and warm and homely.'

'Drink that to warm you and I'll wet fresh tea with the meal,' Nellie said, and Tommy brought some of his treasures to show Meg and Bobby.

'Me dad brought me this boat with the little

men in it,' he said proudly. 'And this drum another time. He told me about the men who live in the jungle.'

Meg and Bobby admired them and Bobby said, 'You've got a good dad, Tom.'

'That's what Miss said,' the child said eagerly. 'I took them to show her and she said I had a good father who took an interest in me.'

'You're a clever boy remembering all that,' Meg said admiringly.

Nellie said quietly to her, 'No wonder. He's said it that many times to people.'

She smiled fondly at Tommy who was standing at Bobby's knee talking eagerly about school.

Nellie felt that there was some special reason for the visit, but Bobby said nothing while they were eating the meal. The apple Charlotte was in pride of place and Nellie had made a sponge sandwich and jelly and custard, to follow the cold meat and pickles and soused herrings.

'Our Nell's a proper good cook,' Bobby said proudly to Meg, and Nellie told them the tale of the apple Charlotte.

'She's a case, the cook. The things she says about Mrs Duncan and them girls, and she doesn't care what she does,' Nellie said. 'I said I'd never tasted apple Charlotte, for all I've made so many, and she just said, "Well, you will now, girl." Mrs Duncan would go mad if she knew.'

'It sounds as if she owes you more than this, our kid,' Bobby said loyally. 'As long as the cook doesn't get into trouble.'

'She doesn't care. She says Mrs Duncan'd never get no one else to cook for what she pays and she knows it. Cook only stays because it suits her.'

After tea Bobby and Meg sat together on the sofa holding hands and he told Nellie the reason for the visit.

'That day you came to Handleys we wanted to tell you we was engaged, so we asked Meg's dad the night before but he said no.'

'But why?' Nellie exclaimed indignantly. 'He couldn't have nothing against you, Bobby.'

'Hang on, Nell, till we tell you,' Bobby said. 'He'd had a few and he got ratty but I asked him again on the Monday and he told me it was on account of me coming back to Liverpool to work that fortnight.'

'But—' Nellie began but Bobby rushed on.

'He said I'd only got lent to Mr Orlando and I might have to come back here when I come outa me time. He doesn't want to come back to Liverpool.'

'He's crossing a bridge before he comes to it, isn't he?' Nellie said.

'It might happen, Nell,' Bobby said. 'I want to stay on in Yorkshire but I'm indentured here, like. I had to own up about that to Mr Sykes and he said he wouldn't come back here and he needs Meg to look after him.'

Meg had said nothing but now she said quietly, 'He's a sick man and he's my father, I couldn't walk out on him,' and Nellie agreed.

'But never mind,' she said. 'You needn't say no more to him about it but youse could sort of behave as if you was engaged. You couldn't get married anyhow till you was out of your time, Bob.'

She went to the dresser and brought out an embroidered sideboard runner. 'Mrs Duncan give me this for waiting on one time,' she said. 'You can start your bottom drawer with it, Meg.'

Meg and Bobby were delighted and he said jokingly, 'Is this what you meant, Nell, when you said about us pretending we was engaged?'

'Not pretending, lad. Just keeping it to yourselves, like. You never know. You might get transferred permanent or Meg's dad might come round. He must know there's nice parts of Liverpool and you could live in them on tradesman's money.'

Bobby stood up and put his arm round Nellie. 'So you're for us, our kid,' he said affectionately, and when Nellie exclaimed, 'Of course,' and kissed Meg, he took a small box from his pocket.

He opened it to proudly display a ring with a half hoop of diamond chippings.

'We got this yesterday,' he said, 'but we wanted to tell you first.' He sat down beside Meg and slipped it on her finger then kissed her tenderly.

Nellie was in tears and Meg and Bobby stood up and put their arms around her.

'Don't cry, girl,' Bobby said, hugging her.

Nellie dried her eyes and smiled. 'You'll think I'm soft, Meg,' she said. 'It's just—I'm that made up. Our Bob reared round here and the

255

way he's got on. An engagement ring!'

'Didn't you have one, Nell?' Meg asked.

Before Nellie could answer Bobby laughed. 'Didn't have no time, did you girl?' he said. 'You was married in five minutes, wasn't you?'

'What do you mean?' Meg asked, looking puzzled.

Nellie blushed but she said quickly, 'I got sent home sick from my place and Janey seen Sam and told him. He come round and said he'd look after me and the next thing it was all fixed up for us to get married before he went back to sea.' She was amazed at the way the words tripped glibly from her tongue but Bobby accepted her explanation.

'I never knew what was happening, although I lived here,' he said. 'Our Nell was so sick and Janey wouldn't let no one near her. Then the next thing she was getting married in Brougham Terrace. I was made up though because I liked Sam.'

'Did he live round here?' Meg asked.

'No, he stayed at the Seaman's when he was ashore. He didn't have no home,' Bobby said. 'He drinks in the Volley though and us kids was always glad when he was home. There'd be a crowd going in the pub and we'd be hanging round asking for coppers. It was always Sam who give us some and he'd give more when he come out. He must've been skint in no time.'

He laughed and Meg said to Nellie, 'He sounds a real good man.'

'Oh he is,' Nellie said. 'He's a good husband and a good father.'

256

'Mind you, he used to be a beggar for fights before he got married,' Bobby said. 'You know how it is when a feller's got a reputation, like, for fighting. Always someone wants to take him on and Sam's mates used to egg him on.'

'It was the mates was the trouble,' Nellie said. 'And then Sam had always had to stand up for himself. He lived rough from he was seven years old.'

'But that's awful. Seven years old!' Meg exclaimed.

Nellie said reminiscently, 'He looked after me an' all. Used to carry the big bundles of washing for me and chased some lads when they was trying to take it off me.'

'So you knew him a long time?' Meg said, and Nellie nodded agreement.

'He's different now since he got married,' Bobby said. 'With the fighting, I mean.'

'He's got different mates now,' Nellie said. 'Real respectable fellers.'

She suddenly noticed Tommy sitting in the corner with a picture book on his knee, listening avidly to the conversation.

'I forgot you was there,' she exclaimed. 'You can go out and play.'

'Ar eh, Mam, it's cold outside,' Tommy said. 'Can't I stay in?'

'Well read your book then. Don't be listening,' Nellie said severely.

Bobby smiled at the child, and Meg said, 'His dad must see a change in him every time he comes home.'

'I see a change in him all right,' Bobby said.

'You should've seen him when he was born. A little red wrinkly thing like a fourpenny rabbit. D'you know I helped to save your life, Tom? If it wasn't for me and Nurse McCann you wouldn't be here.'

Tommy clamoured for details and Meg said eagerly, 'Go on, Bob. Tell us.' But then she turned to Nellie and said diffidently, 'That's if you don't mind, Nell?'

Nellie laughed. 'No I don't mind. I've got to give credit where it's due.'

'Nurse McCann shouted down for me to bring hot water up and when I took the panmug of hot water up she had Tommy in the washbowl then she put him in the hot water then back into the cold water. He was just like he was dead and she kept clouting him. Our Nellie was saying, "Don't don't," ' Bobby said.

He laughed and Nellie said defensively, 'I thought she'd hurt the baby. I was made up though when she gave him a real hard smack and he cried out.'

'So was I,' Bobby said. 'And the nurse said if I hadn't brought the hot water up so quick she couldn't have done it. And look at him now.'

They all looked at the child and he hung his head, blushing, and to take attention from him Nellie said quietly, 'Poor Nurse McCann's real bad, I went to see her and I wouldn't have knew her, Bob. Such a fine big woman but she'd dwindled away. Even her voice.'

She bustled about making a fresh pot of tea before they left and Meg asked if it would be long before Sam came home.

'No, he's homeward bound now from Canada,' Nellie said. 'Another couple of weeks.'

'I hope I can meet him some time,' Meg said.

'Of course you will,' Nellie said. 'You're family now.'

Before they left Bobby told Nellie that he intended to tell Mrs Handley about the engagement.

'That's a good idea, lad,' Nellie said. 'She'd be hurt if she found out and you hadn't told her, and she can make it easier for you and Meg to see each other.'

Meg took off her ring and replaced it in the box before they left. 'Just in case we meet someone on the train,' she said.

She looked sad and Nellie hugged her impulsively. 'Never mind, you and Bob know you're engaged and things will work out for you, you'll see.'

Meg hugged her in return and whispered, 'It'll be lovely to have a sister.'

Nellie was relieved that they left before Janey returned but she was surprised that the old woman, usually so inquisitive, had stayed out for so long. She raked out some of the hot coals from her fire and took them through to the parlour grate, adding some sticks and coal to warm the room.

Nellie was just about to go to bed when Janey returned and flung open the parlour door. 'Who told you you could go rooting round in me room?' she demanded. 'Keep out, d'yer hear, and keep yer bloody nose outa my business.'

'I made a fire because it was so cold out,' Nellie exclaimed. 'I won't bother again.'

She went upstairs raging, but the next morning the old woman said ingratiatingly, 'I didn't mean to yell last night, girl. It was just me body clothes was in the oven and I thought they might get burned.'

Body clothes! Nellie thought scornfully. If she wears any they've been on her for years, but she said nothing and let the incident pass.

She had written to Mrs Handley after the visit there to thank her and her husband for their hospitality, and to thank them for looking after Bobby so well. She was surprised to receive a reply from Mrs Handley written in beautiful copperplate handwriting, telling her that she would be welcome to bring Tommy for a holiday at any time.

Now Nellie decided to write again to Mrs Handley to thank her for the offer and to mention Meg and Bob's engagement. She thought that Mrs Handley might tell her more about Meg's father and she was not disappointed.

Mrs Handley replied describing Meg as a grand lass and saying that she thought Meg and Bob very well suited. Meg's father was not well liked in the village because he was a morose bad-tempered man. She thought he had been different when his wife was alive but she had died when Meg was seven.

He had brought Meg up and been a good father but had never shown her much attention.

Nellie's ready sympathy went out to Meg. Poor girl. To lose her mother so young and to be brought up by such a hard father. Me and Bob will have to make it up to her, she thought. Make a fuss of her.

She looked over at Tommy who was eating fried bread and drinking tea before he set off for school. She pictured Meg at the same age being left without a mother, and Sam, being cast out by his father at seven to fend for himself. And when I was that age what a life I had. Nothing but drudgery and being battered by me ma.

Thank God Tom had had a better life so far. Enough to eat and warm clothes in the winter. Granted this house is very near falling round our ears, Nellie thought, and in summer we're tormented with bugs and fleas. I'm ashamed the way our bodies are covered with bites from them but in the winter they're not so bad. All the walls are wringing wet, but I battle with the bugs and we have the oven shelf to warm the bed in winter. Tom's a lucky boy with a good home and a mother and father who love him.

CHAPTER 14

Nellie was still being plagued by Charlie West. It seemed that almost every time she went out she met him.

'He knows the way I go to work,' she complained to Maggie Nolan. 'If I see him I turn down a different street, but when I get to the bottom he's there waiting for me. He must run through the jiggers.'

'He's off during the day now,' Maggie said. 'You know he got an odd night playing the saxophone in a band? Well, now he's got a proper place in a band. They was playing at Blair Hall last night.'

'Must've gone to his head,' Nellie said. 'I don't know why he bothers with me though. Gertie says girls are always mad after fellers in bands, even him, and he knows I can't stand him.'

'That's probably why,' Maggie said shrewdly. 'He doesn't like the idea someone won't fall for him. And then he's still got his spite in for Sam.'

'I don't know why,' Nellie said, and Maggie laughed.

'I do,' she said. 'One time there was a row in the Volley and Charlie wanted to fight Sam. He tried to hit Sam and Sam just held him off and told him to fight someone his own size, then he walked out. Charlie never got over it but if Sam had hit him he'd have killed him. He was twice the size of Charlie. Bella told me.'

'Everyone seems to know more about Sam than what I do,' Nellie said resentfully.

'I'm going back years now, girl, when you was away in service,' Maggie said. 'When Charlie was going to sea, but fellers like him bear grudges for years.'

'Has he given up his checker's job, then? Is

that why he's always around in the daytime?' Nellie asked.

'I believe it give him up, more like,' Maggie said. 'He was always having days off, so he got his cards, but that doesn't bother Lord Muck. He still seems to have plenty in his pocket, but he's still dodging his round if he can. You want to tell Sam he's pestering you, or tell Charlie you will.'

'I never say nothing to him. I just get away as quick as I can,' Nellie said. 'The cheek of him, to think I'd bother with him when I've got Sam.'

'He looks a proper little dago,' Maggie agreed, 'that sleeked-down black hair and his little pencil moustache and the size of him! He thinks he's the whole cheese though.'

'The answer to a maiden's prayer, Gertie says,' giggled Nellie and went into her own house, laughing.

Sam arrived home a week later bringing some beautiful wooden animals for Tommy, carved by Indians, and soft leather gloves for Nellie. 'You said in the letter about him showing things to the teacher, like,' he said.

'Oh Sam, he'll be made up,' Nellie said. 'He'll be home in half an hour.' Sam looked rough and unkempt, his hair too long and thick and his weatherbeaten face unshaven, but Nellie smiled at him tenderly. She knew that his appearance belied his real nature.

'Didn't you have no barbers among the crew, Sam?' she teased him as she brewed a pot of tea for him.

'Didn't have no time, girl,' he said, standing up and peering into the piece of mirror above the sink. 'It was a cow of a trip. Even docking everything went wrong. I'd better have a scrape before the lad comes home, and I'll go down to Hogan's after.' He ran his hand over his face, then through his thick curls. 'I'll get me money's worth this time anyhow.'

Tommy was delighted with his gifts and told Sam at length about the day he had taken his boat and drum to school. Sam coloured with pleasure when the boy repeated the teacher's remarks.

They had their meal before Janey came home and Nellie told Sam that the old woman seemed dirtier than ever. 'She's up to no good, I'm sure,' she said, 'I often hear people talking in the parlour but she never lets on about them. Maggie says she often sees Charlie West going in the side door.'

Sam's head jerked up. 'Charlie West? Does he come in here?'

'No, of course not,' Nellie said hurriedly, 'Janey keeps the door into here bolted when she's in there at night. Maggie can see a bit of the entry from her bedroom window, that's how she knows he goes in on the sly.'

Tommy began to talk about the visit to Yorkshire but Sam's response to Charlie West's name made Nellie decide to say nothing about him waylaying her.

'You should have seen our Bob's bedroom,' she said instead. 'Spotless, no bugs or nothing and lovely furniture and a big soft bed. And the air, Sam, coming through the window. It was lovely.'

'And the flowers, Dad, and the birds we seen,' Tommy said eagerly, 'and we didn't half have a lot to eat, didn't we, Mam?'

They described the tea party until Sam laughed and said that they were making his mouth water. 'Mrs Handley gave us a bagful of stuff too,' Nellie said. 'I wish we could have saved some of it for you, Sam, but it wouldn't keep.' She said nothing about the tart she planned to make with the jar of damsons, as she meant it as a surprise for Sam.

'We didn't give none of it to Janey,' Tommy said importantly, 'only the eggs. It would have been wasted on her.'

Sam looked at Nellie and grinned, and she said hurriedly, 'Don't repeat that to no one, Tommy.' She turned to Sam. 'There was a box of newlaid eggs and I boiled one each for us but Janey said they were no different to shop eggs. I shared the ham and the chicken and that with Maggie and Katy and give Gertie some parkin and eggs. *They* all appreciated it.'

'It seems to have done Bobby a power of good living there,' Sam said. 'I wish I could see him again. You like his girl, then, Ellie?'

'Oh yes, she's real nice, isn't she, Tom?' Nellie said and the boy nodded.

'I like Mr and Mrs Handley too,' he said.

After the meal Sam said he would go to the barber's. 'Do you want to come, lad?' he asked Tommy, and they went off together, Tommy strutting proudly beside his father. When they came back he carried a balloon given to him by the barber.

'He said me dad done well to get a ship the way things are, and getting worser all the time,' he announced.

'He wasn't very cheerful, was he?' Nellie exclaimed.

'He's right though, girl,' Sam said. 'Me and George were saying we'll have to keep getting down and trying for a ship. No use waiting till we're spent up, like. Won't be no walkover getting a ship the way things are now.'

'You and George do all right though, Sam, being big fellers and known as hard workers. Not like little fellers like Josh Jenkins,' Nellie said.

Sam grinned. 'I laughed at what you said in that letter, Ellie, about Josh Jenkins' wife, and the things the other women said.'

'Bella always sticks up for me,' said Nellie. 'I can't do nothing wrong with her lately. She calls me to sit on the step with her.'

'She's a good one to have on your side, girl,' Sam said, 'especially with having no relations of your own, like.'

'And Tommy's all right going to school with Katy's kids. All Bella's grandchildren look after him,' Nellie said.

Sam looked over to where Tommy crouched before a stool on which he had lined up the animals Sam had brought him, gabbling to himself as he wove stories about them. 'He looks healthy enough, Ellie, but he's still on the small side, isn't he?' he said.

266

'Me dad was small and Dr Wilson thinks Tommy's the spitting image of him,' Nellie said. She spoke without thinking, but when Sam looked at her enquiringly she said quickly, 'I just seen him for something, but it was nothing.'

She jerked her head at the child warningly. 'I'll tell you after. D'you know what he told me? He helped me dad to get me first place for me. Miss Agatha and Mr Ambrose were his friends.'

'He done you a good turn all right, then,' Sam said. He grinned. 'Does he know how often you talk about them?'

Nellie laughed. 'Well, I was happy there. Very different to the life what I had here.'

'Aye, that's true, girl,' Sam said. He stood up and stretched. 'Come on, lad. I'll take you up before I go out.'

'That back room's wringing wet,' Nellie said. 'But I've pulled the bed into the middle of the floor and put the oven shelf in it to warm it for him.'

'Can I take me animals up, Mam?' Tommy asked.

'Just one,' Nellie said but Tommy stood so long trying to decide which one that Sam said finally, 'Ee are, lad, I'll pick one for you. The reindeer.'

When Sam came down after putting Tom to bed he said he was tired out. 'He wanted to know all about the reindeer, and the questions he asked! Took more outa me than a day's work!'

'I know, you answer one question then he

asks you another one about that,' Nellie said. 'But he's real clever, Sam. The teacher is made up with him.'

Sam smiled proudly. 'I'll bet she is,' he said. He had put Nellie's share of his pay-off on the dresser and now he said, 'I'd better get down to the Volley, girl. Get me hand in me pocket or me name'll be mud.'

Nellie went to the door with him, and Gertie who was at her door across the street called, 'Hello, Sam. Welcome home.' Sam raised his hand in salute and walked away, and Gertie came across to Nellie.

'Sam looks smart, doesn't he?' Gertie said. 'I'll bet Tommy's made up to have him home.'

'Oh he *is*,' Nellie said. 'He's just been to the barber's with Sam. You know the fellers always clean up the ship and themselves when they come into dock, but Sam said they didn't have no chance this trip. A cow of a trip, he said, even up to docking. He had a shave though and went to the barber's.'

'He always keeps himself clean and smart, doesn't he?' Gertie said. 'A pity you couldn't go out with him his first night home.'

Nellie looked surprised. 'But he has to go to the Volley,' she said. 'He has to mug the fellers after getting paid off. All the fellers do it.'

'Well, I think it's a pity none of them have the courage to change it,' Gertie said.

'Sam's no coward,' Nellie said indignantly, 'it's just the way things have always been done round here.'

'I'm just talking general,' Gertie said. 'I

know Sam does go out with you and Tommy and that, but some fellers round here—the wives and families never see them when they're ashore. They're in the pub all the time until they're spent up then they're scrounging off the wives for ale money. I think Sam should've had tonight with you and Tom. Plenty of time for mugging them scroungers in the pub after that.'

Nellie said nothing and Gertie hastily changed the subject. 'Do you know what? Mrs Gilligan told me fortune last night,' she said.

'Go way!' Nellie exclaimed. 'What did she say?'

'She said I'm going to have a disappointment but then everything will come right. I think she would have told me a lot more only Lettie come in just when it was getting interesting. She doesn't like her mam telling fortunes.'

'I wonder would she tell mine some time?' Nellie said eagerly.

'I'm sure she would, but we'd have to keep it dark from Lettie. She *is* a gypsy like we thought, Nell. She told me she come up in a caravan for Grand National week, and that's how she met her husband. I'll tell her about you.'

Sam was still sober when he returned from the Volunteer and they went to bed and made passionate love, for once without the thought at the back of Nellie's mind that a baby might be the result.

Before they slept Sam asked about her visit to Dr Wilson and Nellie told him that it was because the nurse had thought Tommy's birth might have caused some damage, but the doctor had said that she was a healthy young woman.

Sam was quite satisfied with Nellie's edited version of her visit, but very sorry to hear that Nurse McCann was so ill.

Nellie snuggled into his arms and they drifted off to sleep. Moonlight was flooding the room when Nellie woke again.

She raised herself on her elbow and began to study Sam's face, thinking of Gertie's words about his smart appearance. The barber had cut his hair very short but it still sprang in tight curls all over his head. He's handsome really, Nellie thought fondly, looking at his wide brow and firm lips, and the little cleft in his chin.

She thought that Sam was unaware of her scrutiny until he half opened his eyes and peeped at her.

'Would you know me again if you seen me, girl?' he teased her.

Nellie blushed. 'Oh, Sam, I was just looking at the way he cut your hair so short. I never noticed that little nick in your ear before. How did you do that?'

'I've always had it,' Sam said. 'Don't know how I got it or even if I was born with it. Didn't have no time to find out before I got threw out.'

He spoke bitterly and Nellie hugged him. 'That's all behind you now, lad,' she consoled him. 'I was only thinking about that when Meg was here. When she told me her mother died when she was seven and I thought it was the same age Tommy is now. Then I thought that

270

you was seven when you had to start fending for yourself.'

'Aye, when you look at him and think I was that age living rough, and Meg without a mother, and the life you had, Ellie. You'd have been better off without your ma,' Sam said.

'Thank God things is better for Tommy anyhow,' Nellie said. Sam smiled. 'Aye, the oven shelf in the bed. I never had no bed!'

'But we're all better off now, Sam,' Nellie said. 'We've got an easy life now, haven't we?'

'We have, girl,' Sam agreed, drawing her close and kissing her tenderly.

It was a very happy time ashore, and Nellie felt that she and Sam had never been so close. They were relaxed together, able to tease each other and finding endless delight in the evidence of their son's intelligence.

Nellie was careful never to give Sam any excuse for jealousy and she was relieved that Charlie West seemed to have vanished. She learned later that he was with the band in Rhyl for a three-week booking.

Although Sam was only home for ten days they had two family outings, to Eastham Woods and to New Brighton. The days were lengthening but the wind was still chill on the day they boarded the ferryboat for Eastham.

Nellie would have preferred to sit in the saloon on the boat, but a quick glance showed her several unattached men standing or sitting there, so she thought it wiser to go on deck with Sam and Tommy.

She was glad that she did. They sat on the

271

rafts on deck, Sam with one arm round Nellie and the other round Tommy, and she enjoyed breathing the fresh salt air and watching the shipping in the river. Questions poured from Tommy about a White Star liner which had dropped anchor in the river and the passenger and luggage tenders which fussed about her.

'God's truth, Ellie, your ears must be wore out,' Sam exclaimed but he answered all Tommy's questions carefully, and explained the work of a dredger that they passed.

The weather was slightly warmer on the Sunday when they went to New Brighton, and they all spent a very happy day there. They watched a Pierrot show and Tommy joined lustily in the singing. 'That's what I'm going to do when I grow up,' he informed his parents.

'I hope it keeps fine for you,' Nellie remarked, but she smiled indulgently at the child.

They went to the fair and Sam won a prize in the shooting gallery, and told Tommy to pick the prize. Sam's score was high so there were several large toys which Tommy could have chosen, but he chose a cup and saucer with Mother picked out in gold lettering on them. Nellie and Sam were both delighted.

While Sam was ashore Nellie served Janey's meals in the parlour, but there were no protests from Janey. She spent most of her time at home in the parlour now, and seemed to have visitors on most evenings. Sam had given her money as usual when he arrived home, and again later in the week, and she seemed content to keep out of his way for most of the time.

Sam and George Adams kept their resolve to apply for ships early in their time ashore, although Buck declared that he was home until he was spent up. The two men spent one fruitless day at various shipping offices, but at their second attempt Sam came home early.

'We tried Lamport and Holt's first,' he said. 'George could've got on but I couldn't, but we got on together on an Elder Dempster ship in the Sandon. The only thing is we had to sign running articles.'

'What does that mean, Dad?' asked Tommy, who was eating his dinner before going back to school.

'Means we haven't signed on just for one trip, lad,' Sam said. 'With running articles we could be away for a long time.'

'But why, Dad?' Tommy persisted.

'Because we'll be trading round. Picking up cargoes. Putting in to different ports, like,' Sam said. 'But wherever we put in, lad, I'll get something for you. Might even bring you a monkey.'

'Oh no, Sam,' Nellie exclaimed before Tommy could speak, and Sam laughed.

'Only joking, girl,' he said. 'But I'll fetch you plenty, don't worry.'

He seemed so cheerful that Nellie realised how worried he had been at the prospect of being without a ship.

She was relieved that he and George would be sailing together, especially as they would be away for a long time, but for herself she was sad at the prospect of a long parting.

Just when we're real close and happy, she thought. No rows or nothing. I'll miss him terrible and so will Tom. She tried to appear cheerful during the last few days, but when Sam was leaving she broke down and wept. She had kept Tommy home from school, and he and Sam tried to console her, but they were all upset.

'It mightn't be all that long, Ellie,' Sam said. 'Who knows. I could be home in no time,' but they both knew that it would be a long separation. It was easier for Sam to console Tommy by making extravagant promises.

'I'll bring you something from every port,' he promised. 'Bamboo whistle and face masks and a proper bongo drum.'

Nellie dried her eyes and tried to smile as she kissed Sam goodbye.

'What should I bring you, girl?' he asked.

'Just yourself, lad, safe and sound,' she whispered and Sam kissed her tenderly. They drew apart and Sam looked at her thoughtfully.

She looked young and slim and attractive, in a dark skirt and a blouse of pretty material with white daisies on a blue background. Tendrils of her curly brown hair escaped from her bun and clustered round her forehead and her big blue eyes were bright with tears.

She's changed, Sam thought. When he'd married her she had been like the child he remembered, with a white face and big frightened eyes but now she was different. Not frightened any more. Making friends in

274

the street and going off on a train journey just with Tommy. Working with them toffs. She looks real posh herself, specially in that coat, but I'm still the same scruff I always was, he thought.

Sam was unaware that Nellie had made a special effort to give him a pleasing picture of herself for him to remember her by, and he felt jealousy like a physical pain gripping him. This was what other fellows would see all the time he was away, he thought, and bitterly regretted listening to George about getting a ship.

All this had flashed through his mind in seconds and yet at the same time he felt ashamed that he doubted Nellie. Although fellers gave her the eye even when she was with him she never gave them no encouragement and she only wore her coat when he was home. Aloud he said, more loudly than he meant, 'You going to stick to the shawl while I'm away, Ellie?'

She looked up at him, startled. 'Yes, of course, Sam,' she said nervously, and he put his arms round her again and kissed her passionately.

'Ta-ra, Ellie. Look after yourself,' he said huskily.

'You too, lad. Come home safe,' she whispered, her arms tight round his neck.

'Can I come up the street with you, Dad?' Tommy asked. Sam said quickly, 'No, lad. Stay here with your mam. Look after her.' He gripped the boy's shoulder, his head averted, then picked up his bag and stepped out of the house.

His mind was seething with various emotions as he strode up the street, nodding mechanically to people who shouted, 'Ta-ra, lad. Good luck.' Now he was sorry he had said that about the shawl. After the way he had battened down hatches on his jealousy all the time he was home, to go away and say that at the end.

It was George who had advised him to fight his jealousy. 'There's no need for it, lad,' he'd said, one night when they were sitting on a hatch cover getting a breath of air. 'Rose says she's a real good girl. Lives for the child and getting the place nice for you coming home. You're a lucky feller and you don't want to spoil it.'

I want to believe him and I want to believe Ellie, Sam thought, but it was little things. The way she let things slip then covered up. Like going to the doctor. Like when she let that slip about Charlie West going in the side door, then went red and wouldn't look straight at him.

And the hints the old one had dropped that day he gave her some money off his advance note. About Charlie West always sniffing round. I told her it was all yarns about girls with that feller. It was lads he liked, but she stuck to her tale. Said he liked a bit of both, especially off married women. Made out he'd cleared off to Rhyl while I was home but he'd be back.

I should've belted her only she was old and she was trying to pay back for the money in her own way, Sam thought. Or it might have been spite against Ellie because she had spoke sharp to the old girl about spitting in the grate.

That's partly why I didn't tackle Ellie about it at the time, and partly because she was that made up about that damson tart she'd done as a surprise. He smiled tenderly as he remembered Ellie standing by the oven after they'd had spare ribs and cabbage, then whipping the oven door open and bringing out the damson tart. She'd been like an excited child, especially when she'd brought in a big jug of custard too.

A crowd of Greek sailors passed him from a ship that had just docked, and he felt bitter envy. If only he was coming home instead of going away. There'd be plenty of fellers home before he docked again, he thought. Plenty of fellers to try to make up to Ellie. I know she doesn't take no notice to them, he thought, but one day there might be one that she'll fall for. He was scowling when he met George by the Overhead to travel to the south docks.

They settled themselves on the train and the older man said sympathetically, 'No joke leaving is it, Sam? You had a good time while you was home, though, didn't you?'

'Aye, but it wasn't long enough. I was a bit sorry I signed. Didn't like leaving the lad,' Sam said. 'He's gonna be changed when I get back.'

'I suppose Nellie was upset too, same as Rose,' George said. 'But at least this way we're looking after them, Sam, and this has got to be better than the last trip.'

'Godstrewth, yes,' Sam said, 'there was a jinx

on that right up to the last minute.'

'I never come off a ship so scruffy,' George agreed.

Suddenly Sam remembered looking in the mirror over the sink and seeing his dirty unshaven face and shaggy hair, and a glimpse in the background of Ellie by the table neat and fresh and clean.

She made a joke of it about the barber, he thought, but I wonder what she really thought about me. We both started rough but she's turned out different to me. Must've been what they learned her in that first place she's always talking about.

He felt miserable again but they went for a pint before going aboard and Sam felt more cheerful when he met some of the crew and had a joke with them. When they went below a few men were already there and Sam was annoyed to see Bert Hagan.

Hagan seemed dismayed to see him and they nodded to each other unsmilingly.

'I never expected to see *him*,' Sam muttered to George, but his friend said quietly, 'Don't worry, lad. He's on a different watch. You won't see him.'

Sam was sitting on his bunk later, looking at the snapshot of himself and Nellie and Tommy taken at New Brighton, when another man paused beside him.

'That your wife and nipper?' he asked, and pulled out a photograph of three children.

'Them's my three,' he said proudly. 'Didn't half carry on when I was coming away. The missus was crying her eyes out.'

'So was mine,' Sam said quickly. The man looked young to be the father of three children but he told Sam that he had been at sea since he was fourteen and he was now twenty-six years old. His name was Billy Olafson.

'It's all right when you're single, like, the sea,' he said, 'But it's different when you're leaving a wife and kids, isn't it?'

Sam agreed. 'Trouble is there's nothing ashore though. Fellers are cutting each other's throats for jobs and it's getting worse.'

'Me kids fret after me, the missus says,' Billy went on. 'I didn't like leaving her neither.'

Sam waited to hear him say that he worried about other men hanging round his wife, but when Billy only stood looking at the photograph Sam said carefully, 'Plenty of people ashore who'll take advantage while we're away.'

'I'm not worried about that. We've got good neighbours and her mam's in the next street,' Billy said. 'It's just the money. Me last trip she didn't get nothing for five months, but she can look after herself and the kids. Made toffee apples and sold them off a handcart to feed the kids, but it's a worry, isn't it?'

Sam felt ashamed. Other fellows seemed to have none of the jealous worries that plagued him. It must be me. I'm bloody twisted, he thought, but soon he was too busy to dwell on anything but the ship.

Billy was on the same watch as himself and George and when they came off watch Billy talked again about his family as they ate their meal. He said that his eldest boy loved horses and was always hanging round the stables at the top of the road, and Sam told him about Tommy and how much he had enjoyed the day in the country.

'Is Nellie going to take him there for a holiday?' asked George who was sitting near by. 'She told Rose about Bobby's landlady asking her.'

'I don't think so,' Sam said. 'She said she wouldn't, like. Might do the wrong thing and make a show of herself and Bobby.'

'I don't see why she should,' George said. 'Bobby managed all right and he hadn't been in good service like Nellie. It'd do the lad a world of good.'

The talk turned to other matters but later Sam wrote to Nellie, urging her to take Tommy on holiday to Yorkshire. He told her what George had said and finished by saying that a holiday would do her good as well as Tommy. 'Don't worry about your job,' he wrote. 'You'll be sure of my money for eighteen months at least so don't take any old buck from the missus. Tell her what to do with her job if she cuts up about you being off.'

Sam felt strong and protective as he read through his letter before sealing it. He could still back Ellie up and tell her what to do even if it was only by letter. And she'd make sure the lad didn't forget him, and tell him it was his dad told her to take him on holiday.

George was right, Sam thought. It was hard being away from them but at least this way they were looking after their families. Even if the money got held up at times they always had it to come. He settled down in his bunk, smiling cheerfully.

CHAPTER 15

Nellie returned to work at the Duncan house, feeling low after parting from Sam, but expecting to be cheered by the cook's salty comments. She found the cook also low in spirits.

'Things have took a turn for the worse while you've been off, girl,' she said.

'What do you mean, Cook?' Nellie asked.

The cook laid her finger to her nose and winked. 'Trouble in store,' she whispered. 'All kinds of carry-on between mister and missus and them girls! Crying and banging round. You never heard anything like it.'

'Perhaps one of them wants to marry a young man what the parents don't like?' Nellie suggested, but the cook scoffed.

'Don't be daft, girl. You read too many of them penny novelettes. I think it's business troubles.'

Nellie looked doubtful and the cook went on, 'You know the missus has never liked parting with money for wages, but for them—it was always the best of everything. Now she's gone real mean and close with the food. Wants to know what's happened to every bite that comes in the house, and saying I could do things cheaper.'

'But they had that big dinner party just before Sam come home,' Nellie said.

'Throwing a sprat to catch a mackerel,' the cook snorted. 'These people don't ask friends round the way the like of us do. They ask people for what they can get out of them.'

Susan, the girl from the orphanage, was peeling potatoes at the sink, and the cook said quietly, 'The missus'll be wanting you to wait on, and you tell her you want parlourmaid's wages. Don't let her give you charwoman's money, Nellie.'

'But I got took on as a charwoman,' Nellie said. 'To tell you the truth, Cook, I'm made up I didn't get the sack for staying off while Sam was home.'

'Don't fret yourself, girl,' the cook said. She nodded at Susan. '*She* got took on to train as a parlourmaid, but she'll never get nearer the dining room than this. They had two couples to dinner while you was off and you never seen the like.' She raised her voice. 'You didn't take to the parlourmaiding, did you, Susan?'

The girl turned round. She was a large awkward girl with big hands and feet and a round face. 'Oh Jeez, it was awful,' she groaned. 'I nearly run out of the place and kep' on running till I threw meself in the river.'

'Mrs Taggart was peeping through the door and she was wetting herself laughing,' the cook said. 'Susan spilled soup on the first feller and she went to pieces. What she didn't drop on

282

them she broke. Mrs Taggart said they was all cringing there, wondering what was going to come flying at them next. Poor Agnes took a dizzy turn, and the missus kept saying, "I'm giving an orphan a home. Trying to train her." None of us was a bit of good after, and I don't know what them lot in the dining room was like. Mrs Taggart said it was the best laugh for years.'

'I'd better go up and tell her I'm here,' Nellie said.

'Well, don't let her walk on you, girl,' the cook advised. 'Stand up for yourself.'

Nellie promised that she would, but she could feel butterflies in her stomach as she knocked nervously at the door of the morning room.

Mrs Duncan had been annoyed when asked for the time off, and had warned Nellie that she risked losing her job, but Nellie had been determined to be at home with Sam.

She was surprised to be greeted with a smile by her employer.

'I trust you are rested, Ellen,' Mrs Duncan said graciously. 'Susan has not proved suitable for training as parlourmaid. I will have to return her to the orphanage unless of course she takes your place in the kitchen and *you* act as parlourmaid.'

Nellie was disgusted. The way they can blackmail you with a smile on their faces, she thought, but aloud she said meekly, 'Yes, ma'am.'

'It will be useful training for you and of course

you can continue to help cook and learn how to cook also.'

Nellie left the room feeling annoyed with herself. Why didn't I say I'd been acting as parlourmaid *and* kitchenmaid for ages *and* running after her daughters as well? I let her make out she was doing me a favour. I'm a right wet lettuce, as Katy would say.

The cook looked thoughtful when Nellie reported the conversation to her. 'She's up to something,' she said. 'Bothering to explain to you. I wonder is she going to get rid of Agnes?'

Mrs Taggart had come down from cleaning upstairs and she joined in. 'I wouldn't put nothing past that one,' she declared. 'Mind you, I think she's trying to put a good face on things. There's trouble brewing here or I'm a Dutchman.'

'I don't know what to do,' Nellie said. 'These hours won't suit me the same. I only really wanted mornings while Tommy was at school.' She saw Susan watching her anxiously and remembered Mrs Duncan's words. She smiled at the girl. 'I won't do nothing for a while anyhow,' she added.

A week later the cook was proved right. Agnes had been with the Duncans for over twenty years, but when she had another dizzy spell she was swiftly despatched to hospital.

'Just like poor Jane,' Mrs Taggart said, but Agnes was more fortunate than Jane because she was able to go to stay with her brother and his wife in Blackpool.

'She won't be going for no rest cure,' the cook said. 'Her brother's fond of her, like, but his wife'll work Agnes until she drops. You know what it's like in them boarding houses.'

The day after Agnes went Nellie was distressed to hear that Nurse McCann had died. She was greatly mourned and the wreath collected for in Johnson Street was one of dozens from grateful patients.

On the day of the funeral the streets were lined with people standing bare headed and silent as the funeral cortege drove slowly to the cemetery, with many women, including Nellie, in tears. She felt that she had lost her last chance of asking advice.

The following day Nellie met Nurse McCann's sister and they spoke about the funeral.

'She loved flowers,' the sister said, 'but I think it might have worried her to see so much spent on wreaths. Now, while people are living so close to the bone.'

'But everyone wanted to show how much they thought of her,' Nellie said. 'Everyone gave willingly.'

The sister smiled sadly. 'It's a comfort to me to know she was so well thought of,' she said. 'Sadie always spoke her mind and some people don't like that.'

'She only said what was true,' Nellie said staunchly, 'and she done it for people's own good.'

'That's true,' said Miss McCann. 'And ill as she was she was very pleased with the flowers you brought her that day. I'm just sorry that she wasn't well enough to talk to you.'

'So am I,' Nellie said more fervently than she intended, so she added quickly, 'I'm glad she liked the flowers. She saved our Tommy's life. I wouldn't have him if it wasn't for her.'

Nellie walked home slowly, thinking sadly of Nurse McCann and of Agnes. She was so deep in thought that it was only when Tommy shouted, 'Mam,' that she noticed him. Katy had made him change from the good clothes he wore for school into a patched old pair of trousers and shirt and he wore plimsolls on his feet.

Nellie was horrified to see how rough and dirty he looked and to see how he scuffled in the gutter with the other boys.

'Come home for your tea, Tommy,' she called sharply but he shouted back, 'I've 'ad it at me Auntie Katy's,' then ran into the entry and a moment later she saw him running along the back walls with the other boys.

Katy had seen her walking down the street and she was waiting at her door with Tommy's school clothes.

'I made him change,' she said with a grin. 'They're playing in that house what fell down, getting covered in muck.'

'I called him,' Nellie said, 'but he said he'd had his tea with you, and run off up the walls in the jigger.'

'Saving his face,' Katy said shrewdly. 'He wouldn't like being shouted for his tea while he was with his mates. They start young round here being the big hard buckos.' She was laughing but Nellie found it hard to smile in return.

'You're not worried about him, are you?' Katy said. 'It'll do him good. Toughen him up a bit, like, Nell.'

She looked anxious and Nellie said quickly, 'No, I'm just feeling down. Nurse McCann—and the maid in work got took to hospital yesterday. Poor old thing. It's the workhouse for them or going where they're not wanted when they're too old to work. I'm glad I'm married, Katy.'

'Aye, I suppose you're missing Sam, too,' Katy said.

Nellie nodded, feeling that if she spoke she would cry, and went off to her own house. She sat on the sofa for a while resting her swollen feet and thinking about Tommy.

It must have started weeks ago, this running wild, she thought, then while Sam was at home he went back to his old self. I've neglected him, working all hours at that place, and for shirt buttons, hardly seeing him while the missus was using me to kid her friends she had a big staff.

She felt bitterly angry when she remembered Tommy running along the back yard walls and the rough way he had answered her. I've put them Duncans before me own child, she thought, and if it suited them they'd throw me off tomorrow.

She thought over the day she had spent there, starting by clearing up the breakfast dishes while Susan helped Mrs Taggart with the rough cleaning. Then helping to prepare lunch and serve and clear it away, then start immediately making tiny sandwiches and fancy

287

cakes for Mrs Duncan's At Home.

'Good job they're dining out tonight,' the cook had whispered to her as they worked. 'When the butcher's lad brought the meat he said he hadn't got to take no more orders until the bill was paid.'

'Go way,' Nellie exclaimed, 'does she know?'

'Yes, I had to tell her. You'd almost feel sorry for her. She went the colour of chalk but give her her due she took it on the chin, like. "The impertinence," she said. "I shall withdraw my custom." I'll bet there'll be high jinks when his nibs comes in tonight though.'

Nellie had left as soon as she had tidied up after the At Home, and now she thought she was glad that she had. It meant that she had been able to see what was happening to Tommy.

He came in a little later, but Nellie only said, 'I've brought your school clothes home, lad. You'd better get a good wash.' There was still hot water in the kettle which she had boiled to make tea, and she poured it into the bowl in the sink. 'Start getting washed and I'll come and finish you off,' she said.

It was only when Tommy was in his nightshirt, drinking a cup of cocoa, that Nellie said quietly, 'I got a shock when I seen you tonight, lad, and the mates you was with.'

Tommy looked down and shuffled his feet. 'They're beltin' mates, Mam,' he said.

'Some of them,' Nellie said. 'But I seen some hard knocks there an' all. I don't want to make a sissy outa you, lad, but I don't want you to

288

be no roughneck neither. Your dad wouldn't like it.'

Tommy said nothing. He now slept in the front bedroom with his mother and she still took him up to bed and tucked him in. When he was in bed and she bent over him, tucking in the bedclothes and saying gently, 'Goodnight and God bless, son,' he suddenly put his arms round her neck and kissed her.

'Sorry, Mam,' he said, and Nellie held him close.

He was still her good little lad, she thought, and from now on she was going to make sure she watched over him. I'll look for another job, never mind staying there to save Susan's job. I got landed with this because of trying to keep Jane's job, but from now on me own come first. No matter what happens or what she says I'm going to keep to it too. Even if I have to be out of work I'll manage on Sam's money.

She set off for work the next morning full of her resolve but when she arrived she found the house in Balliol Road in a state of wild confusion. Mrs Taggart sat at the kitchen table and as soon as she saw Nellie she screeched, 'Oh God, Nellie, what a night,' but the cook transfixed her with a glare.

'I'll tell Nellie, Mrs Taggart. *I was here.*'

She pulled forward a chair. 'Sit down, girl. Do you remember I said yesterday about the butcher?' Nellie nodded. 'And I said there'd be high jinks when the master come home?' the cook went on. 'Well, it must've been the last straw. *He topped hisself!*' Her voice ended in a scream and Nellie screamed too.

'Oh God, no,' she gasped. 'Not dead?'

'Dead as a doornail, and I was the last one what seen him alive. He come in and she took him in her little morning room. I'd come up outa me kitchen to see was the dining room fire all right. I couldn't trust nothing to Susan and when I come out into the hall he was just turning up the stairs. His face was like tallow; but I'd heard the missus carrying on at him.'

'And what did he do?' asked Nellie. 'And where were the girls?'

'At a tennis party, them girls. The missus went up to get ready for going out and me and Susan was in the kitchen. We heard this noise, like, and I said it sounded like something fell. I sent the girl to see and she found him. Hanging from the banisters. He must have put the rope round his neck and jumped off the chair.'

'Oh, poor Susan. Poor kid,' Nellie exclaimed. 'What did she do?'

'Screamed blue murder and I run out in the hall and the missus run down the stairs. I run to the door and be the mercy of God there was a bobby just down the road. He cut him down then he blew his whistle and more came and a doctor.'

'And the missus—what did she do?' Nellie asked.

'Don't talk to me about her,' the cook said in a disgusted voice. 'Poor Susan went into a fit, and no wonder, I didn't know what to do with her but when the doctor come he only took one look at the master then he started to look after

Susan and do you know what that one said? "Never mind her. Attend to my husband." '

'The faggot,' Nellie said.

'Aye, but she got her answer off the doctor. He told her he couldn't do nothing for him but the child needed his care. Shut her up. I was feeling sorry for her till then.'

Mrs Taggart could restrain herself no longer. 'And they was going to leave Cook in the house on her own only she sent a lad for me and I come up and we've sat up all night, haven't we?'

The cook agreed and told Nellie that Mrs Duncan's brother had come and taken her to his own house for the night. The body had been removed and Susan had been taken to hospital. She had seen nothing of the daughters and assumed that they were with their mother.

Mrs Taggart had made tea and as they sipped it she said that they had done nothing but drink tea all night.

'I had to sit up,' the cook said. 'If I'd of laid me head on a pillow I'd have gone outa me mind. The sight of that poor man. I only hope the butcher feels sorry now.'

'You couldn't blame the man trying to get his money,' Mrs Taggart said. 'God knows how much they owed. Speaking of which, do you think any of us'll see the colour of their money?'

'I wouldn't like to bet on it,' the cook said. 'I haven't had me quarter's money and neither has Agnes.'

'She never paid me before I went off,' Nellie

said. 'Said she'd no change but I wasn't worried because of Sam being home with his pay-off.'

'She tried that gag with me, having no change,' Mrs Taggart said, 'but I told her I couldn't stand outa me money. I had me rent to pay. She soon found it when I stood up to her.'

'I'd made up me mind I was going to tell her I couldn't stay late,' Nellie said, 'when I seen our Tom running wild with some real hard knocks yesterday.' She shuddered. 'I'm glad I did go early and missed seeing that.'

'It'll be with me till me dying day,' the cook declared. 'His face!' She began to describe the dead man's appearance but Nellie put her hands over her ears.

'Don't, don't, Cook,' she begged.

The cook stood up. 'Well, being as I was left in charge, like, I'd better see what needs doing.' She bustled out and Mrs Taggart leaned over the table to Nellie. '*She* won't have no need to worry, girl. She's been feathering her nest for years while there was plenty of money here.'

'But how could she?' Nellie gasped.

'Oh, there's ways and means, girl. Fiddling the tradesmen's bills and getting backhanders off them. She'll have a nice little nest egg, don't worry,' whispered Mrs Taggart.

The cook came back. 'You do the steps, Mrs Taggart, and Nellie do the fires in the dining room and drawing room. Don't light them. Just lay them.'

'I'll do me work today then I'll have to see,' Mrs Taggart said aggressively. 'Don't forget, *I'll* be leaving here empty handed.'

Nellie snatched up her sacking apron and her cleaning box and escaped into the dining room, too agitated as she went through the hall to think of what had occurred there the previous night.

The cook had disappeared when she went through the kitchen with the ashes and Mrs Taggart had finished the front steps and was scrubbing the kitchen floor.

'I think she's *packing*,' Mrs Taggart said with a wink, but a moment later the cook came back.

'What about the other fires, Cook?' Nellie asked but the cook sat down and sighed heavily.

'I wish someone'd come and tell us what's happening,' she said. 'We don't know where we are. Never mind them other fires, Nell. Make us a fresh cup of tea, there's a good girl.'

'It give me a turn when I come back through the hall,' Nellie said. 'I could picture him there, like. No wonder you couldn't stay here on your own, Cook.'

'Yes. I couldn't of stayed here without you, Mrs Taggart,' Cook said to the charwoman, who was now sitting by the table.

Harmony prevailed again as they sat drinking tea and discussing their futures.

'I think she might have give me the sack when I said I couldn't stay late, so I'm no worse off,' Nellie said. 'I've got Sam's allotment but this was just to fall back on, like, if it was held up.'

'You could go as a cook general,' the cook

said. 'You've got a real light hand with pastry, Nell, and that's a gift you're born with.'

'I couldn't live in though, Cook,' Nellie said. 'I'll try to find some cleaning.'

'I'm not worried neither,' Mrs Taggart said, laughing. 'When Lady Muck cut me down to two mornings a week I got another two with a lady in Merton Road. That'll keep me going until I get sump'n' else. What about you, Cook?'

The cook shrugged. 'I only stayed here to oblige and because it suited me,' she said. 'Remember, Nell, that fellow from the Cotton Exchange and his wife what often came to dinner? He spoke to me a couple of times. Praised me dinners and half-jokingly said to let him know if I felt like a change. He give me his card though.'

'You'll have no trouble getting another job, Cook,' Nellie said.

The next moment they were amazed to hear a noise at the front door and heavy footsteps in the hall. They all jumped to their feet and Mrs Taggart whipped the teacups into the sink. Nellie snatched up her cleaning box as the door opened and a portly man looked in.

'Ah, Mrs Shufflebottom,' he said. 'In the morning room, please.'

'Yes, sir,' the cook said, hurrying out as he turned away, ignoring Mrs Taggart and Nellie. They looked at each other and Nellie put her fingers over her mouth to stifle a giggle. 'Mrs Shufflebottom!' she said. 'No wonder she told me just to call her Cook.'

Mrs Taggart only nodded then went quickly and lightly up the back stairs.

It seemed only a moment later she reappeared, her arms full of sheets and pillowcases and a pair of men's shoes. Swiftly she whipped off her sacking apron and wrapped the articles in it then slipped out the back door to reappear without the bundle.

Nellie was still standing open mouthed with shock and the charwoman said grimly, 'What I don't get in cash I'll take in kind. Run up and get something for yourself, girl. I'll keep douse,' but Nellie shook her head.

'I couldn't, Mrs Taggart,' she said. 'I'd be too frightened. They might send a scuffer after me.'

'Don't be a fool to yourself, girl. They've got that much they won't miss these. Haven't they robbed everyone blind anyhow to get where they are now?' She pulled a silver cigarette case and a small box from under her voluminous pinafore. 'Here, which do you want? This or the cufflinks?'

Nellie was still shaking her head when they heard the morning room door open and Mrs Taggart thrust her booty back under her pinafore. The cook came back, looking important.

'Mr Thomson says you can go home, Mrs Taggart. I told him as you'd been up all night with me. He says you can come back tomorrow and see what's needed.'

'And wharrabout tonight?' asked Mrs Taggart, but the cook said she would be all right now that she was over the first shock. She turned to Nellie.

'Go and light the fire in the study and dust it,' she said. 'Someone's coming to see Mr Thomson and then you'll have to answer the door to callers. Tell them Mrs Duncan and her daughters will be staying with Mr Thomson and his wife for the present.'

Both Nellie and Mrs Taggart were amazed at the sudden air of authority assumed by the cook, but they said nothing. Mrs Taggart only asked mildly if she should do the study fire so that Nellie would be ready to answer the door, and the cook agreed.

I wonder what will disappear from there, thought Nellie, but she found it hard to condemn Mrs Taggart. It's the way our sort of people have always got even, she thought. I'm just too much of a coward for it.

The expected visitor came and was in Mr Duncan's study for several hours with Mr Thomson and when Nellie took coffee to them she saw that the roll-top desk was open and the table littered with papers which the two men were poring over.

After lunch she was kept busy answering the door and she grew tired of repeating the formula she had been told to use. Some of the callers were genuinely unaware of the tragedy but others Nellie felt were drawn by vulgar curiosity.

She remembered the way the cook and Mrs Taggart had fallen on her like starving men on bread, so anxious were they to tell the dramatic tale. This lot are just the same, she thought, although they think they're posh.

For a few hours during the afternoon she was left alone in the house while the cook went to visit friends among the servants in nearby houses, and she was relieved when the cook said she could go at five o'clock. 'Just come the usual time tomorrow, Nell,' she said.

When Nellie reached Johnson Street she decided to go first to Bella to tell her tale, feeling that it was some return for Bella's kindness to her, to give her the opportunity to be first with the dramatic news.

She was glad that she did later when she went to pay Katy for Tommy's meals.

'Me mam's having the time of her life telling everyone about that poor feller what hung himself,' Katy said with a grin. 'She's out in the back entry now with women from Elliot Street all round her. All coming outa their back doors.'

'It was creepy going past them stairs though,' Nellie said with a shudder. 'I wouldn't fancy staying the night on me own like Cook's going to do. Eh, you know what her name is, Katy? Mrs Shufflebottom!'

'And you never knew all the time you've worked there?' Katy said.

'No, she told me to call her Cook,' Nellie said, and Katy hooted with laughter.

'No bloody wonder,' she said.

Katy had two items of news herself which she was anxious to tell Nellie. The first was that Peter was back at work, and the second that she was almost sure that she was expecting a baby.

'The fourth and last if I am,' she said firmly, but when she saw Nellie's face she said tactfully, 'You might be next, Nell. Our Donald is turned three, y'know.'

They both knew that the gap between her children had been carefully planned but neither mentioned it.

When Nellie returned to the Duncan house the following morning she found Mrs Taggart already there. 'I've got me marching orders,' she announced, 'but at least he coughed up.' She waved two pound notes.

'The house is getting closed up,' the cook said quickly. 'I told Mr Thomson Mrs Taggart and you never got paid, Nell, and he give me that for Mrs Taggart.'

'And what about me?' Nellie asked.

'He wants you to stay for a few days to answer the door and keep the place tidy and then he'll settle up with you. I'm to stay on as caretaker and they'll want me to help for the funeral,' the cook said, preening herself.

'And the house is getting closed up?' Nellie said.

'Yes, he said in the circumstances, as if it was because of what happened, but me and Mrs Taggart are just saying it'll probably have to go for the debts. His wife and Miss Lydia was with him and they went upstairs packing things to take back with them. He opened the door with his key and Miss Lydia never even spoke to me,' and Cook wiped away a tear.

'Never mind. I suppose she was upset,' Nellie consoled her.

'The funeral's going from his house so I don't suppose they'll come here again, the missus and the girls,' Cook said.

The number of callers grew less over the next few days and Nellie assumed that official callers must be going to the Thomson house. On Friday Mr Thomson came and told her that her services were no longer required and gave her three pound notes.

She was not sorry to leave, although she had enjoyed part of her time there, and she was pleased to be given three pounds and thanked by Mr Thomson. The cook seemed unable to talk of anything but the tragedy and Nellie could only offer the same words of sympathy, and say again how thankful she was that the Duncans had planned to dine out, so she had gone home before it occurred.

No one seemed concerned about Susan, and Nellie went to the hospital to see her, only to be told that she had been returned to the orphanage. Nellie asked a nurse if Susan would be sent to another place but the woman said it was unlikely.

'She'll probably go to a home for epileptics, or they might put her to work in the laundry. That's what they do with defectives.'

'But she wasn't defective,' Nellie protested, 'it was only the shock brought the fit on.'

The nurse shrugged. 'I don't know, I'm sure,' she said. 'I don't know anything about the girl.' She hurried away.

Nellie would like to have befriended Susan but she knew so little about her, not even to which orphanage she had been sent. She was glad to go back to her own neighbourhood and put the whole affair behind her.

CHAPTER 16

Nellie was worried when she received Sam's letter telling her to take up the offer of a holiday with the Handleys. Try as she might she was unable to rid her house of vermin completely, and both she and Tommy showed the evidence in numerous bite marks on their bodies. She had noticed Mrs Handley glancing at the fleabites on Tommy's neck during their last visit, and felt ashamed.

There were other things too. How would she know what to do about helping in the house? And when to go to bed and when to get up in the morning? It was all right Bobby saying she was worrying over nothing. These were very real problems to her.

Could she tell Sam now that she was worried about the expense of the journey as well as whether she should offer money to Mrs Handley? Now that her job had gone she might need her savings if Sam's money was held up, yet he had told her they should go.

Before she wrote back to Sam, the problem was solved for her. Bobby's apprenticeship was due to finish and he was suddenly moved back to the Liverpool works. He and Meg came to tell Nellie on a Sunday and Meg wept as they told their news.

'But why, Bob? I thought you was settled there,' Nellie said, looking bewildered.

Bobby shrugged. 'Ours not to reason why,' he said bitterly. 'The job I got sent there for is long finished but I've been doing others for Mr Orlando. He's real narked about me coming back but I *am* indentured here.'

'Tommy's been sleeping with me since Sam went, so your bed's here for you, lad,' Nellie said.

Bobby said hurriedly, 'It's all right, Nell. I'm fixing up a room near the works. You'll need that room when Sam comes home and anyway Tommy's getting a big lad now.'

'And Bob will be able to come and see you often now, Nell,' Meg said gently.

Bobby put his arm round her. 'I'm going to look round for a house or rooms for us an' all,' he said. 'The minute Meg's twenty-one next May we're getting married and her father can't stop us.'

'You'll be able to afford it now you're out of your time, lad,' Nellie said. She felt hurt that Bobby was not coming home yet she could understand why.

Meg went down the yard to the lavatory and Bobby whispered quickly, 'This has come at a bad time, our kid. Her old feller's drinking like a fish. Barred out of the pub and boozing at home.'

Meg came back and he said no more but later when they were going, Meg herself said to Nellie, 'I'm having a bad time with my dad. The drink seems to have got a hold over him. I wish Bob wasn't going.'

'Never mind. May will soon be here and you can be together,' Nellie consoled her.

Bobby was able to find a room in a house near Fountains Road which was a reasonable size, with an alcove containing a gas ring and a sink, and Nellie and Tommy often visited him there.

Nellie was still searching for another job without success, but her search was half hearted.

Sam's money was arriving regularly and she had her savings and the money from Mr Thomson hidden in her mattress.

'I don't think I'll bother until after the school holidays,' she told Katy. 'I've wrote to Mrs Handley to say we can't go so I want to make it up to Tom. Maybe we could all go out together.'

Katy agreed. She had lost her harassed look now that Peter was working, and her pregnancy was going smoothly. There was rich farmland and sandy beaches within easy reach of Bootle, although the people of the neighbourhood rarely ventured there, and Nellie and Katy spent happy days with the children, wandering through the lanes or playing on the sandhills.

On one occasion they took the ferryboat to New Brighton and Tommy bragged to the other children about the day he had been on the boat with his father and all that Sam had told him about the ships in the river.

'He loves the bones of his dad, doesn't he?' Katy said, laughing. 'It's all "me dad, me dad" outa him.'

'Aye, and Sam loves him,' Nellie said. 'They're real good mates. I hope they never fall out, especially with him being the only one.'

'By the time he's old enough to face up to Sam you might have half a dozen others,' Katy said bracingly. 'Me mam knows a woman was married twenty years without any and had her first when she was forty-one.'

'Gee, I don't want to wait that long,' Nellie giggled.

She and Katy enjoyed these outings as much as the children, and they became even better friends. They thought alike on many subjects and enjoyed long conversations.

No matter how freely she and Katy talked Nellie never mentioned a subject which was rarely far from her mind. For years she had put all doubt about Tommy's parentage from her mind and crushed any memory of Leadbetter, but now her fears had been revived.

The married daughter of a neighbour had come home to her mother to await the birth of her first child as her husband was away on the tugs.

A week earlier she had been sitting on the step when Nellie and Katy passed.

'Still here, Josie?' Katy said jokingly.

The girl laughed and grimaced. 'Yes, worse luck. Me mam says I'll need a shot of dynamite to get started. The castor oil she's give me! I'm three weeks overdue already.'

'It'll come when it's ready,' Katy said cheerfully, but as they walked away she said to Nellie, 'Me mam says it must be twins at least, the size of her.'

The baby was born the same night and there was much hilarity among the women gathered round Bella's step when the child proved to be only tiny.

'Must've been all water she was carrying,' Bella declared. 'The Mersey must've rose a foot when she got rid of that.'

Nellie had been in to see the baby and had felt a stab of fear when she saw him, small and red, cradled in Josie's arms. And she had carried him for nine months and three weeks! So it was possible that Tommy, born that length of time after the rape, could have been Leadbetter's. In vain she told herself that her instinct said that he was Sam's child, and that he was like Sam in character, as she knew Sam to be.

That proved nothing, she knew. Look at Katy. Who would think Bella would have a daughter like her? And I hope there's nothing of me ma in me either, Nellie thought, or in Tommy. She had spent sleepless nights since Josie's baby was born, plagued by her old worries.

As she sat on the shore with Katy while the children played among the sandhills, Nellie felt that she must say *something* to Katy to relieve her mind.

'I couldn't get over the size of Josie's baby, being so late and all, yet he was no bigger than Tommy born, was he?'

'Must've been carrying a lot of water, like me mam says,' Katy said, adding casually, 'unless she got her dates wrong. She coulda been a month out.'

Her words caused a rush of joy to Nellie which made her feel almost lightheaded with relief. That was a possibility that had never occurred to her, but now she realised that if the dates were wrong, the birth was a week early, and there were no complications there as there had been with Tommy's birth.

She jumped to her feet, shouting, 'Come on, kids. We'll play rounders.'

For twenty minutes she and Katy joined in the games with the children, much to their delight, and no one suspected the cause of Nellie's sudden high spirits.

As the mothers sat hot and breathless watching the children who still played, Katy said that she thought Tommy had come out of his shell. 'He's not half as quiet as what he used to be. He's one of the gang now, all right.'

'He never wants to come in when he's playing out,' Nellie said. 'I don't want him to get too rough though, Katy.'

'He won't,' said Katy. 'But he needs to stand up for himself.' She laughed. 'Me mam seen him fighting with Jenkins' lad over some ollies and she said he was getting more like Sam than like you. You know what Sam used to be like for fighting when we was young?'

'But he didn't live round here then,' Nellie said.

'I'm talking about during the war,' Katy said.

'He lived in the Seaman's when he was ashore and drank in the Volley and he was always in fights.' She laughed. 'Made a few enemies too, because he always won.'

'I didn't know him then. I was away in service,' Nellie said. 'And once I came home on me day off I never got out to see no one. Me mam had all the jobs lined up for me until it was time to go back.'

'It wasn't Sam's fault,' Katy said. 'It was just because he was such a good fighter any bucko with a few pints down him wanted to prove he could do better than Sam. He's give it up now though, hasn't he?'

Tommy was whirling the homemade bat around his head and yelling with the other children.

'Not much of the timid fawn about him now, is there?' Katy said with a grin and when Nellie looked startled she explained.

'The teacher let our Amy lend a book to bring home. It was all pictures, like, and words underneath them and one was "the timid fawn". It was a little animal, a sort of deer peeping through some leaves, it had big eyes, sort of frightened looking. Our Amy said it was like Tommy but I thought it looked more like you.'

'Thanks very much,' Nellie said in mock indignation. She felt that Katy had given her a lot to think about and answered some questions for her, and she felt much happier.

Nellie was still feeling happy as she cleared away the evening meal while Tommy played out, and she was unprepared for a sudden attack by Janey.

'I see that one over the road went three weeks over. Nine months and three weeks, same time as you was after Leadbetter seen to you,' she cackled. 'And she had one like a fourpenny rabbit, same as you.'

A tide of red rushed over Nellie's face and she stared at the old woman as though hypnotised, saying nothing.

'Mind you, there's only me knows them dates and I wouldn't say nothing—not unless I had to, like. If you or the big feller tried to put me out. I know it's what he wants but he wouldn't like what I could tell him.'

Suddenly Nellie was furiously angry. 'Josie could've got her dates wrong,' she said. 'I'm sick of your hints and threats. Go ahead and tell Sam. He'll think you've gone soft in the head, like a lot of people round here. And don't think I can't put you out. I hold the rent book, don't forget.'

She expected a tirade in return from Janey, but the old woman seemed taken aback by Nellie's defiance. She stared at her from her small red-rimmed eyes, working her toothless mouth, then said ingratiatingly, 'Don't be working yourself up, girl. You took me the wrong way. There's things I could tell you that would rise the hair from your head, worser by far than your bit of trouble, but I know how to keep me mouth shut. No need for us to fall out, girl. I've known you since you was born.'

Nellie stood breathing rapidly as the old

307

woman talked, then feeling that she would be sick if she stayed a moment longer with her, she snatched up her purse and shawl and rushed out of the house.

She went to join the women gathered round Bella's step, where she could listen to the jokes and the gossip until she felt calmer. When she returned later with Tommy the parlour door was closed and during the following days Janey carefully avoided any controversial subjects.

When the children returned for the new school year in September Tommy was moved up to the class of a new teacher at the school, Miss Helsby. He liked his teacher and enjoyed school.

Nellie was delighted when he asked if he could write to his father. She had taken out the steel-nibbed pen and the penny bottle of ink, and sent Tom to the corner shop for a packet of notepaper and envelopes, so that she could write to Sam.

When the boy returned he said diffidently, 'Now you've got a new packet can I write to me dad, Mam?'

'He'll get ink all over him,' Janey warned. 'As if you don't get enough on yourself,' but Nellie ignored her and told Tom he could write when she was finished.

When she had written, 'I hope this finds you well as it leaves us at present,' she sat for a long time pondering and biting the end of the pen before adding a few lines about Tommy growing tall and Bobby doing well, ending with her usual formula.

Although Tommy made many blots, he wrote without hesitation.

Dere Dad
I went to the shop for this paper. Me mam said I cudd write with pen and ink. I brort me composition home. I got ten out of ten. Bert benet and jimm jones had a fite They got took in the hurry up van there wer five poleesmen
love from Thomas Meadows.

'That's the gear, son,' Nellie said. 'You're a clever lad.'

Later when Gertie came with novelettes for Nellie, she told her about Tommy's letter, quoting it word for word.

'Just think,' Gertie said to the boy, 'when your dad's far away in a foreign country he'll be able to read your letter and know about your marks for composition.' She winked at Nellie. 'And all about Bert Bennett and Jim Jones going off in the Black Maria.'

Tommy flushed with pleasure and afterwards often spoke about Gertie's words.

Nellie had still not had her fortune told by Mrs Gilligan, but Katy had called at an opportune moment while Lettie was out and her fortune had been told and so had Gertie's. They had each told Nellie about it.

'She said I would have many troubles while I was young,' Katy said. 'But in later life I would know great happiness. One of my children would be very successful and one would win great honour on the battlefield.'

'You won't mind having troubles while they're young if you know you'll be happy later on, will you?' said Nellie.

'Peter said it's all baloney,' Katy said. 'That bit about the battlefield is out for a start because he'll make sure none of ours goes in the army. You know his brother was badly wounded at Ypres, but he was a wreck even before the wound. Trench foot and rheumatism from lying days and nights in water in the trenches. He was discharged but he was dead in six months.'

'I wonder which one will be successful,' Nellie said. 'I'll bet it'll be your Amy.'

'Might be this little one,' Katy said, patting the bulge beneath her skirt.

Gertie told Nellie that she was annoyed that Peter had scoffed at Mrs Gilligan. 'I believe every word she says,' Gertie said. 'She told me I'd have many good friends and a happy life but I won't marry until late in life. We won't have children but I'll know true love and prosperity.'

'She gives you all the details, doesn't she?' Nellie said. 'Not like that woman I went to in New Brighton. You coulda taken anything out of what she told me.'

'I'll tell you what makes me sure,' Gertie said. Her eyes filled with tears but she wiped them away. 'She told me things about me mam and dad what nobody knows, only me. And Katy's sister Dolly came asking her to tell her fortune but she wouldn't. Said she couldn't see nothing but after Dolly went Prudence was real upset. I think she saw trouble for Dolly.'

'Is that her name, Prudence?' Nellie said.

'Yes, but Lettie likes her called Mrs Gilligan.'

'Lettie's the boss, isn't she?' Nellie said laughing.

'Oh aye, but she's a real good daughter, Nell. Her mam'd be lost without her.'

'I'm dying to have mine told,' Nellie sighed.

Gertie said, 'I think she's got to be in the mood, like, as well as waiting for Lettie to go out and that's only every Preston Guild. I'll keep reminding her about you though, Nell, honest.'

Bobby seemed to have settled back quite happily at the Liverpool works, and one day when Nellie and Tommy visited him at Fountains Road they found him very excited.

'I think I've got the chance of a house, Nell. The boss might swing it for me, being in the trade, like.'

'Where is it?' asked Nellie.

'Lovelace Street. Two up and two down, good solid little houses. I'll have to find twenty-five pounds key money, but I've got me savings and the boss said I can lend off him and pay it back outa me wages if it's more. I'm bursting to tell Meg but I won't say nothing yet in case it falls through.'

'Would you just live on your own there, like, until youse could get married?' Nellie asked.

'Yes, we can't get married until she's twenty-one in May, but if I get the house it'll give me a chance to get some furniture and that.' He bit his lip then with sudden violent anger he banged his hand on the table. 'I wish to God I could bring her here tomorrow away from that bloody old soak. She says he wouldn't hurt her, but I seen the way he wrecked the house.'

'Never mind, lad. May'll soon be here, and even if the house fell through this is good enough to bring her to.'

'Yes, but I'm banking on the house, Nell. I'll go mad if I miss it. Lovely clean little houses they are.'

'Like this,' Nellie said looking round the room. 'Our place has got me heart broke trying to get shut of the fleas and bugs, yet I *do* keep it clean, Bob.'

'Of course you do, our kid. It's them houses. Remember when I first started at Meldrum's and we done all the walls and beds with stuff from work? One of the older fellows told me we was wasting our time. He said them walls are filled with horsehair.'

'Horsehair!' Nellie exclaimed.

'Yes. He seen it when he was knocking down houses in Buttercup Street from the same builder. He said the bugs and fleas had a happy home there.'

'Fancy that,' Nellie said. 'And me and Tommy seem to come off the worst for bites. Must be because we're clean. They never trouble Janey.'

'They'd probably drop dead if they bit her,' Bobby said with a grin.

Bobby walked home with them and they took a roundabout route to look at the houses in Lovelace Street. It was only a short street with the front doors opening directly from the street but each step was scrubbed and a patch of pavement under each window.

'You'd have respectable neighbours anyhow, lad,' Nellie remarked.

'Yes, but listen, Nell. Don't say nothing to no one about this, will you? The boss'll have to pull strings and if it gets out first—'

'Don't worry, lad. I won't say nothing and you won't either will you, Tom?' Nellie said, and Tommy promised.

Although Nellie was thankful that she had her own rent book she was growing more and more dissatisfied with the house in Johnson Street. The endless battle with the vermin, the stink of fish which brought cats yowling round the house every night, the dampness of the walls and most of all the presence of old Janey, made her long to escape. Bobby's news hardened her determination to find another house, but there was still the problem of old Janey.

It was still very hard to find a decent house and 'key money' was always demanded from a new tenant, but Nellie remembered the words of Mrs Hignett the cook.

'There's no such word as can't,' she had told Nellie. 'If you want a thing enough you can do it,' and Nellie made up her mind that she would accumulate the key money as soon as possible. She already had her savings and Mr Thomson's money, and she tried to add a little every time she drew Sam's money, buying only necessities, but any emergency like Tom outgrowing his boots set her back.

She made up her mind that she would leave

no stone unturned to find some work, no matter what it was, but she was growing disheartened until a few weeks later she met Mrs Taggart and through her got two mornings cleaning in a house in Merton Road.

Nellie carefully concealed her reasons for saving from Janey and her small hoard of money. She knew in her heart that no matter how much she saved, the biggest obstacle to moving was the old woman.

She might tell herself that Janey was not a relation and she had no duty to her, but she knew she could not abandon the old woman. If I took her with me I'd make sure she cleaned herself up and kept her room clean too, she thought, but lying awake at night making these plans she faced the real reason why she was afraid to tell Janey.

No matter how she might defy Janey to tell Sam, she knew that while the secret of her hasty marriage lay between Sam and herself, she was in the old woman's power. And there were the hints she dropped about details of Sam's family which could hurt him if told.

Nellie hoped vaguely that 'something would happen' to solve the problem of old Janey, unable to admit even to herself that she wished the old woman dead. Until this problem was solved she would say nothing to anyone about her plans, not even Sam, but continue to save as much as she could, she decided.

When Bobby went to see Meg at the weekend he always brought back a bag of vegetables and eggs for Nellie from Mrs Handley, and these bags and Nellie's new job had not gone unnoticed by some of her neighbours.

Maud Jenkins never joined the group round Bella's step now but she was always at the door of a woman who lived at the other end of the street. Ada Ginley was a member of the Orange Lodge and a great admirer of Pastor Longbottom of the Protestant Reformed Church, but her husband was a Catholic.

Neither of them attended their respective churches but they had titanic fights on the seventeenth of March and on the twelfth of July, and they were despised by the people in the 'respectable' end of the street where Nellie and her friends lived.

Nellie knew that they gossiped about her and tried to avoid the group, but one day returning from the corner shop she was about to cross the street before she reached the group when she saw Charlie West strutting along on the opposite pavement. She chose to pass the group as the lesser of two evils but she was halted by Ada Ginley.

'I can't stand grabbers,' she announced, standing before Nellie, arms akimbo. 'Yer must 'ave 'ouses in the bank. Your fella's money, old Janey's rent, them bags of stuff from yer brother and now the cleaning job. Taking the bread outa people's mouth what need that job more than what you do.'

'Aye, much wants more,' Maud Jenkins said. 'And only one kid.'

'An' you never let on 'ow you managed that neither,' Ada Ginley said. 'We all know your

315

fella's not one to be denied 'is rights, so 'ow did you do it? Some of us'd like to know.'

Nellie tried to turn away but her way was blocked by other women, and she turned back.

'Mind your own business,' she shouted. 'What I do hasn't got nothing to do with any of youse.'

But Ada Ginley went on, 'We know where some of the money goes. On yer back. Dolling yerself up an' gettin' yerself talked about with other fellers.' She surveyed Nellie's clean white blouse and black skirt showing under her shawl and her neat strap shoes.

'Think yer too posh for the likes of us, don't yer, but we're respectable married women, don't forget.'

Before Nellie could answer she saw the women draw back and the smell of fish alerted her to the fact that Janey stood beside her.

The old woman put up her hand to her fish basket and looked round the group with glittering eyes. 'Wot was that? Respectable married women! Don't make me laugh. Youse have all got big mouths, but don't forget. I've got a bigger one an' I might decide to open it. I know something about every one of youse and well you know it.'

Nobody spoke and Janey went on, 'Yiz pick your mark. A girl you think hasn't got no one behind her, but you thought wrong. Maybe I won't open me mouth this time. Maybe I'll tell Nellie what I know about youse instead so she can open hers if yiz start again.'

She looked round the silent women with

316

contempt and turned to Nellie. 'Come on home, girl, and keep away from these. The scum o' the bloody earth.'

They walked away, Nellie thinking that she would never have expected to be so thankful to see Janey. The old woman said she had come home early because of a pain in her back and Nellie was eager to show her gratitude but Janey refused help.

'I don't want nothing, only a cup of cocoa and a bit of bread and cheese,' she said.

Nellie was anxious about her and lay awake listening for sounds from the parlour and regretting her feeling that her problem about the house would be solved if something happened to Janey. She was not really surprised that Janey's remedies seemed to have worked and she appeared as usual the next morning and went out with her fish. She had said nothing more about the revelations she had promised.

Ironically it was Bobby who had his problem solved by a death, that of Meg's father.

'He dropped dead with a heart attack,' he told Nellie. 'He'd been drinking all day and then he went down to the pub carrying on because they wouldn't serve him. I reckon he died of bad temper as much as anything.'

'Meg'll be upset,' Nellie said, although her own first thought had been, thank goodness, now they can get married.

'She is,' Bobby admitted, 'for all she's had such an awful life with him. I didn't tell you but we fell out two weeks ago. I was that worried about her and talking about when we

317

get married in May and she turned round and said she couldn't leave him. He was her father and it was her duty to look after him. I got real narked but we made it up before I come home.'

'I suppose you was both on edge,' Nellie consoled him.

'I want to get married right away but I don't know how she'll take the idea,' Bobby said. 'She seems to have funny ideas where he's concerned.'

'Why don't you get Mrs Handley to talk to her?' Nellie suggested, and Bobby looked relieved.

'That's a good idea, our kid,' he exclaimed.

A month later Meg and Bobby were married and Meg moved into the room in Fountains Road. She looked pale and wan with a persistent cough and Nellie hugged her impulsively.

'I don't feel a bit like a bride,' Meg said. 'I never thought it'd be like this. Married in black and me poor father hardly cold. I don't know what he would think.'

'He'd be glad to see you married with someone to look after you,' Nellie said. 'He always looked after you until the drink got a hold on him, didn't he? Don't let Bob think you're sorry you married him.'

'Oh I'm not, Nell, honest I'm not,' Meg exclaimed. 'It's just—'

'I know. You've had a bad time, but you want to put all that behind you now and think of Bobby.'

Meg promised that she would, and Bobby

received the key to the house in Lovelace Street a few days later. The excitement of moving into the new house soon restored Meg's spirits and Nellie enjoyed helping her. At first they only had the basic items of furniture and household goods, but as Bobby was now receiving tradesman's wages they were gradually able to buy what they needed.

Nellie was happy to have her brother so near and she grew very fond of Meg, who was once again the lively girl who had captivated Bobby. When Meg announced that she was pregnant just after Christmas Nellie quickly stifled a pang of envy and rejoiced wholeheartedly with the young couple.

CHAPTER 17

Nellie missed Sam and longed for his return but her life was full and happy at this time. Although Janey seemed to have decided against telling Nellie the secrets of her neighbours, Ada Ginley and her cronies kept their distance from Nellie, and Charlie West seemed to have disappeared again.

Nellie had still not had her fortune told and she was even more anxious to have it done now because Gertie said that Mrs Gilligan's prediction had come true for her.

'Remember when she told me that first time I would have a disappointment then all would

319

come right?' she said. 'I'd wrote to the doll factory for a job and they said there wasn't no vacancies but I'd be kept on the list. I was real disappointed but this morning I got a letter to start on Monday.'

Gertie enjoyed her job in the doll factory. 'It's nice light work,' she said. 'I'm putting in the dolls' eyes and sitting down to do it. We have a break morning and afternoon too, yet I get five shillings more than me old job.'

She and Nellie went to the pictures twice a week now, as Maggie or Katy would always look after Tommy. They usually chose romantic films and Nellie thoroughly enjoyed them although she was sometimes embarrassed by the way Gertie was carried away by the action. She sobbed loudly at the sad episodes and uttered cries of delight when all went well for the lovers.

After each film Gertie declared that she had fallen for the hero, although Rudolph Valentino was still her dream man, and she had a large photograph of him in her bedroom. She often said to Nellie, 'Imagine lying in his arms,' and Nellie always said she would rather imagine lying in Sam's.

Sometimes Nellie wondered uneasily what Sam would say about her going out twice a week with a single girl but she continued her visits to the cinema. Sometimes Katy came with them but her baby was nearly due now and she found it uncomfortable to sit still for long.

Tommy was still doing well at school. His teacher Miss Helsby was a dedicated woman anxious to improve the prospects of the boys she taught. She tried with little success to teach the boys better habits and to improve their speech, but Tom was one of the few who responded.

He loved words and he had a keen ear for sounds so he found it fairly easy to speak as Miss Helsby instructed. Nellie was amazed one night when he said carefully, 'Please may I have a slice of bread and jam?'

'A jam butty, you mean?' Nellie said, startled, and Janey cackled loudly.

'Got a plum in your mouth, lad?'

Nellie quickly cut a slice of bread and spread it with jam. 'Did the teacher learn you to say that, lad?' she asked.

'Yes,' Tommy muttered, hanging his head, but Nellie said encouragingly, 'It sounds real nice that, Tom.'

He took the bread and a moment later he was in the street with the other boys yelling loudly in his usual speech as they played a noisy game.

'I wonder what Sam'll think about that,' Janey said. 'He'll be thinking he had a lord for a father.'

Nellie made no reply, but when Tom tried out other phrases taught by Miss Helsby she began to worry. Would Sam mind the boy talking posh and think he was growing away from them, or learning to despise them? She mentioned her doubts to Maggie Nolan but she dismissed them.

'I wouldn't worry, Nell,' she said. 'Sam'll be proud of him—if it lasts that long. You know what kids are. Full of a thing one minute and then the novelty wears off or the teacher gets fed up,' and Nellie was reassured.

Maggie was worried about her husband at this time. The weather had been raw and foggy for weeks and now it had turned bitterly cold with a threat of snow. Johnny had been off work several times, racked by coughing during the foggy weather, and now Maggie worried about him being out in the cold and wet.

'It's too cold to snow,' she said to Nellie and Nellie agreed.

She too was suffering in the bad weather. The new cleaning job was proving to be very hard and she often thought wistfully of her early days at the Duncan house, before things went wrong for the family.

A housekeeper, Mrs Grogan, was in charge and Nellie described her to Katy as a real slave driver. Her hours were eight to noon but often she was kept until one or even two o'clock without any extra pay. The amount of cleaning she was expected to do meant that she came home exhausted. For the first time in her life she suffered badly with chilblains.

'I feel as if this winter'll never end,' Maggie said and Nellie agreed. Three young children in the street had died since Christmas and many more were ill. In spite of Nellie's care of him, Tommy began to cough during the night and to look pale and tired during the day.

Nellie begged goosegrease from the cook at Merton Road to rub his chest and dosed him with cod liver oil and malt in spite of his protests.

She gave some of the goosegrease to Maggie who was now desperately worried about Johnny. He was kept awake most nights with his racking cough although Maggie had put a bed in the kitchen for him.

'The damp in that bedroom'd get on anybody's chest,' she said to Nellie. 'I build up the fire so the kitchen's warm most of the night.'

Johnny had been off work several times during the winter and his fear of losing his job made him force himself to go to work no matter how ill he felt, but the morning came when he was unable to rise from the bed.

Maggie had rubbed him with goosegrease and made infusions of friar's balsam for him, and Nellie had brought a bottle of Owbridge's cough mixture but nothing seemed to ease him. Maggie had even brought in a doctor but he could do nothing to help the sick man and Johnny said the bottle of cough mixture he prescribed was not as good as the Owbridge's.

Maggie's two daughters, Susan now eighteen and Josie sixteen, were a great help to Maggie at this time, sharing the nursing and comforting both their parents.

Nellie also shared the nursing at night as she worked only two mornings a week and the girls worked full time in Tate and Lyle's sugar works. They were sure that their father would recover but Nellie and Maggie could see how he slipped back a little every day.

Finally as the two women watched over him one night Johnny opened his eyes.

'Maggie,' he gasped.

She bent over him. 'Yes, lad, I'm here,' she murmured.

'Maggie,' he wheezed again. 'Will you get a priest, girl?'

'Right away, son,' Maggie promised.

'I'll go,' Nellie offered and Maggie came to the door with her.

'Tell them he was born and reared a Catholic until his mam died when he was ten but he hasn't bothered since,' she said.

Although it was only four o'clock in the morning several people were already astir in the street, dockers and women who were ships' cleaners. Nellie hurried to the presbytery after answering a question from one of the women and by the time she returned the news had run round the street.

Women were at their doors and the priest followed a few minutes later.

'Poor girl. God help her,' Bella said loudly, expressing the sympathy they all felt for Maggie.

The two girls had come downstairs and they all crowded into the scullery to leave Johnny alone with the priest. A little later the priest knocked on the door.

'We will all say the prayers for the dying,' he said gently. 'John has made his confession and received Extreme Unction.'

Nellie noticed that the bedclothes had been turned back from Johnny's feet and his feet touched with oil.

It all seemed dreamlike and unreal to her as Susan ran upstairs for the young boys who came down rubbing sleepy eyes. They all gathered round the bed as the priest recited prayers and they answered, 'Amen.'

Johnny was quiet now. His struggles for breath which had made his listeners feel that they were choking too had ended and his breathing was quiet and shallow. The priest raised his hand in a blessing of all the family and when Nellie opened the door as he left she slipped into her own house.

She felt that she would be intruding as the family gathered round their husband and father for what must be his last hours. It was less than an hour later when Josie knocked on her door.

'Me dad's gone, Mrs Meadows,' she said simply and Nellie drew her indoors and wept with her.

Later she went to sit with Maggie and found her calm and resigned. 'He'd suffered enough, Nell,' she said. 'All these years since 1916. Nobody knows. And that time we was on the Parish. It nearly finished him, Nell. He was a proud man and then seeing our Richie with the rickets and Henry bronchial and not being able to do nothing to get them food and that.'

'But he'd had his job a good few years,' Nellie said. 'He was made up about that.'

Maggie twisted a handkerchief in her fingers. 'You know before you come in last night, Nell. He had a good spell and d'you know what he said?' She began to cry and Nellie put her arm round her. 'He was just laying there holding me hand,' Maggie sobbed, 'and he suddenly said, "I've done it anyhow, girl. I've last out until some of them are reared to look after you." That was my Johnny. Always looking out for me.'

She sobbed bitterly and Nellie cried with her, and then as they dried their eyes Nellie said consolingly, 'Anyway, he had a peaceful death with all his family round him the way he would have wanted.'

'I got a shock when he asked for the priest,' Maggie said. 'I knew he was born and reared a Catholic but he never said nothing about it. You was good to go for the priest, Nell. That's why I sent Josie to tell you right away.'

'She's a good girl,' Nellie said. 'They're both good girls.'

'Aye, but Josie's the one I'll rely on,' Maggie said. 'Our Susie's gone to pieces. Mind you, Johnny doted on her and she thought the sun shone outa him. She's just told me that lad she's started courting is a Catholic. Said she'd told her dad but she never said nothing to me.'

'Maybe that's what made Johnny think of the priest?' Nellie suggested.

'Maybe. Me mam would turn in her grave, the idea of a Catholic priest in the house, but I don't bother about nothing like that,' Maggie said. 'I had them all christened, like, but after—it took me all me time to scrat and scrape to keep them alive, never mind worrying about the like of that.'

Nellie encouraged Maggie to talk. She knew that the reality of Johnny's death had not yet reached her and she wanted to postpone the moment as long as possible.

'I don't bother neither,' she said. 'I don't

326

know if I was christened even. I don't think me mam would've bothered but maybe me dad did.'

'Your mam wasn't afraid of God or man, was she? You might have been done before you come here though. So you wouldn't know where to find out. Where you was christened,' she explained, seeing Nellie looked bewildered.

'But I thought I was born here,' Nellie said.

'No, you come when you was a baby. Bobby was born here,' Maggie said.

'So that's what Ada Ginley was getting at,' Nellie exclaimed. 'She said I didn't even belong round here.'

'Your ma and Janey come here when you was new born,' Maggie said, 'from somewhere but nobody never found out where.' She laughed. 'They didn't fancy asking Janey or your ma.'

They were both silent for a moment thinking their own thoughts when Maggie sighed.

'I can't get over Johnny asking for the priest. I'm glad I got him though. Seemed to give him ease, didn't it?'

'I thought it did,' Nellie said. 'He seemed nice, the priest. I was just thinking of Ada Ginley and her husband fighting over religion and they never go near church.'

'You wasn't here when she had the fight with her ma-in-law, was you, Nell?' Maggie said.

Nellie shook her head and Maggie went on, 'It was when her first boy was born. The old woman sneaked a bottle of holy water into the house under her shawl and as soon as Ada turned her back she baptised the baby

Michael. When Ada realised, there was skin and hair flying.'

'But is that legal, like?' Nellie said doubtfully.

'I dunno. Ada'd already had him done William. I've never seen a fight like it, Nell. Everyone in a ring round them and they was rolling all over the road, biting and scratching and tearing each other's hair out. But the funniest thing, when people was taking his mother away she turned back. Her bodice was in shreds, like, and her hair hanging in rats' tails, not a hairpin left in it, and her face was all scratched and bloody.'

'And what was Ada like?' asked Nellie.

'The same,' Maggie said briefly. 'But the old woman turned back and shouted, "Well at least I've saved his immortal soul." The street was up. She was like Sarah Siddons.'

They were smiling when Susan came down-stairs and looked reproachfully at her mother. Misery seemed to sweep over Maggie, and Nellie stood up. Susan came to the door with her and Nellie said hurriedly, 'I was just talking, like, trying to distract your mam's mind a bit. Talking about people in the street who fall out over religion.'

Susan said nothing, staring stonily at Nellie and obviously thinking that nothing could distract *her* thoughts from her father. Nellie hoped that Josie would soon be home.

Nellie felt guilty because she had spent less time with Maggie since she had become so friendly with Katy and Gertie but she resolved to do all she could to help Maggie with her loss.

Johnny's coffin was placed in Maggie's parlour, which they had never been able to use because anything left in it was mouldy within weeks. 'The damp and the cold won't bother me poor lad now,' Maggie said sadly.

Nellie was surprised to learn that Johnny was only thirty-nine years old. 'The same age as meself,' Maggie said. They had both looked so much older.

The day after the funeral Katy's son was born after an easy labour. Bella and Katy's older sister Queenie attended her and they were both there when Nellie went to see the baby.

'Isn't he beautiful?' Nellie exclaimed, cuddling the handsome little boy.

'Yes, not red or anything,' Bella said. She shook with laughter. 'He doesn't take after me, but mind you, our Katy doesn't neither, do you, girl? Queenie's more like me. Falling into flesh an' all.'

Queenie, a woman almost as big as her mother, only laughed, her flesh quivering as Bella's did. Bella had taken the baby and was kissing and cuddling him and Katy said, 'Just look at her. Anyone'd think it was her first grandchild. How many is it now, Ma?'

'He makes twenty-three, but never you mind, our Katy. Every one's as precious.'

'Aye, while they're like that,' Queenie said. 'But give him a few years, Mam, and you'll be clouting him and calling him a bloody nuisance.'

They all laughed, but after Nellie left she found it hard not to envy Katy. To have a lovely little boy like that and her mother and sister to rejoice with her and to have her husband home every night. Nellie thought of when Tommy was born and the fears and worries which had clouded her joy in him.

Tommy's cough had cleared and he seemed quite fit again, but Nellie was growing tired of hearing about Miss Helsby. She was still undecided about the wisdom of allowing Tommy to be trained to speak differently to his parents and neighbours, and although she had mentioned the lessons in a letter to Sam, she had received no letters from him for weeks.

The next day was bitterly cold and Nellie was shivering when she arrived for work at Merton Road. The cook would have given her a hot drink but the housekeeper was waiting for her.

'Get those steps done immediately,' she said to Nellie. 'They're a disgrace. Absolutely filthy.'

'But I cleaned them yesterday, Mrs Grogan,' Nellie said.

'I didn't ask what you did yesterday. I'm telling you what to do today. This minute,' the woman snapped.

I wonder what's gone wrong with her, Nellie thought, but she collected her bucket and scrubbing brush and went to scrub the flight of shallow steps below the front door.

She had barely started when large hailstones began to fall and she picked up her bucket and cloth.

Mrs Grogan appeared in the doorway. 'What do you think you're doing?' she demanded.

'Finish those steps at once.'

Nellie obeyed, her teeth chattering with cold and the hailstones bouncing off her as she scrubbed. She felt chilled to the bone when she was finally able to empty her bucket and go in to the house for further work. The cook was waiting for her with a steaming cup of cocoa.

'Get that down you,' she ordered. 'That one's got a cob on about something, but she's not taking it out on you. Doing the steps in hailstones!'

Nellie gratefully drank the hot cocoa and ate a piece of currant cake. There must be something about me and cooks, she thought. I always get on well with them.

The hot drink revived her but the housekeeper continued to chivvy her about all morning, and to find her jobs such as scrubbing the floor of a stone-flagged unheated storeroom, and cleaning windows inside and outside. She was glad to escape at nearly two o'clock but she had promised to visit Meg on her way home and to do some shopping for her. Meg's pregnancy was not going well. She had been troubled with morning sickness and now she had developed a hoarse cough.

Nellie found her crouched over the fire wrapped in a shawl, sipping a hot blackcurrant drink, and coughing continuously.

'It's bronchitis,' she told Nellie. 'Bob fetched the doctor in last night. He told me to stay in bed but I don't cough so much when I'm up.'

Nellie replenished the coal scuttle and went for the shopping that Meg needed, then made

331

tea for herself and Meg. She was alarmed by her feverishly bright eyes and red cheeks but Meg told her that she had often had bronchitis before and it would soon pass.

Meg was interested to hear of Katy's handsome baby and told Nellie that she hoped that her baby was a boy. 'Just like Bob,' she said fondly. She said that she felt much better after Nellie's visit but Nellie still felt worried about her as she walked home.

Was it only such a short time ago that she had felt so happy, she thought. Lately everything seemed to be going wrong. The weather, the job, illness and death and no letters from Sam. Surely she would be told if something had happened to him.

She was annoyed that both Tommy and Janey were late home and the meal she had prepared was spoiling. 'Where have you been?' she demanded when Tommy came in.

'Miss Helsby said we could stay behind and she'd learn—er—teach us some more. Speech training she calls it and she's learning us manners too.'

'She should learn you to think about your mother,' Nellie said. 'Staying on like that and me worrying. Your tea getting ruined an' all.'

'I'm sorry, Mam,' Tommy said, looking crestfallen. He soon recovered his spirits and chattered to Nellie about Miss Helsby's teaching. 'Around the rugged rock the ragged rascal ran,' he declaimed.

'Wharra you on about?' Nellie said irritably.

'It's what we've got to say to practice,'

Tommy explained. 'And we've gorra stand up when a lady comes in and take our caps off when we go indoors.'

'Daft capers,' Nellie snorted. They had both finished their dried-up hash and Tommy picked up the plates to take them to the sink.

He hesitated for a moment. 'You know when you finish, like, Mam? Miss Helsby says the knife and fork should be laid side by side to show that you have finished your meal, not just put down anyhow,' he said in a sing-song voice, obviously quoting the teacher verbatim.

Nellie gaped at him for a moment then suddenly her temper flared. Her exhausting day, her sorrow at Johnny's death, the worry about Meg and the lack of letters from Sam all came to a head and she jumped to her feet and gave Tommy a stinging blow to his head.

'It's a pity about Miss Helsby,' she shouted, 'telling me what to do. The likes of us don't need no messing about with knives to show we're finished. We're finished when there's no bloody food left on our plates, but she wouldn't know nothing about that, would she? Or the struggle to purrit there neither.'

'Ar eh, Mam,' Tommy protested, hurriedly taking the plates away while Nellie sat fuming.

She moved to sit beside the fire, rattling the poker around the bars of the grate and working herself into a greater fury.

'That settles it. You're not having no more of these lessons. Learning you to turn your nose up at your mam and dad. Your poor dad that's kept you in comfort all these years. Slaving away and then leaving himself short very often, buying you ganseys and boots and toys no less. An' the life he had when he was your age.'

'I never said nothing about Dad,' Tom began, astounded by the fury he had unleashed, but Nellie swept on unheeding.

'You're getting a right upstart. When I think of them Doyles and a few more round here like them. Never know a full belly and being belted and battered every night be the father. We've been too soft with you. Maybe some of that battering woulda done you more good. Learning you to look down on your own flesh and blood.'

She began to cry and Tommy timidly put his arm round her shoulders. 'Don't cry, Mam. I won't go no more,' he said. He flinched back as Nellie raised her head, but she only put her arms round him.

'It's all right, lad,' she said drying her eyes. 'I don't know what came over me. It's all just got too much. Make a pot of tea, Tom, but be careful, lad.'

The boy said no more about Miss Helsby for the rest of the evening but before he went to bed Nellie told him he could carry on with the lessons. 'You can still go back early at dinnertime,' she said, 'but you've gotta tell me if she wants you after school. And don't be trying to learn me. She's supposed to be just learning you them things.'

Later when she lay in bed herself Nellie marvelled at her outburst at teatime. I must've been bottling it all up, like, she thought, and poor Tom got the brunt of it. And the way I carried on about his teacher and it's good of her to give up her own dinner hour and after school for them lads.

Her anger seemed to have purged her of her misery and she felt cheerful again, although nothing had changed. Two days later a large bundle of letters arrived from Sam to give her real cause to feel happy.

Sam was delighted with the two letters he had received from Tommy, and enclosed a letter for him in one to Nellie. She read the letter to Tom first.

Dear Son,
I hope this finds you well as it leaves me at present. I was made up with your letters. You done well with them marks. It is hot and sticky here. You could do with it at home. We seen monkeys hanging off trees be there tails. I have a lot to tell you.
Your Loving Father.
PS Look after your mam.

Nellie's eyes filled with tears. Ah God, she thought. The way Sam must have struggled to think of something to tell Tommy. He must have been that made up with Tommy's letters, and then saying about looking after me.

Her own letters were more stilted but in one of them he told her that one of his mates had died of a poisoned foot. 'A fellow from Elwy Street,' he wrote. 'We took on a lad I used to know from the *Akbar*, said he missed his ship because a witch doctor put a spell on him. He is a real case. We have a good laugh.'

Sam had told her in an earlier letter about Billy Olafson and she knew that George Adams was with him so she was happy that Sam had such good mates, but sad to learn of the man from Elwy Street. I wonder is he married? she thought, trying to imagine how she would feel if she heard such news about Sam.

Tommy was wildly excited when he read his letter. 'The gear,' he shouted. 'I'm *dying* for me dad to come home, Mam. D'yer think he'll be long?'

'Only about another six months,' Nellie said, but seeing the boy look downcast she added quickly, 'It could be sooner than that.'

They went together to see Meg, and Nellie was pleased to see that she looked much better. Her cough had almost gone, but Meg said that she had been worried about Nellie, more than herself.

'I've had bronchitis before and I knew I'd soon get over it but you looked worn out that day, Nell. Frozen to the bone too.'

'I was,' Nellie admitted. 'I thought I'd never get warm again. That one making me scrub the steps in the hailstones. I'm back there tomorrow. I wonder what she'll have lined up for me.'

'I wouldn't stay,' Meg declared. 'I'm sure you could do something else.'

Tommy was playing with Meg's kitten in the corner of the room and Nellie glanced at him and lowered her voice, 'You should've heard the way I carried on at him,' she said. 'And all over

336

nothing really. He didn't know what had come over me. I was sorry after I let fly at him, but I was that fed up that night.'

'Probably all just got on top of you,' Meg said, 'but you'll feel better now you've heard from Sam, won't you?'

Tommy had brought his letter to show Meg and now he carried the kitten to her. 'I wonder will me dad bring me a monkey?' he said.

'Not likely,' Nellie exclaimed. 'I'm not having no monkey in the house.'

'Well, could we just have a kitten instead, Mam?' he wheedled.

The two women looked at each other and laughed. 'I think you're a bit of a crafty monkey yourself,' Meg said.

'Can I, Mam?' Tommy persisted.

Nellie said firmly, 'No. I've got enough with cats yowling round the house all night after Janey's fish. A cat'd be drove mad anyhow in the house with the smell of the fish.'

'How's Maggie Nolan?' Meg asked.

'The funeral's tomorrow,' Nellie said. 'And d'you know what? He's getting buried at Ford!'

'The Catholic cemetery?' Meg exclaimed. 'Oh God, she'll be the talk of the wash-house, won't she?'

'She says it's what Johnny would want with him asking for the priest, like, but there's something else she only told me on the quiet. She had to let her policies lapse when they had hard times. She took out more when things got better but they wouldn't insure Johnny the way he was. She'd have had to find all the money for the funeral herself.'

'That'd take some doing,' Meg exclaimed.

'I know. When they come and told her there was space in Johnny's mam's grave in Ford it solved her problem, like, because some second cousin of Johnny's says she'll pay all the expenses.'

'She must be well off or else she had him well salted,' Meg observed.

'Maggie says she wished she'd knew about her when they was desperate. She always thought Johnny had no family and so did he. Maggie's brother and his wife won't come to the funeral though.'

'You'd think he'd put his pride in his pocket,' Meg said. 'His only sister and her with no sons old enough to look after her.'

'Her girls are good though,' Nellie said. 'I never seen much of them once they was grown up until now.'

'It's not the same as a grown-up son though, is it?' Meg said. 'How old are they?'

'Sixteen and eighteen,' Nellie said. 'The eldest one's proper bossy but maybe it's just as well. They only used to be in for their tea and out again once they started work but they've stuck by Maggie now.'

Nellie suspected there would be some comment from Ada Ginley, especially after she went in the funeral car with Maggie Nolan, and it soon came. A few days later Nellie turned into the street Ada Ginley stepped out of her house with a bundle of washing on her head.

'Here she is,' she shouted as she approached

338

Nellie. 'The one that fetched Father Bunloaf to the Nolans. Went to a pape's funeral at Ford an' all. Maybe yer a bit of a redneck yourself.'

Nellie had walked past with her head high but at that she turned back. 'No I'm not, and I'm not a lemon pelter either. I've got more sense.' She would have liked to add a comment about people fighting over religion who never went to church but she knew it was wiser to beat a retreat before Ada recovered from her surprise.

She was delighted with herself for answering back, and as soon as Gertie returned from work she hurried over to tell her.

'I was just going to come over for you,' Gertie exclaimed. 'I think Prudence will tell your fortune tonight.'

'Is Lettie out?' Nellie whispered.

'Yes and she's only just gone. To Belmont Road to see about a sewing machine or something but she'll be a while. Hang on.' Gertie went to the parlour and came back to say, 'Prudence says give her ten minutes to compose her mind and she wants you to clear your mind too.'

Nellie found this difficult and she was nervous when she was ushered in to Mrs Gilligan, but relaxed as soon as the woman took her hand. She smiled at Nellie then bent her head and studied the palm of Nellie's left hand closely.

She said nothing but eventually released the hand and drew a piece of velvet from a crystal ball which stood on the table between them. She cupped her hands round the crystal ball, still not speaking, but Nellie felt no impatience only a feeling of peace and tranquillity.

At last Prudence spoke. 'I feel fear, fear. Your life has been dominated by fear. Even now.' She stopped and gazed into the crystal. 'Birth and death then a dark cloud of hatred and bitterness. I see a tall woman, or is it a man? Red hair.'

'My mother,' Nellie whispered but Prudence shook her head violently.

'No, no, not your mother. Cleanse your heart of bitterness. A dark cloud but a golden thread stretching through your life. Stretching almost to breaking point but time, time, then it will draw you back. Violence has cast a shadow and will breed violence.'

Prudence took Nellie's hand again then lay back in her chair and closed her eyes. 'You must be strong,' she murmured. 'Great fear and sorrow and misunderstanding. Water, much water, then sunshine and joy. I see a T which will bring joy. Riches and honours.'

She was silent again and Nellie thought she had finished and was about to withdraw her hand when Prudence spoke again.

'Be strong,' she murmured. 'Keep faith and hope. Fight fear. Death will come and much will be made clear.'

'Whose death?' Nellie said urgently, but Prudence only opened her eyes and smiled at her vaguely. She sat up, still smiling dreamingly, and covered the crystal and Nellie felt dismissed.

Gertie was waiting for her and drew her into the scullery. 'Well?' she said eagerly. 'What did she say?'

'She said Tommy was going to bring me joy and riches and honour,' Nellie whispered. 'And she said my life had been dominated by fear.'

'That was true enough, wasn't it?' Gertie said. 'About the fear, and it was good news about Tommy. What else did she say?'

'I can't think properly. Something about a red-haired woman, not me mam, and a golden thread. I'll have to think but I'm made up about Tommy,' Nellie said.

She was anxious to get home and think over what had been said but she was grateful to Gertie and knew that she was proud to have arranged the fortune telling.

'Thanks very much, Gert,' she whispered. 'I'll try to sort it out in me mind and come and tell you all about it.'

Tommy was in the kitchen when she returned home and anxious to tell her about his lesson with Miss Helsby, but Nellie told him impatiently to go out and play. She wanted to remember and think over all Prudence had said and find the meaning of it, and she took her knitting and sat down by the fire.

Violence casting a shadow and a dark cloud of bitterness, she thought. That must have been Leadbetter's violence, and with a stab of fear she remembered that Prudence had also said that it would breed violence. The bitterness and hatred must be what I felt about him, although she seemed to be talking about the red-haired woman with that.

Who did she know with red hair? Nobody, only me mam and our Bobby, she thought. She said it wasn't me mam and I'm not likely to fall out with Bob. Could it be Mrs Grogan? She was grey now but she might have been red haired, but then I've only known her a few months.

She was interrupted by a knock on the door and Gertie came in. 'I couldn't wait,' she said. 'I was dying to know all she told you. We had a narrow escape. Lettie came in just after you went, wrong address or something, and she was raging. She said her mother was like a wet rag and had I been letting my friends pester her?'

'Oh gosh, Gertie, I hope she didn't carry on at her mother,' Nellie said. 'I mean, it's good of Prudence to do it for us, isn't it?'

'No, she wouldn't shout at her mam. She wouldn't take no notice anyhow if she did. It's just that it takes a lot out of Prudence and that makes Lettie mad.'

'I've been sitting here trying to think about what she said, Gert,' Nellie said. 'It wasn't straightforward like with you and Katy, only that about Tommy and about me life being dominated by fear.'

'That was true about you being nervous and frightened, like, wasn't it?' Gertie said.

'God, yes, all my life. I was always frightened of me mam and the other kids and the school board and everyone. Some of the people where I took the washing. The other maid in me last place, remember Lily we met in the queue? She said I was frightened of me own shadow.'

'And Prudence couldn't have knew that, could she?' Gertie said. 'Come on, what else did she say?'

'She said about birth and death and a dark shadow of bitterness and hatred,' Nellie said.

'That must've been Johnny Nolan and Katy's baby, and the dark shadow Ada Ginley and that lot carrying on at you,' Gertie said.

Nellie agreed rather doubtfully, but not really believing the explanation. 'She said something about a golden cord stretching almost to breaking point and drawing me back,' Nellie said. 'And a death and all would be made clear.'

'She talks lovely, doesn't she?' Gertie said. 'Whose gonna die? Did she say?'

'No, I asked her but she just smiled. I think she was finished then, like,' said Nellie.

They heard sounds in the parlour and Gertie stood up hastily as Janey came through to the kitchen, darting a malevolent glance at her. 'I'll see you later, Nell,' Gertie said slipping away.

'What did that soft mare want?' Janey demanded.

'She called over to see me,' Nellie said calmly. Fight fear, she thought. I'll start with this old faggot.

She thought often of all she had been told by Prudence during the following days, but she was still puzzled by much of it. Gertie's explanations seemed too glib.

Only the words about her life of fear and about the future in store for Tommy were clear, and sometimes with a sinking heart she thought of the words about violence which she had told to no one. 'Violence will breed violence.'

CHAPTER 18

Sam felt that he was having a good trip although the tropical heat was affecting several of the crew and the work was harder as a result. He liked most of the men on his watch, particularly Billy Olafson and of course George.

Sam found a ready listener in Billy to his stories about Tommy and his cleverness, and Nellie's skill at homemaking. In return he listened to Billy's tales about his wife and children, although in his heart Sam was convinced that *his* wife and *his* son were far superior to anyone else.

The letters from Tommy were taken out and read and reread until they were dog eared, and shown to anyone who might have missed seeing them on an earlier occasion.

Wherever they put in he bought small gifts for Nellie and Tommy, until his shipmates joked, 'Isn't yer locker full yet, Sam?'

He bought beautifully carved ships and canoes for Tommy and walnut shells fully rigged to make tiny ships, as well as whistles and drums and masks.

For Nellie he bought crudely painted pots and dishes and bowls in inlaid metal, and baskets woven from rushes. When ashore with George and Billy at Sierra Leone they were pestered to buy large bags of soft dyed leather but

Billy and George refused. 'I'm not spending no more,' Billy said. 'These fellers'd have the shirt off your back.'

George refused firmly but Sam lingered. 'Be handy for her messages, one of these, wouldn't it?' he said, and the seller renewed his entreaties for them to buy.

'A bit posh for messages,' George said. 'The old American cloth's all right for spuds and that,' and they walked away.

Neither of his friends was surprised when Sam suddenly turned back to buy one of the bags. 'He's soft about his missus, isn't he?' Billy said to George as they waited for Sam to finish haggling. 'What's she like?'

'A real nice little woman,' George said. 'Very quiet and ladylike. She was in good service and she keeps herself and the lad very nice.'

'I suppose it's easy for her with just the one,' Billy said. 'My missus never has nothing for herself be the time she's rigged the kids out in boots and clobber from Paddy's Market. As long as she's got something to put in their bellies she doesn't care.'

'Aye, well, Nellie does a bit of cleaning an' all, so they do all right,' George said.

Sam rejoined them carrying one of the bags. 'I got him down to half what he was asking,' he excused himself, 'too good to leave at that price.'

'You're a soft ha'p'orth, Sam,' Billy said affectionately and Sam felt none of the anger which such a comment from someone like Hagan would have aroused. As the ship turned for home, Sam looked forward eagerly to presenting his gifts to Nellie and Tommy.

Tommy had moved up from Miss Helsby's class but he still went for the speech training on two nights a week after school. The other boys who had started with Tommy found various reasons for not attending the classes but Tommy enjoyed them.

Some of the boys had left because they were mocked by their schoolmates, but there was a core of obstinacy in Tommy which made him persevere in spite of the taunts. Despite his quiet manner he was always ready to fight, and the combination of his sturdiness and the knowledge that he had been trained by his father made other boys wary of him.

His speech improved rapidly and he soon lost his nasal tone and the exaggerated diction of his first attempts. Miss Helsby began to alter his habits too. Every night he thoroughly washed his face and body as far as the waistband of his trousers, then his feet and legs in a bowl of water in the scullery.

He had always had a bath on Saturday nights in the zinc bath before the fire, but one Saturday he asked his mother for twopence to go to the public baths.

'What d'you want to go there for?' Nellie demanded. 'You've very near got yourself washed away already.'

'I want to have a good soak, Mam,' Tommy muttered. 'Miss Helsby said we should try to have a proper bath.'

'You *do* have a proper bath every Saturday,' Nellie said indignantly, 'and you get a clean gansey and socks every Monday morning an' all.'

'I know, Mam,' Tommy said humbly and Nellie relented.

'All right, but don't think I'm made of money,' she said.

She was more ready to encourage Tom because the previous day when washing her hair she had felt the lump from the stitches which she had received. That doctor didn't care how he done that, she thought. All of them there turning their noses up at me and treating me like dirt. She remembered her humiliation and her resolve that Tommy would always be treated with respect, and it made her feel more warmly towards Miss Helsby's efforts.

If she learns him to speak nice and to behave proper *nobody* won't be able to look down on him, she thought.

Yet sometimes she wondered uneasily what Sam would think of it all. Tommy had started taking some of the blacking she used for the grate to polish his boots every night, and he used a rag dipped in salt to clean his teeth.

Sometimes Nellie watched him, wondering if she had started more than she had intended. Was Tommy going to grow away from them? Perhaps learn to look down on his parents? But she was reassured when she heard him in the street with his mates, yelling to them with his careful speech forgotten.

I'll tell him to talk ordinary when Sam comes

home and to drop all this messing with his teeth and his boots, she decided. He's a sensible lad, and he'll probably be just ordinary with his dad, like with his mates. She had not heard from Sam since she had told him about the lessons.

The school holidays had started but Nellie was not now as free to take Tommy out so he was spending more time with his friends. Meg was having a difficult pregnancy and Nellie spent as much time as possible with her. She also kept Maggie company whenever possible during the day, although Susan and Josie arranged that one or the other of them would be with her every night.

Nellie's cleaning mornings had been increased to four, so her days were full, but she still went out with Gertie twice a week to the cinema. Her time passed so quickly that she was amazed one day when Rose Adams called and said that she had not seen Nellie for over a month.

'I thought I'd just slip round and see if you were all right,' Rose said, and Nellie felt guilty.

'I don't know where the time goes, Rose,' she said. 'Of course, I'm working four mornings now and then with Bob's wife not being well—'

'Never mind. "Better to wear out than rust out," as my mam used to say,' Rose said with a smile. 'I think the lads are having a good trip this time.'

'Yes, and they're homeward bound now,' Nellie said eagerly.

'Aye, doesn't it seem a long time since they went?' Rose said. 'I don't like long trips. You just get used to each other again then it's time for them to be off.'

'I think Sam'll see a big change in Tommy,' Nellie said. 'It's not just that he's grown but he seems more grown up, like. Not a little lad any more.'

'Aye, they're not babies for long,' Rose said with a sigh. 'It must be nice for you having your brother back in Liverpool though.'

'We're worried about Bob's wife though,' Nellie said. 'She had bronchitis in the winter and she got over it but the cough never left her. She's as thin as a rail too, even though she's expecting.'

Although Rose said all the right things Nellie felt that she was not really attending to what she was saying.

Suddenly a strange thought crossed her mind. 'Rose, you haven't come to bring me bad news, have you?' she exclaimed in alarm.

'No, no, nothing like that,' Rose said. She hesitated then put her hand on Nellie's.

'Jealousy's an awful thing, girl,' she said. 'And there's a few jealous of you.'

'Of me?' Nellie said astounded. 'But why, Rose?'

'Oh, because Sam's a good husband. Because you've got your little job. Mostly because, well—you keep yourself nice and tidy and you've only got the one child,' Rose said.

'Well, that's not doing them no harm, is it?' Nellie said indignantly. 'Who was it anyhow, Rose?'

Rose shrugged her shoulders and grimaced.

'That crowd in the wash-house, girl. That's the place for jangle, believe me. They didn't see me because I was round the other side, but I soon came round and gave them what for.'

Nellie stood up and began to move the ornaments on the mantelpiece about in an agitated manner. 'What were they saying?' she asked, and when Rose hesitated she said, 'You might as well tell me, Rose, or I'll be imagining all sorts.'

'They was talking about you keeping yourself nice, like, then one of them said they couldn't put nothing on *their* backs because of finding enough food for the kids but it was all right for you with only one.'

Rose stopped but Nellie said nothing so she went on, 'Another one said they was respectable married women and they didn't need to be dolling themselves up. You know how it is, Nell, one word borrows another and then they say more than they mean. Someone come out with a tale about seeing you and Gertie out with Martha Miller.'

'Good God. We met her one night when we was going to the pictures and walked along with her,' Nellie exclaimed.

'I thought it would be something like that,' Rose said. 'The thing is, Nell—you know Martha's on the game, like?'

'Martha is?' Nellie exclaimed.

'Yes. Hadn't you never heard? Her feller beat her up last time he come home because of it, but she's back on it. Reckons it's *his* fault because he never sends her no money and she's got the kids to keep.'

Nellie sat down. 'So they're saying nobody can't walk along with her, even. Is that it?' she said.

Rose leaned over and put her hand on Nellie's knee. 'They're saying worse than that, girl,' she said gravely. 'Making out you and Gertie was going with her. On the game, like.'

Nellie looked stunned for a moment, then as she realised the meaning of Rose's words she screamed and jumped to her feet.

'Now don't get excited, girl,' Rose said. 'They didn't believe what they was saying. Like I said, one word borrowed another and be the time they all put their penn'orth in—' She shrugged.

Nellie's face was scarlet and she seemed to find it difficult to breathe. 'I'll—I'll— Tell me their names, Rose. The bloody liars. I'll go and see them.'

'It wouldn't do no good, girl,' Rose soothed her. 'I don't know properly who they were. They all mizzled away when I started on them because they was ashamed. They knew it was all lies.'

Nellie sat down again and began to cry. 'Why, Rose? I never do no one no harm that I know of. Why do they turn on me like that?'

'Jealousy, girl, like I said,' Rose replied. 'I only told you so you and Gertie can watch your step and I thought you might hear it from someone else and get upset.'

'I'll have to tell Gertie,' Nellie wept, but Rose advised her to say nothing. 'It was just a bit of jangle to pass the time in the wash-house,' she said. 'And Gertie won't come across any of them women. Anyhow they'll keep their gobs shut after what I said to them. Only, that Ada Ginley was there and I thought she might say something to you, when you was in a crowd, like.'

'Thanks, Rose,' Nellie said. 'I don't know why people are so rotten.'

'Only a few, Nell,' the older woman said. 'You've got plenty of good friends, don't forget.'

A thought struck Nellie and she looked up, her eyes wide. 'Rose, what if Sam hears it?' she said in alarm.

'He won't, girl. Be the time he's home that lot'll be jangling about someone else,' Rose reassured her.

Nevertheless Nellie felt upset for the rest of the day, and for many days afterwards. The thought that anyone could say such things about her just out of jealousy made her look suspiciously at everyone she met, apart from her close friends. Were they one of those who had jangled about her and made out she was a street walker?

She was touchy and bad tempered with Tom and it was difficult for her to show a cheerful face to Maggie, or to Meg when she went to see her.

She was growing very fond of Meg and very concerned about her thinness and her persistent cough. Meg herself made light of it. 'It's an old friend,' she joked. 'It's been with me for years.'

She and Bobby were very happy, looking

forward to the birth of their child and gradually furnishing their little house. 'The only fly in the ointment is the neighbours,' Meg confided to Nellie. 'I think some of them resent us getting this house, because they had their eye on it for one of their family. They complain about everything we do.'

'What sort of things?' Nellie asked.

'Bob putting a new window frame in the back bedroom, for one. It was rotten and he could get the wood cheap but next door said the landlord would expect everyone to do their own repairs because of that.'

'I wouldn't let that worry you,' Nellie said. 'They're only jealous. I have a bit of that with some of them in our street. Just because I've only got Tom and they've got strings of kids. And because I keep us tidy.'

'As if you didn't want more kids,' Meg said sympathetically. 'I think you do wonders with you and Tom and that house. I wish you could get one like this, Nell.'

'So do I,' Nellie said fervently. 'Mind you, I still wouldn't know what to do about Janey.'

'She's a problem, isn't she?' Meg said. 'How do you get on with her?'

'All right. I don't see much of her. She only has a cup of cocoa before she goes out then she has her tea with us at night,' Nellie said. 'I don't have to bother with a fire for her this weather and she's mostly in her own room. She has all sorts in and out that side door but I never see them.'

'She's a moneylender, isn't she?' Meg said.

'I've seen the two fellers she uses to put the frighteners on bad payers.'

Nellie only nodded, unwilling to tell Meg that her own mother had played that role for years. And now Janey needed two men. No wonder I was frightened of me ma, Nellie thought, recalling again the words of the fortune teller.

'Janey done me a good turn one day,' she said aloud. 'When some of them at the top end was carrying on at me. Janey come up and said she'd tell me what she knew about them.'

'And did she?' Meg asked.

Nellie shook her head. 'No, but she must of knew something because they was all frightened she'd open her mouth, you could tell.'

She picked up a carved wooden bowl from the sideboard. 'Did our Bob make this?' she asked.

'Yes, on that little lathe he showed you the other Sunday. Mind you, that's another fault with the neighbours. They moan about him working in the shed in the yard, yet he doesn't make much noise,' said Meg.

'It's a pity about them,' Nellie said indignantly. 'Mr Orlando said he had a gift for it, didn't he? He might as well use it to make a bit extra for you.'

'That fellow in the market took all he'd made but I wouldn't part with that one. That was the first,' Meg said. 'Aren't we lucky, Nell? Everything's going right for us.'

Nellie kissed her impulsively. 'I hope it always does, love,' she said.

Tommy was waiting for her at the end of the

street when she returned home. 'There's letters from me dad, Mam,' he said excitedly. 'I think there's one for me in one of them.'

'I told you they'd only been held up,' Nellie said, trying to hide her relief.

Sam wrote that the ship had put in for repairs but he expected to be home about September.

He wrote to Tommy that he had a lot of things for him and a lot to tell him, and Tommy said gleefully, 'I'll be able to take them to show Miss Helsby, won't I, Mam?'

'Miss Helsby! That's all you ever think about,' Nellie said.

Another boy had joined Tom at the speech training class, and Miss Helsby invited both boys to lunch on Saturday. Nellie's feelings about the invitation were mixed. She was proud that the teacher thought enough of Tom to ask him to her house, but afraid that it was yet another step for him away from herself and Sam.

She was determined that he would do her credit and when he returned from the public baths, lobster red as a result of his long hot soak, she had his clothes laid out ready for him. His best jersey and grey trousers and jacket which she had pressed carefully, hand-knitted socks and his best boots, shining with blacking.

'Ar eh, thanks, Mam,' Tommy said, then recollecting himself, 'That is very kind of you, Mother.'

Nellie cuffed him affectionately. 'Don't talk soft, lad. It's me, remember.'

It was quite late when Tommy returned full

of the wonders of Miss Helsby's house which she shared with her elderly mother.

'The lavvy's inside, Mam, upstairs,' he said. 'And you should see the furniture and all brass ornaments, elephants and all kinds. An' d'you know what? Her father was a ship's captain on the China run!'

'No wonder they was well off,' Nellie commented.

'And the table,' Tommy went on unheeding. 'All sorts of knives and forks and spoons and glasses. We had ginger beer in the glasses. Miss Helsby's mother said something and Miss Helsby said she wanted us to know how a table should be laid and how to behave in this situation. There was a maid too bringing dishes round and we had to take the spuds and stuff out of them.'

'I hope you didn't say spuds when you was there,' Nellie said. 'But you don't need Miss Helsby to learn you about what goes on a table. I was in good service, remember, lad. With posher people than Miss Helsby. I know how a table should be laid and I know about the food to go in them dishes and the wine for the glasses an' all.'

'I never thought of that,' Tommy said. He could see that his mother resented Miss Helsby trying to teach him things which she knew, and he began to talk about his father's return instead.

'Change your clothes, lad, and you can play out for a bit,' Nellie said, wanting to be alone.

When he had gone she sat with her knitting in her hands letting her tears fall freely. Where has he gone, my little lad? she thought. The little lad who used to cling round her neck believing she knew everything. Such a short time ago and we were all his world, me and Sam.

Had she done right to let him go to the classes? Right for Tom maybe, she thought, thinking of him as he stood tall and confident, clear skinned and healthy, speaking so easily about what he had seen. But what about me and Sam? We've lost him, our little lad. She lifted her pinafore to her eyes and cried bitterly.

Before Tommy came in again she splashed cold water on her face to hide the traces of tears and made herself a cup of tea. I should be ashamed, she thought, crying over that when I think of poor Maggie and her trouble, yet still tears welled into her eyes whenever she thought of the change in Tommy.

Nellie might have been relieved if Tommy had told her more about the visit to Miss Helsby's home. He had been disappointed and he felt that the visit had not gone as Miss Helsby had planned.

The other boy, Walter Roberts, was a newcomer to the school and although he had been eager to join Tom for the speech training and to improve himself, he was still uncouth.

Tom had been surprised that he noticed his companion's shortcomings, when Walter wiped his nose on his sleeve and gobbled his food, and that he felt a vicarious shame when Miss Helsby's mother looked outraged.

I must have learned something, he thought, or I wouldn't have noticed Walter doing that. Probably would've been doing it myself.

'Ridiculous, Henrietta,' he heard the old lady say in a low voice to Miss Helsby, 'you can't make a silk purse out of a sow's ear and I hope this display will convince you.'

Tom felt his face grow red and he was not surprised when Miss Helsby hurried him and Walter away immediately after the lunch, although he felt that it was not what she had planned.

I'll show that old one, he vowed to himself. Even if Miss Helsby stops teaching us I'll find out myself how to be posh. And someday I'll get a house like that for me mam. He said nothing of this to his mother.

Nellie made herself a cup of tea and tried to compose herself, then went to the door. Richie Nolan, now aged twelve years, and his ten-year-old brother Walter were playing with a steering cart they had made, and Henry, now fifteen, came out of the Nolans' door and greeted Nellie.

'Hello, Mrs Meadows, are you coming in to see Mam?' he asked, holding the door wide.

'Yes, I will,' said Nellie, pulling her own door closed behind her, and Henry swaggered away up the street. He now worked for the Co-operative Society as a van boy and he was proudly wearing his first pair of long trousers, his hair sleeked down with pomade.

Richie's legs were still bowed and all three

boys bore signs of their early privations, although Maggie's circumstances had been easier for some years. Nellie mentally compared them with Tommy, and thought she must point out to him how lucky he was.

Maggie had been listless and apathetic since Johnny's death but now her cheeks were flushed and her eyes bright.

'I've had murder with that Ada Ginley,' she told Nellie indignantly. 'She was carrying on about our Susan going out with that Catholic lad. I told her to keep her nose outa my family's business and look out for her own daughters. God knows they need watching.'

'Nosy faggot,' Nellie said. 'What's it got to do with her?'

'She said me mam'd turn in her grave. You know me mam used to dress the drums for the Lodge, Nell, until she fell out with them, and she never bothered no more after that. She always made sure I got churched after the kids were born and they got christened, but she never even walked with the Lodge after she fell out with them.'

'Did she know Johnny was a Catholic?' Nellie asked.

'No, because he never bothered about it until just at the last, like,' said Maggie.

Later when Nellie was alone with Josie for a moment the girl whispered, 'It done me mam the world of good having that fight with Mrs Ginley. Brightened her up, like.'

'What'll happen with your Susan?' Nellie whispered.

'I think she'll turn Catholic,' Josie said. 'She likes the lad.'

'Well, in a way it's in her blood, like, with your dad being Catholic,' Nellie said.

'Yes. I don't think Mam'll mind,' said Josie. 'I think it's daft all this fighting over religion, but if it bucks Mam up I'm all for it.'

Maggie came back and they said no more, but Nellie felt that Maggie had a good family who really cared about her.

I hope our Tommy would be the same with me or Sam if anything happened, she thought. We've got all our eggs in one basket.

CHAPTER 19

When Nellie next visited Meg she was surprised to hear that Bobby was negotiating to exchange houses with an elderly couple who lived in a six-roomed house.

'He heard about these people that wanted a similar house and he went to see them right away,' Meg said. 'I've been to see their house and it's real nice, Nell. Three bedrooms, a kitchen, back kitchen and parlour and a big yard at the back with a shed.'

'But won't it be a lot more rent?' Nellie said. 'I thought you were settled here.'

'We can manage the extra rent,' Meg said. 'Bob got narked about this lot next door complaining and he's not as easy going as he used to be, you know, Nell.'

'I've noticed that,' Nellie exclaimed. 'He never used to fall out with anyone and he'd always give way to people, but he's changed.'

'He's gone a bit—a bit harder,' Meg said. 'Not in a bad way, Nell. Not with me, but he stands up for himself more now. Says what he thinks to the boss but they don't seem to mind. Anyhow, he says he won't put up with this lot next door and we'll move *somewhere.*'

'And do you think you'll get this house?' Nellie asked.

'The people are coming to see this one tonight and if it suits them we'll go to see the two landlords. I want to get it settled before the baby's born, Nell. It's in Masefield Street off Peel Road so we still won't be far away from you.'

'If there's anything I can do, Meg, I will,' Nellie promised. 'You don't want to be doing any lifting and packing. I can do anything like that for you.'

Only three weeks later everything had been arranged, and true to her word Nellie went to help them to move.

The removal took place on one of the days when Nellie was due at Merton Road and she intended to ask the housekeeper for the morning off, but the cook advised against it.

'If you ask she'll say no,' she said. 'I'll tell her I've had a message that you're not well but you hope to be in tomorrow. That's the best way.'

Nellie agreed. She hated her job and only the fact that it meant she could save made her continue with it. Except for the cook the servants had changed several times since she started there.

'Nobody'll stop with this one, but she knows better than to try anything on with me,' the cook told Nellie. 'The mistress would turn in her grave if she seen the way her house was run now. She was a lovely lady. The master just doesn't care now since she died, as long as the house is kept decent.'

'He doesn't do no entertaining, does he?' Nellie said.

'No heart for it,' the cook said. 'This one's trying to worm her way in, but the day she gets her knees under his table is the day I leave. Not that she will. She's only a servant as far as he's concerned, for all her airs and graces.'

'I think I've jumped outa the frying pan into the fire,' Nellie said. 'Me last place was fine at first, but then it went bad when he got into business trouble and this is worse.'

When Nellie returned to work on the day after the removal she found the cook all agog. 'What do you think?' she began as soon as Nellie appeared. 'Bessy's scarpered.'

'The kitchenmaid?' Nellie exclaimed. 'But she seemed so quiet.'

'I know, as if butter wouldn't melt in her mouth,' the cook said. 'But Nellie, these young ones'd learn you. She got her quarter's pay two days ago then just mizzled away last night. Never said a word to nobody. I don't know how she got her box out.'

Nellie immediately thought of Mrs Taggart

concealing her bundle outside until she was ready to take it away but she said nothing. 'Good luck to the girl anyhow,' she said aloud. '*She* won't be put on same as the likes of us.'

'The quare one's fit to be tied,' the cook said gleefully. 'Poor Elsie's going mad with a gum boil, but she won't let her go to the dentist. The master's sister is coming to dinner tonight and staying the night.'

Mrs Grogan appeared at the top of the steps down to the kitchen. She ignored Elsie who was crouched beside the fire holding a bag of salt to her swollen face and glared at Nellie. 'So. You've condescended to appear,' she snapped. 'Do you think you can walk in and out as you please? Where were you yesterday?'

'I told you where she was,' the cook said before Nellie could speak. 'I give you her message.'

'Strange that the kitchenmaid disappeared the same night,' Mrs Grogan said. 'You're all in it together. All the same. The scum of the earth. No standards. Well, there are plenty of people who want the job if you won't do it properly.'

Nellie was furious. She quietly took off her sacking apron and folded it. 'Then you'd better get one of them,' she said. 'I'm not going to be spoke to like that.'

There was silence for a moment as the three women stared open mouthed at Nellie, then the housekeeper turned and flounced away.

The cook leaned against the table, shaking with laughter. 'Good for you, girl,' she said. 'The gob on her. If that rolling pin'd jumped

363

up and hit her she couldn't have got more of a shock.'

'What will you do?' Elsie asked indistinctly. Her face was so swollen that her eye was almost closed and she rocked back and forth in pain.

Nellie leaned over her. 'Never mind about me. I'll get something,' she said. 'Listen, Elsie, get your coat and I'll take you to the dental hospital.'

'Oh, I can't think with this pain,' Elsie groaned. 'Me mam'll kill me if I walk out of me job.'

'Not if she seen the way you was,' the cook said. 'You only live in Birkenhead, don't you? Why don't you go home?'

The next moment Mrs Grogan came back to the top of the stairs. 'I've decided to overlook your impertinence this time, Ellen,' she said graciously. 'As long as you promise never to repeat it.'

'Thanks, but I'm not willing to overlook yours,' Nellie said coolly. 'I'm off. I've got two days' pay owing to me.'

'You needn't imagine you'll get *that*,' the housekeeper said, turning away, her sallow face now red.

'Never even looked at me,' Elsie said resentfully. 'She wouldn't care if I dropped dead.'

'Yes, well, have sense, girl,' the cook said. 'Go with Nellie to the dental hospital and get that seen to, then go home to your mam.'

Elsie stood up. 'I'll go then, Nell, and see how I feel when they've fixed this for me.'

'I'd have gone long ago if it hadn't been for thinking of the mistress that's dead and gone. I've had enough,' the cook said. 'But this one's not getting the better of me. What I'll do, I'll go up and see the master tonight and I'll queer the pitch for Mrs High and Mighty. I'll tell him why I'm the only one left.'

'But he must know the way servants never stay here,' Nellie said.

'Gentlemen don't take no notice as long as there's *somebody* doing the work, and this one can tell a good tale,' said the cook. 'But he'll get the whole story tonight and with his sister coming he can talk it over with her. I don't think there's any love lost between her and Grogan so we'll see what we'll see. I'll make sure you get your two days, Nell. Call in tomorrow and see.'

Nellie and Elsie set off for Pembroke Place and just as they reached the dental hospital Elsie suddenly stopped and bent over the gutter. 'It's burst,' she said.

Nellie held Elsie's head, averting her eyes until Elsie finally straightened up and wiped her mouth.

'I'm not going in there now,' she said. 'I'll be all right now.'

'Your tooth will still be bad,' Nellie said, but Elsie was adamant.

'No, I'll go back and see what's happening there,' she said. 'She'll have to treat me all right now because I'm all she's got.'

Elsie's eye was still half closed and her face bruised and as they boarded the tram, Nellie looked at her.

'Nobody'd think that a gum boil done that,' she said. 'You look as if you've been battered.'

'I'd sooner have been battered than that,' Elsie said. 'I never got a wink of sleep last night.'

'Then don't let that one work you too hard,' Nellie advised. 'Mind you, I don't think Cook will let her. I think she's got the upper hand now.'

'What will you do, Nell?' Elsie asked.

'I'm not worried,' Nellie said. 'I can live on me husband's money and I've got a few ideas.'

She got off at the next stop and walked through to see Meg.

One of the ideas she had spoken about had come from Meg and it had made her more ready to throw up her job than she might otherwise have been. Meg had told her that she had been on a charabanc outing with Bob in the early days of her pregnancy and they had stopped at a small transport café.

'We'd all taken sandwiches but the driver went in for a pie,' she said. 'It was a general shop as well so I went in for sweets and I got talking to the woman. The pies were on the counter and they smelled so tasty I bought a couple. She said a local woman made them for her and she sold dozens to fellows off wagons and carts and that. Why don't you do something like that, Nell?'

'But where would I sell them?' Nellie said doubtfully.

'There's lots of places fellows stop on their

way to the docks,' Meg said. 'You'd do well, Nell. The woman had barmcakes as well and she said the same woman done them for her. She said she was too busy to do them herself and it was true. She never stopped serving all the time I was in there. A proper little goldmine it was.'

Today Meg was lying on the sofa when Nellie arrived and she jumped to her feet looking guilty. 'All you done yesterday, Nell, and here's me lying down. I'm not pulling my weight, am I?'

'Don't be daft,' Nellie said. 'I done that yesterday so you could rest today. Plenty of time to work hard when you've got the baby.'

They laughed and as they sipped tea Nellie told Meg about events at Merton Road and brought up the subject of the pies.

'I'd like to do it but I wouldn't like asking in the shops,' she said. 'And I wouldn't know what to charge.'

'I'll come with you to ask,' Meg offered. 'And you can work out how much the stuff to make them costs and then work out what to charge. Bob'll help you. He knows how they cost a job.'

By the end of the week Nellie had worked out the cost of the pies and Bobby advised her to charge threepence ha'penny for them. 'If you haven't left yourself enough margin it'd be hard to raise the price, but if they don't sell at that you can knock a ha'penny or a penny off,' he said.

Meg advised trying to sell them to a shop at

367

the end of Knowsley Road. 'He sells bread and eggs and fruit, and fellows off the wagons and vans go in there for ciggies, so your pies would go well. I'll come with you to see him. We'll take a few for him to try free.'

'You've got a good brain for business, Meg,' Nellie exclaimed, while Bobby beamed proudly at his wife.

Before all this Nellie went back to see the cook as arranged, and found her in high good humour. 'I got your two days, girl, no problem,' she greeted Nellie.

'Did you see the master?' Nellie asked, and the cook chuckled.

'I did indeed although that one tried to stop me. She's gone, Nellie,' she announced dramatically.

'Gone!' Nellie gasped, while the cook and Elsie enjoyed seeing her surprise.

'Tell her, Cook,' prompted Elsie and nothing loath the cook launched into her tale.

'I went up to see Mr La Roche the minute he came in from business,' she said, 'and I told him all that had gone on, everything. The way I was left with no help and his sister coming, and the way the servants have come and gone with that one. I told him what she said to you. She's a respectable young woman, I said, and she just walked out and small blame to her.'

'Cook told him about me gum boil,' Elsie said. 'And you doing the steps in the hailstones.'

'He just kept tut-tutting and saying, "Dear me," but like I expected he said he'd consult his sister. I said the poor mistress would turn in her grave and he very near pushed me out. Upset, y'see,' said the cook.

'And he just told Grogan to go?' Nellie said.

The cook laughed. 'Not then,' she said. 'I done them a real nice meal, pulled meself out, but I was determined and Elsie served it.'

'I washed me mouth out with salt water, Nellie, and Cook told me to lay on me bed for a couple of hours after I got back,' said Elsie.

'Yes, yes, like I was saying, I done them proud and afterwards me and Elsie was washing up—I wouldn't demean meself to let that one help me, and Miss La Roche came to the kitchen. She said I'd done wonders to put up a meal like that and Elsie had done well to serve it.'

'She was lovely, wasn't she, Cook?' Elsie interrupted.

'Yes. Make us a pot of tea, Elsie,' the cook said, and turning to Nellie she drew her away. 'What done it,' she said winking at Nellie, 'I let it drop about Grogan thinking of wedding bells. That was it. Before you could say knife the quare one was packing her bags. Miss La Roche has gone home to close up her house and she's moving in here to look after her brother. Mind you, she never said nothing to me about what I'd tipped her the wink about, or to the master either, I don't suppose. Just that she felt it her duty to run her brother's house for him.'

'No flies on you, Cook,' Nellie said admiringly.

'You've got to have your wits about you,' the cook said. 'I don't know what she'll do about staff, Nell. The master's staying at his club for a few days.'

'Don't worry about me, Cook. I've got the promise of something,' Nellie said.

She had decided to say nothing about the pie-making venture until she knew that it would work. Two days later Meg went into labour so Nellie's plans were shelved.

A young boy came for her. 'Me mam says Mrs Williams could do with you there because she's started. Me mam says Mrs Williams is all right because she's there with her and she's sent for the nurse,' he said, obviously reciting what he had been told to say.

Nellie gave the boy a threepenny bit and dashed to ask Katy to look out for Tommy before hurrying off to Meg's house.

She found the mother of the boy, a widow from next door, with Meg, and Meg was able to smile cheerfully at Nellie.

'We've sent for the nurse but Mrs Williams has got a while to go yet,' Mrs Saunders the neighbour said placidly.

'This is nice timing, Meg,' Nellie teased her. 'You just gave yourself time to get nicely settled in your new house.'

The nurse arrived a few minutes later and Nellie and Mrs Saunders were banished downstairs. They took the opportunity to get acquainted. Nellie made tea and while they sipped it Mrs Saunders told her that she had lived next door since childhood, even after marriage.

'My mam died fifteen years ago,' she said,

'and me and Joe took over the tenancy. We only had it as our own place five years when I lost Joe. Killed in a shunting accident on the railway.'

'Have you just got the one child?' Nellie asked.

'No. I've got two girls married and a girl eighteen and young Stan at home.'

Nellie in her turn told Mrs Saunders that her husband was at sea and she had just one son aged nine. Meg would like a son, she said, but she would be glad to have a healthy child of either sex.

'They're young yet,' said Mrs Saunders. 'Plenty of time for half a dozen more.'

From time to time Nellie went upstairs to ask about Meg and found her tired but still cheerful. After a while Mrs Saunders slipped home and Nellie took out the ironing blanket and began to iron Bob's shirts, but the nurse came downstairs.

'I'm going to send for the doctor,' she said, then seeing Nellie's look of alarm she added, 'just to be on the safe side. She got to this stage quite quickly but she's not making much progress now. It's a small outlet and she hasn't got much strength.'

Nellie put the iron on the hob. 'She had bronchitis bad,' she said, 'but she got over it. She's still got a cough though. Do you want me to go for the doctor?'

'If you don't mind,' the nurse said. She gave Nellie a note she had written for the doctor and Nellie hurried away. Oh God, don't let her die, Nellie prayed as she rushed along. It'd kill our Bob.

She left the message and the doctor was at the house by the time she got back. Nellie had sent a boy to the works to tell Bobby what was happening and he too rapidly arrived.

They were joined by Mrs Saunders and spent an anxious hour before the nurse called Nellie. 'Scald out a bowl,' she said, 'Scald it thoroughly, then fill it with *boiling* water. Doctor may need to use forceps.'

There was another anxious wait before they heard a baby's cry and Bobby rushed for the stairs. The nurse opened the bedroom door a crack as his boots pounded up the stairs.

'A son, Mr Williams,' she said. 'I'll call you in a moment.'

'What about Meg?' Bobby shouted but she had closed the door firmly. He waited a few moments then knocked loudly on the door and the nurse opened it.

'Don't make such a noise,' she reproved him. 'They are both all right but your wife needs stitches.'

Bobby retreated downstairs, still looking anxious, but a little later the doctor came downstairs.

'All well,' he said briskly. 'The child is small but perfectly formed, and your wife is very tired but she should soon recover. You may go up now.'

Bobby seized the doctor's hand in a grip that made him wince and Nellie said involuntarily, 'Be careful, Bobby.'

They all smiled and Bobby bounded upstairs while Nellie escorted the doctor to the door. 'Will she be all right, Doctor?' she asked.

He nodded but asked how long Meg had been coughing.

'I don't know, but she said it's an old friend,' Nellie said.

He pursed his lips. 'Indeed. I've told her I want to see her at my surgery in six weeks' time. Make sure she comes, won't you?' he said and Nellie promised.

Meg seemed exhausted but she smiled at them happily when they went up to see her and admire the baby. His face was bruised and his head slightly misshapen but the nurse assured them that this was because of the forceps delivery.

'That will all be gone in a few days' time,' she said. 'He's a healthy little boy although he's so small.'

The baby had a fuzz of red hair the same colour as Bobby's and his face, although so marked, bore a definite resemblance to his father's, with the same short upper lip and the cleft in the chin.

'You couldn't deny *him*, lad,' Mrs Saunders joked and Bobby, proudly nursing his son, retorted, 'I wouldn't want to.'

The marks on the baby's face faded as the nurse had promised and the resemblance to Bobby became even more marked.

'Your ma had red hair, didn't she, Nell?' Meg said one day when the nurse was bathing the child and commenting on the resemblance. 'Yet your lad is the model of you, and of your dad, Bob says.'

'You must have strong genes in your family,' the nurse laughed, but a feeling of bitter envy kept Nellie silent. If only Tom had shown a resemblance to Sam, all her worries would have been solved. And here, where it didn't matter, Bobby had this tiny replica of himself.

Something must have shown in her face because Meg said quietly to the nurse, 'Mind you, for all Tom's so like Nellie he sometimes has a look of Sam, hasn't he, Bob?'

'Yes, especially when he's squaring up to his mates,' Bobby grinned, and Meg looked warningly at him, but Nellie was too pleased by Meg's comment to care. She sometimes thought that she could see a likeness to Sam in Tom's expression, and felt that it might be wishful thinking on her part but now Meg had confirmed it.

Nellie was pleased that her cleaning job was finished and she could spend much of her time caring for Meg and the baby. She expected Sam home within weeks and as usual she was also busily preparing for his homecoming.

'I'll leave the idea of the pies until Sam's gone back,' she told Meg. 'He'll have a good pay-off after such a long voyage and anyway I think I'll have to find out a lot more before I start the pies.'

Meg was lying on the sofa still looking frail, but she showed immediate enthusiasm for Nellie's plans and wanted to know what Nellie had to learn.

'For a start I don't think any working man is going to pay threepence ha'penny for a pie,' Nellie said. 'I know Bob costed them from what I told him, but I think I see where I went wrong. Them ones I made for a sample were too good.'

'They were wonderful, them, Nell,' Meg exclaimed. 'I've never tasted nothing so good.'

'But they were too good,' Nellie said. 'I used the best meat and stuffed them with it. I could do something as tasty with cheaper meat and less of it in the pies but a real good gravy. I've been looking round at places that sell pies and I'd never get threepence ha'penny for one, never mind what the shopkeeper puts on.'

'Well, you've got time to think about it anyhow,' Meg said. 'Sam won't be rushing back this time, will he? After being away so long and a good pay-off.'

'It seems so long,' Nellie said softly. 'He'll see a big change in Tommy too.'

'That teacher's made a difference in him, hasn't she?' said Meg. 'Doesn't he talk real nice now, too?'

Nellie sighed. 'Yes, eighteen months ago when Sam went Tom was just a little lad, but now he seems different altogether. In the Junior Boys too, as well as all this with Miss Helsby.'

Meg and Bobby decided to name the baby David Robert and asked Nellie to be his godmother. Sam would be godfather if he was home, otherwise Bob's friend from work would stand in.

The baby was very small and Meg and Bobby

worried about him. Each spoke privately to Nellie about their fears.

'He's tiny, isn't he, Nell?' Bobby said one night as he walked her home. 'But your Tom was too, wasn't he? And look at the fine big lad he is now.'

'Yes, and he never ails much, not as much as other kids round about anyway,' Nellie encouraged him. 'Don't worry, lad. Sometimes the smallest babies come on the best,' and Bobby seemed comforted.

Nellie offered Meg the same comfort a few days later when Meg said she was worried because the child was small and delicate. But then Meg went on to say, 'Is it true that you were very ill when Tom was born, Nell, and that's why you had no more?'

Nellie blushed. 'He had the cord round his neck so it made it hard for me, like. Hard for him an' all. He was really born dead and Janey put him to one side but Nurse McCann saved him. She called to Bobby to bring hot water and she doused the baby in it then in cold water and she brought him round. God, when I heard him give a cry! She was a clever woman, Meg.'

'Fancy that, and when you look at your Tommy now!' Meg said. She hesitated. 'And do you think that's why you haven't had no more?'

'I don't know,' Nellie said. 'Nurse McCann said my womb might be tilted but she was too sick to examine me.'

Meg looked down at the tiny child in her arms. 'I hope he's not going to be the only one,' then looking up in time to see the sadness on Nellie's face she said impulsively, 'Oh, Nell, you could still have more, but if you don't I hope my children will be like your own to you.'

Within a very few years those quick words of sympathy would often be recalled with sadness by the two women.

Nellie and Tommy were eagerly counting the days to Sam's return although once again there were no letters from him.

'It's a shame the way they get held up,' Gertie said. 'Why don't you see if Prudence can tell you anything? Lettie's going twice a week to the church hall. She's doing the costumes for them amateur dramatics people.'

'I'd love to,' Nellie said eagerly. 'Will you find out when I can come, Gert?'

Two nights later Gertie called Nellie to her house and took her in to the dimly lit parlour. Prudence sat behind the small table and after greeting Nellie she again took her hand, then looked into the crystal.

She leaned back in the chair, her eyes closed, then suddenly her body was shaken by sobs.

'Prudence. Mrs Gilligan,' Nellie cried in alarm, but the woman sprang to her feet and began to pace about the room.

'Why? Why me?' she cried, flinging her arms in the air. 'I didn't ask for this gift. I don't want it.' She flung herself back in the chair and seized Nellie's hand.

'Don't. Don't try to lift the veil. The strength will come with the sorrow.'

'Sorrow!' Nellie exclaimed. 'Is it Sam? Oh

God, don't tell me I'll never see him again. Please, please, Mrs Gilligan, tell me what you seen. Honest, I'd rather know, to be ready, like.'

Prudence still gripped her hand. She sighed then said in a faint voice, 'You will see him again. Blows, quarrels, partings.' She moved her head restlessly against the back of the chair, her eyes closed. 'Bad, bad, darkness,' she whispered, 'I see you standing alone, but no—the boy. The boy will cleave to you. Money, success, but sorrow.'

She stopped speaking and Nellie leaned forward, her eyes devouring the woman's face, her hands tightly gripping her hands. 'Prudence,' she said urgently, then the woman began to speak again.

'Money, success, sorrow,' she said. 'Water, so much water. Flowing between you, but the golden cord will never break. A stranger in a strange land.'

Her voice died away and they sat in silence, Nellie afraid to speak lest she missed other revelations, until Gertie tapped on the door and looked in.

'All right?' she asked, and Prudence stirred and stood up.

'I should have refused. I won't do this again, Gertie,' she said fretfully.

'But it's a help,' Nellie protested. 'I mean, if something's going to happen it means you can be prepared, like.'

Prudence shook her head. 'What use is it to know now?' she said. 'When sorrow comes the strength to bear it comes.'

'So you saw something?' Gertie exclaimed. 'Come in to my room and have something to revive you.' She led the way into her living room and took a bottle from the cupboard. 'Someone brought this for me from Spain. It'll do us more good than tea.'

Nellie drank the sherry quickly and it seemed to make her feel strong and happy. 'That must be good stuff, Gertie,' she said. 'I feel ready for anything.'

'Has it made you feel better, Prudence?' Gertie asked, and her lodger, who was sipping daintily at the liquid, nodded.

'It's certainly strong,' she said.

'The feller who gave it to me said it was powerful,' Gertie said. 'So I thought I'd save it for when you foretold the future, like. Lettie says it takes a lot out of you, that's why she doesn't like it.'

'I won't do it again,' Prudence said. 'What comes to me I will keep to myself. What use is it to tell of unhappiness? It means living through it twice.'

'Well, I'm glad you told me what was in store for *me*,' Gertie declared. 'I won't be worrying thinking I'll never get married because all the lads have been killed in the war. I know I've got a happy life to look forward to.'

Nellie knew that Gertie was anxious to hear what she had been told but they were unable to talk about it while Prudence was with them.

Gertie brought out a pack of cards. 'What

about gin rummy?' she said. 'We can play for matches.'

They settled down to play with refilled glasses beside them, and they were still playing, all suddenly in high spirits, when Lettie returned.

'We've led your mam down the primrose path,' Gertie giggled. Nellie announced, 'Yes, we're real bad lots, boozing and gambling.'

They expected Lettie to be annoyed but she was in a surprisingly good humour. 'No harm,' she said. 'Some people say play-acting is sinful but there's nothing wrong with the people I've been with tonight.'

Mrs Gilligan stood up. 'If you'll excuse me,' she said grandly, and walked unsteadily through to the parlour with Lettie. Gertie brewed tea for herself and Nellie.

'You can stay, can't you, Nell?' she said and Nellie agreed.

'Once Tommy's asleep it'd take an earthquake to wake him,' she said.

She repeated what Mrs Gilligan had foretold and Gertie looked grave.

'Maybe it's right what she said, Nell. Maybe it's best not to know and to worry ahead. Especially if like she says you'll get the strength to bear the sorrow when it comes.'

'No, I'd rather know,' Nellie said stubbornly. 'I worry anyway when I think of them lot at the other end being jealous of me. Makes me think how lucky I am and if it can last, like. I think Meg feels the same way because everything's going so well for them.'

'What a pair you are!' Gertie exclaimed. 'You

should be enjoying the good luck and making the most of it.'

Nellie smiled and shrugged her shoulders. 'I wonder though, Gert, do you think that lot might be ill-wishing me?'

'No, I don't believe in that,' Gertie declared. 'Nothing's happened to you yet anyhow. And at least it was all good about Tommy and success and money and that. Him sticking to you too.'

'Yes, and she didn't say nothing about death this time,' Nellie said. 'Only the same thing about the golden cord.'

'There you are then. Just take notice of the good bits,' Gertie advised, but Nellie looked worried.

'I'll be glad when Sam's letters come,' she said. 'I don't know whether it's because of the fortune telling but I've got a sort of feeling about them.'

'Don't be daft,' Gertie said robustly. 'You see, they'll all come in a bunch like they did last time,' and Nellie agreed that she was probably right.

CHAPTER 20

Days passed but still no letters from Sam, then when Nellie went to the shipping office for her money she was told that Sam had been put ashore on the Ivory Coast and was in hospital there. He would return on another of the company's ships when he was well again.

Nellie decided to tell Tommy and they spent some anxious weeks until George Adams arrived home and came to see them.

'I don't think he'll be far behind us,' he told Nellie. 'Him and a fella from the Dingle got taken ashore to hospital because they come out in a rash and they was feverish, like.'

'Is Sam very ill?' Nellie asked fearfully but George reassured her.

'No, he was over the worst when he got took off. I don't think the mate woulda bothered only there was this good hospital handy and the rash might have been infectious, like.'

'Is it a proper hospital?' Nellie asked.

'Yes. It's an English doctor runs it. Be all accounts he's got pots of money and him and these students they do research, like, into tropical diseases. Like the School of Tropical Medicine in Pembroke Place. I heard some of the officers talking about it,' said George.

'And they'll look after Sam proper?' Nellie said.

'Oh aye. The doctor's probably made up to get a couple of Englishmen for his testing and that. He's got plenty of money to throw around so the grub should be good anyhow,' said George. 'I wouldn't have minded a touch of it meself. A good rest just laying in bed doing nothing.'

'You'd better not let Rose hear you,' Nellie joked, and George stood up.

'I'd better get back, but don't you worry,

Nell. He won't be more than a couple of weeks behind us and the rest'll do him the world of good.'

Nellie often thought of what Prudence had foretold during the following worrying weeks, particularly about herself standing alone except for Tommy. Was she going to lose Sam? Yet George had been sure that he would soon be better. Then the blows and the darkness and the parting Prudence had spoken about it.

Could that mean that Sam might start fighting at the hospital? Her mind ranged over every possibility as she lay awake night after night. Still no letters had come but finally one short letter arrived. Sam's letters were always stilted in tone but there was a curtness about this letter that made Nellie feel that it had been written by a stranger. It simply said that Sam had been ill and would soon be home.

To add to her worries Charlie West had reappeared. He had been playing in a dance band in Blackpool for the summer season but was now home again. Nellie had come face to face with him in Johnson Street and he had barred her way, asking if she was glad to see him again.

'I don't care one way or the other,' she snapped at him, but he only said admiringly. 'Little spitfire, aren't you?'

The gossip round Bella's step was that he was bragging about being chased by girls all the time he was away.

'That's his story,' Bella said, laughing heartily. 'But we could tell them they was wasting their time. Queer as a nine-bob note, that fella.'

'I think Charlie could be telling the truth though,' Katy said later to Nellie. 'The girls do run after fellas in bands, and me mam says herself, he likes it both ways.'

'I wish one of them girls'd catch him, then, and keep him away from me,' Nellie said. 'Especially now Sam's on his way home. I don't want none of Charlie West's troublemaking.'

She had been told that Sam was once again on his way home on another Elder Dempster ship and she wanted nothing to mar his homecoming. She suspected that West had visited Janey several times, being admitted and leaving by the side entrance, but he had not attempted to enter her kitchen.

Nellie felt Janey was becoming more and more of a problem. Although she had always seemed impervious to the weather, now she came in the back way every day and settled in front of Nellie's fire.

Nellie had offered to make a hot toddy the first time Janey complained of the cold and she had accepted. 'Put the oven shelf in me bed an' all,' the old woman said, but Nellie made the excuse that it was already in Tommy's bed. The next day Nellie bought a stone hot-water bottle from the pawnshop.

'I wouldn't fancy using the oven if the shelf had been in her bed,' she said to Gertie. 'You should see the state of it, but what can I do? She won't let me in to do nothing there, but I feel ashamed.'

'It's not your fault if she won't let you in

to clean,' Gertie said. 'It's a shame you've got to put up with it. One thing about Lettie. She keeps their rooms spotless. She's a real hard worker.'

'Has Prudence kept to it about not doing the fortune telling?' Nellie asked.

'She doesn't like it called fortune telling,' Gertie said. 'But she won't do it now anyway. She told me she's given a glimpse of the future sometimes like her mother was, but she doesn't want the gift. She said her mother could never see anything about her future and she has never seen anything about Lettie's. Strange that, isn't it?'

'I'd love to have that gift,' Nellie exclaimed. 'To be able to see ahead, like. I'm sure I'd be saved a lot of worry.'

'Prudence doesn't feel like that,' Gertie said. 'I feel sorry for her. She sees things about people that she doesn't want to see, but she's not going to tell them no more. She says the things have already happened when she sees them, although they are in the future.'

'I don't understand that,' Nellie said. 'If things are happening in the future you *must* be able to change them.'

'I don't understand it either,' Gertie confessed. 'Although I did when Prudence was telling me. She said when she's talking to someone sometimes she sees a sort of picture in her head if she lets herself accept it. Things that haven't happened yet, and yet they have so nothing can be changed. I can't explain it like she did, Nell.'

'I still think it's a waste if she's got that gift and she won't use it,' Nellie said. 'At least Lettie'll be pleased.'

'I don't think that's why she's given up,' Gertie said. 'Lettie's a lot more pleasant these days. More happy, like. I think she enjoys going to that concert party thing in the church hall.'

'Maybe it's because her mother has given up the fortune telling,' Nellie suggested. 'Yet maybe she'll go back to it,' but Gertie said that Prudence was adamant.

'She's real worried about you,' she said, but when Nellie looked alarmed she said quickly, 'Only because you was the last she done. It's funny Janey feeling the cold now. She's always been as tough as an old boot, hasn't she?'

Nellie realised that Gertie was changing the subject but she said no more about Prudence, and instead talked about Janey.

She was sorry if the old woman was ill but Janey insisted that there was nothing wrong with her. She still monopolised the fire though and accepted hot toddys and the filled hot-water bottle from Nellie, and more and more Nellie resented herself and Tommy being excluded from the fire.

There was also an unpleasant smell drawn from the old woman's clothes and her unwashed body by the heat, but more than anything Nellie was offended by Janey's comments about Sam's illness. She seemed to regard it as something shameful and her hints and innuendoes about Sam and his family made Nellie furious.

If she protested Janey sneered instead about

how Sam would feel when he found his son a gentleman or hinted about Nellie's own family or the doubts about Tommy's birth. 'He he, it's a wise child that knows its own father,' she often cackled, sometimes while Nellie was actually making a drink for her or filling her hot-water bottle.

I'm sick of her, Nellie often told herself, the ungrateful old bitch. I should just make her go in her own room and get on with it. She's nothing to me, no relation, and it's not my duty to look after her, yet she continued to care for the old woman. At the same time she worried about what she could do with her when Sam came home.

Meg and Bob had decided to postpone the christening until Sam arrived home to be godfather. Nellie had knitted a lacy shawl for the baby and Meg had made him a beautiful christening gown in white silk trimmed with lace and a tiny lace-trimmed hat to match.

A week before Sam arrived Tommy brought a note home from Miss Helsby, asking if she could come to see Nellie. Nellie was thrown into panic by the note. 'What does she want with me?' she demanded. 'Have you been up to something, Tommy?'

The boy protested that he had done nothing. 'I think she wants to talk to you about me keeping on with the classes,' he said. 'You'll have to write a note to say when she can come, Mam.'

'I know, I know, clever clogs,' Nellie said, although she was dismayed at the prospect of writing to a teacher. After much thought she wrote,

Dear Miss,

I hope this finds you well as it leaves us at present. You will be welcome to come after school tomorrow, I hope Tommy is a good boy.

Yours respectfully,

Mrs Meadows.

'There, you couldn't do no better than that, and I never went to school hardly,' she told Tommy as she gave him the note.

'Ah, but what about Mr Ambrose?' Tommy said mischievously.

Nellie laughed but she felt uneasy. What would Sam think of the way she and Tommy talked to each other now? Putting himself on the same level as me as if we was the same age, she thought. She would have to warn Tommy about it and tell him to drop his posh speech and the washing and cleaning his teeth while Sam was home. Yet I don't want to deceive Sam, she sighed. It was all very difficult.

The kitchen, newly decorated ready for Sam's return, was looking its best when Miss Helsby arrived. It was a cold day but a bright fire burned in the shining blackleaded grate and drew reflections from the gleaming fire irons. Nellie had spread her best cloth on the table and laid it with china cups and saucers, a plateful of thin bread and butter and a homemade fruit cake.

I'll show her I know how a table should be set, Nellie thought, and there's some things she doesn't need to learn Tommy. She was wearing a clean flowered wraparound pinafore and her hair, worn in a neat bun on her neck, was clean and shining.

She greeted Miss Helsby and offered tea and the teacher immediately set out to persuade her to allow Tommy to sit for a scholarship to the grammar school.

'I'm sure he could do it,' she said. 'His arithmetic was weak but it's improving with my coaching and his English is outstanding. He works hard and I'm sure he would make full use of his opportunities if he reached the grammar school.'

She had been encouraged by the cleanliness of the room and Nellie's neat appearance and reserved manner and she was unprepared for her emphatic refusal.

'No thank you, miss,' Nellie said firmly. 'Lads from round here don't go to the grammar school. We couldn't afford it anyhow.'

'But there would be nothing to pay for fees or books if he won a scholarship,' the teacher said. 'And as for clothes, no need to worry about that. There is a grant available.'

'Charity, like?' Nellie said. 'No, miss, his dad wouldn't hear of it. He's always looked after us proper and we've never been on the Parish. Tommy's never gone short of nothing, even if his dad's gone without himself for him.'

'But it's not charity, Mrs Meadows. It's a *right*,' Miss Helsby said.

Nellie shook her head. 'No, his dad wouldn't like it,' she said. 'And I've seen them lads going to school and Tommy'd be outa place with them. They'd skit at him.'

'Why should they? He speaks as well if not better than most of them. That is the purpose of my classes,' said Miss Helsby.

But Nellie still said stubbornly, 'No thank you, miss.'

'Don't you think you should consult your husband, Mrs Meadows? I know Thomas has received a lot of encouragement from him. I'm sure he would wish the boy to improve himself. To have a better life and the chance of a better job when the time comes.'

'He's away at sea but he thinks the same as me, miss,' Nellie said sullenly. 'Speaking nice is one thing, but—the grammar school. We don't want him to go out of his class and get laughed at.'

'But haven't I just explained? He wouldn't be laughed at, and class! What is class?' Miss Helsby said in exasperation. With an effort she controlled her temper. 'Thomas has shown that he would benefit by a better education,' she said quietly. 'It would broaden his mind. Open new horizons for him. I think he deserves the chance.'

Nellie had been sitting with her head bent, rubbing her finger back and forth on the tablecloth, but now she raised her head. Here comes the real reason, thought Miss Helsby.

'I don't want Tommy to get big ideas,' Nellie said. 'Him and his dad think the world of each other now, I don't want Tommy learned any different. To look down, like, on his dad, thinks

390

he's better than him. No, I'll leave things the way they are.'

Miss Helsby was about to argue further but she recognised defeat in the stubborn set of Nellie's mouth and only said with a sigh, 'A pity, because there are so few boys with Thomas's gifts, but of course the decision rests with you.'

'Will you have another cup of tea, miss?' asked Nellie and Miss Helsby accepted, trying to crush down her anger at the denial of the chance for what seemed to her a trivial reason. She said that she hoped that Thomas would continue to come after school for speech training and coaching in arithmetic and Nellie promised that he would.

She was aware of the teacher's disappointment and she said diffidently, 'You've made a lot of difference in him, miss. The way he talks, like, and keeping himself clean. He enjoys being learned all these things too.'

'It's very rewarding,' Miss Helsby said. 'He's so intelligent and eager to learn, and very proud of his father, and of you too, of course.'

She sighed involuntarily and Nellie said defensively, 'Sam's a good father to him. He had a hard life himself, living rough and being knocked from pillar to post, but he wants better for Tommy. Doesn't begrudge it, like, although he had such a hard time himself. I won't let Tommy turn his nose up at him, being just a deck hand and that. He's our only one an' all.'

She felt that she had explained badly but Miss

Helsby thought that she had a much clearer picture now. I must tread as warily as Agag but I *must* try to help this boy, she thought.

She spoke in glowing terms of Tom's schoolwork and his behaviour and before she left she said gently, 'If you reconsider, Mrs Meadows, there is still plenty of time for Thomas's name to go forward,' but she was unable to resist adding, 'I hope that Thomas will not resent being denied this chance.'

When Tommy came in, his mother told him the purpose of the teacher's visit, but concealed the arguments that she had used against it.

'Did you say I could try, Mam?' Tommy asked.

'No, you don't want to get mixed up with them snobs, lad. You'll get a good job without that,' Nellie said.

'Me dad doesn't want me to go to sea,' Tommy said.

'There's plenty of jobs apart from the sea,' Nellie said. 'Plenty of time before you need to worry about that, anyroad.'

Later Maggie Nolan came in and she agreed with Nellie.

'You'd get skitted soft, Tom,' she said. 'By them stuck-up kids in the grammar school and then by the lads round here when you come home. You'd be neither fish, fowl nor good red herring, lad.'

When Maggie had gone Nellie saw Tom scribbling in his exercise book and looked over his shoulder.

'Neither fish, fowl nor good red herring,' she

read aloud. 'That's what Mrs Nolan said. What are you writing it down for?'

'I've never heard it before and I like it,' Tommy said defensively. 'I've written it down so I won't forget it.'

'You're a funny lad, Tom,' Nellie said affectionately, ruffling his hair.

Miss Helsby told Tom's present teacher, Mr Morton, about her unsuccessful visit to Tom's home.

'Quite frankly I think you're wasting your time,' he said bluntly. 'You can't help these people. They're stubborn and ignorant and they've no ambition for their children.'

'I don't agree,' Miss Helsby said sharply. 'The boy is very well cared for and she told me she was grateful for the training I've given him. She was very clean and respectable and she seemed to have done her best with a quite dreadful house.'

'But she won't allow the boy his chance?' Mr Morton said.

'No, but there was *something*. If I'd had her twenty years ago I could have made something of her. She just seemed very protective towards the father, afraid the boy would come to despise him.'

Mr Morton laughed. 'You know my opinion, but still, you might prove me wrong. Still time if they reconsider anyway.'

Tom showed no sign of resentment at his mother's decision, and continued to attend Miss Helsby's coaching after school, but a few days later he brought home a composition on 'A

Night at Sea', which his teacher had marked 'Excellent—10 out of 10'. 'Miss Helsby asked sir if I could bring it home to show you,' he told his mother.

Nellie recognised the teacher's motives, but when she read through the essay she was impressed by Tom's knowledge and his choice of words. 'How did you know that about the stars being so big and the warm wind?' she asked.

'Me dad told me about when they were in the Med, and they used to go up and sit on a hatch cover when they came off watch,' he said.

Nellie felt a twinge of jealousy. Sam never talked to me like that, she thought, but then she felt ashamed. She should be thankful that Sam and Tommy were so close.

She told Meg about the essay on her next visit to her and the baby. 'Sam never has much to say but he must talk his head off when he's out with Tommy,' she said. 'Mind you, I suppose Tom never stops firing questions at him.'

'That teacher must think a lot of Tom too, giving up her time to learn him even though he's in the Big Boys now,' Meg said.

'She didn't like me saying no to her,' Nellie said. 'But I'm not chancing him turning his nose up at his dad.'

'I'm sure he'll never do that, Nell,' Meg protested. 'They seem such good friends, I'm looking forward to meeting Sam.'

Nellie sighed. 'It's been such a long trip, and then the hospital on top of it,' she said. 'You know, I feel all worked up, Meg. I hope I don't feel strange with Sam.'

'I'm sure you won't,' Meg comforted her. 'Maybe for the first five minutes but that's all.'

'Only a few more days now anyway,' Nellie said. 'I think Tommy's as worked up as me, waiting for him. His dad'll have a lot to tell him this time anyhow.'

The final few days before Sam arrived were very trying for Nellie and Tommy, who were both very tense. They felt that they had been waiting such a long time for his return, deferred by his time in hospital, and subconsciously each wondered whether they would be like strangers when they met Sam again.

Tommy showed his tenseness by being aggressive towards his schoolmates and came home one night with a black eye and a cut lip.

'The state of you!' Nellie exclaimed. 'What's your dad going to say, seeing you like that? Who was you fighting?'

'A lad two years older than me,' Tommy said proudly. 'Me dad won't mind me fighting. He might be mad though that I dropped me guard and got this shiner after all he taught me about defence.'

'Here's me getting new clothes ready so you'll look nice when he comes and look at the cut of you! *I'm* mad, never mind your dad,' Nellie said.

In spite of her words to Tommy, Nellie herself relieved her tense feelings by a bitter quarrel with Ada Ginley. She had almost forgotten Rose's warning about the wash-house gossip linking herself and Gertie with Martha Miller and her trade, until Ada Ginley shouted across the street to a neighbour as Nellie passed, 'Some in this street are bloody well dressed and we know how, don't we, Jinny? On Martha Miller's game.'

At another time Nellie would have walked on, ignoring her and shedding tears later in the privacy of her home. But now she confronted Ada Ginley, arms akimbo.

'You watch your dirty lying tongue, Ginley, or it'll be the worse for you,' she yelled at her. 'People in glass houses can't throw stones. I heard about you and your gang in the wash-house. You want your mouths washed out with soap.'

A group of women immediately collected round them.

'That's right, Nell,' one woman shouted, 'you give her what for, girl.'

Ada had been silent with surprise but she soon recovered. 'Yer can't deny it,' she shouted, 'you and that soft mare across from you, Gertie. Youse were seen going on the game with Martha Miller.'

'We walked along with her for a bit on the way to the pictures,' Nellie said. 'No law against that, is there?'

'Ho, ho, a likely story,' Ada scoffed. There were shouts of encouragement for her now as well as for Nellie from the women gathered round them.

'Wharra we supposed to do? Cross the road when we seen her?' Nellie yelled. 'Anyhow, you've no call to look down on Martha after what I've heard about you.'

Ada screeched and attempted to run at Nellie and bury her hands in her hair, but Bella put her vast bulk between them.

'Cut it out, the pair of youse,' she said with authority. 'I thought you had more sense, Nellie Meadows, taking notice to what this one says. And you, Ada Ginley, your tongue'll get you hung before you're finished.'

Ada tried to break free of the women who held her to get at Nellie, but Bella said warningly, 'Don't forget who lives with Nellie. Do you want Janey on yer back?'

The women swiftly melted away, and even Ada only made a token show of resistance as she was drawn back to her own house.

'I never knew they was all so afraid of Janey,' Nellie said to Bella.

'Aye, well, maybe they think they'd better not take no chances,' Bella said. 'I know Janey's not the woman she was but she still has a hold over a lot of them.'

Nellie went back to her house, wondering how many people believed Ada Ginley's gossip. What if Sam heard of it?

Gertie heard about the row and came over to see Nellie. She was just as angry as Nellie had been when she heard the details, but surprised that Nellie had challenged Ada Ginley.

'I don't know what came over me?' Nellie confessed. 'I just flared up, and the things I

397

said! I didn't know I had it in me.'

'A good thing you did,' Gertie said loyally. 'Maybe she'll think twice before she jangles about you again.'

'I don't think she's worried about me, but they all seem afraid of old Janey,' Nellie said.

'I'm that mad,' Gertie said, 'I'd like to do what our supervisor did. She sent a solicitor's letter to some woman what was calling her. It only cost seven and sixpence.'

'That might be better than what I did. Screaming like a fishwife,' Nellie said, but Gertie shook her head.

'No, I'd never live it down if I done that,' Gertie said. 'Nobody round here wouldn't never speak to me again. I could go mad though, Nell.'

'So could I,' Nellie said. 'Just because we didn't treat Martha like a leper.'

'I don't know why we should worry anyhow,' Gertie said. 'People who know us know it's not true, and the others'll soon find out.'

'I'm worried in case Sam hears some fancy tale about it, on top of being worried about that troublemaker Charlie West being back.'

'Oh, to hell,' Gertie exclaimed suddenly. 'Why should we waste our lives worrying over what might never happen? I'm sure Sam won't believe any tales about you. You should be on top of the world now with him nearly home after all this time.'

'I am,' Nellie said, smiling again. 'Bob and Meg are having the christening on Sunday so Sam can be godfather. I've never been a godmother before. I'm real excited.'

With an effort Nellie pushed all her fears to the back of her mind and happily made her final preparations for Sam's homecoming.

CHAPTER 21

Sam had been eagerly looking forward to returning home to see his wife and son again, and he was dismayed to find a rash spreading over his body as the ship was turning for home. He felt ill and feverish, and feared that his illness might delay his return.

His shipmates 'carried' him for a while, but then another man developed the same rash. The ship was putting in to Freetown and there was a hospital run by an English doctor not far from there, so it was decided that the men would be put ashore for treatment. The doctor had come aboard to examine them and had offered to admit them to his hospital.

Sam protested strenuously that his rash was going and he was feeling better, but to no avail. George tried to console him. 'Just as well to get it seen to, lad,' he said. 'Then you'll be fighting fit be the time you get home.'

'That doctor just wants us to practise on,' Sam said bitterly. 'The mate doesn't care. He's took on them two that were hanging round, backed off their own ship. I'll be as right as rain in a couple of days and I'll

399

bet I'd do more work than them two put together.'

'Don't worry. We won't have no skivers on this ship,' George said grimly. 'Just make the most of the rest, lad. Just think. Be the time you're home we'll be spent up and ready to go back and you'll still have it all to come. I'll go and see Nellie and tell her about you.'

The hospital was much more comfortable than Sam and the other man, Jimmy McGregor, expected, but they were irritated by the constant tests and questioning by the doctors.

'I never knew me pee was so interesting,' Jimmy said to Sam. 'That's three times today they've took samples of it, and then the blood tests and even me *seed,* like.'

'I know, and the questions!' Sam said. 'They want to know every bit about you from the minute you was born.'

'My dad scarpered when I was a nipper,' Jimmy said, 'I don't know nothing about him, but the things they keep asking me.'

'The boss man, Dr Fairbrother. He's the worst,' Sam said. 'I felt like a wrung-out rag by the time he'd finished.'

'I heard him going on about when you was a kid,' Jimmy said.

'Aye, I said to him, "What's that got to do with me rash?" but he said, "Privations in childhood can affect you all your life." '

'I reckon we're just guinea pigs for him,' Jimmy said. 'He's made up to get some white men to practise on.'

400

'My rash is nearly gone, and when that goes I go,' Sam declared, but Jimmy said he was in no rush to leave.

'Good food and comfort here,' he said. 'Better than what I'd get at home, never mind on board. Me ma's always in the alehouse, so I can put up with the tests, and they've got to run outa questions some time.'

'I want to get home to my wife and kid,' Sam said. 'I won't know me lad if I'm away much longer.'

The young doctors, four white men, showed no sign of running out of questions and one of them was always beside Sam and Jimmy as soon as they awoke in the morning. One of them in particular, Dr Doyle, chatted to Sam on a variety of subjects and made copious notes on his answers.

He was a big awkward young man, always falling over objects or knocking things down, and Sam and Jimmy often made jokes about him. They had all questioned Sam about his hardships as a child, when he had slept rough and often been cold and hungry.

One day when Sam was sitting in the garden Dr Doyle came to him, carrying the huge folder of notes. He chatted to Sam for a few minutes about his general health then looked through the voluminous notes.

'Bad luck to have to endure all that as a kid,' he said casually. 'Then to have to suffer the effects in adult life. Being sterile is one of the worst things that can happen to a fellow, isn't it?'

Sam gaped at him. 'Sterile? Me?' he stammered. 'I'm not sterile. I've got a lad nearly ten.'

'A stepson?' Dr Doyle said, looking flustered.

'No. Me own son,' Sam shouted.

The papers slipped from the doctor's knee and he bent to retrieve them. 'Sorry,' he muttered. 'I've got it wrong. Misread the notes.' He gathered up the notes and left hurriedly, and Sam sat staring after him, his thoughts in a whirl. Before he could recover from the shock and begin to think clearly, Dr Fairbrother arrived.

'I fear my young colleague was too hasty in his assumptions, Sam,' he said smoothly.

'I'm not what he said,' Sam growled. 'I don't pick up women in port, like, but me and me wife—' He turned away, his face red with anger and embarrassment.

The doctor said blandly, 'Of course, of course, my dear chap. Just a little misunderstanding.'

He told Sam that they had been studying a group of natives. 'They are apparently virile men yet they father very few children and the tribe is dying out,' he said. 'We thought we might find a link with white men with poor backgrounds, although of course your deprivations cannot compare with what these natives have endured—constant gross malnutrition with the resulting bone malformation and ulcers, and endemic diseases carried by flies.'

'I never had nothing like that,' Sam muttered.

'Of course. Will you tell me again about your

childhood illnesses? Just as a matter of interest, you understand.'

'I don't know,' Sam said. 'I was sick sometimes, I suppose, but I felt pretty bad most of the time, hungry and cold and that, but I just got on with it.'

'I understand. And when you were at the reformatory?' the doctor said.

'I had pleurisy but I got over it. I was days in an open boat, torpedoed, when I was fifteen, and I got over that and all. There's nothing wrong with me,' Sam growled.

'Of course,' the doctor said soothingly. 'Your rash has almost cleared and your temperature is down too.'

'So, I'm ready to go, then?' Sam said.

'Nearly,' the doctor said. 'I'm sure you are anxious to return to your wife and child. A boy, isn't it? What's his name?'

'Thomas. We call him Tommy,' Sam said.

'And how old is he?'

'Ten in November,' said Sam.

'So you'll miss his birthday? A shame, but I suppose that often happens in seafarers' families,' the doctor said.

He stayed talking to Sam, drawing him on to tell all about Tommy's cleverness and the letters he wrote to his father.

'This teacher keeps him after school or in the dinner hour and learns him sums and how to talk and that,' Sam said proudly, and the doctor said that Tommy must be an exceptional boy.

Later Sam said to Jimmy, 'The old doctor's

all right. Got some manners, like, and talks sense. Not like that other soft get, Dr Doyle.'

His shock and outrage had been soothed by Dr Fairbrother's swift response, but later when he was alone, they returned. For the rest of the day and the following night he thought of nothing but Dr Doyle's words.

He meant that all right about me, he thought grimly. He just never seen that in the notes about Tommy or he wouldn't of said it. The old fellow was just smarming me over. The implications of what he had been told filled his mind until he felt that he was going mad. Tommy could not be his son, and Ellie had tricked him.

All these years of boasting about Tommy to his mates and bragging about the home Ellie had made for him, and all the time it was a lie. Tommy was another man's son, and Ellie who seemed so straight and honest and loving had just been using him.

He avoided Jimmy and the doctors and found a secluded corner of the garden where he retreated like a wounded animal. On Dr Fairbrother's orders he was not disturbed and one of the doctors played backgammon with Jimmy to keep him away from his friend.

All night Sam tossed and turned and by the following morning his temperature had risen alarmingly and he was delirious.

'He keeps shouting out for his wife and the lad,' Jimmy told Dr Fairbrother.

The doctor ordered cold compresses to be applied to Sam's temples and his body sponged down, without comment, but he was furious. He sent for Dr Doyle.

'You damned young fool,' he said. 'We could lose this man thanks to your loose tongue, and think what that would mean to my hospital. He came here recovering from a slight fever and the officers on his ship knew that. Why the hell didn't you read the notes properly?'

'But the tests. His semen,' the young doctor stammered.

Dr Fairbrother made an impatient gesture. 'The notes showed he had been married and the child born the same year. Are you a complete fool? I drew my own conclusions and so should you have done. You could even have established whether he knew of the sterility before blurting that out.'

'But I looked through the notes afterwards. There was no date of birth,' Dr Doyle said defensively.

'You could have established that quite easily by discreet questioning, as I did,' Dr Fairbrother said cuttingly, 'but discretion is not your strong suit, is it?'

Sam's temperature dropped again and he gradually recovered. He lay in bed surly and uncommunicative and on Dr Fairbrother's orders he was not questioned again, although the tests continued.

In all the many questions no one had asked Sam about the illness on the trip after his marriage, and Sam had thought they were only interested in childhood illness.

Had he realised that his swollen neck during

that illness meant that he had mumps, and known that mumps in an adult male could cause sterility, so much heartbreak for himself and Nellie could have been avoided.

Dr Fairbrother arranged that Sam and Jimmy returned home on the first available ship. Dr Doyle also returned on the same ship, but he avoided Sam as he had done since his gaffe.

Sam was silent and morose throughout the voyage, his mind dwelling constantly on his problem. The thought of Ellie and Tommy was always in his mind. He never doubted that the doctor was right, and Tommy was not his child, but how could he have come so close to another man's son? He thought of Tommy as a baby clinging to him, his arms around his neck and his soft cheek pressed to his rough one.

Then when Tom was a bit older, standing beside him again with his arm round his neck asking questions and eagerly listening to Sam's tales of his voyages. Trotting along beside him holding his hand and saying proudly even to strangers, 'This is my dad.' At this point Sam's pain would feel unbearable and he would groan and cover his face with his hands.

He often recalled an old Irish flower seller who lived at the other end of the street saying as he and Tommy passed hand in hand. 'God love him. Sure he's the core of your heart, sir.' And it was true, Sam thought. It was still true. He couldn't stop loving Tommy.

And Ellie. His little Ellie. He thought of their childhood days, two neglected children clinging together for comfort, but then as he thought of his marriage he felt bitter anger at the way it had been so quickly arranged.

No wonder they called me Soft Sam, he thought. I just went into it blindfold, made up that I could look after her again and all the time she was tricking me. Palming off her baby as mine when she knew it wasn't.

Who was Tommy's father? Could it be Charlie West or was it someone she'd been walking out with when she was in service?

Sometimes he felt that his head would burst with these thoughts. His memories of the fellows in the Volley skitting at him, his vague feelings that something was wrong. That Ellie was keeping something from him. The way she looked at old Janey sometimes when the old one came out with some queer remark.

It was old Janey what put Ellie up to it, he thought. I hate that old one. I'll have her outa the place the minute I'm home. Home. Could he go home? I'll kill the whole lot of them when I see them, he thought. Janey, Ellie, Charlie West. They're all in it together. Making a fool outa me, thinking I'm just Soft Sam, but I'll show them.

All except Tommy. Tommy had been tricked same as he had, poor little lad.

Yet sometimes softer thoughts invaded Sam's mind. Thoughts of Ellie standing in her bright kitchen welcoming him home, his chair ready with Woodbines and matches beside it. The good meals and Ellie sitting across from him in front of the fire, smiling at him as she darned his socks.

The days out with Ellie and Tommy. The Overhead. New Brighton. Then Ellie lying in his arms, loving him. Suddenly he would feel sure it was all a mistake. True there had been no more children but the nurse and the doctor Ellie had gone to thought that was because of women's troubles. They could be right and that fellow in Freetown wrong.

Sam's mind swung back and forth wondering what he should do when they docked, but eventually he decided he must go home. He must have it out with Ellie, and if it was that Charlie West, break him in two, yet in his heart he knew that he was going home because he was desperate to see Ellie and Thomas again. He could sort his mind out better when he saw them, and maybe even go to see that Dr Wilson Ellie saw.

Jimmy McGregor was not offended by Sam's moroseness, and chattered about his affairs as they neared port. He told Sam that he had backed off in Canada on a previous voyage. 'You should've seen me book. The things I'd been logged for,' he laughed. 'I got over the border from Canada into America and I gorra ship to Southampton. I said me book had got pinched and I got another one, so I'm in the clear.'

Sam said nothing, only stared glumly at the floor, but Jimmy went on undeterred.

'You should've seen the Judy I picked up in Southampton. Real hot stuff she was, but I wanted to get back to the 'Pool and me mates. I think she fell for me. She folleed me to Liverpool.' He preened himself and Sam glanced at him.

Jimmy was a squat, ugly little man and Sam thought briefly, she must be hard up, but he was not really interested.

'She might be waiting for me when we dock,' Jimmy went on. 'She liked the 'Pool, but she might've gone back to Southampton be now.'

'Probably has,' Sam growled.

'Aye, we've been away a long time,' said Jimmy. 'Thought we was set there for a good long holiday but the way he suddenly turned and couldn't get rid of us quick enough. Must've had his eye on someone else.'

Sam said nothing and Jimmy wandered away but he was back beside Sam when the ship docked in Liverpool.

'Look over there, Sam,' he said excitedly, 'there's that tart I was telling you about. There, the red-haired one with the sort of cloak thing and a big 'at.'

Looks a real tart, a bit of no good, Sam thought, but he said nothing.

'I told you she was struck on me,' Jimmy said complacently, but when they went ashore the girl put one arm through Jimmy's arm and the other through Sam's.

'I'm froze,' she said smiling up at Sam, 'should we go for a drink?'

Sam had decided to confront Ellie as soon as he arrived home but suddenly he wanted to postpone the interview and he turned willingly into the pub. The girl, whose name was Madge Kenyon, she told Sam, ordered brandy and feeling suddenly reckless, Sam ordered the same.

'Aye why not?' Jimmy said cheerfully. 'We've got a hell of a lot of drinking to catch up on, haven't we, Sam?'

Sadness had settled on Sam again and he longed to go home but Jimmy had bought the first round so he felt obliged to stay until he had bought his round. The brandies were trebles and by the time Sam had drunk the second, quickly followed by a third and fourth, he had abandoned all thought of returning home.

It was Friday night and the public house was full, mainly with seafarers and dockers, and Sam and Jimmy bought drinks for all around them. At the end of the night, when Sam, Jimmy and Madge were equally tipsy, willing hands helped them into a taxi and they drove off to the sound of drunken cheers.

'See you in the Volley, tomorrer,' Jimmy and Madge shouted as the taxi driver hauled Sam from the cab and propped him up against his door. He knocked on the door before driving away.

Nellie only knew that Sam's ship would dock at the South End docks and she had expected him to arrive via the Overhead Railway at any time from early morning. There were no other local men on the ship so she had no one to ask, but when Sam had not arrived by ten o'clock at night she sent Tommy to bed, promising to call him when his father arrived.

When she heard the taxi and the knock on the door she went to open it but Sam pushed it open and fell into the room, knocking her back

410

against the wall. Tommy had fortunately run downstairs and between them they managed to get Sam on to the sofa.

They were engulfed in a reek of brandy fumes and Tommy said in amazement, 'He's drunk, Mam. Me dad's drunk.'

Nellie only nodded as she untied Sam's neckerchief and unbuttoned his shirt.

'Get that zinc bucket, lad,' she said. 'He's not used to brandy. He might be sick.'

She felt stunned. Nothing like this had ever happened before. Other men might call into the pub on their way home and stay for hours but Sam had always come straight home, knowing that she and Tommy would be eagerly waiting to see him, and eager to see them.

He must've fell in bad company, like, she told herself and determined not to blame Sam until she knew what had happened. She wondered briefly if she should send for her brother to help her to get Sam to bed, but quickly decided against it. This must be kept from everybody except herself and Tommy.

'Do you think we can get him upstairs to bed, lad?' she asked Tommy, and he said he was sure they could.

'I'm real strong, Mam,' he boasted, but he as well as his mother was exhausted when they finally got Sam upstairs and on to the bed.

Nellie lit a nightlight and kept it burning all night and the bucket beside the bed, as she was sure Sam would be sick, but he slept without waking until ten o'clock the next morning.

He stumbled downstairs to drop into the chair

by the fire, holding his head.

'Do you feel bad, Sam?' Nellie said timidly. 'See if this makes you feel better.'

She put a pint mug of tea beside him and Sam gulped from it, then made a headlong dash to the outside lavatory.

He came back wiping his face and put his head under the cold water tap, sluicing his head and face for several minutes. 'That's better,' he said, wiping himself on the towel Nellie handed him.

He sat down again and Tommy said loudly, 'Hello, Dad.'

'Hello, lad,' Sam said, trying to smile at the boy.

'It's the christening today and you're the godfather,' Tommy said.

'Hush, lad, don't bother your dad till he feels better,' Nellie said. 'I can send and tell them you're not well, Sam, and someone else can do it.'

Sam looked at their concerned faces and felt ashamed. His other problems had receded although he felt in a muzzy way that something must be sorted out when he felt better.

'No, it's all right, girl,' he mumbled. 'What time is it?'

'The christening's not until three o'clock and it's only just after ten now,' Nellie said.

'I'll be all right be then,' Sam said. 'I think I'll stretch me legs. Get a bit of fresh air.'

Without comment Nellie took a dry flannelette shirt from the drawer and gave it to him. 'That one's soaking,' she said.

'And you slept in it,' Tommy said, but Nellie shook her head at him reprovingly.

Sam stopped in the act of pulling off his wet shirt. 'Who got me up to bed?' he asked.

'Me and Tommy. We didn't want no one else to know,' Nellie said quietly. It was the nearest to a reproach that she had uttered and Sam's face grew red as he hurriedly pulled the dry shirt over his head.

Tommy seemed to take it for granted that he would accompany his father, and Sam was surprised to find how much the boy had grown.

'You're very near as big as me now, lad,' he said, as they walked along.

'I'm taller than Mam although I'm only ten,' Tommy boasted.

'Aye, well, your mam was always small and dainty, like,' Sam said.

'We had an awful job getting you to bed,' Tommy said laughing. 'You were a dead weight. Where had you been, Dad?'

'We docked at the South End. Went in for a brandy to warm us, like, and one folleed another. We come home in a taxi.'

'In a taxi from the South End!' Tommy gasped. 'That must've cost something, Dad.'

'Aye, I think I remember dashing him a five-pound note,' Sam said laughing. 'He probably got another one off Jimmy.'

He felt better able to walk and was able to eat his dinner when he returned. Nellie had pressed his suit and laid out a clean white shirt with it, but she told Tommy to get washed and changed first, then to read while she and Sam got ready.

Lettie had made a blue dress with a white collar for Nellie and with it she wore her blue coat, now rather faded, and a new hat.

'You both look real posh,' Tommy said when they came downstairs. Nellie was relieved that Tommy was speaking in what she thought of as an 'ordinary' voice, instead of the improved speech taught by Miss Helsby.

Before they left Sam unpacked from his seabag the presents he had brought home for Nellie and Tommy. He still intended to sort things out with Nellie but he found it harder than he expected. I'll get this christening over and maybe me head'll be better later on, he thought. Anyhow, I want her on her own when I tackle her, with Tommy out of the way.

When they reached Bobby's house he was introduced to Meg and she proudly showed him the baby. 'He's only small but I believe your Tommy was too and look at him now,' Meg said, smiling.

Sam's face had darkened at the reminder of Tommy's birth but it went unnoticed as Nellie and Meg fussed over the baby.

Meg had already dressed him in his christening robe but now they wrapped him in the shawl knitted by Nellie then put on his hat and pinned a baby veil to it.

'The shawl looks real nice, doesn't it?' Meg said. 'And the veil should keep any smuts off his face.'

At the church Nellie made her responses clearly as the minister baptised the baby David Robert, but Sam was grim and unsmiling, speaking only in a deep mumble.

Afterwards there was a small party at the house with a few of Bobby and Meg's new neighbours, some of Bobby's workmates and Nellie, Sam and Tommy.

'Are you the only relations?' Mrs Saunders asked Nellie.

'Yes, Meg only had her father and he died just before they was married,' Nellie said. 'There was only me and Bob in our family.'

'Funny, isn't it? People have either got dozens of relations on each side or hardly any. Doesn't your husband have no one belonging to him?'

She looked at Sam who was sitting quiet and morose in the corner, and Nellie said quickly. 'No. No one living.' She was anxious to distract attention from Sam, until he had recovered from his surly mood, although she had no idea what had caused it.

Meg and Bobby had provided a sit-down meal and most of the guests stayed on for the evening. Tommy was the only young boy there and Nellie asked Meg if she would mind if he left.

'He's like a fish out of water with no other lads here,' she said. 'You don't mind if he goes to his mate's house? He can stay the night there.'

'That's a good idea,' Meg said. 'Then you and Sam can stay as long as you like.'

Tommy went to say goodnight to his father and Sam growled, 'How often does this go on? You sleeping out?'

'This is only the second time,' Tommy said.

'But I'll be home before you're up in the morning, Dad.'

One of the young men had produced a mouth organ and everybody sang to the music. Bobby was going round refilling glasses and Nellie was alarmed to see how frequently Sam's glass was refilled.

He had stayed in the same corner, not joining the group round the mouth organ player or joining in the singing, and Nellie was helping Meg to hand round snacks. As she passed Sam he caught her arm. 'Come on. We're going,' he growled. 'I wanna get down to the Volley and see me mates, and I wanna talk to you too.'

Unfortunately the musician chose that moment to play 'All the nice girls love a sailor', and one young man who had tried hard to be the life and soul of the party said jokingly, 'Hey, Sam's a sailor, isn't he? A girl in every port, eh Sam?'

Nellie smiled nervously but Sam said nothing and the young man went on, 'Well, what's sauce for the goose is sauce for the gander, I say. How about it, Nellie?'

Everyone laughed but the next moment the young man was knocked flat on his back by a blow from Sam's fist.

'It was only a joke, for God's sake,' several people exclaimed, and willing hands helped the young man to his feet.

Bobby confronted Sam and Nellie had never seen her normally placid brother so angry. 'Don't come the big fellow here, Sam Meadows,' he said furiously. 'I know you had a name round the pubs for fighting

416

and our Nellie can't move for your jealousy, but by God you'll behave yourself in my house.'

The two men squared up to each other and Nellie and Meg clung to them to keep them apart.

'We'll go,' Nellie said, weeping with shame. 'I'm sorry, Meg.' She glanced at the young man's cut lip. 'I'm sorry,' she murmured.

'It's not you should be sorry,' Bobby said, and Sam turned back as though to fight again. Nellie hung on his arm and Bobby said angrily, 'Don't you come here no more, Sam Meadows.'

Nellie managed to draw Sam away and she wept bitterly as they walked down the street.

'Aye, you might well cry, you whore,' Sam said. 'I can see now what you get up to while me back's turned.'

Nellie stopped dead in amazement. '*What* did you call me?' she said in disbelief.

'A whore,' he shouted. 'You think I'm soft, don't you? I'll soon learn you I'm not. Leading that feller on.'

Suddenly Nellie was furious too. 'Maybe you know your own tricks best,' she said. 'Maybe that feller spoke the truth about sailors.'

Sam staggered as he turned to look at her. He grabbed her arm and thrust his face close to hers. 'Ya hard-faced bitch,' he snarled, but before he could say any more they were surrounded by a group of men.

'Welcome home, Sam,' one of the men called jovially, and looking up Sam realised that

417

they were outside the Volunteer. He hurriedly dropped Nellie's arm and she averted her face and hurried away, while Sam went into the public house with his friends.

CHAPTER 22

Nellie was relieved to reach the haven of her own home, where she could weep in private and try to make sense of Sam's remarks and behaviour. Calling me *that* word, she wept. It can't be because of Ada Ginley's gossip because he hasn't seen anyone who would tell him.

He's been in a queer mood ever since he came home, she thought, and then going drinking on the way home. He never done that before yet he gave me and Tommy presents. I can't make him out.

She felt hot with shame as she thought of the scene at her brother's house. What would Bobby's respectable neighbours think of her and Sam? She was only thankful that Tommy left before the fight, but Sam disgraced all of us, she thought.

He didn't like me saying he knew his own tricks best. Not that I think he carries on with other women but I don't have nothing to do with other men, yet he's always accusing me. That jealous and suspicious. It's not fair. He should trust me like I trust him.

After a while she dried her eyes. I'm a fool,

418

she thought. Sitting here crying me eyes out while he's in the Volley enjoying himself and not worrying about nothing, but she was wrong.

Sam had been treating all his mates in the Volunteer and drinking with them, but the numerous drinks, added to those he had consumed at the christening, only made him more and more morose.

His mind was clouded and confused by the drink he had taken but he felt vaguely angry and hard done by. His resentment grew as scenes from the christening began to come back to him and he tried to remember all that had gone before.

He had been tricked, he knew, and he was angry with Ellie and he struggled to remember the details.

Madge Kenyon and Jimmy McGregor were in the Volunteer and had joined him as soon as he went in, but Sam retreated more and more into a world of his own as the night went on and he grew more drunk.

Suddenly he slipped to the floor and lay full length. Madge screeched and hung over him, and Jimmy and another man tried to pull him to his feet without success. A barman came and effortlessly hauled Sam up and over to the door.

'Better outside, lad,' he said briefly, and took Sam round to the side of the Volunteer. He propped him sitting on the ground, his back against the wall.

Madge and Jimmy had followed and Madge crouched beside Sam who lay with his head sunk

419

on his chest, oblivious to what was happening.

'Are you all right, Sam?' she asked but he made no answer.

'I'm going back inside. We can't do nothing till he sobers up,' Jimmy said, but Madge said she would stay with Sam.

'He's got nearly all his pay-off on him. He might get robbed if we leave him on his own,' she said.

'More likely to get robbed if you stay with him,' Jimmy muttered, but he left her with Sam.

After a while, as Sam showed no sign of recovery, Madge filled her cupped hands with water from a horse trough and threw it in his face. He shook his head in a dazed way then opened his eyes and looked at her.

'Wharra—' he began then staggered to his feet and over to the gutter where he was violently sick.

'Oh God, oh God,' he muttered and Madge steered him to the horse trough where he splashed his face and head with water.

He sat down on a nearby wall and Madge sat beside him stroking his leg. Jimmy came out again followed by two of his married brothers who had also been drinking in the Volunteer.

'You all right, Sam?' Jimmy asked.

Sam only grunted and Madge said brightly, 'He's been sick. He put his head in the horse trough, didn't you, Sam?'

'God, I feel bad,' Sam groaned. 'Must've been something I ate at that christening.'

Jimmy and his brothers roared with laughter.

'More like something you drank, lad,' said one brother. 'You haven't half had a skinful,' but Sam had sunk into a daze again.

Madge had been sitting close to Sam brushing the pub-floor sawdust from his coat, but unseen by Jimmy and his brothers she had slipped her other hand to the inside of Sam's thigh and was gently stroking him.

He was still sitting with his head hanging low and one of the brothers said to Jimmy, 'Berra gerrim home, lad, he's goin' to go off again. Where does he live?'

'Johnson Street, the end house,' Jimmy said. 'His wife's named Ellie or Nellie.'

'Nellie Meadows? I've heard about *her*,' one of his brothers said. 'The missus heard she's on the game with Dusty Miller's wife.'

The three men tried to get Sam to his feet but they were all small men and Sam was a dead weight. They let him slip back again on to the wall and one of the brothers said, 'To hell with this. I've left me drink and some bloody minesweeper might've swigged it.'

'Aye, he's out for the count, we'll never shift him,' the other brother said and they went back into the Volunteer.

Sam had heard the man's words about Nellie without comprehending them at first, but as his head began to clear a little his rage grew. 'I knew it. I bloody knew it,' he muttered. 'On the game. The lad sleeping out.'

He struggled to his feet and with Madge and Jimmy supporting him on either side he began to make his unsteady way home. Jimmy had Sam's arm round his neck and was so engrossed in keeping him on a straight course that he was unaware that Madge, although she was holding Sam's arm, had also slipped her other hand to Sam's crotch.

'Don't worry, lad,' she was whispering in his ear. 'Why shouldn't you have a bit? *She's* on the game.'

When they were a few doors away from his house Sam stood up straight.

'All right. I'm all right,' he said thickly. 'You can—you can go back.'

'OK, as long as you're all right,' said Jimmy.

Madge reached up to kiss Sam, pressing herself against him and skilfully opening his lips with her tongue.

'Here, you're my girl,' Jimmy protested, dragging her away.

She took his arm, saying soothingly, 'Only being friendly with your mate, Jimmy.'

Nellie had meant to wait up for Sam but the stresses and upsets of the two days had exhausted her. Her head ached so much that she felt unable to keep her eyes open and finally she left the door open for Sam and went to bed.

She was lying in the darkness half asleep when she heard stumbling footsteps on the stairs and Sam lurched into the bedroom.

'Is that you, Sam?' she asked nervously.

Her innocent question seemed to be all that was needed to bring Sam's fury to a head. All the years of subconscious doubt, the taunts of his shipmates, the revelation by the doctor, the words of Jimmy's brother and his feeling of being tricked and betrayed, added to the poison dropped in his ear by Madge as she skilfully aroused him, came to a head to burst like a boil, and brought him mad with humiliation and the desire to wreak his vengeance on the body of his wife.

'Yes, it's me. Who did you expect?' he snarled, throwing off his trousers and flinging himself on the bed. He seized Nellie and shook her then tore her nightdress from her and fell upon her.

'Sam, Sam!' she screamed now fully awake and terrified.

She struggled to push him away but she was helpless beneath the weight of his heavy body as he forced himself upon her, his lips bruising her mouth and his teeth biting her neck and her breasts.

Nellie lay helpless, shock and fear depriving her of the power to speak or struggle. This was worse, far worse, than the rape by Leadbetter, because this was Sam—but a Sam she had never known or dreamed existed, snarling obscenities and saying over and over again, 'Am I Soft Sam? Am I Soft Sam?' as he thrust himself upon her like a madman.

Finally he turned away from her and fell on to the floor, and Nellie lay moaning and shuddering, feeling as though she was living through a dreadful nightmare, yet knowing by the searing pain of her body that it was only too real.

Presently Sam began to snore and Nellie, feeling like an old, old woman crept from the

423

bed trying to gather the rags of her nightdress around her. She listened fearfully for a change in the rhythm of Sam's breathing as she drew another nightdress from a drawer and crept downstairs.

She locked herself in the scullery and shivering uncontrollably, she tried to wash away evidence of the rape. She was shaking and crying so much that in the end she lifted the bowl to the floor and sank down beside it. Her body felt on fire from all that Sam had inflicted on it, yet her teeth chattered with cold and she could scarcely hold the flannel.

I'll never get over it, never, she cried as she covered her face with her hands, weeping as though her heart would break. That Sam, *Sam*, could do this to her. She felt as though the solid ground had opened beneath her feet. It was the shock and humiliation that affected her far more than the physical pain.

Eventually she managed to dry herself and put on the clean nightdress, then she went into the kitchen and flung her shawl around her. She had wrapped the rags of her other nightdress in newspaper and was about to put them in the fire she had stirred up, but she thought that the smell of them burning might bring Janey out to investigate.

She hid them in the coal bucket instead and made herself a cup of tea, crouching over the fire, still weeping and shaking. Her only consolation was that Tommy had been out of the house and had seen nothing. Would Sam have restrained himself if Tommy had been at home, she wondered, but she felt that it would have made no difference. Sam was beyond reason, as though he had suddenly gone out of his mind.

The tea restored Nellie and she began to think more rationally. What had happened to make Sam like that, she wondered? He had been angry when he left her outside the Volunteer, but nothing like the lunatic who had arrived home.

At the thought of what had happened her fragile calm deserted her and she sat moaning and sobbing, rocking herself back and forth distraught with grief and horror.

Time passed unnoticed until she heard sounds from the parlour and realised that she would soon have to face Janey. She rose stiffly and looked into the mirror over the sink. Her face was bruised and swollen, her mouth distorted and one eye almost closed.

Desperation made her think quickly. She kept clean rags in a drawer as bandages for Tommy's frequent cuts and grazes, and she took one of the largest out and tied it round her face, under her chin, tied on top of her head.

She drew her shawl over her head and when Janey emerged she was sitting by the fire, her hand to her face.

'Good God, girl, what's up with you?' Janey exclaimed.

'A gum boil,' Nellie said indistinctly. 'I've been up half the night. Outa me mind with the pain.'

'I'll give you something,' Janey said, going

back into the parlour and returning with a small black bottle.

'That'll deaden it, girl, but you won't be right till it bursts.'

Nellie thanked her and asked her to get her own cocoa before she went out, still crouching over the fire with her hand to her face.

'He he, your wits must be addled,' Janey cackled. 'It's Sunday, girl. You'd better go and lay down till that works.'

'No, I'll stay here until Tommy comes in,' Nellie said.

Janey pottered about, making her cocoa, but eventually she went back into the parlour and Nellie heard her shoot home the bolts inside the door.

Nellie lay back in the chair feeling dazed, either due to the dose from Janey or to shock, her mind empty of thought. Presently the bandage round her face irked her, and she took it off. Tommy might arrive at any moment, but he would be easier to convince about the gum boil.

She felt sleepy, as though the dose Janey had given her had not only dulled the pain but had drugged her, but she was determined to stay awake until Tommy came home. There was no sound from the parlour and she thought Janey must have gone out.

She closed her mind to all thought of Sam or the bedroom and she was taken by surprise when there was a sound on the stairs and he suddenly appeared. She sprang to her feet, cowering away from him in terror, her shawl falling back from her head to show her bruised and swollen face.

Sam stared at her in horror. 'Oh God,' he said, then stumbled through the scullery into the yard. She heard the back gate open and his uncertain heavy footsteps receding and she sank into her chair trembling and weeping bitterly.

Tommy had still not arrived and presently she dragged herself to her feet, and up to the bedroom. Whimpering with pain, and with horror at the state of the bed, she managed to take off the soiled sheets and roll them into a bundle.

She felt too weak to make up the bed, and only drew the bedspread over it, then stumbled downstairs. Fear of Tommy returning gave her the strength to fill the dolly tub with water and immerse the soiled bedding in it, then she returned thankfully to the chair.

She was sitting there in a daze when Tommy returned.

'I'm sorry I'm late, Mam,' he was saying as he came in, but he stopped, gasping in horror, when he saw her face.

Nellie had drawn her shawl close and snatched up the bandage to hold to her mouth when she heard him, but he could see enough of her bruised and swollen face and her almost closed eye to alarm him.

'Mam, what's happened? What've you done?' he exclaimed.

'It's a gum boil, lad,' Nellie said indistinctly, 'like poor Elsie in me last place.'

'Will you have to go to the dental hospital?' he asked.

'No. Janey's give me something to make it burst,' Nellie said. 'I'm going to take the rest of it and lay down. You see to yourself, son.'

'Where's me dad?' Tommy asked.

'Gone out to see his mates,' Nellie mumbled, and Tommy looked downcast. 'I thought he might be in bed. Billy's dad was going to take us to the park for a game of footer but I wanted to get home and see me dad.'

'I can't talk,' Nellie mumbled, standing up and moving to the stairs trying to conceal the stiffness of her limbs.

'Should I bring you a cup of tea, Mam?' Tommy said eagerly, but Nellie refused.

'And don't touch me washing that's in soak,' she said, afraid that Tommy might try to help by doing the washing.

Upstairs she drank the small amount left in the black bottle and with a shudder of revulsion lay down on the bedspread. She felt that she would never sleep easily in that bed again, but the drug worked and soon she had fallen into an uneasy sleep.

Sam walked unsteadily away from the house, keeping to the back entries or streets lined by warehouses. He was unshaven and unkempt and he had no wish to be seen by the respectable people making their way to morning services. He felt light headed with reaction, weak and drained of emotion by what had passed, and bitterly ashamed.

As long as he lived, he felt, he would never forget the sight of Ellie's damaged face or her instinctive terrified shrinking from him. He pounded his fists on the walls at the thought, and felt such self-hatred that he wished he was dead.

Gradually he realised that he was attracting curious glances from the few people he passed as he staggered along, and he felt that his weakness was increasing. He tried his usual remedy of sluicing his head and face in a horse trough but it made no difference.

He found himself near some cocoa rooms and went in and ordered a pint of tea. He had eaten nothing since leaving the ship except his dinner the previous day and a little at the christening, but he was unable to eat. A crowd of dockers surged in, in high spirits at getting Sunday overtime, but Sam ignored them.

He crouched in a corner drinking the scalding liquid. Deliberately he tried to close his mind to what had happened in the bedroom and all that had gone before it, but the sight of Ellie cringing away from him in fear refused to leave him. He must have gone mad, he thought.

He stood up, unable to bear his thoughts, and leaving the cocoa rooms he drifted along aimlessly, unable to think or plan, only to suffer.

His attack on Nellie seemed to have purged Sam of all bitterness, but left him instead filled with shame and remorse and a deep feeling of rejection, of being an outcast.

Suddenly there was a delighted scream of,

'Sam!' and Madge Kenyon came teetering over the waste ground in her high-heeled shoes. She grabbed his arm.

'Oh Sam, I'm that pleased to see you,' she said. 'I've done nothing but think about you all night. You'd got me right up to the boil kissing me, then you went up into your house. I was desperate for you, Sam.'

Sam said nothing but tried to pull away from her. She clung even more tightly to him.

'You look bad, Sam,' she said. 'What about a wet? The Oak's only round the corner?' Sam allowed himself to be led into the public house where Madge ordered brandy for both of them. As the spirit burned like fire down Sam's throat he began to feel more alive.

'That's better,' Madge jollied him, 'you looked like you'd lost a tanner and found an 'a'penny when I first seen you.'

Sam still said nothing and Madge began to talk about the job she said she had in the matchworks. She had noted Sam's instinctive withdrawal from her talk of sex and she was too experienced to pursue it, but she had already decided that he was going to be her means of escape from her life in Liverpool. There were too many creditors ready to demand their money and even worse, two moneylenders to whom she owed money. It was time to go, and with Sam.

She had hung on waiting for Jimmy McGregor, hoping that marriage to him would solve her problems, but he had made it clear the previous night that he had no intention of marrying.

'I've seen what it done to me brothers,' he said. 'I can kip at me old one's. She's no cop with the grub but I can get that anywhere.'

She plied Sam with drink, paying with the money she had taken from him the previous night and which he seemed not to have missed, and bought some bottles to take with her.

Gradually Sam slumped lower and lower in his seat and when he seemed to be almost asleep she roused him enough to get him to his feet.

Even in his fuddled state he resisted her attempt to lead him along the pavement outside.

'I can't go home,' he mumbled, pulling away from her.

'No Sam, we're going the other way. I've got to get something from me room,' she said soothingly. A taxi had dropped some foreign seamen and she hailed it and managed to push Sam into it.

Her landlady poked her head out from the cellar kitchen as Madge steered Sam up the steps of the house.

'I wanna see you, lady,' she said threateningly.

'I'll see you later. Me friend's not well,' Madge said glibly.

'Humph. See you do,' the woman said going back to her kitchen.

In her room Madge lowered Sam on to the bed where he promptly fell asleep.

Madge waited until she was sure that Sam was unconscious before she checked that he was carrying his seaman's book, then she cautiously withdrew his money from his pocket, leaving only loose change. She sighed with satisfaction as she counted the notes. Added to what she had stolen from him the previous night it would be enough to take them back to her home town of Southampton for a fresh start.

She pushed the notes inside her brassière and quickly changed from her flamboyant clothes into a plain and shabby coat and skirt, and covered her hair with a black hat. Sam stirred and grunted and she quickly filled a cup with brandy but he had fallen asleep again.

As she made her preparations for flight, packing an old carpet bag with her clothes and trinkets, she watched Sam warily, and gave him small amounts of drink whenever he woke. She would have to wait until darkness fell, and she wanted Sam drunk enough to be unable to realise what was happening, but not incapable.

When she judged that the time was right she roused him and led him downstairs, but the noise he made alerted the landlady. 'Where d'yer think you're going?' she demanded, and Madge skilfully dropped the carpet bag behind her.

'I was taking him home for his seabag,' she said meekly, 'but I think I'd better send a lad. He's too shaky.'

The word 'home' had penetrated Sam's muzzy mind and he made a clumsy gesture of protest, but Madge said quickly, 'All right, lad. Sit on the step. I'll send a lad.'

Quickly she called a boy and told him quietly to go to the house in Johnson Street. 'Say a big fella sent you,' she whispered. 'And you're to take the bag to the Seaman's. Bring it here and

432

I'll give you sixpence.'

In a short time the boy was back with the bag. 'Who give it to you?' Madge whispered.

'A young lad. Said his mam was asleep,' the boy said, snatching his sixpence and racing away. Madge had already taken the carpet bag back upstairs and now she sped lightly up to her room with Sam's bag.

Quickly she transferred her clothes and trinkets into it then took it downstairs. 'Here's your bag, Sam,' she said loudly as she regained the front door where Sam sat slumped on the step, and as she expected, the landlady looked out again.

Like a bloody cuckoo in a clock, Madge muttered to herself, but aloud she said, 'He's got his bag. I'll put him in a cab to the Seaman's.'

Stepping out she hailed a passing taxi. 'The Seaman's,' she said loudly, 'but hang on.'

She got Sam to his feet and into the taxi then went back for his bag. As she threw it into the cab she jumped in after it and slammed the door. 'Never mind the Seaman's. Lime Street,' she said. As she looked back she could see that the landlady had run up the area steps and was standing, hands on hips, screaming after her.

The taxi driver could also see her in his mirror and he winked at Madge. 'Eloping, are yer?' he said.

'Something like that,' she said with a laugh.

The man nodded at Sam. 'You'll have to sober him up before he'll be any use to you, girl,' he said lewdly.

'Don't be hard faced,' Madge said, annoyed

that the man had so quickly summed her up. He wouldn't talk like that to Sam's bloody wife, she thought.

There had been some discussion about Nellie and Sam in the Volunteer the previous night, and most people had disagreed with Jimmy's brother's comments about Nellie being 'on the game'.

'That's wash-house jangle,' George Adams' brother Harry said. 'Our Rose said Nellie and her mate met Dusty Miller's one when they was on the way to the pictures, and walked along with her, like.'

'Aye, Nellie's a real respectable little woman and Sam thinks the world of her,' another man said.

'No smoke without fire though,' Madge had giggled.

'No, you've only got to look at Nellie to see she's not on the game,' Harry Adams said. 'You can soon pick out the ones that is.'

He had looked at Madge with contempt, and remembering that look Madge was even more determined to get Sam away. She managed to buy two single tickets and get Sam on to the platform, but he seemed to rouse and he looked about him in a bewildered way.

'Wha—wha's happening? Where are we?' he asked thickly. 'We're getting a train, lad,' Madge said quickly. 'You can't go home. Your wife's threw you out and got her fancy man in. He brought your bag.'

Sam looked at his bag but before he could speak Madge put a bottle of overproof rum to his mouth and tilted it so that the fiery spirit ran down his throat.

Sam was in a drunken stupor when she got him on to the train with the help of two burly passengers and a porter.

As the train began to move Madge sank down beside him with a sigh of relief. She'd done it, she thought triumphantly. She'd got him away right under the nose of his mealy-mouthed wife and his mates and there was no way she would ever let him go.

She would have the time of her life now with Sam as her protector, and on her home ground. She took a swig herself from the bottle of rum and began to hum a bawdy song.

CHAPTER 23

In later years, whenever Tom heard the word 'interminable' he was reminded of that Sunday. While his mother lay in her drugged sleep upstairs he sat in the silent house, expecting that at any moment his father would return, and afraid to leave the house in case he missed him.

Gradually as the slow minutes crept by, the conviction grew in him that something was horribly wrong, something much worse than his mother's gum boil and his father's absence. There was a strange feeling in the house, he felt.

From time to time he sneaked upstairs to look at his mother but she slept on, making a strange guttural sound as she breathed. She was lying on the bedspread covered only by her shawl and Tom could see the extent of the damage to her face. Could a gum boil do this? he wondered.

Downstairs again he watched the hands of the clock which seemed scarcely to move, and listened to every footstep that approached the house, hoping it was his father's, but he was always disappointed.

From time to time he cut thick slices of bread and spread them with jam for himself, and went upstairs to ask if his mother wanted food but she still slept.

At last there was a quiet knock on the front door and Tommy flung it open eagerly, but only a ragged young boy stood there. 'Some big fella sent me for his seabag,' he said. 'He's gonna give me sixpence if I take it to the Seaman's.'

'Was it me dad?' asked Tommy, but the boy shrugged.

'Just a big fella,' he said. 'Give us it quick. I wanna get me sixpence.'

'Me mam's asleep,' Tommy said doubtfully.

'I don't want yer bleedin' mam,' the boy said impatiently. 'Give us the bag. There it is.' He pointed to where the bag lay in a corner and Tommy gave it to him.

Several times he had knocked at the parlour door but there was no answer and now he tried again but without success.

Darkness had fallen completely when he

436

heard a sound then his mother came shakily downstairs.

'Oh, Tommy lad, how long have I been asleep?' she asked in a dazed way.

'*All day*, Mam, and me dad hasn't come home,' Tommy cried, 'and Janey's out too.'

Nellie sank into her chair. 'Fetch me a wet flannel, lad,' she said and the boy rushed to bring the flannel and towel.

'Has it burst, Mam?' he asked.

Nellie looked bewildered. 'What burst, lad? What do you mean?'

'The gum boil,' Tommy said, and she made a visible effort to collect her thoughts.

She dabbed her face with the wet flannel and wiped it with the towel then handed them to her son.

'Not yet, lad,' she said. 'Did you get sump'n' to eat?'

'Yes, jam butties. Why is me dad at the Seaman's, Mam? When's he coming home?'

'The *Seaman's*?' Nellie exclaimed, looking wildly at him. 'Who said he was at the Seaman's?'

'The lad that come for his bag,' Tommy said, and as Nellie gave a cry of pain he shouted, 'Mam, Mam, what's going on? What's happening?'

Nellie put her arm round the boy. 'It's all right, lad,' she said. 'Who was the lad? What did he say?'

'I don't know. He was just a scruffy kid. He said a big fella told him to take the bag to the Seaman's and he'd give him sixpence. I asked if he was me dad and he didn't know.'

Nellie had been sitting with her hand over her mouth, thinking, and now she said hopefully, 'Maybe it was just a trick to steal the bag, Tom. Your dad might've talked out of turn when he was drunk and someone got the idea to rob his bag. Not that there was much in it, mind you.'

'He'd took our presents out,' Tommy said.

'He might've left his book in it, even his pay-off,' Nellie said, and Tommy looked alarmed. 'I shouldn't have give it to him, but I couldn't wake you, Mam, and Janey was out too.'

'It's all right, lad. I'm not worried about the bag,' Nellie said. 'I just wish I knew. He's probably just drinking somewhere.'

'Should I see if he's in the Volley?' Tommy asked and Nellie agreed.

The boy sped away but he was soon back, looking downcast.

'The barman said he hasn't been in all day,' he said.

'Oh God, where is he?' Nellie murmured despairingly and they clung together crying. 'Your poor dad,' Nellie wept. 'He's not well, Tom, not himself, like. I don't know what they done to him in that hospital.' She dried her eyes. 'I'll have to go and see is he in the Seaman's,' she said firmly.

The next moment there was a knock at the door and they looked at each other in wild hope, neither stopping to think that Sam would just have walked in. Tommy darted to the door but when he opened it only his Uncle Bobby stood there.

'Your mam in, lad?' he asked, stepping in, then as he saw Nellie's damaged face he shouted in horrified anger, 'Did *he* do that? I'll bloody murder him.'

Nellie's shawl drawn close under her chin hid her neck and her bruised arms but there was no way that she could hide her face. She stood up and faced Bobby with dignity.

'It's not your business, Bob,' she said quietly, 'it's between me and Sam.'

'Of course it's my business. You're my sister, aren't you?' Bobby said angrily. 'Where is he?'

Tommy was about to speak but his mother glanced at him and shook her head. 'He's not here,' she said.

'And that happened after you left my house?' Bobby said. 'I was mad enough about him belting me mate and upsetting Meg, but to do that to you! He's not getting away with it, our kid.'

'This hasn't got nothing to do with the christening,' Nellie said. 'It hasn't got nothing to do with you at all.'

'How can you stick up for a fella what done that to you?' Bobby exclaimed angrily. 'Well, I tell you this. He never sets foot in my house again. You're always welcome, Nell, but I don't want him there no more.'

'No, thank you,' Nellie said quietly. 'I don't go where me husband's not welcome.'

'But good God, after he done that to you,' Bobby said. 'You're a fool if you stick to him, Nellie, I tell you straight. You're always welcome though, girl. You done a lot for me

439

and Meg and I don't forget it.'

But Nellie was adamant. 'I don't go where Sam's not welcome,' she said again.

'I'd better go, then,' Bobby said, 'but don't forget. If I meet that fella I'll learn him to batter me sister, whether you want me to or not.' He flung out of the house and Nellie sank back weeping, into her chair.

Tom crouched beside her. 'Why is Uncle Bob so mad, Mam?' he asked, looking bewildered. 'It's not me dad's fault you've got a gum boil, is it?'

Nellie dried her eyes. 'I'd better tell you the truth, lad,' she said with a sigh. 'It's not a gum boil. Your dad done it but he didn't know what he was doing. It's that illness he had, or something them doctors done to him. It's kind of turned his brain, like.'

The boy said nothing for a moment then he asked quietly, 'Should we go to the Seaman's, Mam, and try to find him?'

Nellie put her hand up to her face. 'Better not, lad. I don't want to make a show of him with me face like this. Anyhow, the more I think of it the more I think it was just a trick to pinch his bag. People get up to all kinds to rob seamen. We'll hang on and wait for your dad to come home.'

She felt sure that Sam was drinking somewhere and would return eventually, but she was also sure that there would be no repetition of the horror of the previous night.

The slow minutes crawled by as they waited for Sam or for some message from him but

440

nothing happened. After a while Nellie boiled an egg for Tommy and made a bowl of bread and milk for herself. She found it difficult to eat even this, but she felt stronger after she had eaten it.

At ten o'clock Nellie sent the boy to bed, promising to call him if anything happened. He went obediently and lay awake straining his ears for any sound, but time crawled by and he heard nothing.

Nellie sat downstairs thinking of Sam as she had seen him that morning but she blocked out the details of the rape from her mind. Strangely she felt no hatred or revulsion towards him for the attack on her. It all seemed too unreal, too completely alien to Sam as she had always known him.

She felt that a stranger had suddenly entered her bed, and she believed what she had told Tommy, that Sam was suffering from the effects of his illness and the doctor's treatment.

He wasn't right from when he first come home, she thought. Even when he took them presents out he looked as though he didn't know properly what they was. As if he'd forgot what he'd bought for me and Tommy. And to go drinking on his way home when he came ashore. He'd never done that before, always come straight home to them, yet he'd tried. Walking with Tom and standing up with her at the christening. Wearing his good suit and his white shirt as though everything was all right.

Poor lad, she thought. He must have knew something was wrong but been too moithered to know what. And something must've happened to his poor head last night, she thought, her mind shying away from any detailed memory. The picture of Sam as she had seen him last rose again in her mind.

The anguish of his expression as he looked at her and his involuntary groan of, 'Oh God,' before he fled convinced her that he had been possessed by something beyond his control when he attacked her.

She built up the fire and from time to time bathed her face in salt water. It made the wounds sting but she felt that it would make them heal more quickly. When weariness overcame her after midnight she lay down on the sofa, wrapping herself in her shawl, and dozed lightly, starting up at any noise from outside the house.

She had not heard Janey return but the following morning the old woman came into the kitchen from the parlour. She stared at Nellie's face and Nellie said wearily, 'All right, Janey. It wasn't a gum boil. Sam battered me.'

She was determined that no one would ever know what had really transpired.

'I never thought it was,' Janey said, 'but I thought me bottle'd do some good.'

'It did,' Nellie said, 'especially the second dose I took. I was doped all day.'

'The dregs is always stronger,' Janey said. She went back into her room and brought another small bottle and a jar of ointment. 'Where is he, the quare fella?' she asked.

442

'I don't know,' Nellie said. 'He never come home.'

She knew that it was useless to try to conceal anything from Janey, but the old woman only said, 'Did you get your money out of his pay-off?'

'Not yet,' Nellie said. She was still hoping for Sam to return and she was sure that he would never leave her without money.

'You're a fool, girl. You shoulda made sure of it right off. Plenty round here who'll help him to spend it,' Janey said.

She drank her cocoa and left saying she would keep her ears open for news of Sam, and as soon as she left Nellie took the rags of her nightdress from the coal bucket and burned them. She knew that Tommy, who had stayed awake so long, had now fallen into a heavy sleep.

She had opened the evil-smelling jar of ointment that Janey had given her and closed it again, deciding instead to use Zam Buck ointment on her wounds. It doesn't smell much better than Janey's stuff, she thought as she spread the pink ointment, but it helped to cover the smell of the burning rags.

From time to time as she pottered about, she envisaged Sam as she had last seen him, with the look of anguish and horror on his face, and she regretted her instinctive recoil from him. She little knew then how often that picture of Sam would fill her mind in the years to come.

She drank frequent cups of tea but she felt too tense and tightly strung to eat. If only Sam would come home.

It was midday when Tommy woke and came downstairs. 'Has me dad been home, Mam?' he asked eagerly, and his face fell when Nellie shook her head.

'Maybe he was at the Seaman's after all,' she said.

'But he'd be awake now though,' Tommy said. Nellie made bread and dripping for him and a cup of tea without replying and Tommy said coaxingly, 'I don't have to go to school this avvy, do I, Mam?'

'Good God, I'd forgot it was Monday,' Nellie exclaimed. 'No, I could do with you here with me, lad.'

She longed to go out to find any news of Sam but she was ashamed to let her neighbours see her face, yet she dreaded waiting alone for news.

Shortly after two o'clock Katy called. She made no comment about Nellie's face but only asked Tommy to go to the corner shop for her.

'I wanted him out of the way,' she said quickly when the boy had gone. 'Sam wasn't home last night, was he?' Nellie shook her head and Katy took her hand. 'Listen, Nell. I hate telling you this but I think someone should let you know. You don't want to hear it in the street.'

'Hear what?' Nellie asked fearfully.

'Me mam got told Sam was on Lime Street Station last night with that tart of Jimmy McGregor's,' Katy said. 'He was paralytic drunk and some fellas helped her to get him on the

444

train to London. He had his bag with him.'

'Sam? You're sure it was Sam?' Nellie asked.

'Me mam said the feller knew Sam what told her,' Katy said sadly.

Nellie sat in stunned silence for a moment then she said in a bewildered way, 'But Sam. With that woman. He never knew her.'

'She met them off the ship, and they was drinking together in the South End,' Katy said. 'Her and Jimmy McGregor was in the Volley with Sam on Friday night. He got put out and they brought him home.'

Nellie sat twisting the edge of her apron in her fingers, unable to speak. Sam. Sam with another woman. She couldn't believe it.

Katy looked anxiously at her. 'I thought you might have knew, Nell, and I'd be talking out of turn, but we're mates. I didn't want you sitting here not knowing nothing or getting it thrown at you by the likes of Ada Ginley.'

'I know. Thanks, Katy,' Nellie murmured.

'She's a real bad lot, that Madge Kenyon,' Katy said. 'She come here with Jimmy McGregor when he put in to another port before he came home, but she hung on here after he'd went back to sea. Me mam said she was a pro but she was up to her eyes in debt and she had to scarper. God knows why Sam went with her though. Mind you, me mam said he was that paralytic he was very near lifted on to the train.'

Nellie knew that her friend was rambling on to give her time to recover, but her mind felt paralysed and she sat in silence. She realised that Katy was looking at her face and she felt that she must think of a story which excused Sam, but her mind was blank.

She was glad when Tommy arrived back with Katy's message, to distract attention from her, but the boy began to tell Katy about Sam's seabag.

'I want to go to the Seaman's to look for me dad,' he said. 'But Mam won't let me.'

'Better not, lad,' Katy said gently.

'But me dad's sick. He needs us,' Tommy said.

Nellie roused herself. 'It's all right, Tom. We'll sort it out. Go out and play, lad, while I talk to Mrs Rimmer.'

When the boy had gone Nellie said quietly, 'I seen you looking at me face, Katy. Sam done it on Saturday night but he didn't know what he was doing. I've never seen him that drunk but I think it was more than that. There's something wrong with him, Katy. That illness while he was abroad or whatever that doctor done to him. He was out of his mind, like.'

'It wasn't like him to do that,' Katy said. 'Or to get mixed up with that bad lot. Jimmy McGregor was saying she was supposed to be his girl but his brothers told him he was lucky to be shut of her, and he said she'd tried to get him to marry her but he wasn't having any. Maybe that's why she latched on to Sam.'

'Sam bashed a fella at the christening,' Nellie said. 'Our Bobby was round here swearing vengeance on him.'

'Maybe Bob could find more out for you,' Katy said, 'although, mind you, no one's better

446

at that than me mam. She hardly moves out of the house but she gets to know everything that goes on.'

'I'm glad to know what's happened although I can't believe it,' Nellie said. 'Sam with another woman. He's never looked at anyone else, not even women in ports, like. But there's nothing worse than sitting here waiting and wondering. Thanks for telling me, Katy.'

'I'm only sorry it wasn't better news,' Katy said. She stood up and kissed Nellie impulsively. 'Chin up, girl,' she said. 'You've still got plenty of good mates.'

When Katy had gone Nellie was suddenly taken by a fit of trembling which made her shake like a patient with St Vitus's dance. Gradually she managed to control it, gritting her teeth and gripping the arms of her chair, but she felt weak and drained.

She knew that it was the result of shock and that if she was not to break down completely she must close her mind to all that had happened. She would tell Tom his father had gone then refuse to discuss it any more.

When Tommy came in he found his mother busily cooking eggs and bacon for their meal. She turned to him.

'Your father's gone. He's took a train,' she said. 'I don't want to hear no more about it. It's over.'

'But, Mam,' Tommy began and Nellie thrust her face close to his.

'Not another word, I said. It's over. Behind us,' she hissed at him, her eyes glittering.

447

Shocked and frightened the boy ate his meal without speaking again, darting nervous glances at his mother. Was she going out of her mind too? he wondered. Nellie's lips were still swollen and obviously it was painful for her to eat, but she doggedly chewed the bacon and ate slices of bread and butter.

For once she was pleased to hear the thump of Janey's fish basket being put down, but when the old woman came into the kitchen she said nothing about Sam. She seemed engrossed in her own troubles, crouching close to the fire and complaining bitterly about the cold weather.

Nellie poured her a mug of tea and Janey took a bottle of rum from her fishwife's pocket and poured some into the cup. 'You wanna try some of this, girl,' she said. 'Do you the world of good. Get rid of yer troubles.'

'Maybe I will, then,' Nellie said grimly. She dished up the bacon and eggs for Janey and the old woman peered at her face. 'That looks better. Was it me ointment? Did you take me jollop?'

'No, I'll take the lot tonight,' Nellie said. 'Knock meself out.'

Janey could only eat a little of the eggs and bacon Nellie cooked for her, and soon decided to go to bed. Nellie filled her hot-water bottle and made her a hot toddy with some rum, and for once the old woman seemed grateful.

'You're a good girl,' she said. 'You don't deserve none of these troubles.' She was wheezing as she breathed and Nellie looked at her anxiously.

'Will you be all right, Janey?' she asked. 'I've built up your fire.'

'Aye, I'll be all right,' Janey said. 'I'll sweat it out of me. Be all right in the morning.'

Nellie sent Tommy to bed early and soon followed him. No matter how she tried to close her mind to all that had happened, thoughts of Sam with Madge Kenyon kept breaking in.

Sam with another woman. All her compassionate thoughts of him, her belief that his illness and treatment had unbalanced his mind and caused him to act out of character, were forgotten and she was filled with a primitive bitter rage.

Sam unfaithful, after all she had put up with over the years because he had unjustly suspected her of what he was now doing himself. The rows because of his jealousy, and the way she had always tried to soothe him although she had never looked at another man.

Was that why he had been so angry when the young man at Bob's house had made a joking remark about sailors and girls? Perhaps even then he was planning to run off with this prostitute. I'll never forgive him, never, she thought.

She drank the whole of the contents of the bottle Janey had given her, feeling that if she could not soon find oblivion she would go mad, and suddenly fell deeply asleep.

Janey slept too in her frowsty bed, drugged by the rum, but Tommy lay awake. He knew now that something had happened, something that meant that his father would never come again, although his mother refused to talk about it.

He loved his father so much and had looked forward to his return for so long that now he was filled with grief and disappointment. The shock was all the greater because he had always looked up to his father and now it seemed his father had done something which made his mother so angry that she refused to speak of him.

And it's all my fault, Tommy thought. It was me made my dad so mad that he did whatever he did. Mam had told me not to talk posh in front of me dad, and I didn't when I went for the walk with him, but at the christening I did it just to show off.

That's what made me dad mad. That started it all, him punching that fella in Uncle Bob's, then getting drunk and belting Mam. It's all my fault.

Guilt and misery brought tears to his eyes, and although he felt that at ten years old he was too old to cry he was unable to stop the tears and he cried himself to sleep.

The following morning Nellie went about the kitchen tight lipped and grim, frying bread for Tommy's breakfast and making cocoa for Janey, who had come through from the parlour as usual.

Tommy was afraid to speak and Nellie said nothing until she said curtly, 'Get off to school.'

Tommy escaped thankfully. It seemed that the previous morning when they had comforted each other belonged to another age.

Katy came and offered to do Nellie's shopping but she refused help.

'I'll go myself,' she said. 'I'm not the first round here with a black eye and I won't be the last.'

She went to the shops wrapped in her shawl, her head high, looking so forbidding that no one dared to ask any questions. Even her friends felt unable to offer help or comfort because they were intimidated by her manner.

The shock of hearing of Sam's flight with another woman seemed to have suddenly changed Nellie from the gentle timid girl she had been into a grim hard woman. Over the following days she seemed to withdraw into a world of her own, brooding on past incidents to fuel her feelings of anger and betrayal.

Her outrage at the thought of Sam with another woman hardened her so that she seemed to become encased in an inflexible shell. She rejected any offer of sympathy and rarely spoke even to Tommy or Janey.

Tommy was bitterly unhappy. He felt that he had lost his mother as well as his father and blamed himself for all that had happened.

He stopped going to Miss Helsby's class and spoke as roughly as the most neglected urchin, and soon began to look like one. He rejected all the training in cleanliness and manners and pride in himself which Miss Helsby had taught, feeling that the lessons had been the cause of the trouble.

Withdrawn into her own misery and indifferent to all that was happening, Nellie failed to notice the change in Tommy, and nobody dared to point it out to her. Messages sent to

451

his mother through Tommy were thrown away as soon as he left the school.

Nellie's only concession was to watch eagerly for a letter from Sam, which might have explained his flight, but as the days passed it was clear that this was a vain hope. She often thought of a phrase quoted by Mr Ambrose, 'Hope deferred maketh the heart sick.'

A letter had arrived from Meg shortly after Nellie's quarrel with Bob. Meg wrote that she was sorry about the quarrel and although she must stand by Bob she would always be grateful to Nellie. It was clear that she would not be visiting Nellie but to Nellie, immersed in her larger grief, it was unimportant. She put the letter aside indifferently.

Later she heard that Meg had been found to be suffering from tuberculosis and she and Bob and the baby had returned to Yorkshire, but Bob had not contacted Nellie before they went.

CHAPTER 24

Two weeks had passed since the fateful Saturday night when there was a loud knock on the door and Nellie opened it to find a policeman standing there.

'Mrs Meadows?' he asked.

Nellie's hand flew to her heart and she said faintly, 'Sam.'

'Does a Jane Hitchmough live here?' the

policeman asked.

Nellie looked at him stupidly then as her mind adjusted she said with relief, 'Yes, old Janey.'

'She's collapsed in the street and been took to Belmont Road and she's given you as next of kin,' the policeman said. 'Will you want to go and see her?'

Nellie nodded and he told her that Janey was on an urgent note and could be visited at any time.

'So she's bad, then?' Nellie said.

The policeman shrugged. 'Well, an urgent note, missus,' he said. 'What relation is she?'

'No relation but she's lodged here since my ma lived here,' Nellie said.

'Better not tell the sister that,' the man said. 'She's a Tartar. Mightn't let you in.'

It was eight o'clock at night and for the first time Nellie realised that Tommy was not in and that she had no idea where he was. She called a boy and asked him, but he could tell her nothing. 'If you see him tell him I've had to go out and to go to bed,' she said. The decision to keep her affairs to herself was instinctive but totally different to Nellie's attitude before her troubles.

Belmont Road was a workhouse hospital and Janey was in a long bleak ward with the beds very close together. The sister confronted Nellie. 'What relation?' she snapped.

'Niece,' Nellie said, remembering the policeman's warning.

'Then you should be ashamed of yourself,' the sister snapped. 'My nurses had to take a

453

scrubbing brush to your aunt. She was in a filthy state.'

'How is she?' Nellie said, ignoring her remarks.

'Very ill. Very little chance of recovery,' the sister said triumphantly.

'And less since she's been scrubbed,' Nellie said, walking to Janey's bed and leaving the sister open mouthed. The days when I was frightened of them sort are over, Nellie thought grimly.

Janey was propped up on high pillows wearing a calico nightdress. Her breathing was shallow and her face flushed but she looked at Nellie and grinned, 'What did you say to that one?' she asked. 'I seen the gob on her.'

Janey's bed was against the wall and although the bed on the other side of her was almost touching hers the occupant of it seemed to be unconscious, so Nellie quietly told Janey what had happened.

She grinned again and wheezed. 'Yer getting hard faced in yer old age, girl.'

'What happened to you?' Nellie asked. 'You shouldn't have gone out this morning with that chest.'

Janey drew her closer. 'It wasn't really me chest,' she whispered. 'I got set on. Woulda been knifed only for the copper on the beat. I just collapsed, like, and he had me fetched here.'

Nellie laughed. 'You crafty old beggar,' she whispered, 'and they've put you on an urgent note.'

The patients in the ward seemed to have

454

been settled for the night and Nellie said she would go.

'Come and see me tomorrer,' Janey begged and Nellie promised that she would.

'I'll bring you something to eat,' she said, and Janey asked for a pig's trotter.

'I just fancy a trotter,' she said and Nellie promised to bring one.

The next day she seemed to be gasping for breath as Nellie approached the bed, but she whispered that it was just an act. 'Don't want them taking the urgent note off me,' she said. Nellie had brought the pig's foot and some bread and butter, and Janey devoured them.

When she had finished she looked searchingly at Nellie. 'You look as if you need a good feed yourself, girl,' she said, and suddenly Nellie felt her eyes fill with tears.

'You're not crying over Sam Meadows, are you?' Janey said. 'Listen, girl, you're well rid of him. There's things I could tell. Bad blood. You know all them children died young. All what was born after Sam.'

'I know. They was an unlucky family,' Nellie said.

'Unlucky me arse,' Janey whispered. 'It was because his da picked up some disease from some foreign woman and fetched it home to his poor wife. Lucky it was after Sam was born but none of the others lived and she died before she was thirty.'

Nellie's eyes were wide with shock. 'But Sam thought it was TB. He thought that was why the neighbours never took him in.'

'No, it was on account of what they all died of,' Janey said. 'The first one took fits and the others—there was a little girl, she was an object, and then a lad and he died at six months. Looked a hundred.'

'But Sam?' Nellie whispered.

'He was all right. Born when they was first married and his old fella was a steward on the liners—when they was well off. Never showed for years with the old fella but then his brain went funny and he turned against Sam and threw him out.'

'And what about Sam's mother?' Nellie asked.

'She died just after Sam got threw out,' Janey said. 'A terrible death and the old fella went like a bag of bones. Signed on a dirty old tramp and two days out of Liverpool he went over the side. Supposed to be an accident.'

Nellie felt stunned but the talking seemed to have exhausted Janey. She lay back with her eyes closed and although there were many things Nellie longed to ask her, she felt that the old woman was too tired.

When she stood up to go Janey gripped her wrist. 'A fella might come for some stuff. Let him take it.'

'Yes, all right,' Nellie agreed. 'I'll come and see you again.'

'Come tomorrow. I've gotta lot to tell you, girl,' Janey wheezed.

Nellie felt dazed as she walked home. Could she believe old Janey? It all seemed so farfetched. Was this what she had been hinting about when she said she knew things about Sam's family?

Nellie reached home at five o'clock and found that Tommy had been in from school and had gone out again. She prepared their meal, her mind still full of Janey's revelations, and before Tommy came back she opened the side door to the parlour with her key, and pushed back the bolts on the door into the kitchen.

She looked round the parlour in disgust, at the pile of dirty blankets on the truckle bed in the corner, and the general dirt of the room. She had forgotten to ask Janey what the man might come for, and she could see nothing that seemed of use to anyone. She would have to see what the man asked for.

Tommy came in and bolted his meal then darted out again.

'Don't you be late,' she shouted after him but she thought he had already gone out of earshot.

It was dark when she heard a banging on the side door which she had relocked, and then a loud knock on her own door.

The man who stood there looked at her aggressively. 'Where's old Janey?' he snapped.

'If you mean my aunt she's in hospital,' Nellie said coolly.

'Yer aunt. I thought she was yer lodger,' he said.

'I don't let lodgers live rent free,' Nellie said. She felt that she needed to assert herself with the man before she allowed him into the house.

'I've got some stuff here and I want it,' he blustered.

'So me aunt said,' Nellie answered. 'You can

457

come in.' She led the way into the parlour and lit the gas, her eyes never leaving the young man.

He went directly to an old shawl which was thrown on a corner cupboard and lifted it, taking out a red bandanna handkerchief tied at the corners and opening it to show a pile of jewellery. Nellie's mouth fell open in amazement but by the time the man had checked the jewels and turned back to her she had recovered.

'Don't you say nothing about this to anyone,' he growled.

'Don't worry. I don't know nothing about it and I don't want to know,' Nellie said. 'Don't you come back no more either.'

'Will *she* be coming back?' he asked, less aggressively.

'Of course, but things will be different,' Nellie said. She unlocked the side door and let him out, then shot home the bolts before going out of the side door, locking it and going round to her own front door. I don't want no one walking through here into the parlour when I'm out, she thought. Her own door was never locked.

So that was what Janey had been up to. Them's stolen jewels or I'm a Dutchman. Good job I never knew or I'd've been worried to death, she thought.

She slept little now and that night while she lay awake she thought over Janey's revelations about Sam's family. I'll make sure I never tell Sam about them, she thought, but immediately she realised that she would never tell Sam anything ever again.

Suddenly the thought struck her that history might be repeating itself. Perhaps Sam had picked up a disease from a foreign woman and that was why he had been in hospital. Why he had behaved so strangely when he came home.

But Sam never went with those women, she thought, but then she gave a grim smile. What a fool she had been, believing all he had told her. That he never picked women up abroad and then he had picked up that tart right here on his own doorstep. I'll never trust anyone again, she vowed, and never cry over him no more either.

She was impatient to see Janey again to learn more from her, but the old woman was dozing when she arrived and seemed disinclined to answer any questions. She roused herself when Nellie produced sandwiches and told her about the man who came for the jewels.

'I never knew that was what you was up to in there, Janey,' Nellie said.

'No harm, girl. Just doing a favour.'

Nellie began to ask questions about Sam's family but Janey's replies were vague and sometimes contradicted what she had said the previous day. Nellie began to wonder whether she could believe Janey. She knew the old woman was a liar, and Sam was convinced that his family had been wiped out with TB, yet why would Janey tell such lies?

'Why didn't you tell me before about Sam's

dad?' Nellie said. 'You've kept it quiet all these years.'

'You've been good to me, girl,' Janey mumbled. 'You don't want to be crying over the quare fella. Maybe he's the same as his old fella.'

Nellie felt even more confused. Could Janey have told this tale to stop her grieving for Sam? Her mind was so twisted that it was possible, Nellie thought.

She stood up to go but Janey gripped her wrist.

'Don't go, girl,' she said urgently. 'I wanna tell you this in case I go.'

'You've got plenty of time yet,' Nellie said, 'you can tell me tomorrow,' but the old woman seemed agitated and Nellie was curious so she sat down again.

'It's about yourself,' Janey whispered. 'Harriet wasn't your ma. That's why she hated you.'

'Not me ma?' Nellie gasped. 'Who was?' For a wild moment she thought that Janey might claim her, but the old woman leaned closer.

'A girl what lodged with us where we lived before. A nursery maid in a big house, she'd been. Walked out with your da when he was home from sea. She fell for you after he sailed.'

'So me da really was me da?' Nellie said.

Janey nodded. 'She had to leave her place. Kept herself be sewing. Harriet took her as lodger. She was expecting herself to a Norwegian but he scarpered.'

She lay back, breathless, and Nellie gave her a

drink of water. She was determined to hear the end of the story from Janey. 'What happened to me mother?' she asked.

'They was going to get married but she was in labour when he come ashore. She died the next day. He was out of his mind.'

'And Harriet?' Nellie prompted her.

'She'd just had hers. Born dead. She was mad about Tom, that's your da, mad about him. That's why she took Helen's baby in, so she'd see Tom.' The old woman's face twisted in a sneer. 'Harriet. Soft cow. Tom never looked the side of the street she was on.'

Nellie looked bewildered. 'But how did I—?' she began but Janey flapped her hand, gasping for breath.

'Wait wait,' she panted. 'She wanted Tom. Any road. Any road at all. Said she'd take the kid and rear it. He'd have to marry her. Give the kid a name.'

'The kid? That was me?' Nellie said.

'Yes. We shifted to Johnson Street,' Janey said.

Her voice was faint and she seemed to be falling asleep or unconscious but Nellie leaned over her.

'Janey, just tell me this. Did me da marry me mother before she died?'

'No. Told yer,' she said fretfully, 'in labour. Died next day.'

It was clear she could say no more and Nellie left, planning to go again the following day.

Her thoughts were chaotic but she never doubted the truth of this tale. It made sense

461

of much that had always puzzled her. She felt enormous relief that Harriet, who had always hated and ill-treated her, was not her mother, yet it meant that she was illegitimate.

The part that was hard to believe was that Harriet was in love with her da. That that big rough bully, who terrified Janey's clients and everyone else in the neighbourhood could feel such an emotion was incredible, yet Nellie believed that it was true.

The transformation in Harriet when Da came home, her new clothes and her meekness and efforts to please him, although he slipped away from her like quicksilver. Even the different treatment of Nellie and her new clothes while her father was home were explained.

I must find out more about my real mother, Nellie thought, but then another thought struck her. Bobby. What about Bobby? Who was *his* mother?

She could think of nothing but Janey's story as she lay awake during the night, and fresh questions constantly rose in her mind.

She was so impatient to see Janey that she went to see her in the morning, braving the sister's disapproval.

'I thought I could see me aunt any time on an urgent note,' she said. 'She thought she wouldn't last through the night.'

I'm getting as good a liar as Janey, she thought as she went to the bed.

The old woman was breathless and exhausted but she seized Nellie's hand.

'I'm glad you've come, girl. The nights are

the worst. I'll be all right in a minute.'

'I can't get over what you told me, Janey,' Nellie said. 'I keep thinking of things to ask you. What about our Bob? Who's his mother?'

'Harriet,' Janey said with a wheezy chuckle, 'and your da's his da.'

'But I thought—?' Nellie said.

'He couldn't stand her? Wasn't as bad as that. She just wasn't Helen and then she frightened him off throwing herself at him.' She panted for breath, closing her eyes but still gripping Nellie's hand.

'She got her way. You know what they say, girl? All cats are grey in the dark.' She chuckled again wheezily. 'So there was Bobby.'

Janey had asked for rum on Nellie's first visit but she had thought it might harm the old woman. Now, however, she gave Janey the parcel of sandwiches then slipped the medicine bottle of rum and water from beneath her shawl.

'I hope it doesn't do you no harm,' she whispered, but in one swift action Janey pulled the cork from the bottle and drained it.

'Harm, girl?' she said. 'Rum never harmed me, only the want of it.'

It seemed to give her a new lease of life, and she settled down to tell Nellie scandals about the neighbours. Her knowledge had been held over them like the Sword of Damocles for many years, but now she poured it out to Nellie.

'Don't take no more old buck from that Maud Jenkins. If she opens her mouth tell her you'll shut it for her. She daresn't go out to work and

463

leave that fella of hers with his own children or he's into their beds like a ferret down a rabbit hole.'

'Mr Jenkins?' Nellie said thunderstruck.

'The very same and he's not the only one. That Norton woman on the other side. She's supposed to be rearing twins. Not a bit of it. Her husband had her and the eldest girl in the club at the same time. Three days between them babies. The girl went to her grandmother's and when Dolly Norton was due she went an' all and that's how they worked it.'

The nurses were at the other end of the long ward and no one disturbed Nellie and Janey, as details of long-buried scandals poured from the old woman.

She told Nellie of a neighbour who had been a prostitute, of another who had been in gaol for theft and another who was a compulsive gambler, whose husband bought in the food and doled out pennies to her for necessities.

'He takes a bagful of clothes to work with him or she'd have them pawned for a bet,' she said. 'And that old one that lodges with Jessie. She seen off her first four babies for the insurance. Supposed to have overlaid them accidental, like, but I know the truth and she knows I know. Because of the likes of her they brought it in a few years ago that you could only insure a baby for a penny a week.'

'Four of them, Janey,' Nellie exclaimed. 'How did she get away with it?'

'Easy. Some people have got away with more than that. Bob Coleridge. He done his first wife in because she was carrying on with another fella. Stabbed her. His sister was there and she run out screeching Daisy had cut herself. Two fellas put her on a handcart and run to Stanley Hospital with her while me bold lad slid out to his mam's.'

'But I heard about Daisy Coleridge,' Nellie said. 'Bella told me to be careful with knives. Said Daisy had an accident with one and died.'

'Aye, they covered it up well. His mam got rid of his clothes and he put his brother's work clothes on and sloped into the foundry in place of his brother. They said they'd changed shifts.'

'But how do you know all this?' Nellie asked.

'I know a lot more,' Janey said. 'A so-called widder that's lived over the brush for years. A schoolteacher married years and kept it dark to keep her job. Lots more, I'm telling you, girl, because it'll give you a hold over them. Power!' she said triumphantly. 'They think if I go they're safe, but you tell them, girl.'

She suddenly seemed exhausted and Nellie bent over her. 'I'd sooner hear about me mam, me real mam and me da, Janey,' she said urgently, but the old woman turned her head away.

'I'm tired,' she said. 'Ask that Dr Wilson. Bring me more rum tomorrow.'

Nellie promised to do so and left.

Janey seems to think she's done me a good turn telling me them things about the neighbours, Nellie thought, but they won't go no further. God knows I've got enough trouble in me own life without stirring it up for other people.

That night she was visited by two burly men who said they 'looked after' Janey and wanted to know when she would be home. Nellie faced them calmly.

'I don't know,' she said. 'But it'll be a while before she can go out with her fish,' and they went away.

I'd have been terrified of them not long ago, she thought, but now she seemed to have grown a hard skin. She had recognised them as the bullies that Janey used to collect bad debts, and wondered again that they were needed to replace Harriet. And yet Harriet, bully though she was, had her weak spot. I'll have to ask Janey about them two tomorrow, she thought.

As she lay sleepless in bed Nellie decided that she would refuse to listen to any more tales about neighbours, and insist that Janey talked about her mother and father. I don't care what other people have done, she thought. I don't know how much is true anyway, but I believe all this about my real mother. It explained so much that had always puzzled her.

The tale of the babies being killed for the insurance money stayed in her mind and she shivered as she thought of it. Maybe because it was true, she thought. She remembered when the insurance man came for the sixpence a week she paid for Sam and herself and said to her, 'Are you going to insure your baby, love? You can only put him in for a penny a week because people have been tempted, like, when they've had too much insurance on a child.'

At the time she had only thought of getting rid of the man quickly in case Sam was told about him but now she could remember the whole conversation. Picture the man standing there and even smell the wet woollen mitts he wore on his red chapped hands.

She felt too restless to sleep, with all these thoughts tumbling about in her brain, and she went downstairs for a cup of tea. The hearth was covered with cockroaches which scuttled away as she lit the gas, and more were under the table and by the sofa legs.

I hate this house, Nellie thought. I'll never get it clear of them things and the bugs, no matter what I do. And all I done to make it nice for Sam and for what? Her tears fell but she wiped them away angrily.

The following morning she arrived at the hospital before nine o'clock, and a nurse darted out to intercept her. 'You're Miss Hitchmough's niece? Sister wants to see you.'

She took Nellie to Sister's office. 'Sit down, Mrs er—I'm sorry to tell you that your aunt died at four o'clock this morning.'

'Died,' Nellie echoed. 'But I thought—I thought she'd get better.'

The sister sighed. 'I warned you,' she said with a long-suffering air. She picked up a piece of paper from her desk. 'Before she died Miss Hitchmough told me that she had made arrangements for her funeral. She said

467

that there is an envelope in the drawer with the details. Here is the name and address of the undertaker. You may collect her belongings and the death certificate later today.'

She stood up and ushered Nellie to the door, and Nellie left feeling dazed. So now she had lost the chance to hear more about her real mother. Why had Janey kept all this to herself for so long? she thought angrily. Just so that she could gloat over knowing something that no one else knew, and because she was a sly and scheming old woman.

Nellie felt no grief for the old woman, only anger and frustration that she had concealed so much until it was too late to tell all she knew.

Back home she went immediately to Janey's room and to the drawer in the dilapidated corner cupboard. There was a stiff manila envelope there stamped with the name of Rae and Dobson, the local undertakers.

It was as grubby as the other papers in the drawer, but sealed, and Nellie decided to take it directly to the undertakers.

'A grand old lady,' Mr Rae said as he glanced quickly through the papers. 'Not many reach the biblical three score years and ten and she lived nine years beyond that. You are not a relative, Mrs Meadows?'

'No. She put me down as next of kin so I could get in to see her in the hospital, but she only lodged with us. I don't think she had any relations,' said Nellie.

'No, she thought not. That's why she made these arrangements, with commendable

468

foresight, I may say. She dreaded a pauper's funeral. You may leave everything to me, Mrs Meadows.'

As Nellie walked home she felt suddenly free. She could go where she liked and do what she liked without considering Janey or anybody else. She had no hope or expectation that she would ever see Sam again.

The rumours flying about the neighbourhood about him and Madge Kenyon had made Nellie aware that he was now living with Madge in Southampton, and the fact that he had not written to her convinced Nellie that he had cut himself off from her completely.

The Sam she had known was gone and a stranger had taken his place and Nellie's hurt pride helped her to bear her grief.

There's just me and Tommy now and I can look out for us. I don't need no one. Even our Bobby is only me half-brother. Maybe I'll be like Janey and keep that to meself until it suits me to tell him, and it'll be long enough before I go near him again anyway, she thought.

Maggie Nolan was at her door when Nellie walked down the street.

'Have you been to see the old girl, Nell?' she asked. 'How is she?'

'She died early this morning,' Nellie said, and when Maggie exclaimed she said, 'She left word she's paid for the funeral. With Rae and Dobson.'

'Good God, when did she do that?' Maggie exclaimed.

'I don't know. She never said nothing to me

about it but I'm glad she did. Now I won't have to do nothing,' Nellie said.

'Fancy never saying nothing, all the years she lived on your floor,' Maggie said indignantly. 'She was a crafty old mare, wasn't she? Deep as a drawn well. People have kept asking me about her but I never see you these days, Nell.'

'I know, Mag,' Nellie said, putting her hand on Maggie's arm. 'I had to try and sort meself out. This on top of everything else. I've been moidered.'

'I know, girl. That's what Katy said to me and Gertie, you'd have to have time to yourself, but we was all worried about you, girl. Never mind. Time's the great healer, so they say.' She sighed. 'I hope they're right.'

Nellie knew she should say something about Maggie's grief for Johnny but suddenly she felt that she must be alone.

'Tell people about Janey, will you, Mag?' she said. 'Mr Rae's going to let me know about the funeral.'

She escaped into her own house before Maggie could answer. Running upstairs she flung herself on the bed and began to bite at the bedspread, in order to stop herself from screaming hysterically. It all seemed more than she could bear.

I must be going out of my mind, she thought when she was calmer, but she knew that hard work was the best cure for a troubled mind. She moved the black kettle over the fire for hot water and wrapped herself in an old pinafore and a sacking apron, before starting to clean out Janey's room.

I don't know where to start, she thought, looking round the filthy room, but she decided to start with the bed. She could hear a rag man shouting and she gathered the dirty blankets and threw them out in to the entry for him to take.

She was about to drag the mattress out there too when she felt a weight in one corner and thrust her hand inside the mattress. There was a canvas bag there and when Nellie opened it she saw that it was full of silver and gold coins and screwed-up notes.

She had left the door ajar and the rag man looked in. 'These for me, Ma?' he asked. 'Anything else?'

Nellie thrust the bag in the drawer. 'There might be. I'm only starting,' she said. 'Come back after.'

She left the bag in the drawer and searched quickly for more money in the mattress before putting it out in the entry.

Remembering how the man had lifted the shawl to take the jewellery, she systematically searched the room but could find nothing else. The papers from the drawer she put in her own coal bucket with the bag of money, then she called the rag man into the room when he returned.

'You can clear all this,' she said. 'The bed and the bits of furniture. The old woman's died.'

The rag man gleefully loaded up his handcart with the truckle bed, the rickety chair and table, and the corner cupboard. He even took the ancient rag rug and the neck shawl which had covered the jewellery but Nellie told him to leave the curtains. 'I don't want people nosing in,' she said, and the man paid her half a crown and left well satisfied.

Nellie locked the door after him and went back to her kitchen. The bare parlour was filthy but it could wait, she thought, as she made herself a cup of tea, and the money could wait to be counted until after dark.

Fleetingly she thought that even a few weeks ago she would have refused to touch the money because of the way it had been accumulated, but now she thought hardily, there's nobody got more right to it than me, and I don't care where it comes from. It can be the rent she owed me. I'm finished with being soft.

She suddenly remembered that she must go to the hospital and quickly washed and changed. When she reached there she was given the death certificate and a brown paper bag with Janey's skirt and bodice and shoes, and the pad she wore to support her fish basket.

'What happened to her fish basket?' Nellie asked but she was told to ask at the police station.

She went there and was told that the basket had been stolen when Janey collapsed.

'The word is there was a lot of money in it,' the policeman said. 'But we haven't nabbed anyone yet. Was she a moneylender?'

'I don't know,' Nellie said. 'I don't know what she done when she went out. She never let on.'

'That kind don't,' the policeman said. 'Well,

472

if she was, there'll be a few people won't be sorry to see her go.'

Including me, Nellie thought as she walked away, but I'll tell Maggie about this and she can spread it round in case any of them are wondering about Janey's money.

Maggie was talking at Bella's step and Nellie told immediately where she had been. She showed the woman the brown paper bag and the death certificate.

'You'll want that for the insurance,' one woman said, but Maggie and Bella said together, 'She didn't have no policies. She paid for her own funeral to Rae and Dobson's.'

'It was only when they give me the things and I saw the pad I thought about the fish basket. The sister told me to go to the police station and d'you know what the copper said?' Nellie said. She paused dramatically, and the women watched her eagerly. 'He said the basket got stolen when she collapsed and the word was there was a lot of money in it, but they hadn't nabbed anyone yet. He asked me if she was a moneylender. I said I didn't know, but he thought she must've been because of all the money, like. He said people wouldn't be sorry to see her go.'

'He spoke a true word there,' said Bella's neighbour, Dolly Norton, and Nellie immediately thought of Janey's tale of her twins who were not twins.

'I'd better go,' Nellie said. 'I feel wore out with all the traipsing round.'

'You're a good girl, doing all the running

round and going to see her in hospital when she was only your lodger,' Bella said. 'And all you done for her before that.'

'She wouldn't let me do much. Wouldn't let me in the parlour to clean,' Nellie said. 'The rag man's just cleared all her bits and you know what he give me? Half a crown. Carrying all that money round and she wouldn't spend an 'a'penny to give herself some comfort.'

'And never paid you an 'a'penny rent neither,' Maggie said. 'You was too soft with her, girl.'

'She never offered and I didn't like asking,' Nellie said. 'I don't know what she done when me ma was alive.'

'You won't be any loss for her going, Nell,' Maggie said. 'The good fires she always had in her parlour, although she was never outa your kitchen sitting by your fire and eating your food.'

'And spending her money on her funeral and carrying the rest round to get robbed,' Dolly Norton said. 'It was the price of her.'

'She spent enough on her gin and rum,' Nellie said. 'She didn't mind parting for that. I'm glad I took her a drop of rum in to the hospital. Sneaked it under me shawl in a medicine bottle. She said it never did her no harm, only the want of it.'

The women laughed and Nellie left them, knowing that she had squashed any rumours about Janey's money before they started. I'm getting as crafty as her, she thought.

474

CHAPTER 25

Tommy showed little interest in Janey's death and grumbled when his mother told him he must help to clean out the parlour. At any other time Nellie would have been dismayed by the rapid change in her son, by his rough speech and manner and his untidy appearance, but it all seemed part of the strange world in which she was living.

Linoleum broken in places covered the floorboards and Nellie decided that they would take it up. 'We can burn it,' she said, 'Then you can brush the walls down and I'll scrub the floor.'

Tommy worked enthusiastically once he had started tearing up the lino and stacking it in the coal place, and then he brushed the walls with such vigour that plaster fell from it in lumps and powder filled the air.

'Leave it, leave it,' Nellie said irritably. 'The whole bloody place is falling down.'

Tommy glanced at her in surprise but said nothing, and he darted away when she told him he could go.

She had noticed that a floorboard by the fireplace was loose and as soon as Tommy had gone she prised it up.

In the cavity below there was a black box and an envelope and Nellie opened the envelope first. It was filled with ten-shilling and one-pound notes and four white five-pound notes, all badly chewed by rats or mice. The tin was full of silver coins with a few gold sovereigns among them and a small bag which contained five magnificent rings.

Nellie hurriedly replaced the tin and the floorboard but she pushed the envelope into the pocket of her skirt. Janey must have left it undisturbed for ages, she thought, or surely she would have protected it from the rats.

She went back into the kitchen, and making sure the door was locked and the curtains drawn sat down to count the money in the canvas bag. The sovereigns she put on one side, not sure whether they could still be used, but the rest of the money came to fifty-four pounds six shillings.

Nellie felt weak. It was a fortune and there was still the money in the tin and the notes in her pocket. She felt frightened and wished that there had been less money. It was all more than she could manage, and suddenly she felt more alone than she had ever been.

She was trembling as she pushed the canvas bag under the coal in the bucket. She would have to find a safer hiding place for it, but meanwhile she made herself a cup of tea and sat down to compose herself and try to plan.

She smiled wryly as she thought of the savings she had so painfully scraped together for key money for a different house. Money that they were now using to live on.

With that thought came another. This money

could be the means of escape from this house! Now there was only herself and Tommy to consider. She was free. Free to do as she liked and now she had the money to do it. She jumped to her feet too excited to sit still.

She brushed out Janey's room then took a bucket of water and scrubbed furiously at the floorboards. By the time she had finished she felt exhausted but calmer and when Tommy came in she could behave normally.

She had still not counted the money in the tin but the rings in it made her feel nervous about taking it out again.

Mr Rae had written to Nellie with details of the funeral arrangements and suggested that as Miss Hitchmough had provided for six mourners, Nellie might select five friends or neighbours to accompany her. 'If you have anything to ask me,' he wrote, 'please don't hesitate to call.'

Nellie asked Maggie and Katy but Bella refused, 'Because of me legs, girl,' she said, and Gertie was working. Nellie thought of asking two of the women whose secrets had been told to her by Janey and wondered how they would feel as the coffin was lowered, but she decided to ask two of Bella's daughters to make up the number.

Everyone was surprised at the magnificence of the funeral. Janey had arranged for a glass-sided hearse, horses with black plumes and bearers in top hats and frock coats. Two horse-drawn cabs were provided for the mourners and a funeral breakfast at a local café. Nellie was thankful when it was all over and she could start afresh, but Mr Rae's kindness encouraged her to ask his advice about the rat-gnawed notes.

She sat down nervously in his office. 'It's not about the funeral really,' she said. 'Only Janey—Miss Hitchmough—she never paid me rent, like, but she said I could have this money she saved.'

She felt herself blushing as she told the lie but Mr Rae appeared to notice nothing. She drew out the envelope with the tattered notes. 'The trouble was she left them where the rats could get at them so I don't know if they're any use.'

Mr Rae sorted them out. 'Eighty pounds!' he said. 'But all the numbers are here fortunately.' He put the notes in a firm's envelope and scribbled a note for Nellie.

'If you take this to the bank across the road they'll give you fresh notes for these,' he said. 'A pleasure, Mrs Meadows,' as Nellie thanked him profusely.

She exchanged the notes with ease in the bank and put them in the tin box when she returned home. She had decided that this was the safest hiding place and the box now held all the silver coins which she planned to exchange gradually for notes.

The sovereigns from the tin and the bag she had put together in the canvas bag and hidden it in her own mattress, unsure whether they were legal tender. Altogether she now had nearly two hundred pounds plus the sovereigns and the five rings.

I could buy a house! she thought, but she told herself she must be cautious. No one must guess how much Janey had hidden away. At present the neighbours believed that the lavish funeral and the money stolen from her fish basket accounted for the savings which they believed Janey had, and Nellie decided that she must show no sign of sudden affluence.

Some of the neighbours felt that they should have been chosen as mourners and one of them grumbled to Bella. 'We've known her longer than what your daughters have.'

'You know very well, Sarah Jones, that you'd only go to dance on her grave,' Bella retorted. 'Along with a lot more round here,' and nothing more was said.

Nellie was unperturbed by the comments, obsessed as she was with the thought of leaving the house.

She was still living on her own savings although they were now almost used up, but she told her friends that Sam had left her money from his pay-off.

'A good job, girl,' Maggie said. 'You'd have been on Queer Street otherwise with no job or nothing.'

Nellie had not forgotten the idea of making pies, and immediately after Janey's death she had thought that she and Tommy could live in the parlour and she could keep the kitchen for pie-making. Now with the discovery of the money her plans were changed.

She had rebuffed Katy and Gertie when they tried to console her after Sam had gone, and only used Maggie to spread the tales she wanted spread, and they were hurt, but tried to be understanding.

When she announced that she was taking two rooms for herself and Tommy in Grey Street Katy and Gertie both came to see her.

'It's not the time to go away from your friends, Nell,' Katy said. 'We'd help you out the way you helped me out if you was short.' She looked at Nellie so anxiously that for a moment Nellie was touched, but then she hardened her heart.

'I had to stay here while Janey was here,' she said, 'but I'm sick of this place. The bugs and the cockroaches and it's falling down round me head.'

'True enough,' Katy said. 'But how will you live, Nell?'

'I've got the promise of a cleaning job, through the cook in me last place,' Nellie said.

She marvelled at how easily lies came to her now, but before she could dwell on it, Gertie said emotionally, 'Oh Nellie, all Prudence told you has come true, hasn't it? But remember she said strength will come with sorrow. I'm sure it will, Nell.'

'I can't remember all she said,' Nellie said but Gertie pulled a piece of paper from her pocket.

'I wrote it down,' she said. 'Most of it, anyway. She said, "Birth and death and a great cloud of hatred and bitterness, a red-haired man or woman". Another time she said, "Death will come and all will be made clear". That must be your Bob and his baby and Janey's death, mustn't it?'

'Will you leave me that bit of paper, Gertie?' Nellie asked. 'That much has happened, like, I can't remember proper what she said.'

Both women tried to persuade Nellie not to act hastily.

'Sam might come back,' Katy said. 'That one only took advantage of him while he was drunk, me mam said.'

Gertie said sentimentally, 'All your happy years, Nellie. He can't just forget them. And poor Tommy. He needs his dad.'

'Don't tell *me*, Gertie,' Nellie said forcefully. '*I'm* not the one who cleared off. Anyhow, I don't want him back. It suits me to live me own life.'

She was determined not to tell them that Rose Adams had been to see her and told her that George had heard that Sam was living in Southampton with Madge Kenyon and working on the docks. 'It's better to know, Nell, than to live in hope, isn't it?' she said gently, and Nellie dully agreed.

Now she hid the agony the news had caused her, but as Katy and Gertie left Katy said, 'She's that upset she doesn't know what she's doing. She's better here where we all know her and feel for her, and want to help her. Especially now she's fallen out with her brother.'

'She should take a lodger,' Gertie said. 'Someone like Prudence who'd be company for her.'

481

'Perhaps she wants to get Tommy away. Kids are cruel and he's in fights all the time about things said about his dad,' but Gertie disagreed.

'He's not changing school,' she said.

Nellie stubbornly went ahead with her preparations. She packed up clothes and household goods and had them taken to Grey Street by a boy with a handcart. Her furniture, the rickety table and chairs, Sam's chair and the dresser and beds were loaded on a cart ostensibly to go to her new home, but she had sold them to a secondhand dealer. She was determined to discard the bed and the chair, which brought back so many memories.

Using some of the silver coins she bought new beds and a few items of solid furniture. She told herself that she was leaving the house in Johnson Street with no regrets, blocking from her mind memories of happy years with Sam and Tommy.

Nellie sometimes felt that she was two people in one. On the surface a hard capable woman able to plan and scheme and show an unconcerned face to the world, and underneath a distraught humiliated woman who felt that she had been wounded past bearing.

During her long wakeful nights the softer woman took control and sometimes Nellie felt that her suffering was more than she could bear. She felt that she had never realised how much she loved and depended on Sam until she lost him.

She was bitterly hurt that Sam had made no

attempt to get in touch with her. Every day she had watched every post hoping for a letter, until sick at heart she had decided that Sam had forgotten her. He must be sober by now, but he had chosen to stay with that woman. Even in her thoughts she was unable to say Madge's name.

Nellie had never lived in rooms so she knew none of the disadvantages but she soon found them. The rooms were clean and the area more respectable but she felt hemmed in and restricted.

Tommy hated them and spent as little time as possible in them. He had a longer walk to and from school and as soon as his meal was over he escaped back to his old companions.

Nellie had been vague about her address, but Katy asked for the number of the house and came to see her. Fortunately Nellie had found a temporary job cleaning offices in Dale Street so she could tell Katy that she was managing very well.

'Maggie Nolan thinks the woman who got your house found some money hidden in the parlour,' Katy said. 'Maggie said the kid told their Walter that his mam found gold doubloons in the wall. She tackled the woman and told her that if she found anything it was yours be right but the woman swore blind the kid was making it up. I don't believe her though.'

'If she's found anything she's welcome to it,' Nellie said. 'The way Janey got her money I don't want it.'

'But the rent she owed you, Nell,' Katy protested.

'I don't care. I only wish Maggie had found it,' Nellie said. She still felt amazed at the ease with which she could lie.

Katy said nothing about the new furniture but Nellie told her that her old furniture was too big for the rooms and she had exchanged it. They were ill at ease with each other and when Katy left Nellie felt that she would never come again. I showed her I didn't want her, she thought, and I don't. It was her brought me word about Sam and that woman, and I don't want reminding about it.

Without putting the thought into words she felt vaguely that if anyone talked about Sam it would breach the wall she had built up between herself and other people. Even Tommy, and the boy seemed to recognise this and never spoke of his father.

It had been easier for him to avoid Miss Helsby's classes after school because she had slipped on the icy pavement in March and sprained her ankle.

Sunk in her own misery his mother had paid no attention when he told her about the teacher, nor had she asked about her since. When Miss Helsby returned she sent messages to Tommy which he ignored but one night when he dashed out of school she was waiting for him.

'Come with me, Thomas,' she said briskly, and old habits of obedience made him obey, although sullenly. She was walking with the help of a stick and she gave him a bag of books to carry but she said no more until they reached her house.

She took him to her study. 'Sit down,' she said. She handed him a glass of ginger beer and sat down opposite to him, her legs planted firmly and her hands on her knees.

'Now, Thomas, tell me why you have been avoiding me and why you have become a hobbledehoy?'

'I don't know, miss,' Tom mumbled.

'Miss Helsby,' she corrected him. 'Now I'm not a fool, Thomas, and neither are you. Tell me what has caused the change in you.'

He said nothing, staring down at his glass with his lower lip outthrust, but in spite of himself the familiar surroundings affected him.

When Miss Helsby said quietly, 'Are you worried about your father?' it was like the breaking of a dam. All his pent-up guilt and misery flowed out, his feeling of shock and betrayal at his father's disappearance in such circumstances, even the fact that his mother had turned against him.

'She knows it's my fault me dad went, miss,' he said.

Miss Helsby had listened quietly, without interrupting him but now she said briskly, 'Nonsense, Thomas.' She handed him a handkerchief and when the boy had dried his eyes and seemed more composed she said gently, 'There is never one simple explanation for anything that happens. No one knows all the reasons why a person acts as he or she does, not even the person concerned. If you are to be a writer, Thomas, you must understand that. Try to explore minds and motives, but remember only God knows the secrets of all hearts.'

Tommy looked at her wide eyed. 'A writer, miss?' he said.

Miss Helsby looked at him quizzically. 'Don't tell me that the thought has never entered your mind, Thomas,' she said.

His face grew red. 'I—used to like—' he mumbled.

'Exactly,' Miss Helsby said, well satisfied. 'Now I will lend you a book which exactly describes your feelings so you will know that they are common to everyone who suffers bereavement.'

'But my dad hasn't *died*,' Tommy said in alarm, 'at least I don't think so.' But Miss Helsby quickly reassured him. 'Desertion for whatever reason is similar to bereavement, Thomas. Those left have the same feelings of guilt. That they are to blame. That they should have done more for the one who has gone, in addition to the feeling of loss. The book will help you to understand.'

She rose and went to the bookcase and Tommy said shamefacedly, 'Me hands are dirty, miss.'

'Then go to the bathroom and wash them,' Miss Helsby said. 'You know where it is.'

In the bathroom Tommy washed his hands and face then examined himself in the mirror. I look a proper cut, he thought, trying to smooth down his unruly hair. He looked around him, at the large bath in a mahogany surround, at the lavatory with the pan patterned with flowers and the ornate handle of the chain. Some day I'll get

486

a bathroom like this for Mam, he vowed.

Downstairs Miss Helsby was waiting for him with the book wrapped in brown paper. 'Remember, Thomas, you must comfort your mother,' she said. 'You have gone through the first stage and you are now entering on the stage where you must pull yourself together and start again. I will expect you on Saturday morning at nine o'clock.'

'Yes, miss,' Tommy said, then with a grin, 'Miss Helsby.'

She smiled. 'You'll do, Thomas,' she said. 'Away with you now and don't forget what I've said.'

Tommy ran home feeling light hearted but when he went into the living room his mother was crouched by the fire in an attitude of despair.

'*Mam*,' Tommy exclaimed, crouching down beside her and putting his arms round her, 'Mam, what's happened? What have you heard?'

'Nothing, lad,' Nellie said wearily. 'It's just—oh, everything.' She looked at his face close to her own and sniffed.

'Vinolia Soap, Mam,' Tommy said eagerly. 'I've been to Miss Helsby's and I got washed in her bathroom with her soap.'

'I thought you didn't go there no more,' Nellie said. 'Wasn't she sick or something?'

'She sprained her ankle but I'd stopped going anyway,' Tommy said. 'She was waiting for me outside school. Mam, she thinks I'll be a writer.'

Nellie looked at his beaming face and suddenly

487

burst into tears. 'Oh Tommy, lad,' she wept while Tommy held her and rocked her.

'Don't cry, Mam,' he begged her. 'Miss Helsby thinks we're over the worst. I told her all about, y'know, thinking it was my fault me dad went, and she said everyone thinks like that. She's give me a book about it.'

'You never told *me* about that,' Nellie said.

'I did, Mam, but you never listened,' Tommy said with a touch of resentment. He took the book from the brown paper and showed it to her.

'*Life After Bereavement,*' she read, then looked up startled. 'Your dad isn't *dead,* lad.'

'No, but Miss Helsby said the feelings are the same. Fancy her saying I could be a writer, Mam.'

'Fancy,' Nellie echoed, looking at him fondly. He's only a kid, she thought. I've been talking to him as if he was a man, then with a shock she thought, I haven't been talking to him at all.

She stood up. 'It's only corned beef for tea. I can't cook nothing properly here, Tom. I miss me kitchen, bad as it was. It's all scrap meals here.'

She watched Tommy covertly as she prepared the meal. His long tangled hair, his torn jersey and trousers.

I must've been outa me mind, she thought. Fussing over leaving the house an' all that and me poor lad going to the dogs.

Tommy was still talking about his visit to

Miss Helsby's house.

'She said I'm over the first stage, Mam, and I'm starting the second where I have to pull meself together and start again.'

'Oh aye, then you can start by washing your hair,' said Nellie. 'Then get down to John Henry's and get it cut. Where's your other gansey?'

'It won't go near me, Mam. It's like a strait-jacket,' Tommy said.

'Give me that one, then, and I'll mend it,' Nellie said.

Tommy set off clutching the penny for the barber, whistling and leaping in the air from time to time with pure happiness. Everything was going to be fine, he felt, and he was going to be a writer. His dad would be proud of him when he came home, as he was now sure he would.

At home Nellie had tidied the room then sat down to read the book. There was much that was not relevant to her situation but with a shock of surprise she realised that she too had been blaming herself for Sam's desertion. How often she had thought of Sam as she had last seen him, the shock and despair on his face as she cringed away from him.

I've been thinking that was why he went, Nellie thought, and blaming myself, but he wouldn't have gone just for that. Or at least he wouldn't have stayed away. At the thought she began to cry again but she quickly dried her eyes when she heard Tommy on the stairs.

'That's more like it,' she said when he came in, looking at his clean face and clean short hair and his mended jersey. Tommy was still in high spirits and Nellie managed to appear cheerful until just before he went to bed.

She had come across the paper on which Gertie had written down the forecasts by Mrs Gilligan, and remembered the glib explanation Gertie had found that they related to Bob and his baby and Janey's death.

She might have been right about Janey's death, 'all will be made clear', Nellie thought, but the rest is about when *I* was born. She turned the paper over to read the forecasts made on her second visit.

'Strength will come with sorrow. Blows, quarrels, partings. I see you standing alone. No. The boy will cleave to you. Money, success, sorrow, water flowing between but the golden cord will never break. A stranger in a strange land.'

Did this mean Sam or Tommy? Alone but the boy will cleave to you, Nellie thought, and suddenly flung her arms round Tommy weeping bitterly.

'Oh lad, there's only you and me now,' she cried, and Tommy held her close and cried with her.

'We'll be all right, Mam,' he said. 'I'll look after you.'

Nellie wept even more bitterly as she remembered Sam standing before her twisting his cap in his hands and saying, 'I'll look after you, Ellie.' Finally she dried her eyes and tried to smile.

'That's it now, lad. I've cried meself out. I'll be all right now.'

'That's good,' Tommy said with such evident relief that his mother laughed.

'Yes, I'm finished with crying now, lad,' she said. 'Miss Helsby got it right. It's time we was putting all this behind us, and making a fresh start. You'd better get to bed and leave me them trousers to mend.'

It was true. This was a watershed for Nellie, the time when she accepted that Sam was lost to them, and put the past behind her. She might weep in the privacy of her bed in the small hours of the night, but by day she set about making a new life for herself and her son.

She and Tommy were close again but there was a subtle change in their relationship. He was no longer the child clinging to her hand, but a strong companion standing beside her and helping her.

For Tommy too it was a fresh start. The boy he had become during the past unhappy months, the hobbledehoy as Miss Helsby had described him, was alien to all that he had been taught during the first ten years of his life. Thankfully he turned away from that boy and reverted to his own true nature.

He would never forget his father and always cherish a hope that Sam would come back to them, but until then he would look after his mam. He felt with a thrill of excitement that life was opening out before him.

CHAPTER 26

Sam slept most of the way to Southampton, helped by drinks from the bottle of rum held by Madge every time he stirred. She dragged him off the train with difficulty at Southampton and into a cab, giving the address of a lodging house in a street near the docks.

A postcard she had sent ensured that there was a room there for them, and the landlady greeted them at the door and helped her to steer Sam to the first-floor back. Once in the room he immediately collapsed on the bed and began to snore.

'He can't half sleep,' Madge said giggling breathlessly. 'I'm glad you had a room, Kitty.'

'I had a first-floor front too but I thought the back might suit you better,' Kitty said. She dug her elbow in Madge's ribs. 'Unless you've changed,' she said meaningly, but Madge only laughed.

'I'm that dry,' she said. 'Any chance of a cup? He'll sleep for hours.'

They went out of the room locking the door behind them and down to Kitty's basement kitchen.

'Well, what happened?' Kitty asked, pouring tea. 'I thought you were going to marry that fella you followed to Liverpool?'

'So did I,' Madge said. 'He went off on a

long voyage, nearly two years, and when he came back he was hopeless. A real skinflint. I never saw nothing hardly of his pay-off, but this fella's different.'

'I'm glad to hear it,' Kitty said dryly.

Madge said immediately, 'Don't worry. I'll see you all right.'

'If you're going back to it you'll have to watch yourself,' Kitty said. 'Big Eddie's taken over more since you went. He doesn't like anyone on his patch.'

'Sam's a match for Big Eddie,' Madge boasted.

'Sam? That his name?' Kitty said. 'Hope he's good with the knife, then. Doesn't seem to know where he is.'

'That's just the drink,' Madge said. 'He'll be all right.'

She felt that Kitty was asking too many questions and soon went back to the room.

It was some time before Sam woke then he sat up looking around him with bleary eyes and passing his tongue over his dry lips. Madge poured him a glass of water from the jug on the washstand and he gulped it down.

'Where's this?' he asked. 'Where are we?'

'Southampton, Sam,' Madge said.

'Southampton?' he shouted. 'What the hell are we doing in Southampton?'

'You wanted to come here, Sam,' Madge said softly. 'Don't you remember you said you wanted to get away and I said why don't we go to Southampton?'

Sam looked bewildered, clutching his head

493

and groaning. 'Me head's splitting in two,' he said. 'I only remember Lime Street. The noise and the steam. Did I get on the train? Why?'

I had a narrow escape at Lime Street if he woke up that much, Madge thought, but aloud she said, as though unwillingly, 'Your wife threw you out, Sam.'

'*Ellie?* Threw me out?' he said. 'Don't talk daft.'

'Well, not her. It was her brother and her fancy man done it. You'd wrecked the place and very near murdered her,' Madge said glibly.

Sam looked up. 'Murdered her?' he said sharply. A memory of Nellie cringing away from him rose in his fuddled mind and he groaned.

'Two years is a long time away, Sam,' Madge said. 'You was just that mad at what'd been going on. You're better away from Liverpool for a while. I'll look after you, Sam.'

'Her fancy man,' Sam said. He sat scowling at the floor and Madge said nothing. 'I must be going bloody mad,' he said finally. 'I don't remember none of it.'

'It'll come back,' Madge said. 'Mind you, you weren't half carrying a load of drink. I've never seen a fella so drunk, or maybe you got a knock on your head in all the fighting.'

She sat down beside him and put her arms round him but he pushed her away and got to his feet unsteadily. He poured the remaining water from the ewer into the bowl and sluiced it over his face and head, but his mind remained muzzy.

How could all this have happened and yet he remembered nothing of it? Perhaps he did get a knock on the head.

'I'm going out,' he said. 'Clear me head.'

'All right, Sam. I'll come with you,' Madge said. He made a gesture of dissent but she said quickly, 'You don't know where you are.'

'Too bloody right,' Sam growled, but they had only walked a short distance when he felt so ill that he was glad to return to the house. He refused the drink Madge offered him and lay in the bed trying to sort out his thoughts, but they were still as muddled, and finally he fell asleep.

When he woke Madge was beside him, her arm around him, but he slid away from her and went to open the dirty window. His mind was beginning to clear but his memory was patchy. He tried to think back to his last trip and suddenly he remembered the hospital and the doctor telling him that he was sterile. He groaned aloud, striking the window ledge with his fist so hard that the windows rattled.

Madge woke. 'Sam, what's the matter?' she cried jumping out of bed and coming to him, but he thrust her away.

'I've gorra gerrout,' he said, pulling on his boots.

'I'll come with you,' she exclaimed.

'No you won't,' he said roughly. 'Just tell me the address.'

He went out and walked about trying to think. Had he faced Ellie with that? He couldn't remember. Was that why he had beaten her and wrecked his house? Once again he remembered her cringing away from him and her battered and bleeding face. Oh God, he groaned aloud.

And she had a fancy man. Was it the fellow he fought with in her brother's house? He could remember that all right. His anger grew. So Bobby had helped to throw him out of his own house. But it wasn't his own house.

He thought of old Janey and her hints. What a fool he'd been. Soft Sam. Diddled all along the line. He began to feel ill again and turned back to the house where Madge was waiting for him. She was a tart, he thought, but more straight than Ellie. Looking so innocent as if butter wouldn't melt in her mouth and tricking him all the way, he thought savagely.

Madge was surprised when he returned and spoke quietly to her.

'Come back to bed, Sam,' she coaxed him, and once in bed she exerted herself to rouse his desire.

He took her roughly with none of the tenderness he had shown to Ellie before that last terrible night, but Madge seemed to enjoy his roughness.

'Never mind about them lot in Liverpool,' she whispered afterwards. 'They don't care about you, Sam. Just out for what they can get out of you. Double crossing you and learning that lad to be a snob. They think you're not good enough for them, but I love you, Sam. We'll be good together.'

Madge had only heard a stray reference to Sam's son and his extra lessons, but she was well satisfied with the effect of the remark on Sam.

'He used to think the sun shone outa me,' he muttered. 'I suppose she's learned him different now.'

Madge was too experienced to pursue it further.

'Are you hungry, Sam?' she asked.

'Yes, I am,' he said in surprise. He picked his trousers off the floor and put his hand in the pocket, pulling out a handful of silver and copper.

'This is all I've got,' he said in dismay.

'Yes, they cleaned you out proper, Sam, and the good pay-off you must've had from that long trip too. Never mind, I've got enough.'

She went out and soon returned with four baked potatoes and a screw of salt, and another bottle of rum.

'Where'd you get these this hour of the night?' Sam asked, and she smiled.

'This is me home town, remember,' she said.

Sam felt better when he had eaten two of the potatoes but he refused the rum. Madge had replenished the water jug and he drank some but soon his unbearable thoughts made him seize the rum bottle and gulp from it.

He was sitting on the side of the bed and Madge sat beside him and put her arms round him. 'Oh Sam, I'm crazy about you,' she murmured. 'I fell for you the minute I saw you. I've never known a man like you before. You're my dream man.'

As she talked her hands roamed round his

body skilfully arousing him until they fell back on the bed. Although he treated her roughly Madge responded to him with cries and moans of delight.

Suddenly Sam remembered his last night with Ellie and turned away from Madge with a groan of self-disgust. What the hell is wrong with me? he thought. I'm not bloody fit to live.

Madge was clutching him, leaning over him and kissing him frantically.

'I'm sorry, girl,' he muttered, but she only clutched him more desperately.

'I don't mind you being rough, Sam. I like it,' she murmured. 'I like it anyway with you. I'm mad about you. I *need* you, Sam.'

He pulled away from her clutching hands and pulled on his trousers and his boots. 'I've gorra gerraway, gerrout,' he said desperately, and blundered out of the room and into the street.

He walked quickly for hours, trying to escape from his thoughts until he was exhausted.

Sam was a deeply unhappy man, more unhappy than he had ever been during the hardships of his past life. His tough exterior concealed a profoundly insecure and vulnerable personality, and his suffering was intense.

A man like George Adams growing up in a close and loving family and repeating the pattern in his own marriage would never be troubled by the doubts which tormented Sam.

The insecurity caused by his father's rejection and his loveless childhood had been the reason for his doubts and his jealousy of Nellie, yet he had been happy since his marriage.

Proud of his wife and son, of his comfortable home, and basking in Tom's uncritical love and admiration, Sam had grown confident and happy.

Now all that confidence had gone. All the doubts aroused by the ill-natured teasing of his drinking companions on the night of Tommy's birth, old Janey's malicious hints, and the shattering revelation by the doctor of his sterility, made him an easy target for the lies told by Madge.

The picture of Ellie as he had last seen her was constantly in his mind, filling him with self-loathing, and he despised himself for responding so readily to Madge. Yet her declarations of love and admiration for him, and her apparent desperate need for him, was balm to his wounded self-esteem, and he was unable to resist her, especially when he had been drinking.

Madge had lit the gas fire and was sitting by it when he went in and she immediately picked up the bottle of rum.

'I don't want none of that,' Sam muttered. 'I want me head clear. Did I bring me book with me, me seaman's book?'

'No, Sam,' Madge lied, feeling that she needed to know his plans before she produced it.

'I must've left it or lost it,' he said. 'I'm gonna get a job. I'm not living off you. Anyhow your money must be very near gone.'

'It is, Sam, but Kitty's found me a little job,' Madge said quickly.

'I feel buggered now but tomorrow I'll try the docks,' Sam said. 'I might go after round the shipping offices. See if I can get a new book. Have you got any notepaper?'

'No, but I can get some as soon as she opens,' Madge said.

Later she bought pen and ink and notepaper and pretended to approve of Sam's idea of writing to his son. 'You don't know what they've told him but you can tell him your side, Sam,' she said.

Sam sat for a long time looking at the notepaper then finally he wrote. 'Dear Tommy, I hope this finds you well as it leaves me at present. Look after your mother. Your loving father, Samuel Meadows.'

Madge managed to be ready to go out as he finished it.

'I'll post it for you, Sam. I pass the post office and I'll get a stamp. If I get the next post he should get it tonight or tomorrow morning.'

Once away from the house she read the letter then tore it and the envelope up and scattered the pieces.

Sam had fallen asleep when she returned and she took the opportunity to slip his seaman's book into his bag. No use hiding it if he was going to get a replacement but she was determined to keep him with her as long as possible.

Sam watched the post eagerly for the next few days but at the end of the week he said to Madge, 'I think he'd have wrote be now, don't you?'

He said nothing of the other hope he had that if his wife knew his address she would write to him.

'Sam, they don't want to know about you, lad,' Madge said. 'Why don't you forget them? *I* love you, Sam. I'm mad about you.'

He had been round the shipping offices but was unable to get a ship without his book, but he got half a day's work on the docks on the first day he tried. His illness and his prolonged bouts of drinking had left his powerful body thinner and weaker than usual, but sheer determination carried him through the long shift.

Madge was surprised and relieved to know that he had been working. She had been afraid that he had gone, perhaps even back to Liverpool, although she knew he had no money for the train fare. Sam kept his thoughts and plans to himself and told her little, and he was so moody and unpredictable that she was afraid to ask.

He got another job barrowing coal for a coaster and Madge took advantage of his absence to bring clients into the room. The landlady turned a blind eye as long as she was given her cut of the money, and no one saw the men entering or leaving her house by the back way.

Sam gave Madge most of his earnings but he was surprised by the amount of money she seemed to have.

'Must pay well, waiting on,' he said one day when she was wearing another new dress.

'I get good tips, Sam,' she said glibly.

Often when he returned home she was burning

501

a joss stick, and when Sam complained she said they made her feel sexy, and immediately began to prove it to him.

The landlady laughed when Madge told her. 'You're a caution,' she said. 'But you sail close to the wind. You'd better watch out for Big Eddie.'

Madge tossed her head. 'Sam's a match for Big Eddie,' she said, 'he's got fists like ten-pound hammers.'

'He'll need to be good with a knife and all,' Kitty said. 'Not many better than Big Eddie.'

When Madge went back to the room Sam had thrown the joss stick out of the window and fallen asleep in the chair. The smell of the joss stick hung in the air masking other odours.

Madge sat down leaning her arms on the table and devouring Sam with her eyes as he slept. He was all she wanted in a man, she thought, big and strong and rough, yet easily manipulated and believing all she told him about his wife. She felt angry when she thought of his wife and the way he still worried about her, and as though on cue Sam stirred and murmured, 'Ellie, Ellie.'

Madge pressed her lips together and clenched her fists in fury, but she controlled it and slipped to her knees between Sam's legs. One sure way of making him forget his milk-and-water wife, she thought, waking him by stroking and kissing him.

'For God's sake,' he exclaimed as he woke. 'Don't you ever get fed up?'

'Not with you, Sam,' she wheedled. 'I'm mad about you,' but for once it failed to work.

He turned away. 'I'd rather have a cup of tea,' he said jokingly, and was amazed at Madge's reaction.

She screamed and yelled, beating her fists on the floor, and Sam said anxiously, 'Stop it, for God's sake. You'll have the house up,' but she continued her hysterics.

When she screamed at him, 'You wouldn't say that to your bloody wife,' Sam glared at her so ferociously that she fell silent.

'Keep your bloody tongue off my wife, d'you hear?' he said menacingly, and she nodded, shrinking back from him.

Sam went to the window and stood looking out, trying to control his temper, and Madge slipped out of the room.

She came back with some stew from the cookshop.

'Kitty's using the kitchen,' she said. 'So this was all I could get.'

Sam took his cue from her and said nothing about what had happened earlier.

'Smells good,' he said. 'Better than the oodle we had on board.'

Later they went out together to a public house, but stayed only a short time before moving on to another one, and then another. Madge wanted as many people as possible to see her with Sam.

In spite of her brave words to the landlady she was nervous of Big Eddie, a huge coloured man who ran a stable of girls, and kept them in line with his expertise with a knife. He also used his knife to discourage any opposition.

So far she had been lucky. Many of the local prostitutes were amateurs, supplementing meagre wages or housekeeping money, but she had been having as many customers as the professionals run by a minder. Sooner or later she would be challenged about it, but she hoped that the sight of Sam would make them think twice.

She was lucky too that she was able to use her room. For a cut of the proceeds Kitty was prepared to turn a blind eye but Madge knew she would repudiate her without hesitation if she was ever found out.

She feared Sam's reaction if he ever learned of her activities, but she was unable to stop. She craved the money and the luxuries it bought, and even more the satisfaction of her insatiable desire. That's why they keep coming back to me, she thought. They know I need it as much as they do.

Although Sam told himself that he was finished with everyone in Liverpool, whenever he heard a Liverpool accent he could not resist questioning the speaker. So far he had found no one who knew people he knew, or Johnson Street, until he met a man in a dockside pub during his break from work on the docks.

'You from Liverpool?' he asked, and the man grinned.

'Aye, you an' all be the sound of yer.' He held out his hand. 'Purrit there, wack.'

He told Sam that he lived in Kirkdale

and drank with his mates near Derby Road occasionally.

'Where else do you drink?' Sam asked, and felt as though his heart missed a beat when the man said, 'The Volunteer.'

They discussed the landlord and barmen and various customers and at last Sam brought the conversation round to Johnson Street.

'Me mate lives in the next street,' the man said. 'They were talking in the Volley about some girl from Johnson Street going to college. Some fortune teller told her ma about it, they said.'

'Did you see anyone from the end house?' Sam asked. 'A little woman and a lad?'

'Where the moneylender lived?' the man exclaimed. 'The fella from there was drinking in the Volley. On his own. Drinking brandies and never offering anyone a wet. The lads were talking about him when he went out. They reckoned he'd found some of the old girl's money after she died, behind a brick in the wall. The lad let the cat outa the bag but the fella said he was making it up. A fortune in gold sovereigns, they said.'

Sam was silent with shock. So it was true. He thought he had accepted Madge's tale about Ellie with another man, but now he realised how much he had hoped she was wrong. And a swine who calls me lad a liar, he thought, but then like a hammer blow he remembered the doctor's words. Tommy was not his lad.

He realised that the man was looking down at his empty glass and he said hurriedly, 'Have another. Have a brandy or a drop of rum.'

'No thanks. I'll stick to the ale,' the man said. He was obviously trying to think of something else to tell Sam and finally he said, 'I think the lad's name was Tommy.'

'Did you see him?' Sam asked eagerly.

'No, only the landlord said young Tommy was the one should have gone to college. It was wasted on a girl because they only got married anyway. Another fella said Nellie could've rigged Tommy out for college with the money, only they were keeping it dark about finding it.'

He could remember no more and Sam thanked him and went back to work, his mind in turmoil. He was working in the hold of a ship, with a cloth tied round his nose and mouth to protect him from the grey dust which rose in choking clouds. His eyes smarted and his misery and anger grew.

Another man sitting in his chair, lying in his bed with Ellie. He ground his teeth at the thought. No wonder I never got no answer to me letter. Maybe they kept it from him. And old Janey died. Good riddance, he thought.

It was her fault I got married, I could have still been drinking with me mates when I was ashore and staying in the Seaman's only for her. Sometimes he had thought of going back to Liverpool, just to see how the land lay, he told himself, but now he swore that he would never return. He had served his purpose there and he wasn't wanted now.

His anger made him shovel furiously until a man tapped him on the shoulder.

'What are you trying to do? Do other fellas out of a job?' he said unpleasantly. 'Leave some for the next shift.'

Sam mumbled an apology and slowed down but another man leaned across him to talk about his brother who had only managed one half day's work in the week.

'Bloody strangers taking the bread out of our mouths,' he said.

Sam was tempted to crash his fist into the man's face but he restrained himself. They won't see much more of me, he thought grimly. I'll get a ship if I have to camp out in the offices. Get on board with proper mates, not like he was here, a resented outcast.

He was morose and taciturn when he went back to the room. Madge said nothing, only gave him a mug of tea generously laced with rum. While he ate his meal she chattered about her mythical job as a waitress, until his mood lifted a little and he agreed to go with her to a public house.

It was one that Madge knew well, with an alley at the back which she found very useful. She saw many men she knew there and glanced at them sideways as she walked in behind Sam.

While he ordered drinks she was able to exchange a few whispered words with one of the men, and before long she touched Sam's arm.

'Just going round the back to the lav,' she whispered and slid out of the door.

Before long she was joined by the man she had spoken to, and she returned to Sam a little later, with the money in her pocket increased.

Sam's gloomy mood had returned and he steadily drank himself into a truculent, vicious state of mind.

Meanwhile Madge had visited the alley four times with different men, the spice of danger of being caught out by Sam adding to her pleasure. Absorbed in his own misery Sam had noticed nothing, but a sudden silence alerted Madge.

Big Eddie had walked in, his wide-brimmed trilby at a rakish angle and his coat swinging from his shoulders. Two henchmen walked a step behind him. Big Eddie approached Sam.

'You got big ideas, man?' he asked smoothly.

Sam swung round and as Eddie's hand went to his pocket Sam's fist flew out and connected with his chin. All the frustration and anger that had been building up for months was behind the blow and there was an audible crack. The coloured man seemed to be lifted off his feet and fell spreadeagled on his back.

The knife had clattered from his hand and his henchmen bent over him anxiously. The pub was silent but the landlord moved swiftly.

'*Out,*' he roared, and as though by magic, four hefty men appeared and manhandled Sam to the door.

The landlord grabbed Madge and flung her after Sam.

'And don't come back,' he shouted. 'I seen you in and out all night like a blue-arsed fly. This isn't a bleeding knocking shop.'

'I've got a weak bladder,' Madge shouted,

and the men laughed derisively as they went back inside.

The combination of the drink and the fall on the cobblestones stunned Sam temporarily, but when Madge tried to help him to his feet he pushed her away.

'So that was the game?' he said bitterly. 'Right under me nose too.'

'He's wrong, Sam. I've got a weak bladder,' Madge cried, trying to take his arm, but he pushed her away. He set off at a furious pace for the lodging with Madge running to keep up with him. 'Honest to God, Sam, it's not true,' she moaned.

They reached the room and Sam snatched up the water jug and poured the water over his head into the bowl then splashed his face with it.

'You make me mad the way you do that,' Madge shouted, 'like a bloody horse,' but immediately she flung her arms round him. 'I'm sorry, Sam. I didn't mean it, I love you, Sam,' but he pushed her away.

'Gerroff,' he yelled. 'I must be bloody thick. All this time. The money, the clothes...'

'It was tips, Sam,' she said.

'Tips!' he said scornfully. 'You must think I'm a right bloody gull. Believing everything you told me.'

He dragged his bag from under the bed and opened it, then looked in disbelief at the seaman's book lying inside it.

'Me book was here all the time,' he said. He turned to Madge. 'You knew it was here,' he accused her.

509

'Honest, Sam, I didn't. I thought you must've left it behind,' she said, but he looked at her with disbelief.

'I could've gorra ship. I thought I'd have all the messing getting a new book and it was here all the time.'

He began to fling his gear into the bag with Madge crying and trying to impede him, but he was soon packed.

He seemed to have sobered up, and he looked in disgust at Madge as she screamed and flung herself about hysterically.

'What's going to become of me?' she howled grabbing at his bag. 'Don't go, Sam. Don't leave me.' She managed to fling her arms round his neck. 'I won't go with no one but you, Sam,' she whimpered. 'I'll get a proper job. Stay with me. We're good together.'

He pulled her arms from his neck and held her at arm's length. 'I don't care,' he said roughly. 'Do what you like. I'm just mad to think what a bloody fool I've been. Couldn't see what was sticking out a mile. Joss sticks!'

He hoisted his bag to his shoulder and went to the door, but she still tried to cling to him. He shook her off.

'*Women,*' he said, 'I'm finished with the whole bloody lot of you.'

Kitty was peeping from her kitchen but she quickly withdrew as he clattered down the stairs.

Sam walked down to the docks thinking that he would find somewhere to doss down for the night, before trying for a ship the next day. He stopped at an all-night stall and bought a pint of coffee and a bacon sandwich and asked the man about lodging houses for seamen.

'There's a common lodging house just across the road there,' the man said. 'Only sixpence a night but you'd have to watch yourself. They'd cut your throat for your bootlaces, never mind your boots.'

'They wouldn't try twice,' Sam growled.

'No, I don't expect they would,' the man said.

The lodging house was comfortless but clean and Sam went to the same stall for his breakfast after having a wash and shave for twopence. Strangely he felt more like himself than at any time since he came ashore from his last trip, and he chatted easily to the stallholder and other customers.

He told them that 'she' had hidden his book but he had found it and was now looking for a ship.

'Women,' the stallholder said, shaking his head. 'And that's why you wanted the doss house.'

'You done right,' another man said. 'I tell you what. The *Adair*'s leaving for New York today and one of her crew got knifed last night. In hospital. If you're ready to go you might get taken on.'

An old man with a flowing beard and an overcoat tied with string said sonorously, 'There is a tide in the affairs of men, which taken at its flood leads on to fortune. Grasp the chance, young man.'

Sam took his advice to such good effect that before nightfall he was on the *Adair*, his gear stowed in his locker and ready to start his watch as the ship headed out to sea. He was back in familiar surroundings among men he understood and where he was accepted, but he was surly and morose and made no friends.

He brooded constantly on his wrongs. His mother had been right with her constant cry when he was a young child.

'If you take to the sea, son, keep away from bad women in ports.'

I've got bad women in two ports, he thought grimly, Southampton *and* Liverpool.

Madge was an out-and-out old tail but Ellie was no better, taking another man into the house before he'd turned his back hardly, and maybe while he was away at sea.

The idea grew in his mind that he would back off when the ship reached New York, and never go back to England. When they docked he drew as much money and took as much gear off as he could without arousing suspicion.

With his reputation as a loner it was easy to evade his shipmates and he struck away from them into the teeming streets near the docks.

He held up his head and strode along. He was finished with his past life, he thought, and one thing for sure, no one would ever call him Soft Sam again. No one would ever find him an easy mark again.

CHAPTER 27

Although Nellie bravely decided to put the past behind her and make a fresh start it was not easy. She might replace her furniture and alienate her friends so that she was not reminded of Sam but in the still hours of night her heart betrayed her.

Then she lay wakeful night after night weeping bitter tears for the husband she had lost, as she remembered past happiness and wondered whether she would ever see him again.

She tried to weep silently, now that only a curtain divided her bed from Tommy's, but sometimes she thought that on the other side of the curtain her son too wept for his father.

It was never mentioned between them and during the day they both tried to appear cheerful and it was easier for Tommy because new horizons were opening for him. Miss Helsby had told him that it was too late for him to try for a scholarship but there was no reason why he should not fit himself for a good position in life.

She encouraged him to join the public library and gave him a course of reading, and he was invited to her house every Saturday morning. There she coached him in mathematics and started to teach him Spanish, and he was always invited to lunch.

It was only some time later that he realised that Miss Helsby had used this time to inobtrusively teach him table manners and polite behaviour.

She corrected his speech too on these Saturday morning visits and discussed the books he had read and suggested others, opening up for him a world far removed from the bleak and poverty-stricken world he had been born into.

Nellie still hoped to carry out her idea of supplying pies to small shops, but the enquiries she made showed her that it was not practicable.

'I couldn't do it while we was still here with no proper kitchen,' she told Tommy. 'But even if I could I think I'd be out of pocket. It seems they'd want all the profit for themselves nearly and I'd have to stand the loss of any they don't sell.'

'We'd be better with a shop of our own to sell them, Mam,' Tommy said.

'Oh yes, lad, and pigs might fly,' Nellie scoffed, dismissing the idea but gradually it grew on her. She could use some of Janey's money to get started.

Her cleaning job had finished and until now she had been afraid to use more than a few shillings of the money, feeling that it was all that stood between herself and Tommy and destitution. Now she thought, nothing venture nothing gain, and began to look for suitable premises.

After a long search she found the ideal place. It was really a big old house, but the ground floor consisted of a large front room which had

514

been used as a shop, a living room and a roomy kitchen. Upstairs there were three bedrooms and a bathroom and attics.

Best of all it was on one of the routes to the docks. There was also some waste ground behind it and a water tap by the side of the shop. 'Carters could stop to water their horses and come in for a pie,' Nellie told Tom, as he now wished to be called.

After some bargaining she managed to rent the property and paid fifty pounds key money. The landlord agreed to have the house cleaned for her, and she and Tommy distempered all the rooms in cream.

'You never get no time to play, lad,' Nellie said remorsefully, 'between this and all the stuff for Miss Helsby.'

'I've enjoyed doing it, Mam,' Tom said.

Neither of them acknowledged that they were pleased to have every moment occupied with hard work so that they had no time to brood, and to be so exhausted every night that they slept soundly.

Tom was excited at the prospect of having his own bedroom again, and Nellie, who had decided to open a general shop in the front room, was busy arranging for counters and stock.

She was dismayed by the amount she was spending but she told herself that she still had plenty of money and the sovereigns and rings if she was desperate.

When her mind became more balanced she had worried about the source of the money,

515

but she gradually realised that old Janey must have been a receiver of stolen goods, particularly jewellery, and she hoped that the money she had found had come from these activities rather than from moneylending.

I don't mind handling that money, she thought. It would be rich people what got robbed and they don't care how they make their money. Grind the likes of us down while they do it, but moneylending's different. Blood money off poor people. She hoped that the moneylending money was in the basket which was stolen, or was the money hidden in the wall and found by the tenants who followed her.

Nellie managed to square her conscience in this way and spent the money with an easy mind. She was too hard worked and worried at this time to have much time to brood and in later years she often thought that this had been her salvation.

The thought of Sam with another woman was always a nagging pain in her mind and it was almost a relief when she was told Sam had sailed for New York and abandoned his ship there.

She avoided her old neighbourhood, but one day she had been to a wholesaler's in Stanley Road when she met the landlord of the Volunteer.

He tipped his hat and walked on then he stopped and called, 'Mrs Meadows!'

Nellie turned back.

'I don't know whether you know this. One of them McGregor lads was saying that Sam signed on for a New York trip and he backed off there. Thought you might like to know.'

Nellie thanked him quietly and walked on, pain tearing at her as fresh as when it was new, although it was now over a year since Sam left. At least he was not with that woman, Nellie thought, but in some ways he seemed almost more lost to her. She told Tom what she had heard and he looked hopeful.

'I don't think my dad will like it there, Mam,' he said. 'Since the Wall Street Crash in 1929 the whole of America is in a bad way. No work and farmers losing their jobs and wandering the roads. Dad might be glad to come home.'

'Did Miss Helsby learn you all that?' Nellie said in amazement.

'No, Mam, I read about it,' Tom said with a grin.

Nellie told Tom that a lady she had worked for was providing the money for the shop, and she was glad that she did when Tom met Bella. She questioned him about his mother's venture then said bluntly, 'That all costs money, lad. I hope your mam's not going into debt for it, Tommy.'

Tom told her the tale Nellie had told him, and Bella said she hoped Nellie would do well. 'Tell her our Amy's at the high school. She looks real posh in her uniform,' she said.

On earlier occasions Tom had met Gertie and Katy.

'I suppose your mam's made new friends now, Tommy,' Gertie said resentfully, and Tom told her that his mother never left the Grey Street rooms, which was true.

517

Katy had only said, 'I haven't been back to see your mum, Tommy, because I didn't think she wanted to see me. She'll need time to get over it, I know. Tell her I'm always here if she wants me.'

Tommy had not given his mother the messages, only told her he had seen the neighbours. He sensed that his mother was ashamed of being deserted, and wanted to avoid people who knew of it, so hurt pride on both sides kept the friends apart.

I know I made them feel unwelcome when they came to Grey Street, Nellie thought, but I don't care. I don't want nothing more to do with that part of me life.

She had decided to open her shop as a general shop at first and only started making and selling pies when she was used to ordering goods and serving in the shop. Trade was slow and after a week she rose at five o'clock one morning and made two dozen pies to sell.

Tom was at school and Nellie had no one to confide in. She became increasingly agitated as only five pies were sold during the morning. This was a daft idea, she thought, but suddenly there was a rush of customers and by one o'clock all the pies had gone and she could have sold more.

As soon as Tom came home she left him to serve in the shop and rushed out to buy more ingredients, and the next morning she made four dozen pies. Only two were left at the end of the day and she and Tom ate them for their evening meal as she had no time to cook one.

Tom's theory that on the first day the sudden rush was caused by carters who had bought pies telling others seemed true and most of the pies were bought by men on wagons. One of the men commented that the pies would be nicer hot and Nellie felt frustrated. She could have warmed the pies in the oven but she was unable to leave the shop.

The man who had supplied Nellie's stock had given her a card which read, 'Please do not ask for credit as a refusal often offends.'

'Put that up behind your counter, lass, and stick to it,' he advised her. 'I know a lot of small shops keep going by giving tick but you need to know your customers and you don't know yet who you can trust.'

'That's something I never thought of,' Nellie said dismayed, and the man told her that it was important.

'You'll get a lot trying it on because you're new,' he said. 'Just be firm. Later on you could oblige some of your regular customers, but get rid of the scroungers first off.'

Nellie was glad of his good advice when various people asked for their purchases to be put 'on the book', but the word soon went round that the new woman was as hard as nails and the scroungers went elsewhere.

'You done right to refuse them lot, girl,' one of her regular customers said. 'I knew they'd try it on, thinking you was soft. I'm glad you were able for them.'

She was a fat woman named Bessie and Nellie became friendly with her as the weeks passed. She was able to tell Nellie details about her other customers which made them more interesting to her.

Nellie was particularly interested in a thin dark girl named Jean Hughes. She was a widow with two young sons, and something in her barely concealed sadness gave Nellie a fellow feeling for her. She bought little and carefully and Nellie sensed her desperate poverty.

Bessie told Nellie that Jean's husband had been a clerk in a weighing office at the docks and had been knocked down and killed by a wagon carrying cotton bales, as he returned home.

'She never got no compensation because he'd left work, see. All she's got to live on is her ten-bob widow's pension, and five bob for the eldest and three for the other lad. Not much left to feed and clothe three of them after she's paid six bob a week rent. She feels it more because they was well off before.'

Nellie had just brought a fresh tray of pies through one day when Jean was in the shop with her children. The pies smelled appetising and Nellie saw the eldest child looking longingly at them then plucking his mother's arm and whispering to her.

Jean shook her head and counted out the pennies for her purchases from her thin purse. This is how I'd be, having to refuse Tom, if I hadn't found that money, Nellie thought, and longed to give pies to the children, but she feared to offend Jean's pride.

The next day when Jean came in for bread,

accompanied as usual by her boys, Nellie said suddenly, 'Jean, will you do me a favour? Will you come behind the counter for me while I put more pies in to heat up? They sell much better when they're hot but I can't leave the counter.'

Jean agreed willingly and Nellie spent ten minutes in the kitchen, taking out hot pies and putting others in the oven.

The two little boys, proud of being allowed behind the counter, were peeping in at her from the doorway and Nellie called them in and gave each of them an apple, then she quickly broke the crust a little on two of the pies.

'Will you hide these in your tummies for me?' she asked, and the boys nodded wide eyed. She carried the tray of hot pies into the shop followed by the boys carrying the apples and pies.

'What have you got there?' Jean said sharply and Nellie winked at her.

'Two of my disasters,' she said. 'They're going to hide them in their tummies for me.'

Jean looked doubtful but the children's delight was so patent and Nellie seemed so unconcerned, that she accepted the situation. 'I'm sure you could sell them, damaged or not,' she said.

'What, and let people know I'm not a perfect cook?' Nellie said laughing, and Jean was forced to smile.

Nellie made a tentative attempt to offer her payment but Jean said quickly, 'No thanks, I was glad to help, and you've given to the boys.'

Later Nellie told Tom about the incident, and she was surprised when he flung his arms round her and hugged her.

'What's that for?' she asked.

'Because you're like you used to be,' Tom said. 'You wouldn't have bothered to do that a few months ago, Mam.'

Nellie was about to make an indignant reply until she thought, the lad's right. I wouldn't, but I'm coming out of it now.

She looked proudly at her son. How tall and strong he had grown, and what a comfort to her. He was old for his age too, she thought, and she could talk over all her problems with him.

'You've got an old head on your shoulders, lad,' she said. 'That's my fault.'

Tom laughed. 'Miss Helsby says I'm mature for my age, Mam. It means the same but it sounds better, doesn't it?'

Nellie smiled too. 'Well, seeing as you're so *mature*, you can tell me what you think of my idea.'

She told him that most of her profit was coming from the pies but now that the weather was cold they sold better hot.

'I've been thinking that I might close the shop and open the front room as a café. What do you think, Tom?'

'Just selling hot pies?' he said doubtfully.

'No, I'd do other things. Pasties and apple pies, and big pans of pea soup and scouse. I could get Jean to help me with the serving and I could sell pies to take out.'

'It's a good idea, Mam, but you don't want

to kill yourself trying to do too much,' Tommy said. 'I wish I could leave school and help.'

'Don't be daft. I'll enjoy doing the cooking and if Jean'll help—' Nellie said. 'I'll keep the shop going till I've made me plans.'

'I think you've got most of them made already,' Tom said with a cheeky grin.

It was true and Nellie realised that subconsciously the idea had been in her head for some time.

She took Jean aside and asked if she would be willing to help and Jean agreed eagerly.

'My sister'll mind the boys for me,' she said.

Nellie warned her that it was a gamble at present, but she was surprised at how quickly everything fell into place.

The man who supplied the dry goods for the shop advised her to keep her counter for a while. 'If you're going to sell pies to take out you'll need somewhere to put them,' he said. 'And you could have a tea urn where your shelves have been.'

Nellie took his advice and also continued to buy the groceries for the café from him. She bought second hand tables and chairs and covered the tables in American cloth which would wipe clean.

Accompanied by Tom she went to the mug market and bought thick serviceable dishes and two huge pans. At Tom's suggestion she also bought cruets and cutlery, and ashtrays.

'I would've forgot about them,' she told him. 'I don't know what I'd do without you, lad.'

Tom also helped her to lay linoleum on the bare floor boards and to set up the tea urn.

Nellie had engaged a fourteen-year-old school leaver to serve in the shop for the last few weeks, while she was occupied with her plans, and then to help with the café.

'I want to see how she shapes before I open the café,' she told Jean. 'I'm hoping I'll be too busy then to train anyone.'

The girl, Winnie, was small and timid but a very willing worker, and she soon gained confidence. Nellie was pleased one day when she was in the kitchen to hear Winnie dealing firmly with someone asking for credit.

'No, Mrs Meadows is dead against it. She might give me the sack if I done it,' she said, and the woman went away empty handed.

Nellie closed the shop on a Saturday and by Monday morning the café was ready for opening. It was a bitterly cold day, but a bright fire burned in the big grate and steam from the bubbling urn made the room even warmer.

Winnie and Jean had both come in early and there was a large pan of scouse and one of pea soup ready, a pan of potatoes and one of cabbage and dozens of pies and pasties.

'Oh, God, Jean, what if nobody comes?' Nellie said nervously, looking at all the food.

'Don't worry, they will,' Jean said confidently.

Their first customer was a foreman from a demolition gang. Nellie had placed a card in the window giving details of the food available and the prices, and put a similar card on the wall of the café. The man looked at it.

'Got any bacon butties?' he asked.

Nellie and Jean looked at each other but Jean said swiftly, 'They'll be a few minutes yet. Wouldn't you like a pie?'

'No, don't seem right for me breakfast,' the man said. 'I might have one for me dinner.'

Back in the kitchen Nellie sent Winnie running to the grocer's for bacon and cut thick slices of bread. Meanwhile Jean had brought the man a mug of tea, and he had opened a newspaper. He had secured a chair near the fire and seemed in no hurry for his sandwiches, but Nellie managed to produce them within a few minutes.

'I've never fried bacon so fast in me life,' she gasped to Jean.

'I've never run so fast neither,' Winnie giggled.

The next two customers were more accommodating and ordered pea soup and a pasty, but the smell of the bacon hung in the air, and both men asked if bacon butties were on the menu.

'We'll have them tomorrow,' Nellie promised. 'We only opened this morning.'

'This'll put a lining on me stumick,' one man said as he finished his generous helping of pea soup. 'But I might have bacon or sausage butties tomorrow. Smells tasty.'

Trade was slack for a while, but as the dinner hour approached the tables filled up, and Winnie was also kept busy serving pies and pasties to take out. They took their own meals as they could, and all worked well together. At the end of the day Nellie was amazed to find only a few pasties were left and some apple pie.

Tommy had come home from school and he and Winnie were washing up while Nellie and Jean sat at the kitchen table preparing vegetables for the scouse and pea soup.

'I never thought all that scouse and pea soup would go,' Nellie said. 'The size of them panfuls I made!'

'And all the pies,' Jean said. 'We'll have to have more potatoes ready for tomorrow and more cabbage.'

Nellie agreed although she said soberly, 'It might have been just the novelty, like, today. We can't count on every day like that.'

They all laughed together over the bacon butties episode and Jean suggested that they had some bacon and sausage sandwiches ready when they opened. 'There mightn't be much call for scouse and stuff early on, more for dinner time,' she said.

They shared out what was left of the food, and Winnie surprised them by saying darkly, 'I'm going to hide these for our Cath and our Vinny. Me mam'll only give them all to *him.*'

'Who do you mean, love?' Nellie asked, and Winnie told her she meant her stepfather.

'We all hate him,' she said frankly.

Nellie said no more, but later Tom said that Winnie had told him that her mother had remarried two years after her father's death, and now had two children to her second husband.

'She said he wanted her to go into service so she'd be out of the house. He wants her sister and brother out too. Her brother was sixteen and was going to join the army as a boy soldier.'

'Poor kid,' Nellie said indignantly. 'What can her mother be thinking of?'

Nellie's fears that the first successful day was only a flash in the pan proved unfounded and the café was a success from the start. She continued to make the pies and pasties to take out as they were so popular. She was up early every morning, baking and cooking throughout the day to replenish the food which was so quickly sold, then up late doing the books after preparing vegetables and meat for the following day. Jean and Winnie worked hard and willingly and Tom helped as much as possible but Nellie carried the greater part of the burden.

No matter how hard she worked she could never stop grieving for Sam. If only she could turn back the clock and tell him how much she loved him. She reproached herself for not trying harder to find him and bring him home when he went to Southampton.

He was a sick man and needed her, but she had let him be taken advantage of by that harpy, she mourned, just because of her foolish pride. She blotted the memory of the rape from her mind, and thought only of her happy times with Sam. For some reason the memory she returned to most often was of his rescue of her when they were both children.

As Christmas approached she thought often of her brother too and of Meg and David.

'I wish I'd wrote back to Meg that time,' she told Tom. 'I was just that moidered at the time.

And David me godchild and he must be four by now.'

Tom had left school and was due to start work in a newspaper office in January, but he suggested that he and his mother should go to Yorkshire when the café was closed for Christmas. Nellie readily agreed and wrote to Mrs Handley but there was no reply.

'Never mind, you know what you say, mam,' Tom said. 'Nothing venture, nothing gain.'

They set off early in the morning but when they arrived at the little railway station they were told that Mr and Mrs Handley had died in July within two weeks of each other. Nellie asked for Bob Williams and the man told her that he lived in a cottage not far from the railway with his little son.

He said nothing about Meg and Nellie was afraid to ask, as she feared the worst. When they reached the cottage she knocked timidly and there was no reply, but when Tom banged the knocker, Bob opened the door.

He looked haggard and untidy and Nellie stared at him in dismay.

'Oh, Bob,' she said and the next moment they were in each other's arms.

'Meg?' Nellie said fearfully, and heaved a sigh of relief when Bob said Meg was in a sanatorium.

A tiny boy was peeping from the door of the living room and Tom slipped past his mother and uncle in the hall and went to the child.

He picked up the boy. 'Hello, David, I'm your cousin Tom,' he said gently. Nellie and

Bob were still clinging together weeping, then Bob drew Nellie into the living room where Tom was standing holding David in his arms.

Nellie looked with dismay round the dirty neglected room, and Bob looked shamefaced.

'We're in a bit of a mess, our kid,' he said. 'There's that much to do and be the time I go and see Meg and see to David...'

He shrugged and Nellie said quietly, 'I feel ashamed, lad. Why didn't you let me know?'

He mumbled that he didn't like to after what had happened, and Nellie took David from Tom's arms.

He's as light as a feather, she thought in consternation, but the child snuggled happily into her arms as Bob told her that Meg had not recovered her strength after David's birth and her cough had grown worse.

'I think she had an idea about the consumption, like,' Bob said. 'She wasn't surprised when we got told. That's why we come back here. Thought the air would do her good but it never made no difference. She's been in the sanatorium a year now.'

'And you've been trying to manage all that time?' Nellie said.

'We was all right at first. Mrs Handley seen to everything and she kept David there while I was at work, but she died in July.'

'The man told me,' Nellie said. 'Her and Mr Hanley in two weeks. What happened?'

'She was at a funeral and there was a thunderstorm. She was soaked and she got a cold and it turned to pleurisy and she died.

529

He just sort of give up and his heart give out. They'd been real good to me. I was proper cut up,' Bob said.

'And how do you manage now?' Nellie asked.

'I've got this girl comes in. Supposed to look after David and do a bit, but to tell you the truth, Nell, I worry about leaving him with her. She's a bit backward, like, but I can't do nothing else. The people here—there's no neighbours like at home. You know the way everybody'd take a kid from a family in trouble.'

Nellie leaned her cheek on David's hair, her eyes full of tears, and Bob looked distressed.

'I wasn't getting at you, girl,' he said. 'It's my fault we never seen each other all this time.'

'No, it was me. I'm sorry, Bob.' She was unable to say more and tried to wipe away her tears without alarming the child on her knee.

Bob looked at the clock. 'It's time I went for the hospital,' he said. 'Hetty's supposed to be here by now. I nearly always have to go for her.'

'Knock and tell her not to bother. We'll look after him,' Nellie said. She found a shirt among the ironing and ironed it for Bob and told him to tell Meg she would see to things now.

'He looked better already than when we came,' Tom said when Bob had gone.

'Aye, that shirt looked as if it had been washed in pea soup and dried up the chimney but at least it was ironed,' Nellie said.

Nellie had made tea and fried two eggs for Bob before he left and now she boiled an egg for each of them while Tom made toast at the

530

bright fire. Tom made soldiers of toast for David with his egg and for the first time the little boy smiled.

'Poor little lad, he hasn't had much luck, has he?' Nellie said. She had filled the copper and boiled water and now she washed some shirts of Bob's and clothes of David's, then thoroughly cleaned the kitchen and the scullery.

Tom cleaned the windows, with David standing beside him handing him cloths and smiling shyly at him from time to time. Nellie could find nothing in the larder except eggs and cheese to make a meal and some vegetables stored in an outhouse.

By the time Bob came back the room was bright and clean, David had been bathed and changed, and there was a panful of leek and potato soup bubbling on the hob. Nellie made savoury pancakes to follow and she was pleased to see both Bob and his little boy eating with obvious enjoyment.

Bob said that Meg had been delighted to hear that Nellie and Tom had arrived and she could stop worrying about Bob and David now.

'What will you do, Mam?' Tom asked quietly as he and Nellie washed up.

'Does Uncle Bob expect you to stay? What about the café?'

The same thought had been worrying Nellie. There had been no opportunity to talk at length with Bob and she wondered how to broach the subject of the café, but before she spoke of it, Bob said, 'I haven't asked you anything about yourself, Nell, I've been that glad to see you.

You've given me the heart to carry on now, our kid, until Meg gets home.'

'How long do you think it'll be?' Nellie asked.

'The spring, the doctor said, if everything goes all right,' Bob said, 'but I'll be all right now, Nell. What about you? Have you got a job?'

'Not exactly,' Nellie said, and began to tell him about the shop and the café.

'I'm made up to hear that,' Bob said, 'You and Tommy could've starved for all I knew and I never bothered. I feel that ashamed, our kid.'

'It was six of one and half a dozen of the other with us,' Nellie said firmly. 'But all that's behind us now and we won't talk about it no more. I'm worried about you though, lad.'

'You needn't be,' Bob said. 'I *was* down but you've give me fresh heart, Nell. I'll be all right. Hetty was playing on me. She's not as daft as she looks and I'll see she does what she gets paid for from now on.'

'Could we take David back home with us? Would that help, Bob?' Nellie asked but Bob refused.

'He might fret after me. Y'know, with his mam going and then losing Mrs Handley,' he said.

Before they left it was arranged that Bob and his son would come to stay for Christmas with Nellie and Tom.

Sam had not been mentioned but when Bob was saying goodbye to Nellie he said awkwardly, 'I'm made up to see the way Tom's turned out,

Nell. His dad would be proud of him.'

Nellie's eyes filled with tears and she hurried away.

The Christmas visit was a great success. Nellie had furnished the roomy third bedroom with a double bed and a walnut bedroom suite for Bob and David and on Christmas morning Nellie and Tom went in to see David opening his Christmas stocking. They were all caught up in the child's delight.

David was excited about everything—the contents of his stocking, the small tricycle his father gave him, the Christmas tree decorated by Tom, and the Christmas dinner when his father carved the goose cooked by Nellie. He seemed to have become quickly attached to Nellie and Tom, and sat as close as possible to Tom.

Bob was interested in the layout of the café, and while Tom played with David, Nellie and Bob caught up with all that had happened in the lost years. Bob said that his employers had been very good to him, allowing him to transfer to the Yorkshire branch when he needed to take Meg back there for the air.

'The trouble is they need me in Liverpool and there's not much work for me in Yorkshire. I can see they think I should move back and there's nothing to stop me, only I can't get a chance to look for somewhere to live,' he said. 'At least where I am I'm getting David looked after.'

'But what about when Meg comes home? Won't she need the air?' Nellie asked.

'It didn't do her no good before,' Bob said

bitterly. 'Anyhow, she'll be cured when she comes home.'

An idea was born in Nellie's mind but she said nothing then.

Bob and David returned to Sudely and the following Sunday Nellie and Tom travelled there again. Tom stayed with David while Nellie accompanied Bob to visit Meg.

She was shocked to see how thin and frail Meg looked although she seemed in good spirits. She and Nellie hugged each other, both near to tears, then Meg stood back and looked at Nellie.

'I don't think you've changed, Nell,' she said. 'Bob thought you had.'

'Not in her looks, like,' Bob protested. 'Just sort of—more grown up, sort of.'

'Harder, he means,' Nellie said, but she smiled as she spoke.

'I'll have a walk round,' Bob said, 'leave you two to talk.'

He went out and Meg said quietly, 'He's made up to see you again, Nell, and so am I. We *have* worried about you, y'know, although we never done nothing about it.'

'You had too much else on your plate,' Nellie said. 'I suppose it was the same with me.' She sighed. 'The years just go past.'

'Bob says Tommy's grown a lovely lad, and a good son. Do you ever hear anything of Sam?'

For a moment Nellie was shaken by Meg's directness then she said quietly, 'I've heard that he sailed to America and backed off there. He was a sick man when he come home that time, Meg. You know he was sick on that trip to the Ivory Coast and they put him off at some hospital? I don't know what they done to him but he wasn't himself when he got home.'

'We don't know what happens in them foreign places,' Meg said. 'They might have given him stuff they get from them foreign plants, or anything.'

'They done *something*,' Nellie said sadly. 'He wasn't the Sam I knew when he come home.'

'Never mind, you've got a good son,' Meg comforted her.

Nellie smiled again. 'I wouldn't change a hair on his head,' she said.

Bob came back and Nellie said, 'Now while you're both here, what do you think of this idea? What about Bob getting his Liverpool job back and him and David staying with us while he looks round for a house? Me and Jean and Winnie could keep an eye on him during the day, or he could go to Jean's sister who looks after Jean's boys. They're very happy with her. She's only young but real motherly.' She stood up. 'I'll go and have a walk round now and leave you to talk about it. I won't be offended if you say no.'

She went out and about ten minutes later Bob came looking for her. He put his arms round her and hugged her.

'We think it's a wonderful idea, our kid,' he said. 'If you're sure?'

'I wouldn't have said it if I wasn't,' Nellie said.

Meg was as enthusiastic as Bob and as grateful to Nellie.

'It's been fretting me to think of David with that half-baked Hetty while Bob's at work,' she said. 'I want him to grow up like Tom so he might learn by his example.'

It was quickly arranged. Nellie had been worried to find David so frail on her first visit, but he seemed to improve every day, spending his days happily with Jean's sister and settling in with Nellie and Tom and Bob as though he had always lived there.

The arrangement worked well from the start. Bob had moved back to the Liverpool works and after work he was always ready to lend a hand with the work of the café. For Nellie it was almost like being a family again, although the memory of Sam still filled her heart.

CHAPTER 28

Nellie had said nothing of her circumstances, even to Jean, and it was generally assumed by her customers that she was a widow. Sometimes it seemed to Nellie that this might be the truth. Would Sam disappear so completely from her life if he was still alive? Surely he would want to see Tommy even if he no longer cared about her.

She remembered what had happened to her father and wondered if Sam had met a similar fate. Or if that mysterious illness, which had so changed his personality in her opinion, had also claimed his life. She knew that Tom still hoped for his father's return so she said nothing to him which might destroy his hope.

During Tom's last year at school he had entered two national competitions and had won prizes in both. One for an essay on animals organised by the RSPCA, where the prize was a lavishly illustrated book on dogs, and the other for the RNLI, where the prize was a certificate and a book on seafaring.

Miss Helsby had encouraged him to enter and she also encouraged him to keep a journal. He still wrote down phrases which interested him from the racy conversation he heard all around him, and again urged by Miss Helsby entered competitions in the children's pages of magazines and newspapers, often successfully. For many of the stories he wrote he drew on the tales his father had told him of faraway places and people of other lands.

All this and some discreet help from Miss Helsby had secured Tom a job as office boy for the *Courier* newspaper. His duties were all the most menial, making tea, emptying wastepaper baskets, delivering parcels and letters to various places, even placing bets for one of the reporters with the bookie's runner who operated in a nearby entry.

Nothing dimmed his enthusiasm and his notebook rapidly filled with new phrases. Nellie had watched proudly as he set off on his first morning wearing his first suit with long trousers and carrying a small case containing his lunch and a notebook and pencil.

She never tired of hearing his tales of what happened in the office and often wondered how she and Sam had produced such a clever son who looked such a gentleman. Miss Helsby had learned him manners and how to speak, but that look was Tom's own, she thought.

Buried under all her memories of Sam was the thought of her employer Joshua Leadbetter who had raped her, and one wakeful night she found it impossible to thrust the memory away. He had belonged to a rich and well-bred family even though he had behaved so badly towards her, and the thought that he might be Tom's father troubled her.

The date of Tom's birth made it unlikely but possible, yet all her instincts had always told her that he was Sam's son.

She slept little but the next day Jean helped to allay her doubts.

'Doesn't Tom look smart in his new suit?' Jean said. 'He looks quite the gentleman.'

'I don't know where he gets it from, or his cleverness,' Nellie said incautiously.

'What was his father like?' asked Jean.

'He was big, broad shouldered, dark curly hair,' Nellie said, not correcting Jean's assumption that she was a widow.

'So Tom takes after you altogether,' Jean said. 'He's even got your refined air.'

'Me, refined?' Nellie exclaimed. 'There's nothing refined about me, Jean. I wish there was.'

'Of course there is,' Jean insisted. 'I thought that as soon as I saw you, that you looked ladylike. And you can't say you haven't got brains running this place.'

Nellie coloured with pleasure but more because of the suggestion that Tom had inherited her refinements than for the compliment to herself.

She was growing very fond of Jean, who in addition to being a good worker possessed a practical good sense which often helped Nellie.

Before the café reopened after the first Christmas Jean and Winnie, Nellie and Tom discussed what they had learned and made plans for the future. Tom thought his mother was doing too much and the others agreed.

Jean said she thought that they were being too ambitious in trying to supply anything that was asked for.

'Bacon butties,' Winnie said giggling.

'That was a good idea but I don't think we should try to serve them all day,' Jean said seriously.

'Just for breakfast, you mean?' Nellie said, and Jean nodded.

'And now we're doing liver and onions, spare ribs and cabbage and anything else anyone wants, as well as all the different puddings. It's too much for you, Nellie.'

After some discussion it was decided that they would serve bacon and sausage sandwiches and pea soup until ten o'clock then stop making sandwiches and serve pea soup, scouse, and pie or pasty served with potatoes and vegetables and a rich gravy.

'We could do one pudding each day,' Jean suggested. 'Apple pie or boiled fruit pudding with custard, or jam roly-poly. One each day, not a choice of any of them.'

Nellie agreed. 'I could do a couple of big rice puddings for them that wanted something cheap,' she said. 'That'd be no trouble.'

The customers readily accepted the more restricted menu. The café had become so popular that men were being turned away or waiting around outside until there was room.

Life became easier for Nellie with the smaller menu and with more help. Winnie's sister had left school and came to help in the kitchen, and when Bob came to live there he took over many jobs which Tom had done, like peeling potatoes for the following day.

Tom did the books after work, but they all worked as a team, everyone willing to do whatever was necessary at the time.

Before Bob came Nellie told Jean that she was not a widow, and was surprised to find that she already knew.

'From something Tom said,' Jean said calmly. 'But it's your business, Nell.'

Nellie told her what she had told Meg of Sam's illness. She had told it to herself so often that she truly believed it and it made Sam's desertion easier for her to accept.

'In a way it's worse than being a widow,' Jean said. 'If you're widowed you know where you stand. You know that though you never really stop grieving it must get better with time. I suppose you worry about him too.'

'I do,' Nellie said. 'I don't think I'll ever see him again and I think he might be dead, but—'

'But there's always a hope,' Jean said sympathetically.

'Yes. I know it's daft but a fortune teller told me I would see him again, and I think of that. I don't really believe in them things but some of the things she said have come true.'

'You'll just have to live from day to day and see what happens,' Jean said practically and Nellie agreed.

Bob and Nellie decided that he would look for a house when there was definite news of Meg's discharge from hospital but the date was constantly put back.

Nellie and Bob visited her frequently, often taking David and sneaking him into the grounds where Meg could spend some time with him, although children's visiting was discouraged.

'You'd have been too terrified to do this at one time,' Bob said to Nellie.

'I'm frightened of nothing now,' she said grimly.

'I believe you,' Bob said.

Many of the men Nellie dealt with either as customers or in business seemed to think that as a widow she was easy prey. With her slight frame, her big blue eyes and deceptively gentle voice Nellie seemed very vulnerable, but they soon found their mistake.

'Some of them try it on,' she told Bob. 'They

see a nice little business and think they'll get their knees under the table, but they don't get very far with me. Still, I'm glad you're living here, Bob. That should frighten them off.'

I think they need to be more frightened of you than me, Bob thought, but he said nothing. He could see that Nellie had changed but he knew it was only a façade. To David and Meg and himself she was still a loving elder sister.

Almost unnoticed the years slipped away, filled with hard work and growing success for the café. Soon after his arrival Bob had arranged for his firm, Meldrum's, to knock through some sculleries and walk-in pantries to enlarge the café and the kitchen. Nellie had bought the house at a reasonable figure as a sitting tenant only a month earlier.

Before long the extra tables were filled every day and more food needed. Nellie had engaged two girls to wait on the tables and a woman to help with the cooking. Winnie and her sister were still unhappy at home and when they told Nellie that their stepfather tried to force his way into their bedroom, she converted the attics into a flat for them.

When at long last Meg was discharged from hospital in 1936 she told Bob that she felt nervous about running a house, so they stayed on with Nellie. David moved to share Tom's bedroom and it seemed that the family simply expanded to take in Meg and went on as before very happily.

'It's no wonder she feels out of touch,' Nellie said to Tom. 'All those years shut away.'

Tom laughed. 'You're a fine one to talk,' he teased her. 'All that's been going on in this city and the world and you've never paid any attention. The Tunnel opening the year before last, the celebrations for George V and Queen Mary's Jubilee last year and now King George dying last month and a new King, and you never even noticed, did you?'

'Why should I?' Nellie said. 'It's got nothing to do with me. This is what I'm interested in, my café and my family.'

'Mam, you're incorrigible,' Tom said laughing. 'You should go to the pictures sometimes with Jean. See the Pathé Gazette and a film.' He leaned over her chair and whispered, 'And leave Meg and Bob on their own.'

Nellie only pushed him away, laughing, but later she thought over what he had said, and suggested a trip to a cinema to Jean. It was the beginning of a regular outing, and Nellie began to be more aware of what was happening outside her own little world.

Tom was now sixteen and when a reporter left to join the International Brigade, he was offered the job of junior reporter but he declined it.

He told his mother that although he wanted to write it was not as a reporter.

'It's not for me, Mum,' he said. 'Interviewing people after a tragedy when they want to be left alone, or trailing round garden fêtes and presentations. I've applied for a job in a shipping office. I think I've a good chance.'

'But what will Miss Helsby say?' Nellie said dismayed.

'I've told her and she approves,' Tom said. 'She said she taught me Spanish because she thought it would help me to get a job with a line trading to South America, only she thought the newspaper office might appeal to me more.'

'He knows his own mind, doesn't he?' Meg said.

Nellie sighed. 'He had to grow up too fast, Meg,' she said. 'The way I was.'

'It hasn't done him any harm,' Meg said staunchly. 'If our David turns out like him I won't grumble. He's got a good chance with Tom learning him all the time.'

Nellie only smiled but she thought to herself that David was not the only one learning from Tom. She listened to him correcting David's speech as Miss Helsby had corrected his, and realised the faults in her own speech. Without saying anything to anybody she tried to correct them. It was easier for her because Jean spoke well so the improvement in her own speech was less noticeable.

Tom secured the job and was happy in the shipping office, finding romance in the documentation he did for ships sailing to various parts of the world. He also hoped that in this milieu he might hear something of his father, but he was disappointed.

He was still writing short stories and sending them to the many magazines which printed such pieces and he was often successful. Nellie almost burst with pride when the stories were published and copies of the magazines were passed from hand to hand in the café.

As always on such occasions she thought of Sam and how proud he would have been. She went in to serve in the café from time to time to see that her customers enjoyed the food and were well served, and one cold morning when trade slackened she went in.

Tables occupied the space where the tea urn and counter had been, and there were three tea urns in the extended kitchen. A man sat near the door, a tall man who must once have been as well built as Sam. Now his shabby clothes hung loosely on his emaciated frame and his skin seemed stretched over the bones of his gaunt face. Most of the customers ordered pie and potatoes and vegetables, followed by pudding of the day, but Nellie also did a cheap meal of scouse or pea soup and bread, and rice pudding for twopence, and this was what the man had ordered.

Was this what Sam was like now? Nellie wondered as she looked at him. She had never forgotten Tom's words about the Depression in America following the Wall Street Crash.

She filled the bowl of scouse as full as possible and cut large hunks of bread to go with it, and then gave him a massive helping of rice pudding. Tea was not included but she said to the woman in the kitchen, 'Fill a lot of mugs with tea.'

The woman looked surprised but no one argued with Nellie and she rapidly filled the pint mugs. Nellie went back to the café.

'Mugs of tea on the house,' she said. 'A new woman's made a mistake.'

'Keep her on, missus,' one man said jovially.

'Buckshee tea tastes twice as good.'

Nellie laughed and rapidly distributed the mugs of tea, even those who had one already accepting the free one. I must be mad, she thought. A dozen mugs of tea just so I can give this man one, but he smiled at her gratefully when she put the mug on his table.

'Are you working round here now?' she asked, seeing flour on his sleeve.

'No, I'm just casual on the flour wagon for the day,' he said. 'The regular man's off.'

'Well, I hope you get a few more days and we see you again,' Nellie said. 'Good luck. I hope something else turns up if that doesn't.'

'Thanks, missus,' the man mumbled turning his cap in his hands, and Nellie saw with horror that he was near to tears, and made an excuse to hurry away. Oh Sam, Sam, she thought, if you're down on your luck, lad, please God someone will give you a bit of help or a word of comfort. She dashed upstairs to the bedroom and locking herself in cried as though her heart would break.

She bathed her eyes and busied herself in the kitchen but later Jean whispered to her, 'Is something wrong, Nell, or have you just been thinking about Sam?'

'Just thinking,' Nellie whispered but she was unable to say more.

When Nellie bought the house Bob studied the deeds and discovered that some of the waste ground behind the house was included in the sale. Now he was urging Nellie to build an extension to the café and a kitchen on this land.

'I'd chip in, Nell,' he said, 'and we could build a flat over it for me and Meg and David.'

Nellie thought it a good idea as it would give them a home of their own yet they would still be near at hand and Tom agreed with her but Meg seemed strangely reluctant. Nellie wondered if Meg was experiencing symptoms which she was concealing from them.

Although she tried to help she seemed to tire very easily and even talking seemed to exhaust her. She preferred to sit reading or listening to the radio, not even paying much attention to David or Bob.

David had been at school for nearly three years now and he looked very different to the frail little boy who had arrived at Nellie's house. He was still like a replica of Bob, with red hair and a deep cleft in his chin, but now he had the same sturdy body as his father and his eyes were bright with intelligence and health.

His best friends were still Jean's two boys, Leslie who was older and Douglas younger than him, and the woman who worked in the café often said, 'Youse are like one big family.'

She said it to Meg one day and Meg smiled sadly.

'Just as well, I think,' she said. Nellie overheard her but said nothing then. Later when they were alone she took Meg's hand.

'Is something worrying you, love?' she asked gently.

Meg's eyes filled with tears. 'I think I'll have to go back to the sanatorium,' she whispered. 'You know I was having periods when I came home, but they've stopped and I've brought up blood a couple of times.'

'Perhaps the periods have stopped because you're pregnant?' Nellie said, but Meg shook her head.

'No, even when I first came home I couldn't,' she said sadly. 'I think it had been so long. Poor Bob, he got a bad bargain in me.'

Nellie hugged her. 'Don't ever say that. You wouldn't say it if Bob was the one ill, would you?' she said. 'Bob loves you. He'd only be worried about that on your account. Does he know about your symptoms?'

'No, I've tried to keep it from him but I think he might suspect. The way he looks at me sometimes.'

Nellie stroked Meg's hair gently. 'Do you have to go back to that place?' she said. 'I'm sure sleeping out on that balcony in cold weather can't be good for you. Why can't you be nursed at home? Just stay in bed here and rest. I'll do whatever's needed.'

'No, it'll be too much for you,' Meg said. 'But thank you anyway, Nell. You've been a good sister to me and Bob.'

'We'll see what the doctor says,' Nellie said briskly, 'but you can go to bed now and rest and don't worry about David. Whether you stay in bed here or you have to go away for a bit we'll look after him—if I can get him away from his friends for long enough. He's such a favourite with everyone.'

'I know I needn't worry about David,' Meg said. 'You know, on Saturday when I saw him and Jean's two lads going off with Bob to watch Tom playing football, I felt so thankful. I thought of what a lonely little boy he'd have been if he'd been if he'd stayed in Sudely. God must have sent you that day, Nell.'

Nellie put her arm round Meg. 'I only wish I'd gone sooner,' she said, 'but I'm thankful I went. It's meant a lot to me and Tom to have you and Bob and David here. Our own family.'

She suggested that Meg went to bed, as the talking seemed to have exhausted her, but Meg wanted to talk to Bob before she went. Nellie made her comfortable in the armchair until Bob came home from work.

As Meg had expected Bob was not surprised to hear of her symptoms.

'I'm only surprised that they let you come home from the hospital, love,' he said, 'but I'm glad they did.'

He went for a doctor and had a talk with him before returning to the house. The doctor was a Polish Jew, a refugee from Hitler's Germany, and although his English was imperfect he was a clever and compassionate young man.

He agreed that Meg could be nursed at home but told Nellie that Meg's dishes must be sterilised and kept separate from the rest of the family's.

'You too must have care,' he said. 'The washing of hands. Much antiseptic. Only a few weeks I think then hospital it must be.'

The extension plans were postponed, and Nellie engaged another cook and a waitress so that Jean and two cooks did all the cooking, and she was able to stay away completely from the café.

Once her illness was confirmed, Meg seemed to decline rapidly. It was the autumn of 1938 and everybody in England was breathlessly waiting for war to be declared but the minds of Meg's relations were filled with her struggle. She was brave and uncomplaining and pathetically grateful to be nursed at home.

Nellie knew how much she dreaded a return to the hospital and how much it meant to her to be at home, so when the doctor said he thought the time had come for Meg to be moved to hospital Nellie pleaded for her to be left at home a little longer.

She was always glad that she did and that the doctor agreed.

Two nights later the doctor had been on one of his frequent visits and Nellie and Bob were settling Meg for the night.

All was peaceful and Nellie had gone to the window while Bob bent over Meg gently smoothing back her hair. Suddenly there seemed to be an alteration in Meg's breathing and Bob said in a scared voice, 'Nellie,' but she was already beside him.

Meg's breathing had ceased and stunned Nellie said, 'She's gone, Bob.'

'She can't have,' Bob said distractedly.

He rubbed Meg's cheek and her hands and lifted her in his arms but Nellie said gently, 'It's no use, lad. She's gone just like that. No struggle.'

She saw Tom, aroused by some sixth sense, peep into the room then she heard him running down the stairs. Time had ceased to exist and it seemed only a moment later to Nellie that the doctor was gently moving her and Bob away from the bed.

He bent over Meg then turned and put his hand on Bob's shoulder.

'A peaceful end. I hoped for this. Be grateful.'

Bob only stared at him wildly and Nellie said, 'She just seemed to stop breathing, Doctor.'

He shrugged and put out his hands, palms upward. 'The disease or the heart. The heart has been first. A kinder death so be happy for her.'

David had wakened when Tom left the bedroom and now Bob insisted on bringing him in to kiss his mother's cheek.

'It's all wrong,' Nellie said tearfully to Tom, 'the poor child.'

Tom said soothingly, 'Better this way, Mam. Now he's seen her just lying peacefully in her bed. Much better than that ghoulish habit of lifting children up to coffins.'

The very peacefulness of Meg's death seemed to make any noisy grief unseemly and Nellie and Bob talked quietly together until she persuaded him to lie down on the sofa.

'I won't be able to sleep,' he said, but within minutes he had fallen into an exhausted sleep.

The café staff were sad to hear of Meg's death but all agreed it was a merciful end. One of the helpers, Mrs Evans, said thoughtfully, 'Somehow she never seemed as though she was here to stay. Always a bit apart, like.'

Jean wept when Nellie told her. 'That poor little boy,' she said. 'And he's such a darling.' She dried her eyes. 'And poor Meg to go so young and with so much to live for. At least though it was peaceful and in her own bed as she would have wished.'

'I'll always be grateful to the doctor for that. He's been so good,' Nellie said. 'He's only got a few patients so far but I hope he does well.'

'I suppose after what he must have been through he can feel for other people,' Jean said. 'Like you and I can feel for Bob because we've been through it ourselves.'

Jean seems to forget sometimes I'm not a widow, Nellie thought, but maybe she's right. Yet it was impossible for her to abandon hope completely.

CHAPTER 29

Two days after Meg's funeral the Munich Agreement was signed. On newsreels and in newspapers the Prime Minister Mr Chamberlain was shown waving a piece of paper which he said would mean 'peace for our time'.

Most people were delirious with joy that war had been averted but Tom and Bob were sceptical.

'That doctor doesn't think we can trust Hitler, and he should know,' Bob said. 'He thinks we've been conned.' But these views were unpopular. Everyone wanted to believe that the threat of war was over.

Bob grieved sincerely for Meg but he threw himself into the planning of the extension. He thought that they should still have the rooms built over the new dining room and kitchen, although he and David would stay with Nellie.

'They can be used as storerooms for now,' he said to Nellie. 'I think you should stock up, Nell. If war comes all the stuff you use will be scarce,' and although Nellie thought he was being pessimistic she agreed to order extra supplies.

Everyone at the café made an extra fuss of David to make up for the loss of his mother, especially Jean and the two 'little mice' as Jean and Nellie called Winnie and her sister Cathy. They were as quiet as mice and very happy in their flat in the attics, and David was always a welcome visitor there.

Both girls had worked very hard, and often returned in the evening to help while Nellie was absent nursing Meg, but Jean had shouldered most of the responsibility. Nellie was very grateful to them and wondered how to show her appreciation, but it was Tom who suggested how to do it.

The sale of pies to take out had been discontinued due to lack of space but Nellie knew that there was still a demand for them, and she had asked Bob to include a narrow room to serve as a shop against the wall of the new kitchen in the plans.

Now Tom suggested that the sisters should be given charge of the shop with a commission on everything they sold there, in addition to their wages for their help in the café. Winnie and Cathy were delighted with the idea, but said that they were willing to run the shop without commission.

'You've already done so much for us,' Winnie said. 'Honest, Mrs Meadows, I don't know what would have happened to us without you. Our stepfather'd changed his mind about wanting us out,' ('And we know why,' Cathy interrupted) 'and he wouldn't have let us leave home to go in rooms. He couldn't stop us taking the flat although we were so young because he was afraid of you.'

'Afraid of *me*?' Nellie said laughing.

'Well, you'd have soon seen him off if he tried, wouldn't you?' Winnie said seriously.

It amused Nellie that Winnie who had been such a giggler was at twenty a tall girl with a serious manner, and plump Cathy was now the giggler.

Nellie had already decided on a plan for Jean, and Tom and Bob were both enthusiastic about it. 'Jean's been in with me from the beginning and she's been a tower of strength to me. I think I should make her a partner,' Nellie said.

She put the idea to Jean one evening when they had been to the cinema and returned to Jean's house for supper.

'But I can't put money in, Nell,' Jean exclaimed.

'I don't want you to,' Nellie said. 'You've

put more than money in. You've backed me up and worked like a slave for the business, even though I could only pay peanuts at first. I couldn't have done it without you, Jean, and I should have suggested this long ago.'

'But the money you used to start up,' Jean said. 'It must have been very hard for you to get that together.'

Nellie hesitated then she said, 'I'll tell you something, Jean, that no one else knows, not even Tom. You mightn't want to go in with me when you hear it.'

She told Jean of the money she had found, and about Janey and her moneylending and receiving. 'At the time it just didn't bother me,' she said. 'I told myself that I was entitled to it because I'd kept Janey and had no rent from her, but now I wonder. I think the money I found came from the receiving not the moneylending.'

'Why do you think that?' Jean asked.

'Because I want to, I suppose,' Nellie said honestly. 'Somehow it doesn't seem so bad because it's stolen from people who are not too scrupulous themselves.'

'Like Raffles or Robin Hood,' Jean said laughing.

'The moneylending money is *really* tainted,' Nellie said. 'Taken from poor people who are desperate, but I hope that was stolen when her basket was pinched. The police seemed to think there was a lot of money in it although I don't know how they knew. They didn't get it back. The people who took my house found sovereigns behind a brick by the fireplace too.'

'She must have been rolling in money,' Jean exclaimed.

Nellie agreed. 'And she never spent a ha'penny on herself or any comfort,' she said. 'Well, now you know about the money, what do you think?'

'I see nothing wrong in you having it,' Jean said. 'As you say, you kept her for years, and then she had no relations so the money would only have gone to the Crown.'

'I meant how do you feel about the partnership?' Nellie asked.

'I'd be made up and I think you're very good to ask me,' Jean said, kissing Nellie impulsively.

Before Christmas it was all arranged, to take effect from January 1st 1939.

Tom was very pleased about the arrangement. He felt that now with Jean to share the responsibility for the café, and with his uncle and cousin living with them, he could relax some of his anxious care for his mother. He was convinced that war would come and that as he was now eighteen years old he would be eligible for war service.

He knew that he would pass any medical examination. Although he had blue eyes and brown hair and fair skin which burned easily in sunlight, like his mother, he was tall and broad shouldered, though less burly than his father.

He often thought about his father and wondered whether he was alive or dead. None of the enquiries he had made about him had produced any news of Sam since he left his ship in New York. Tom had only confused memories of Sam's brief time at home when he last saw him, and he felt unable to ask his mother for any details.

He had heard the rumours and gossip when Sam left, it was alleged with another woman, and heard Nellie's explanation to Bob, but he felt that some vital link was missing. He often went over in his mind the stories Sam had told him and his memories of his father, and used them for the stories he wrote.

He was now very successful, and sold his work with ease. It provided a useful supplement to his salary as a shipping clerk, but more than that it was something he enjoyed doing, and it was still a thrill to see his work in print.

David had now moved back to his father's bedroom so Tom had his room to himself, and he spent all his spare time there scribbling, often far into the night. He had started a novel but he told no one about it, not even his mother.

One of the first stories Tom wrote was based on what he had heard of his father's childhood. He had called it 'Little Boy Lost' and he had sent it to a highbrow monthly magazine, the *Quill*. It had been returned with a letter which Tom treasured, and which encouraged him to try to write a novel.

The editor wrote that the story was interesting and unusual, and he was impressed by the lyrical quality of the writing, but the subject and setting were not suitable for his magazine.

'I suspect that you are quite young,' he wrote.

'You possess talent which with perseverance will ensure success. I wish you well and expect to hear more of you in years to come.'

Tom put the letter away with the treasured letters from his father and as with them it was taken out and read and reread, although he knew the words by heart. The novel was well advanced and he was spending as much time as possible on it, as he felt there would be little chance of writing if he was called up.

David was very proud of Tom's success and bragged about him to all his friends. Like Tom he loved reading and Tom tried to guide his choice of books as Miss Helsby had guided his.

He told Miss Helsby of this on one of his now infrequent visits to her.

'So your influence goes on,' he said smiling.

'That is as it should be, Thomas,' she said seriously, 'knowledge passed from generation to generation.'

Tom told his mother of the conversation. 'Mind you, Mum, it's not exactly a generation, is it? Eight years between us. David's more like my younger brother.'

A shadow crossed Nellie's face. 'Aye, I remember when he was born. I'd always wanted more children and poor Meg said if I couldn't have them her children would be like my own to me. Poor Meg. We often talked about that in those last few weeks.'

Tom would have liked to ask why he was an only child but he knew that he dared not. Close though they were there was much which his mother kept to herself and shared with no one, not even him. Although Tom loved David without reservation he was often annoyed with Bob. He felt that his uncle was too free with criticism of the way his mother ran the café and took her sacrifices for him for granted.

He was surprised to find that Jean agreed with him. He had gone to her house with a message from his mother and stayed for a cup of coffee with her. It was just after the partnership had been suggested, and Jean said she was pleased to be able to talk to Tom alone.

'Are you sure you like the idea, Tom?' she asked. 'I know your mum says she makes her own decisions but I'd like to be sure you agree.'

'Of course I do,' Tom said. 'One hundred per cent. Mum needs you.'

'And what about Bob?' Jean asked. 'He might have expected to be offered it. I mean, he's family and with all he's done on the extension and everything.'

'Oh no. Bob's interest is in his own job. He's only fussing about the extension because Meldrum's are building it. He's got nothing to do with the café—although he keeps putting his oar in,' Tom said resentfully.

He expected Jean to protest but she said, 'Yes, I know he does. I don't know where he gets the idea that he knows better than your mum. The way she's built it up from scratch, the chances she's taken, and he comes when everything's going smoothly and tries to tell her what to do.'

She was flushed with indignation and Tom leaned towards her.

'I'm glad someone else can see it,' he said. 'He's pushed this extension and I'm sure Mum didn't really want it. She was quite happy with the café the way it was when she could do all the cooking herself, well, with a bit of help.'

'But she was completely in charge and she could keep everything to her own standards,' Jean said. 'I think she went along with the extension idea because of the flat for Bob and Meg.'

'And now Bob's decided they'll stay with us. Don't get me wrong, Jean. I like Bob, he's a good fellow, but he just takes Mum for granted. Doesn't ask what she wants, just tells her what he's decided.'

'I know what you mean,' Jean said. 'I know he was grateful to her for nursing Meg, and so was she, poor soul, but he never seemed to realise what a sacrifice she was making to do it. Cutting herself off from the café that had been her whole life, for what could have been months. It turned out to be weeks, but that doesn't alter what I mean.'

'Mum didn't mind, I know,' Tom said. 'She was glad to do it. To keep Meg at home. But it was Bob's attitude. As though it was the obvious solution. As though the café was a hobby that she could just lay aside like knitting. He wouldn't have dreamt of taking time off work, yet she has far more responsibilities at work than he has.'

'The trouble is she makes it all look so easy,'

Jean said. 'She never says anything about how she's affected so I suppose we all take advantage of her in some way. But I wish she wouldn't take Bob's advice when it's so often wrong.'

'Only on trivial things,' Tom said. 'Anything she really cares about no one could tell her what to do.'

'It's this idea that men know best even if they're as thick as a plank,' Jean said. 'And women like your mum and myself, Tom, we think we're independent but we've been indoctrinated. At the back of our minds we think they are right.'

'Not you, Jean,' Tom said. 'And not Mum, I think, although where we lived when I was a kid the men were always the big boss. They'd batter any woman who defied them, so the women went along with it. We've lived in our own little world in the café but perhaps those years *did* affect Mum. Not that my dad was like that.'

'Not only in your neighbourhood,' Jean said. 'We lived in a nice district. Dad had a small business but he thought the world revolved round him. Monarch of all he surveyed. He treated my mother like a slave and she let him. Do you know, Tom, he never poured a cup of tea for himself in his life.'

'Then how did you grow up so independent?' Tom said laughing, but Jean looked serious.

'Because of what I saw,' she said. 'My mother used to kneel at his feet unlacing his boots and taking them off and putting his slippers on his feet. I offered to do it to save her, although I hated him, but he wouldn't allow it. I think he liked to see her kneeling before him. More than once he kicked out at her because she was slow or the slippers weren't warm enough. It wasn't the only time he hit or kicked her either.'

'Is he still alive?' Tom asked.

'No, thank God. He died of apoplexy carrying on at a workman. I bet the man had a good laugh. My mother died just before I was married.' She stood up and put coal on the fire. 'I'm sorry, Tom, you didn't expect to get your ears pounded like that,' she said.

'I enjoyed hearing it. You know how nosy I am,' Tom said.

'Is that what you call it? I know you're interested in everything and everybody,' Jean said. 'I suppose you'll use that in a story.'

'Bits of it maybe,' Tom said with a grin. 'I didn't mean to go on about Bob. He's all right really.'

'Neither did I. It's just that I care about your mum,' Jean said.

Tom said nothing to his mother about the conversation but he asked her about Jean's husband.

'I think he was a good man,' Nellie said. 'She seems to have been happily married although I never knew him. It was sad her being widowed so young.'

'Has she never thought of remarrying?' Tom asked. 'She's a smart woman, isn't she?'

'I think a few have wanted her to,' Nellie said. 'Stan Norris, who supplied the chairs, I know he asked her out, and a traveller who used to come, he was very keen and I thought she might have been tempted but it was when Winnie and Cathy left home. She said she'd never bring a stepfather in to her boys.'

They were alone and Tom said softly, 'Would you, Mum? If Dad had been killed?'

She shook her head.

'But you think Jean should?' he persisted.

'Maybe, but I'm sure I'm a widow,' she said. 'Anyway I'm what they call a one-man woman.' She moved away and began to tidy magazines. 'Do you want all these?' she asked.

Conversation closed, Tom thought wryly, and said no more.

Although Tom was well liked in the office and was a member of the office football team, he made no close friends. So much of his free time was spent on writing that he had little to spare for a social life.

The colleagues he went with to lunch often tried to persuade him to join them playing billiards or dancing but he always refused, and he never showed any interest in the girls in the office.

'You love words more than women,' one man said in exasperation but Tom only laughed and agreed. When I've finished my book, he promised himself, but he still confided in no one about the novel.

Bob usually brought David and Jean's boys to watch Tom's team playing football and when the football season finished Tom often took the three boys swimming on Saturday afternoons or he and Bob played cricket or football with them in the park.

Tom and Bob both worked until one o'clock on Saturdays so Saturday afternoons were precious.

'I know the lads are made up to be with you,' Bob said one day. 'But haven't you got no mates you want to go out with, Tom?'

'No, this suits me,' Tom said. He forbore to say that an afternoon with his friends would mean going on to a pub and probably arriving home after midnight and no writing.

He put his book aside for one friend that he made in the spring of 1939. Winnie's brother Vinny came home on three weeks' leave and stayed in the flat with his sisters. He was a regular soldier and had served on the North-west Frontier and in Palestine and there was instant rapport between him and Tom. They spent much of his leave together.

Sometimes they went to a cinema or a theatre with Winnie and Cathy or went to a pub, but what they both enjoyed most was sitting in the flat with a few bottles of beer to lubricate their dry throats as they talked, often far into the night.

'They're perfectly matched,' Winnie told Nellie, 'Vinny likes talking and Tom likes listening.'

'I think Tom's mad,' Nellie said, 'staying up so late. I know Vinny's on leave but he's got to go to work the next morning and so have you and Cathy. Do they disturb you?'

'Nothing disturbs me and Cathy once we get our heads down,' Winnie said. 'Tom says he's used to being up late writing anyhow.'

'I never thought anyone could get him away from that,' Nellie declared.

Winnie smiled. 'You should have seen Tom the other night. He was sitting there saying "The Khyber Pass" over and over again. Rolling it round his tongue like something nice to eat.'

It was as well that Nellie was unaware that Tom stayed up long after returning from the flat, filling notebooks with details of Vinny's tales.

The three weeks of Vinny's leave soon passed, but before he left he came to see Nellie, bearing a large box of chocolates.

'I want to thank you for what you've done for my sisters, Mrs Meadows,' he said. 'Winnie told me what happened. You saved them from that fellow, and you've been good to them ever since.'

'I got the best of the bargain,' Nellie said. 'They've helped me a lot. We all pull together here and they more than pull their weight. And they're so quiet. We call them the little mice.'

'I went to see that fellow,' the boy said gruffly. 'He wasn't worth soiling me hands on.'

'Water under the bridge now, lad,' Nellie said. 'The girls are happy. That's the main thing. I'm very fond of them.'

The summer of 1939 was beautiful, with sunny days and balmy nights, and everyone tried to enjoy it to the full. Most people felt that they had been reprieved from the threat of war but as autumn approached it was gradually accepted that war was inevitable.

All the talk in the café was of preparations

for war, of the warehouses being emptied and of cargoes no sooner landed than they were whisked away.

'There's some won't go short. Them with money,' one man said, but another said, 'Stow it, Jimmy. Change the record. Everybody'll get it this time with aeroplanes dropping bombs like in Spain.'

'We'll be all right here,' several men told Nellie. 'The planes won't be able to get over the Pennines and if they come by sea they'll get shot down before they get here.'

Nellie hoped that they were right but her first concern was for Tom. At his age he would be called up to serve in one of the three services and she was relieved when he told her that he intended to enlist in the army. She thought it was unnatural for anyone to fly in the air and she often thought of Sam as a boy of fifteen spending days in an open boat when his ship was torpedoed.

Tom was influenced by Vinny's tales of army life, but he found most of his colleagues in the office were applying for either the Royal Air Force or the Royal Navy. A fellow member of the football team, who was as tall as Tom, went with him to Renshaw Hall to enlist, as he also wanted to join the army.

They had thought vaguely of the Cheshire Regiment or the King's Liverpool, but because of their height they were recruited into the Grenadier Guards. The other men at the office told them horror stories of the Guards' training but Harry and Tom laughed at them.

'Anyone who thinks he'll have it soft in any of the services will have his eye wiped,' Harry declared.

'Anyhow we're both fit. We can take it,' Tom said.

Tom had at last finished his novel a few weeks earlier and sent it to be professionally typed. He could hardly bear to part with the crisp immaculate pages when they were returned, but he parcelled them up and sent them off to a London publisher.

Within weeks his call-up papers arrived. Nellie wept and recalled stories of the Western Front, and of Johnny Nolan's sufferings, but Tom comforted her by saying that this was a totally different war.

'They'll have learnt by the mistakes they made last time,' he said optimistically. 'No gas, and everything's mechanised now. No horses pulling gun carriages through mud.'

'It's not the horses I'm thinking about,' Nellie said tartly, but she was proud of her son when she saw him in uniform on his first leave. Tom was dismayed to find a parcel waiting for him containing his manuscript.

'In these uncertain times and with the prospect of paper rationing,' the publisher wrote, 'we feel unable to accept a first novel.' He added a few encouraging words and Tom parcelled up the novel and sent it off to another publisher.

'He might be more willing to take a chance,' he said to his mother. 'I'm not waiting around for better times. The war might last a long time.'

'But everyone thinks it'll be over soon,' Nellie said in dismay.

'They're probably right, but I'll get it off again anyway,' he said hastily.

Tom looked well and told Nellie that he was enjoying army life. After years of feeling that he was the man of the house and responsible for his mother, and then of spending nearly all his free time writing, he enjoyed being without responsibility.

Everything was decided for him now. The way he spent his days, his meals, his sleeping arrangements and even to a certain extent his companions, and there was no privacy for writing. His interest in people was still as strong though, and he enjoyed mixing with men from many different backgrounds and mentally storing away their conversation.

He and Harry had travelled down to the Guards' depot at Caterham together and had been put in the same squad. For the first few weeks they were so exhausted by the training that they were just content to drop on their beds every evening. Their muscles soon hardened and when they had passed the first inspection by the company commander and they were allowed out they were ready to enjoy themselves.

Drinking, visits to the cinema, lightheartedly dating girls, they enjoyed it all, and as they became more fit even enjoyed the drilling.

By the end of three months, when they had been inspected first by the adjutant and then by the commandant and had passed, they were swaggering past the new recruits as though they had spent a lifetime in the army.

Tom had always received more letters than anyone else in the squad, but shortly after they moved on to the training battalion he received letters from nearly all his correspondents on the same day. He looked through the pile, recognising the various handwriting.

His mother, Jean, Bob, David, Winnie and one posted on from Vinny. He opened his mother's letter first.

She told him that Bob had asked Jean to marry him, and they were going to be married in September.

I'm very glad for them. Jean was only young when she lost her husband and so was Bob when he lost Meg. I think they were both lonely. The three lads get on well together. The stuff could be moved out of the rooms over the extension but it wouldn't be big enough for them really and neither would Jean's house. Bob thinks they should make a fresh start anyway, so they've got a nice house in Lucinda Street.

Tom dropped the letter on his knee. Bob and Jean! Well, it was on the cards, I suppose, he thought. He left his mother's letter and opened Jean's.

She wrote that he might be surprised to hear that she and Bob were to marry.

I know I said that I would never inflict a stepfather on my boys, but Bob has been like a father to them for years, just as you have been like an elder brother, Tom, and I'm very grateful. The boys are very fond of Bob and you know how I love David. With Les ten and Doug eight, David at nine fits in perfectly and they are all good pals.

PS I'll make sure that Bob appreciates your mum!

Tom read the letters from Bob and Winnie and they all said much the same thing, that the three boys were already like one family. Winnie said that Nellie would miss David and Bob and Lucinda Street was farther away than Jean's present house, but not too far. 'Don't worry about your mum, Tom,' Winnie wrote. 'Cathy and I will see she's not lonely.'

At least *somebody's* thinking about Mum, Tom thought. He picked up his mother's letter again and reread it, feeling a lump in his throat. Oh, Mum, he thought. Happy for the three boys, happy for Jean and Bob because they were lonely. Not a word about how it would affect her, of her own loneliness, yet now with me away and David and Bob gone she will be more lonely than ever before. If only Dad would come back! Yet as the years passed it seemed more and more unlikely.

Tom loved his mother with a fierce protective love and longed for her happiness, but close to her as he was he understood how she suffered.

Other people might think that she had put the past behind her and made a success of her life but he knew the truth. He knew how often she wept in the night for his father and saw the sadness in her eyes even when she smiled.

He remembered once while he was still at school he said bitterly to his mother, 'Dad didn't love us or he wouldn't have gone away.'

'He loved you, Tommy. You were the core of his heart,' his mother had said softly. 'It was me he left.'

He remembered that he had protested that she was wrong. His dad had loved her, but she shook her head.

'He was sorry for me, lad,' she said with a sigh, 'I loved him though and I never knew it till now.'

Now he sat on his bed, the letter in his hand, oblivious to everything around him. My poor little mum, he thought, what a life she's had. A phrase came into his mind. 'A life of hectic endurance'—that's what hers had been. Quiet and uncomplaining she had worked hard from morning till night, willingly shouldering any burden, providing for old Janey, nursing Meg and caring for David and Bob like a mother.

The sacrifices she's made for me too, Tom thought. When I was little and times were hard it was bread and margarine for her and an egg for me. Then the awful daily jobs she stuck at so that I could have the best of food and clothes, money for the slipper baths or toothpaste or writing paper and books. Anything that Miss Helsby suggested for me. Uncomprehending but willing, praising me yet never claiming any credit for herself.

Tom felt ashamed that he had not tried harder to trace his father when he grew old enough, and wondered whether it was still possible. He recalled the gossip when his father left but he was sure that his father must have been tricked in some way.

He liked to drink with his mates when he was ashore but Tom felt sure he never looked at any other woman than his wife. Perhaps Mum was right and the illness was the cause of Dad going, thought Tom.

He had sat so long staring into space and thinking, that Harry came across.

'Bad news, Tom?' he asked.

Tom started. 'No, good news really. A wedding in the family. Just got me thinking.' He hastily gathered up his other letters. 'I'll have to read these later.'

He wrote the same night to congratulate Bob and Jean and wish them well, and wrote a long letter to his mother. He had made up his mind that he would write a few lines to his mother every night, and send them twice a week so that she would know he was always thinking of her.

He also decided to find out as much as possible about his father on his next leave and start some enquiries about him, perhaps even write to the British Embassy in New York. America was not yet at war and *someone* there might at least tell him where to look for his father.

CHAPTER 30

Sam had no clear plan of what he would do when he left the ship, only that he must get away from the places where he had been tricked and humiliated and make a fresh start. America was supposed to be the land of opportunity but Sam had no great ambition or desire for success.

He only wanted to earn enough for food and lodgings, but he soon realised that he had chosen a bad time. America was in the grip of the Depression, and he saw lines of gaunt and ragged men and women standing in line outside a soup kitchen, and roaming the streets.

As night drew near he realised that his good boots and the bag he carried were being eyed hungrily by some of the desperate men, and he changed his mind about sleeping in a lodging house. He began to make his way back to the waterfront and the Seaman's Home, confident that he could look out for himself until he reached there.

He was unprepared to turn a corner and to be pushed against a wall with a knife to his throat. Three men surrounded him, but Sam kept his eyes on the knife holder and his head still, and suddenly kicked out with his heavy boots. One man yelped with pain and fell back and Sam kicked and punched the other men, at the same

573

time shouting at the top of his voice, 'George, Buck, Tommy. Over here.'

The men ran off and Sam hurried away keeping to the middle of the road, and darting glances all around him until he reached the Seaman's Home where he managed to get a bed.

Later as he lay on his bed he thought over the incident. The way those names had come to his tongue! George, Buck, Tommy. He thought of his old mates George and Buck and wondered where they were and what they thought of him.

I suppose me name's mud in the Volley, he thought, for what I done going off with that one. I'll be a laughing stock too after Ellie fetching that other fella in. And Tommy. I shouted for him too, me posh son that turns his nose up at me now.

Suddenly he was struck by the thought, never far away, that Tommy was not his son. Couldn't be. He groaned and rolled over burying his face in his pillow. Ellie, Ellie, how could you do this to me? he thought, then close on came another thought.

If only he had never seen that doctor or he'd kept his bloody mouth shut. I could've gone on not knowing, being happy and seeing me lad grow up. He clenched his fists. That new fella had better treat Tommy right or he'd have him to reckon with.

Images from the past filled his mind and invaded his dreams when he briefly slept then woke again. Ellie as a ragged barefoot child looking trustingly at him as he shared out the food she had been given or he had bought. The rare treat of fish and chips when in spite of everything they had been happy.

His homecomings to the cosy kitchen with his chair with Woodbines and matches beside it and savoury smells filling the air.

Tommy as a baby standing on his knee with his soft cheek against his face and his little arms around his neck. Later holding Ellie in his arms, making love to her gently, afraid to hurt her because she seemed so fragile and innocent. *Innocent.* He groaned aloud and pounded his fists on the pillow in frustration and despair and the man in the next bed leaned over.

'Stow it, mate,' he said ferociously. 'Fellas are trying to sleep.'

Sam mumbled an apology and eventually slept.

The next morning he left early, still determined to turn his back on his past but uncertain which way to go. A man was approaching the Home as he left it and they stopped in mutual recognition.

'Chancer!' Sam exclaimed.

The other man said, 'Samson!' which had been Sam's nickname at Heswall.

Chancer turned back and they strolled along together catching up on the years since they had been boys together in the reformatory.

Sam talked of his experiences during the war and the ships he had sailed in since but he said nothing about his wife or Tommy.

'I've knocked about all over the world,'

Chancer said frankly. 'In the war I was torpedoed twice and in an open boat. The second time I was put ashore at Nova Scotia, in a bad way, but I got all right. I've never settled anywhere long though.'

'Been here long—New York?' Sam asked.

'No, only just come. Me longest spell was in Chicago. I done well out of Prohibition but it's on its last legs now,' said Chancer.

'That why you left there?' Sam asked and Chancer laughed.

'No, there's Prohibition all over,' he said. 'No, it's got a bit too hot for me. Too many people thinking I'd look better on a slab.'

You couldn't look much worse, Sam thought, glancing at Chancer and thinking that his looks had not improved with time.

His ginger hair, close cropped when Sam had last seen him, now was a tangled mane and he had acquired a broken nose and a scar which pulled down the corner of his eye and gave him a sinister expression. Probably useful, Sam thought, as they seemed safe from attack.

They were getting away from the most slummy area now and by common consent they turned into a comparatively clean eating house.

'Can't get over this, Samson,' Chancer said. 'D'yer know, you're the first Heswall lad I've met again in all these years.'

'I met a couple during the war. None since,' Sam said.

They began to reminisce about the reformatory, the harsh discipline, the floggings, the spartan diet.

'Nothing seemed as bad after,' Sam said. 'Maybe that was the idea.'

'When you think of it, bread and a pint of tea was all we had between midday dinner and the next morning,' said Chancer.

'And the other meals weren't up to much neither,' Sam said. 'I remember me first ship. When I seen what the cook give me and the lad to take to the fo'c'sle I couldn't believe me eyes. Bacon and eggs, bread and butter, coffee, and the crew were *moaning* about it.'

'Same with me,' Chancer said. 'I was mess lad and when the cook was ladling the bacon and eggs into this great big dish I thought he was never going to stop.'

'I bet they didn't all reach the fo'c'sle,' Sam said.

Chancer grinned. 'I scoffed five eggs between the galley and the fo'c'sle,' he said, 'an' shoved some bread up me gansey too, but there wasn't no need to pinch food on that ship.'

'You never got six cuts like we got at Heswall for pinching a slice of bread,' Sam said. 'When you think of it. Mind you, I was only there in the first place for pinching a jar of jam. *You* pinched bread or spuds many a time and got away with it, didn't you? No wonder you got the name Chancer.'

'Aye, but then I'd get six cuts for nothing,' Chancer said indignantly. ' "Looking insolently at an officer," for God's sake. Not even opening me mouth to him.'

They finished their meal and left the eating house and Chancer asked about Sam's plans.

577

Sam shrugged, and Chancer asked if he fancied shipping on a coaster.

'I know where one's taking on,' he said. 'Have you got your book?'

'Aye. What about you? You'd swallered the anchor, hadn't you?'

'I've got *a* book,' Chancer grinned. 'For this voyage I'm James Huron.'

'*If* we get on,' said Sam.

'Just leave it to me,' Chancer said confidently.

Sam left him to do all the talking when they reached the coastwise ship and they were both signed on.

Sam found Chancer a good companion and a staunch friend. He still had the ability to acquire items and manipulate situations to make life more comfortable, which had earned him his nickname, and he ensured that Sam benefited too.

The crew were of many nationalities but they got on well together, and the food and the crew's quarters were reasonably good. The officers were more easy going than British officers and Sam and Chancer had time and opportunity for many long talks together.

They usually discussed the ships they had known and the voyages they had made and found that at different times they had sailed in the same ship.

'Dirty old scow, wasn't it?' Chancer said. 'And the grub was bloody putrid.'

'Aye, I was almost glad when I was too sick to eat it,' Sam said with a grin. 'God, I was bad that trip. I was like as though I was on fire and me neck all swelled up. I was like something out of a sideshow.'

'Maybe you got poisoned with the grub,' Chancer said.

'I don't know what it was,' Sam said. 'But me neck! I couldn't swallow—couldn't hardly speak.'

'Sounds like mumps,' Chancer said.

'No, that's only for kids,' Sam said. 'I was twenty-one, twenty-two. First voyage after I was married.' He stopped, realising too late what he had said. Neither he nor Chancer had spoken of their personal affairs, but Chancer made no comment now, and Sam hurried on. 'I had two real good mates with me, Buck Madden and George Adams, and they looked after me great. The rest of the lads were good too, carried me, like, till I got all right again.'

'Nothing like a good mate,' Chancer said quietly. They were leaning on the ship's rails, smoking, and he hurled his cigarette stub over the side. 'I've just lost a good mate,' he said.

'Hard lines, mate,' Sam said quietly.

Chancer lit another cigarette and they smoked in silence for a while. Then Chancer said, 'That's another reason I left Chicago. He stopped a cop's bullet there.'

'Were you together long?' Sam asked.

'About nine years,' said Chancer. 'We split up once or twice. Had a dust-up and split but we soon got back together. He watched my back and I watched his. The Professor, I called him. Clever fella.'

'We used to call George the Professor because

he was always reading,' Sam said.

'Ah, but Spence really *was* a professor,' Chancer said. 'From a university, but he told me once he got fed up with the scheming and the backstabbing, trying to get on by treading on someone else. He said there had to be more to life and he took to the road.'

Sam felt that he owed it to Chancer to be as open with him.

'My wife,' he said. 'She's in Liverpool. It's all over.'

Chancer nodded. 'Any kids?' he asked, but Sam shook his head.

'Have you?' he asked.

'Probably,' Chancer said. 'Scattered round, like, but no wife.' He grinned at Sam. 'I can still get the girls, you know, even with this kisser. A few have tried to pin me down but I ducked out. Mind you, I was thinking of going home, settling down, until I bumped into you. That's why I was going in the Seaman's.'

'Some girl's had a narrow escape,' Sam said.

He had never known Chancer well at Heswall but now he found that the more he knew of him the more he liked him.

Chancer seemed to understand when a black cloud of misery descended on him and how to lift his spirits. It was good to be with someone who had known him as a lad, Sam felt, and he knew that Chancer felt the same.

When the ship paid off they stayed together, going wherever their fancy or the available work took them. Chancer was too restless to stay long in one place and Sam drifted along with him, taking each day as it came and trying to avoid thinking of the past or the future. As Chancer had said of his previous mate, they 'watched each other's back', and this was important. The roads of America were dangerous at this time, roamed by the hungry and the dispossessed, but together they could deal with any danger.

Chancer could nearly always find work for them, enough to provide food and lodging, or a dry barn to sleep in and a chicken under his coat to be cooked for their meal when they were away from the farm.

He had his own peculiar code and though he would never steal from a fellow unfortunate, anyone else was fair game, and they usually lived well. Sam was too indifferent to care one way or the other.

Months slipped into years as they wandered, working on farms or in canning factories, sailing on ships trading along the coast or on the Great Lakes, working on railways or in logging camps.

Wherever they wandered Chancer would always manage to pick up a girl, and this was the only point on which they disagreed.

'What have you got against dames?' Chancer would demand. 'Are you a monk or something, Samson?'

Soon after they met, Chancer had reminded Sam that when they were at Heswall Sam had told the lads that his mother had warned him not to go with women in ports.

'We thought you was mad,' Chancer had laughed, 'we was all only waiting for the chance.'

Now he often reminded Sam of this when Sam had refused to join him on his hunt for a girl. 'Your old lady done a good job on you,' he would say in disgust. 'She might as well have got a knife and chopped them off for you.'

Sometimes he pretended to be afraid to sleep near Sam. 'Am I safe?' he would say. 'Fellas that don't fancy dames sometimes fancy fellas,' but whatever he said Sam refused to take offence and only grinned and smoked silently.

His violent temper, once so easily aroused, seemed to have been damped down with the rest of his emotions, and he only fought if it was necessary to protect them, and never with Chancer.

Gradually over the years his perception of Ellie had changed. Now he saw her not as a woman who had tricked him but as a victim of circumstances or of people more crafty than herself. The mental picture that had troubled him, of her cringing away from him in terror and her bruised and swollen face, had gradually faded.

Now when he thought of her he saw the white face and huge eyes of the starving child, or the busy happy wife and mother, serving the meals and watching proudly as they were enjoyed. He thought of his days ashore, going to the market, with Nellie's hand in his arm and her face smiling proudly up at him.

All too often that memory was followed by another, of him raging jealously at Nellie because a stallholder spoke to her. Of his time ashore spoiled by rows caused by Charlie West and people like him. Why had he listened to them? Why had they picked on him? Because I was an easy mark, he would think.

They knew that I would take notice to them and they done it for a laugh. A laugh! And the life I used to lead Ellie because of them tales. Because I was a sucker, a jealous fool that wouldn't trust me own wife.

These thoughts seemed to occur most often when he and Chancer were sitting peacefully beside a camp fire and he would get up and fling away, tramping for hours, exhausting himself but unable to escape from his thoughts.

Chancer never said anything when he got back, only brewed up a dixie of coffee for him in wordless sympathy. He never asked questions and Sam said nothing of his reasons for misery, or gave any details of his wife and son.

In turn Sam respected Chancer's silence about his family. He knew from talk in the reformatory that Chancer had been placed there by his father who complained that he was out of control, and that the father held a good position, but Chancer never volunteered any information about his early life and Sam never asked for it.

It was in the Fall of 1937, when their wanderings had taken them to a ship on the St Lawrence and from there to Prince Edward Island, that Sam first spoke of Tom to Chancer. They had seen many beautiful sights during their wanderings, but never anything like the glorious colour of the maple leaves.

'My God, my lad would love this!' Sam exclaimed.

For a moment there was silence then Chancer said calmly, 'An artist, is he?'

'No, he just loved anything colourful, like,' Sam said. He hesitated then said awkwardly, 'I didn't tell no lie when I said I never had a child. He wasn't mine but I sort of helped to rear him.'

'So he'd be like your own,' Chancer said. 'I wish I could paint this, but I'd never get these colours right. No one would.'

They had been hired to saw wood and all day as they worked Sam's mind was filled with memories of Tommy. Tommy as a baby, as a toddler strutting proudly beside him, of playing football with Tommy or teaching him to box.

At the end of the day as they relaxed after their meal he was unable to resist talking about him to Chancer.

'He was real clever, you know, Tommy. Even when he was a little tiddler the questions he used to ask! Never got tired of hearing about places I'd been or things I'd seen.'

'How old will he be now?' Chancer asked.

'Let's see. He was born November 1920. God, he'll be seventeen very near,' Sam said amazed. 'A young man. I never realised.'

Suddenly like a dam bursting the whole story poured out. Ellie as a child, of their wedding after Janey had waylaid him outside the Volley. The night Tommy was born. The taunts of his so-called mates.

Chancer listened in sympathetic silence as Sam sat with his head bowed and his clasped hands between his knees, words pouring from him. He

584

spoke of Nurse McCann saving Tommy's life and how tiny he had been. 'But he come on. Got real strong. The times we had. I learned him to box. Wanted him to be able to look after himself. He was a bit small like his mam but he was strong. She used to wash him in scenty soap when he was a baby, always kept him nice. Always a new gansey and boots for me coming home.'

He stopped, smiling to himself, and Chancer said quietly, 'He had a good mother, then?'

Sam's head jerked up. 'The best,' he said emphatically. 'She was a good wife too. If me money was held up he never went short. She got cleaning jobs. Worked real hard.'

He stood up and went to lean on the door jamb looking out at the darkening countryside, and Chancer said softly, 'Sounds like a good wife too. What was she like?'

'Ellie? She was little and thin, quiet like. Quiet voice. Big blue eyes. She had the place lovely when I came ashore. Me chair be the fire and Woodies and matches beside it, and something real tasty cooking.'

They were both silent for a while, Sam occupied with his thoughts and Chancer looking puzzled but asking no questions. Suddenly Sam crashed his fist into the palm of his other hand.

'I just wanted to look after her,' he exclaimed, 'from I first seen her as a kid. That's all I wanted. To look after her.'

Chancer looked even more puzzled. 'I'd say you were doing that all right, Sam, as far as you could as a seaman, and she was doing her side of it. I can't see what was wrong?'

'It was me. Me bloody jealous temper,' Sam groaned. 'I spoiled them good years. Listening to them in the Volley, Bert Hagan and them lot, and old Janey coming out with things. Making out I'd been tricked.'

'I don't get it,' Chancer said, 'You're no fool, Samson. Why did you take any notice?'

'It was Tommy—she only went eight months for him, and he wasn't nothing like me,' Sam muttered.

'But that doesn't prove anything,' Chancer said. 'Do *you* think she'd trick you?'

'No, she was straight, Ellie. I'm sure she was. She must've got tricked herself some way,' Sam said. 'But we got over all that. Oh, I was still bloody jealous, and that runt Charlie West hanging round, but we was happy. And me and Tommy. They all used to say about us round there, the way we were together. An old one at the top of the street—she said he was the core of me heart.'

'And still is, I think,' Chancer said. 'You know, Samson, if the Prof was here he'd tell you you'd been jumping to conclusions. You could claim Tommy as your son.'

Sam groaned and put his hands over his face. 'Oh God, I wish to God I could, but I can't,' he said with anguish. 'I took bad on me last voyage. Got took to hospital and the doctor there—he said I was sterile.'

Chancer whistled softly. 'By God that's a facer,' he said.

'Aye, it is,' Sam said grimly, and they said no more. Chancer often quoted philosophical comments which had been made by the Professor, but he could think of nothing to fit Sam's tragedy.

Sam was stiff and self-conscious the next morning when he remembered all he had said, but Chancer's manner was the same as usual, and soon Sam was behaving naturally.

During the following months he gradually filled in the details of his story. Chancer was a perfect confidant, always ready to listen and make sympathetic comments, but never pushing Sam further than he was ready to go.

It was a great relief to Sam to talk freely about what he had brooded on for so long. He even told Chancer about Madge and Southampton.

'I can't believe now that I did that. I must have been bloody mad. Knocked sideways by that doctor, I guess.'

One thing he never spoke about and even avoided thinking about was the attack on his wife immediately before he left home. Instead his thoughts dwelt fondly on the other happier homecomings, and especially on their outings as a family, and the nights of passionate lovemaking.

Despite what he had heard of the other man moving in immediately, of the tales Madge had told him of Tommy becoming a gentleman and despising him, and Nellie being 'on the game', something within him obstinately refused to believe that the Ellie he knew was not the true one.

If only he had realised how much he loved her. Now when it was too late he was filled with love and longing for her, and longing for his son. Chancer had said that being a father to Tommy until he was ten made the boy his son, more than the blood tie, and Sam had grasped eagerly at the idea. Tommy's unknown father had never shown any interest in him, yet Sam had always loved him.

But it was Ellie he longed for even more than his son. He remembered the way she had clung to his arm when they were out together, her pleasure in the little gifts he bought her. The way she nestled in his arms and kissed him, and he wondered whether she ever thought of him.

He wondered this aloud one day when he had been talking about his wife to Chancer and Chancer thought she probably did.

'But the way I walked out on them,' Sam said. 'And Tommy's a young man now with his life before him, and Ellie's made a new life for herself.'

'With the brandy drinker?' Chancer said. 'I've been thinking about that, Sam. Hasn't your old lodger just died? Maybe the fellow had just taken the room. If he found the money and he was drinking it. Didn't the landlord say something about the lad should have had it?'

Sam stopped dead in amazement. 'I never thought of that,' he said. 'I wish I'd talked about all this years ago. You've got a good headpiece on you and I'm so bloody thick.'

'No, it's just what they say, "The onlooker sees most of the game," ' Chancer said laughing.

'The Prof always said things should be looked at from every side before any conclusion was drawn. He was a brilliant man, Sam. He studied Kant, you know, and when he talked the world seemed different.'

'Aye, and you could understand him. You're an intelligent man yourself, Chancer, but me—I'm just like an animal that can feel pain but can't understand why.'

'And that's as profound a thought as any of the Prof's,' Chancer said.

Sam and Chancer spent the autumn and winter working on farms and in canning factories but only enough to provide food and lodgings, then they wandered on. In the spring when the ice melted they worked on ships trading on the Great Lakes and when they tired of this they thought they might go back to America.

They had been back and forth over the border several times over the years but even Chancer was unable to get them over this time and they turned back to Canada. By now it was 1938 and talk of war was everywhere until the Munich Pact was signed.

'It'll come through,' Chancer said, 'stands to reason. Even in '36, the last time we were in the States, things were picking up. More work, more prosperity, and all because of armaments. The same everywhere.'

Sam agreed. 'That Cockney lad on the ship. He reckoned England was getting better. More chance of a job, though it had a way to go.'

'Only one reason. Armaments. They're piling them up and they've got to be used so they can make more, and that means war,' Chancer said.

Sam sighed. 'I hope to God you're wrong but I guess you're right,' he said. 'And they told us ours was the war to end wars.'

'That wasn't the only lie they told us, was it?' Chancer said.

A few minutes later Sam said thoughtfully, 'It's just struck me. If it comes, Tommy'll be old enough to fight.'

'The same thought had struck me,' Chancer said.

He had filled his pockets with apples earlier and now he and Sam sat down in a clearing, their backs against tree trunks, munching the apples.

'Do you get fed up listening to me about all this?' Sam asked. 'I mean, all these years I've never said nothing about it, and now I never stop.'

Chancer pulled off his battered cap with a flourish and sketched a bow. 'On the contrary, dear sir, I am honoured to be chosen to hear it,' he said.

The contrast between the flourish and the flowery words and Chancer's distorted face was ludicrous and although Sam laughed he thought with fierce loyalty, I hope people see past his kisser to see what he really is. Pure gold. The best mate a fellow could have.

He felt that although he and Chancer had wandered the roads for so many years as the best of friends they had both kept part of themselves separate and private. Since he had talked of his past their relationship had altered and become deeper, and he had realised more clearly Chancer's tact and kindness and his intelligence.

He wanted to tell his friend how much he appreciated his response to his revelations but he was unable to frame the words.

'Thanks for taking an interest, like, Chancer,' was all he could say.

Chancer threw the apple core into the undergrowth. 'I've often thought lately, Samson, you and me, we're in the same boat in some ways.'

'How do you mean?' asked Sam.

'The Prof always said that what we experienced in childhood, even as babies, set the pattern of our behaviour for the rest of our lives.' He shrugged. 'I reckon we both had the same experiences.'

'Heswall, you mean?' Sam said.

'Before that. We were both thrown out by our fathers, and our mothers—well, they were no help. Mine died when I was born and yours seemed to do a good job of twisting your ideas about women,' said Chancer.

'I don't blame me ma,' Sam said. 'She was always sick and she couldn't stand up to me dad, but him! He hated me.'

'So did mine,' Chancer said.

'How old was you when he threw you out?' asked Sam.

'Well, that's the question,' said Chancer. 'He sent me to prep school when I was four and I ran away, then to three other schools over the next few years, but I never stayed long anywhere. I was down for his public school but he told me he wouldn't let me disgrace him there. Turned me over to the police as being out of control. That's how I landed at the reformatory in Heswall.'

'I never knew you were posh really,' Sam said. 'You talked like us and made out you'd lived rough and that.'

'Protective colouring,' Chancer said with a grin.

'You tried to abscond a few times, didn't you? Never made it,' said Sam.

'I didn't like the punishments either,' Chancer said grimacing. 'I soon realised I hadn't much chance of getting away, so I just made life as bearable as possible.'

'I remember,' Sam said dryly. 'That's how you got your name Chancer.'

'What I'm saying, Sam, is you shouldn't blame yourself too much for the way you behaved. You couldn't help yourself.'

Sam shook his head. 'I couldn't blame nobody else,' he said. 'I never even told Ellie what that doctor said. Never heard her side of it. And I never even said ta-ra to Tommy.'

Chancer said nothing for a moment then he leaned forward.

'Listen, Samson, why don't you go back? Go and see them. I think you want to.'

'Don't see how I can,' Sam said gruffly. 'After all these years. They'll have made their own lives without me.'

'But you could just go and see. Don't even

have to make yourself known. Just go and see and you'll be easier in your mind. You can always come back if you want to.'

'Might stop me going on about them,' Sam admitted. 'You know, I battened down hatches on it for all these years, although I did think about them, like. Since I started talking about them. I can't think of nothing else.'

'I think you should go,' Chancer said. 'It's not as if you feel bitter about them, but you'd like to know how they are, wouldn't you?'

'But what about you?' Sam said.

'I might just settle down,' Chancer declared. 'Let one of the dames catch me. Those twinges of rheumatism I had last winter. Maybe they were a warning it was time for the old rocking chair.'

'When I see you in it I'll go,' Sam joked, but they both knew the decision had been made.

CHAPTER 31

When Tom came home on fourteen days' leave from the training camp his first outing was to the shipping office where his father had been paid off after his last Liverpool voyage. The clerk he spoke to was anxious to be helpful to anyone in army uniform. He told Tom that his son serving with the Cheshire Regiment had been killed at Dunkirk.

Tom gave as many details as he could

without revealing why his father had sailed from Southampton, but the man could offer little hope.

'He could have signed on with another line from New York, even if he decided to come back to his home port,' he said.

'I know it's just a chance,' Tom said. 'But I've got to try.'

'Come back in a couple of days and I'll check where I can,' the man said. 'If I can find anyone who can help you I'll send them to see you.'

'My mother doesn't know I'm doing this,' Tom said hastily. 'I'm on fourteen days. Could you just send a message and I'll meet them? You could tell me when I come back.'

When he returned the man told him that he had no news of Sam signing on but he gave him the address of a man who had sailed in and out of Southampton for a couple of years. 'He's had an accident. Staying with his mother in Juvenal Street,' he said.

Tom hurried to the address and the man said he was willing to tell Tom all he knew but he warned him that he might not like it.

'Never mind. Tell me,' Tom said, and the man said he had heard about Sam.

'Big fellow with a fist like a sledgehammer, is he?' he asked and Tom nodded. 'Well, lad, this is only what I heard. Could be wrong.'

He hesitated and Tom said, 'I know there was a woman involved.'

'Well, in that case. This fellow lived with a tart. She used to be run by some pimp. Big black man called Big Eddie. There was a fight one night in the pub and Big Eddie drew a knife and the fellow hit him. Broke his jaw and the landlord got him put out.'

Tom's face had gone first red then very pale and the man said anxiously. 'I'm sorry, lad, but you said you wanted to hear it.'

'I do,' Tom said. 'I want to know anything you can tell me.'

'Well, I got told the fellow signed on for New York the next morning, and he backed off in New York. The tart got slashed and she disappeared when she came out of hospital. Sorry I can't tell you no more, lad, but as far as I know he was never in Southampton again.'

'I'm very grateful for all you've told me,' Tom said. 'My dad was very ill on his last voyage from Liverpool. He got put ashore to a hospital abroad and he was a changed man when he came home. We think it might have damaged his brain. What happens when a man backs off?'

'Different things, lad. Some fellows have a good time, then sign on anything they can get. Some fellows go travelling round or find a shore job. Just depends.'

Tom stood up. 'Thanks a lot. I'm glad to know what happened. Better than guessing.'

He tried to put money in the man's hand murmuring, 'Have a drink,' but the man refused it.

'Keep your coppers, lad,' he said. 'I done all right with the compensation.' He winked. 'The old lady said I shoulda been on the stage.' He ushered Tom to the door. 'Hope you find your

595

dad, lad, and he's got all right,' he said.

Tom returned home feeling despondent but he was pleased to find one of his mother's old neighbours sitting with her.

'You remember Mrs Rimmer, Tom, Katy Rimmer and her daughter Amy that used to take you to school?' his mother said.

'Gosh, I'm glad to see you,' Tom said enthusiastically, and both women laughed.

'I'm glad to see you too, Tommy,' Katy Rimmer said. 'You look great and writing stories too your mam tells me.'

'How's Amy and Bernie and Don?' Tom asked.

'The lads are at sea and Amy's in the Wrens. A cypher clerk,' Katy said proudly. 'There's only Alan at home now.'

'She won the scholarship, remember, Tom?' Nellie said. 'She was always clever.'

Tom stayed for a few minutes chatting but he felt that his mother and her old friend wanted to catch up on all the news.

He excused himself and went up to his bedroom to write down all the seaman had told him. Just in case, he thought, although unless his mother asked him directly he would never tell her what he had learnt.

Nellie told him later that she had met Katy by chance when she had been queuing for tomatoes.

She spoke tearfully about her pleasure in meeting Katy again and hearing all about her old neighbours. 'What do you think, Tom? Mrs Gilligan and her husband are back together again, and Lettie's working as a wardrobe mistress or something with the Royal Court and doing very well.'

'Mrs Gilligan?' Tom said.

'The woman that used to tell fortunes. Prudence, Gertie called her. A lot of them have come true. She told Katy about their Amy doing so well when Amy was only a little girl and she said Gertie would marry late and be very happy and that's come true an' all.'

'Who was Alan she talked about? Is that her husband?' Tom asked, to show interest.

'No, Katy's husband is Peter. Alan was the last little lad she had. She told me about Maggie Nolan. She's give up her house. Gone to live with Josie and her husband, and Susan and her husband are only round the corner from them.'

'What about the lads?' asked Tom.

'Henry and Walter are both at sea and Richie's working in the Meccano on war work. Him and Henry are both married and Walter's courting. Maggie's very happy with Josie.'

Tom laughed. 'You seem to have got all the news,' he said. 'I hope you'll keep in touch with Mrs Rimmer, Mum.'

'Of course. I'm only sorry I lost touch but that was my own fault. Katy's not the kind to bear grudges though.'

'I think it was my fault really, Mum,' Tom said looking guilty. 'I was given messages that I didn't tell you about. Thought they might upset you.'

'Oh well, it's water under the bridge now

anyway,' Nellie said cheerfully, and Tom felt that he would worry less about leaving her when this leave ended.

The second publisher had returned his novel, again with an encouraging letter and blaming paper shortages, and Tom wondered if he should wait until the war was over to send it out again.

There had been an air raid in September and houses near the docks had been demolished and people killed or injured. The café had escaped but Tom heard men talking about the raid.

'This is only the beginning,' one man said, 'stands to reason Bootle and Liverpool are going to get it. Look at the stuff we ship in and out,' and men at other tables agreed with him.

Although Tom worried about his mother and family and friends if this was true, he also worried about his manuscript. Nellie had put the parcel into a tin box when it came back, but now Tom thought that he would send it off again.

It was as likely to be buried in rubble in London as in Bootle, but at least, he thought, another publisher would have looked at it.

Tom had visited Jean and Bob and David in their new house, and Winnie and Cathy in their flat and they all assured him that his mother was quite happy.

'We won't let her be lonely,' Jean said, but she was pleased that Nellie had met her old neighbours again, and she liked Katy when she met her.

'I might be lonely myself soon,' Jean said with

a sigh. 'Bob's applied for the Air Force. Ground crew.'

Although Bob was now prematurely grey he was only thirty-four and would be liable for conscription and Tom thought he was wise to plan ahead.

The three boys were clamouring to talk to him and Tom laughed at Jean. 'Lonely! With this crew?' he said.

'D'you know Tucker who brings the bread?' Jean's son Leslie demanded. 'Do you know what he said to my dad? He said are they taking grandfathers now? Just because my dad's hair is grey.'

'I hope your dad gave him a flea in his ear,' Tom said but his eyes met Jean's and they smiled at each other at the boy's unselfconscious use of the word dad.

This is one marriage that's working out very well, Tom thought, and I'm made up. Jean told him that the café was still busy, but not as much as it had been.

'It's not that we haven't got the customers,' she said, 'it's the supplies.'

'I suppose that stuff that was stocked up was a help,' Tom said, but Jean said it had been used very quickly.

'Mind you, it's not only the supplies,' Jean said. 'We can't get the help so easily now. The Meccano and Crawford's, places like that, they're all on war work and paying good money. You can't blame the women going there.'

'It's a good thing you still help there and the

"mice" are there,' Tom said, but Jean blushed and looked away.

'I don't know what'll happen about that, Tom,' she said. 'You see, I'm almost sure I'm expecting a baby.'

Tom kissed her impulsively. 'That's *super*, Jean,' he exclaimed. 'Congratulations to both of you.'

Jean smiled. 'I'm sort of ninety-nine per cent sure but so far only Bob and I and your mum know about it.'

'I won't say anything except to Mum,' Tom assured her.

His mother told him that she had wanted to tell him but thought it was Jean's privilege to do so, but she was delighted with the news.

Tom went back off leave feeling that although he had not succeeded in tracing his father, it had been a successful leave. He felt much happier about his mother. Although he could still detect sadness in her eyes, there had been a new serenity about her in the past few years, and now she would be happy to be reconciled with her old friends.

It was true that Nellie was no longer beset by the doubts and fears that had haunted her for so long. All her instincts told her that Tom was Sam's child and now she trusted those instincts and regretted that she had ever allowed herself to doubt his parentage. Leadbetter was now only a hazy memory of an evil man.

Nellie always felt a pang when she looked at her son and thought how proud Sam would have been of the fine man that Tom had become.

She had allowed Tom to go back believing that she was surrounded by friends and would never be lonely, but it was not the whole truth. Katy, Jean, Winnie and Cathy, Bob and David, they were all considerate and loving towards her, but they had their own lives to live.

Katy had Peter and her family, Jean and Bob and the boys had each other. Winnie and Cathy would inevitably go, first to war work then perhaps to families of their own. Even Tom she hoped would marry one day.

Sam was the only person in the world who could cure the aching loneliness inside her and he was never far from her thoughts. She had believed that what she felt for Sam was affection and gratitude but long ago she had realised that the bitter pain and sense of loss that she felt like an open wound inside her was caused by her deep love and longing for Sam.

If only she could see him even once, she often thought, just to tell him how deeply she loved him and had always loved him, but it seemed he was lost to her for ever.

No one suspected that she suffered. The absence of doubt had given her a serenity, and although quiet she was always capable and cheerful, with a pleasant greeting for her customers, and an easy and friendly manner with her staff.

Tom sometimes looked at her anxiously, but on this leave at least she had managed to convince him that she was perfectly happy.

Tom went back off leave to be moved to the service battalion.

Their first duty was guarding an airfield, and they soon discovered that it was only a few miles to a small town. Transport was easily arranged and soon after they arrived they were invited to a concert in the town.

'I'll try anything once,' Harry declared and he and Tom and a group of friends travelled in.

The concert was given by the usual mixture of amateur singers and comedians, a vicar who recited Ghunga Din, and a once famous singer.

His career had been ruined by drink but he still had the power to touch an audience. He sang 'Because' and 'Love's Old Sweet Song', then as an encore, 'Just A-Wearyin' For You'.

The audience was quiet and intent, and as he sang the words, 'Wishing for you wondering when, You'll be coming home again,' Tom felt a lump in his throat.

After the concert the local ladies provided tea and coffee for the service personnel, and Harry and a few others began to joke and flirt with a group of WAAF's.

Tom stood aside, still affected by the sadness of the final song and disinclined to join in. He only realised that he was blocking the way to the table when he heard a quiet voice saying, 'Excuse me.' He turned to see a small dark girl in the uniform of a nurse trying to pass him.

'Sorry,' he said with a grin. 'I'm in a dream.'

'I hope it was a pleasant one,' she said as he moved aside.

She was with a small group of nurses and one of them called, 'And another coffee, Roz.'

'How many hands do you think I've got?' she called back.

Tom said quickly, 'Can I help?'

She blushed furiously as Tom helped her to carry the coffee, to a chorus of wolf-whistles from his friends.

The room was so crowded that all the groups were close together and Tom knew that the nurses were listening as Harry shouted, 'Hey Tom, look what I've caught. A Liverpudlian.' He had his arm round one of the Air Force girls, a plump girl with a loud braying laugh and an affected voice, whom Tom disliked on sight.

She was staring up boldly into his eyes and he felt obliged to speak to her.

'Which part of Liverpool?' he asked.

'Scotland Road,' Harry said before she could answer. 'Haven't you seen her selling mint outside St John's Market?'

She tossed her head and wriggled away from Harry's arm. 'I come from Childwall, actually,' she said, still staring boldly at Tom.

He could not resist it. 'I come from Bootle, *actually,*' he said. 'Near the docks. You know, Bootle where the bugs wear clogs.'

'I don't believe it,' she said flirtatiously, 'with that accent.'

Tom noticed Harry edging away and he said quickly, 'Yes, I'm Bootle born and bred. Harry's more your class. Born in Woolton.'

He turned away and realised that the nurses had been listening to the conversation and were all giggling.

Tom was too hemmed in to move so he

tried to carry it off. 'Any more coffee, girls?' he said breezily, and three of them asked for more. 'Will you help me?' he asked the girl they called Roz.

They managed to squeeze through to the table and Roz said quietly, 'Is that true? That you come from Bootle?' and when he said it was she told him that she had been brought up near Knowsely Road.

'We lived near there for a while,' Tom exclaimed, 'we had rooms in Grey Street. Now my mother has a café near Worcester Road.'

'I was brought up by my Nin,' Roz said, but at that moment they were joined by Harry.

'Hi,' he said. 'Whew, what a praying mantis. I've unloaded her on to Dick White. Is there more coffee going?'

He took one of the cups of coffee from Roz and carried this with his own back to the nurses. 'Whose is this?' he asked and Roz said it was for Dot, as she and Tom distributed the others.

'Hi, Dot,' Harry said. 'I'm Harry and I'm badly in need of a nurse. Will you cool my fevered brow?'

'More likely to give you one,' one of the other girls said, and soon the repartee between Harry and the girls was fast and furious. Tom and Roz stood apart talking of all the places they knew in Bootle and trying to find mutual friends.

Soon one of the nurses reminded the others that they were due back at the hospital and Harry and Tom left with them. Roz told Tom that her parents were dead, and she had lived with her grandmother since she was two years old.

Before they parted Tom learned that her full name was Rosalind Palmer, and that she loved nursing but hated leaving her Nin.

'She doesn't cry but I know how upset she is, and I hate leaving her. She's always been so good to me, and I'm all she's got now,' she said.

Harry and Dot seemed to be getting on well, to judge by the laughter, Tom thought, and they all agreed to go in a foursome to the hop held on Saturday nights.

Tom went back to the camp with his head in the clouds, and Harry forbore to tease him for once. What a smashing girl, Tom thought. So quiet yet so open and he liked the way she had talked about her grandmother. Although she had dark hair and eyes she reminded him of his mother. She was small like her and had the same quiet voice and gentle manner. I can't wait to see her again, he thought.

When they all met again on Saturday Roz told him that she should have been on duty, but Betty, whom he had met at the concert, had swopped with her.

'She's married, you see,' she explained. 'She enjoyed the concert but she doesn't mind missing the dance.'

Betty, who was incurably romantic, had told Roz that she thought that Tom was her 'Mr Right', but she said nothing of this to Tom.

Harry and Dot danced sometimes with other people but Tom and Roz danced every dance together until the interval. After that they told their friends that they were going out for a breath of air, and they walked with their arms round each other, or sat on a grassy bank, talking.

Tom had said nothing about his father either in the shipping office or to his army friends, but now he found himself telling Roz all about Sam and about his unsuccessful efforts to trace him.

'He could be suffering from amnesia and if his memory comes back he will come home,' Roz said.

Tom agreed although he knew that Roz was only trying to comfort him.

She told him that her grandmother had had a hard life. 'She was widowed when she was thirty-five, with five children. Three of them died of diphtheria within weeks of each other then her daughter died of a twenty-four-hour fever when she was eighteen. My father was her last child and she says he died from stubbornness.'

'Stubbornness!' Tom exclaimed. 'I've never heard that before.'

'She said he was always talking about working-men's wrongs, addressing meetings and that. He was speaking at a meeting in the park and there was a cloudburst. Everybody ran for cover but he was too stubborn. He'd gone to speak and he was determined to do it. He was soaked to the skin and died of pneumonia a fortnight later.'

'And what about your mother?' Tom asked.

'She died of TB when I was two,' Roz said.

She smiled. 'You know, she'd been reading a story where the heroine was called Rosalind, just before I was born. That's how I got my name.'

'I think it's a lovely name,' Tom said. 'Just right for you, somehow.'

They thought that they had spent only a few minutes outside and they were astounded to hear the band playing the national anthem. It was the same every time they met. Time flew past before they could say half of what they wanted to say to each other, but dragged unbearably in between their meetings.

Tom had written at length to his mother about Roz and Roz had written to her grandmother about Tom, and in April it seemed that they might have the chance to meet. Tom was due for a week's leave and Roz would finish one part of her training then and have leave before moving on.

Tom had heard that his battalion might be moving, so he was less upset about Roz moving on but he was very anxious for his mother to meet her, and Roz wanted him to meet her grandmother. They were delighted when they managed to wangle leave at the same time. They met at a local railway station and in the deserted dusty waiting room Tom held Roz in his arms.

'Roz, I love you,' he murmured, kissing her and holding her close. 'Will you marry me?'

'Of course I will,' she said and they both laughed at her matter-of-fact tone.

'It's these romantic surroundings getting to

you,' Tom joked, looking round the grimy room, but then as they kissed the surroundings were forgotten, and they were in a magic world of their own.

All the way to Liverpool they made plans for their future. They decided that Roz would choose an engagement ring on this leave.

'After we've met each other's family though,' she said. 'We should involve them.'

'Although we'll get engaged even if everyone's against it,' Tom said masterfully.

'Do you think they will be?' Roz exclaimed in alarm, and Tom assured her that his mum and all his family would love her.

Before the journey ended they had decided that they would marry on Tom's next leave in three months' time, when Roz would have finished her three-month course, and that after the war they would have a house with a garden and at least four children.

'We're both only children with hardly any relations. You've only got one uncle and I've got no one so our children will need company in their own generation,' Roz said seriously.

When the train drew in to Lime Street Station Nellie and Roz's grandmother, still unknown to each other, were among the crowd waiting behind the barrier.

'Mum usually waits at home for me and the lads come to meet me,' Tom said. 'I suppose she can't wait to see you.'

'It's the same with Nin,' Roz said laughing. 'This is the first time she's met me off the train.'

As they hurried down the platform Roz pointed out her grandmother, and Tom his mother, and they decided that Mrs Palmer was taller than Tom expected and his mother was smaller than Roz had expected, but each privately thought they would like the relations.

The next moment Tom was hugging his mother and Roz her grandmother, then there were introductions.

'It's funny, I thought you might be Tom's mother,' Mrs Palmer said. 'I liked the look of you.'

'I was wondering about you for the same reason,' Nellie said in her quiet voice.

'Should we all go over to Lewis's for a cup of tea?' Tom suggested, then looked at Roz and laughed.

'I've told Tom you always took me to Lewis's soda bar for my birthday,' she said, 'and he took his mum when he got his first job.'

'You'd have a lot to talk about coming from the same place,' Mrs Palmer said.

She looked approvingly at Tom and he smiled back at her. He liked what he saw.

She was a tall spare old lady, with little sign in her face of the tragedies she had suffered. Her hair, now white, was as curly as Roz's, and she had the same dark eyes, but she was more forthright in her manner. Tom thought that anyone who hurt her granddaughter would get short shrift.

At the same time Roz was deciding that she liked Nellie, and Nellie was looking at her with relief and appreciation. Tom had been too

609

engrossed in his writing to spend time with girls before he went in the army, and she had been afraid that he might be too inexperienced to choose wisely.

From his first letter after meeting Roz it was clear to his mother that he had lost his heart completely and hoped to marry Roz. She liked what he told her of the girl but she had spent sleepless nights worrying whether Roz was right for him, and felt about him as he did about her, or whether there was unhappiness in store for her beloved son. Now she felt reassured.

CHAPTER 32

They were all secretly amazed at how easy they felt in each other's company. Even Nellie, still shy with strangers except in the café, chatted easily to Roz and her grandmother.

'I love Lewis's,' Roz said, looking round. 'Remember, Nin, when you used to bring me here to the Soda Fountain for my birthday? I always had a banana split.'

'It's only the last few years I've come into town regular,' Nellie said. 'I came with a girlfriend once or twice when I was young for a special frock or something but I always felt out of place.'

'It was my son made me come in,' Mrs Palmer said. 'Rosie's father. He was a proper firebrand. When I said I didn't like coming here he marched me into town to C & A. He said I was as good as any of the tuppence ha'penny toffs in the shops.'

'And so you were, Nin,' Roz said. 'I don't know why you felt like that.'

'Because some of them would look sideways at you if you wore a shawl, wouldn't they?' she appealed to Nellie. 'These young ones. They don't know what it was like. They don't know they're born.'

'You're the same, Mum,' Tom said. 'Even when you're giving people business and they should be laying the red carpet for you, you behave as though they're doing you a favour. You've got no confidence in yourself.'

'Maybe I had it knocked out of me when I was a kid,' Nellie said.

Tom smiled at her and at Roz and her grandmother.

'You both did a good job with Roz and me anyway,' he said. 'Gave us confidence in ourselves.'

Tom took Roz's hand and leaned over to her grandmother. 'Roz and I would like to get engaged, Mrs Palmer,' he said. 'Do you approve?'

'I do, lad,' she said heartily, and leaned over the table to kiss him, then Tom put his hand on his mother's cheek.

'And what about you, Mum?' he said softly.

Nellie put her hand over his, her eyes full of tears. Oh *Sam,* she thought, if only you were here now, but she smiled at Roz and kissed her.

'I'm made up,' she said. 'I think you're just right for each other.'

There was excited discussion of their wedding plans and both the older women thought they were wise to marry quickly.

'This isn't the time for long engagements,' Nellie said, and Mrs Palmer said they should make the most of their happiness.

'I know I've only just met you, Tom,' she said, 'but Rosie's told me a lot about you and I'm pretty good at weighing people up. I'll die happy to see her with a good man like you.'

Nellie was more restrained but she held Roz's hand and told her that she felt that she knew her because Tom had told her so much about her.

'I knew he was head over heels,' she said, 'and I'm so happy now I've met you.'

'I'm crazy about Tom, too,' Roz whispered to her.

'You'd better look after her, lad,' Mrs Palmer said mock ferociously as they stood up to go. 'That girl's my world.'

'Oh, *Nin*,' Roz protested and they left laughing.

Before they parted it was arranged that Tom and his mother would visit Mrs Palmer's house for tea on Sunday, then they would all go back to Nellie's house and Jean and Bob and the boys would join them.

'Call me Gwen,' Mrs Palmer said to Nellie.

'My name's Nellie.'

'Ellie?' Gwen said.

Nellie said hastily, 'No, *Nellie.*'

It was like a stab at her heart, but Gwen said

cheerfully, 'I'm going deaf in my old age.'

Tom and Roz chose the engagement ring, a half hoop of diamonds, on the following day and it was the start of an idyllic week for them. They tried to divide their time equally between Gwen and Nellie during the day and the older women were understanding about their need to spend time alone together at night.

'I'm finding it hard to wait,' Tom groaned one night when they were locked in each other's arms near a bombed house.

'Only three months, Tom,' Roz said. 'I'd rather do things properly.'

Tom sighed. 'I would really,' he said. 'But we *know* we'll be married soon. It'd only be bringing it forward.'

'But my Nin and your mum, they'd be so upset if anything went wrong,' Roz said.

'So would I,' said Tom, releasing her and sitting up to light cigarettes for both of them.

The tea party in Gwen's house was a great success. It was a tiny four-roomed house with a lean-to kitchenette containing a sink, a gas cooker and a mangle with large wooden rollers.

'I've put *some* washing through that mangle,' Gwen told them. 'I took in washing to keep us, one and sixpence for a big caseful and I think they must've sat on the cases to get the lids shut. The washing'd spring out when I opened it.'

'My ma took in washing,' Nellie said. 'Mostly from publics and big houses. I used to have to fetch and carry it and do most of the washing too. I was a proper drudge for her.'

The two women began to reminisce and Tom

613

heard details of his mother's early life that she had never told him, including the way his father had rescued her when they were children.

'I was terrified of them rough lads,' Nellie said. 'But I was more terrified of me ma. If that washing had got muddy!! Sam chased them away and wiped me eyes on me pinny. He often used to help me carry the washing after that, and he looked after me the same way when we married.'

'He sounds a good man,' Gwen said. 'When did he die?'

'He's not dead,' Nellie said. 'He was ill on a voyage and he had some trouble when he came home. He sailed for New York and he backed off there. I've never heard no more from him, but I feel sure somehow he's alive. A fortune teller told me that water would flow between us and the golden cord would stretch but never break.'

'I'm sure he'll come back,' Gwen said. 'When you've lived as long as I have and seen what I've seen, well, you know that anything can happen in life. Like I heard someone say, truth is always stranger than fiction, and I've heard of men come back from the dead more than once.'

The meal had been laid in the back room which had a grate shining with blacklead and a row of brass ornaments along the mantelpiece with a copper kettle at either end, but then they moved into the tiny front room.

This had a tiled grate with a wooden surround and a mahogany sideboard and corner cupboard

614

and a walnut sewing table. They all shone, and Nellie looked round.

'You've got some beautiful furniture,' she said.

'It was me mother's and her mother's before her,' Gwen said. 'Mother came from farming people out Burscough way and she brought them with her when she got married. I've put some elbow grease on them, I can tell you.'

'They show for it,' Nellie said. 'And so does your brass.'

'Aye, well, elbow grease costs nothing, I always say.' She smiled at Roz. 'I don't know how much she'll put on them when they come to her. You can have them, girl, as soon as you get a home of your own.'

'Thanks, Nin, but I wouldn't take them from here while you were here,' Roz said.

Later they all often spoke wistfully about this conversation.

In the evening they went to Nellie's house, and Bob and Jean came with the three boys, then later Cathy and Winnie came. Everyone liked Roz and her grandmother and Bob and Gwen discovered that her husband had worked for his boss's father many years earlier, so they enjoyed a long chat.

Bob was due to leave for the Air Force the next week, and Gwen said, 'You give them Germans hell, lad. The way they've knocked Bootle about.'

'I hadn't the heart to tell her I was only ground crew,' Bob said later.

Tom and Roz made as many arrangements as

615

they could for their wedding in three months' time although they could only give a provisional date.

'I feel as though it makes it seem that much nearer and more definite,' Tom said and Roz agreed.

Before they left there were two air raid warnings on April 23rd and 24th but no bombs were dropped.

'Perhaps the raids are over in this area,' Roz said optimistically. 'I know other places are getting it but maybe the Germans think they did enough damage to Bootle up to Christmas. It's been fairly quiet since then.'

Tom said nothing. He knew that Roz was trying to convince herself as well as him that there was less need to worry, but the devastation that they saw on the way to Lime Street Station made both of them fear for their loved ones.

It was fortunate that they knew nothing then of what was to come. A few days after they returned, both Liverpool and Bootle, and the other bank of the River Mersey, were bombed ferociously for eight consecutive nights.

The news bulletins said only that a north-west city had been attacked, but a man returning from leave in Birkenhead and another from Walton told what was happening.

'Liverpool's like a bloody inferno,' the Birkenhead man said. 'Lewis's has gone and Blackler's and the docks. You wouldn't believe the damage.'

Later that day Harry came to Tom, white faced, to tell him that he was going home on compassionate leave.

'My mum and my sister were slightly injured when our house got it, but it's my dad. He was fire-watching in Dale Street and he's got shrapnel in his spine. Your mum must be all right, Tom, or you'd have heard.'

Tom did what he could to help Harry to get away quickly, thinking what a good friend he was to think of reassuring him at such a time.

Shortly afterwards a driver came looking for Tom with a letter from Roz telling him that she was going home as her grandmother's house had been hit and she was in hospital.

Letters in grimy envelopes came for Tom from his mother and Jean and Winnie, all telling him not to worry as they were all right, but he was in a fever of anxiety. It was almost a relief to hear that his mother was in hospital with a broken arm and to be given compassionate leave.

He was stunned to see the extent of the damage in Liverpool and the number of houses damaged in Bootle. He stopped by an ARP man who was with a gang of men carefully searching through some rubble.

'How many came over, for God's sake?' Tom gasped.

'Hundreds, mate,' the man said. 'They came in relays, the buggers, bombing into the places they'd already set on fire.'

Another man shouted, 'Alf, quick, there's someone here,' and the man hurried away.

Tom went to Walton Hospital and was told his mother had been sent home. 'Her house is standing and we need the beds for tonight,' a harassed nurse told him.

He dashed home to find the house still standing although most of the windows had been hastily boarded up as the glass had been blown out. The glass of the attic window, crisscrossed with brown paper, hung out waving like a flag.

The house was filled with WVS ladies and other people setting up a temporary rest centre to replace others that had been bombed, and Tom found his mother, her arm in a sling and a dressing on her head, taking teapots from a cupboard.

'Tom!' she exclaimed, bursting into tears as he took her in his arms, but she soon dried her eyes. 'I'm sorry. I've got nothing to cry about compared to some,' she said. 'I'm just so glad to see you.'

'Shouldn't you be in bed, Mum?' Tom said anxiously.

'No, I'm better up. That hospital, Tom. Those poor people. You know Bob's away but Jean and the lads are all right. They've got an Anderson shelter.'

'Have you seen Roz?' Tom asked.

'Yes, she came to see me. Poor Gwen. Her house has gone, Tom. All that lovely furniture, but still, she's alive, that's the main thing,' Nellie said.

Tom went to look round and found that though the strong old house had stood, the extension was completely demolished. He met Winnie with a tray of cups and she told him that she was staying downstairs with his mother as the attic flat was uninhabitable.

'It was the incendiaries on the roof,' she said. 'What isn't burned is soaked with water.'

'You've had a bad time,' Tom said, and Winnie said it was impossible to describe it.

'The worst night was when the *Malakand,* you know, the ammunition ship, was blown up in Huskisson Dock. That's the night Gwen's house got it.' ·

'I don't know where to start looking for Roz,' Tom said.

'She'll be at the hospital. Belmont Road. That's where Gwen was taken,' Winnie said.

'Belmont Road!' Tom exclaimed and Winnie told him that people were taken to anywhere the ambulances could get through to.

'Where's Cathy?' Tom asked.

'At work. She works in the ROF factory in Long Lane now,' Winnie said.

'You don't mean to tell me people are still going to work in all this?' Tom exclaimed.

'Of course. People are going out to places like Maghull and Huyton to sleep but they come back for work,' Winnie said. She picked up the tray of cups she had put down to greet Tom. 'I'd better go through with these,' she said, but she turned back to say, 'Don't worry about your mum, Tom. She's better pottering. I'll make her lie down if she gets too tired.'

Tom went to Gwen's house, thinking that Roz might be there, and stood stunned with shock at what he saw. Where Gwen's house and the house next door had stood there was only a hole in the ground, and the houses on either side had walls blown away to show bedrooms open to view.

And this was what Roz had seen, he thought, desperate to find her and comfort her.

He found Gwen first at Belmont Road Hospital. Her head was bandaged and her foot was in a splint but she seemed comparatively cheerful.

'This was the price of me, wasn't it?' she greeted Tom. 'Talking about bowing out and leaving Rosie me furniture. The bloody Huns got it instead. Is your mum all right, lad?'

'Yes. I went to the hospital but she was at home, organising teapots,' he said.

'That's the stuff,' Gwen said. 'I tell you the buggers aren't going to get me down either, Tom. Our Rosie's helping on one of the wards. Ask Sister.'

He found Roz kneeling beside one of the makeshift beds crowded in the corridors, a Catholic priest beside her bending over the dying man on the bed, and he stood back to wait until she was free.

After a few minutes the priest drew the sheet over the man's face and moved on to comfort others and Roz came to where Tom stood by an office door. As his mother had done, she came into his arms and wept for a moment, then took a deep breath and dried her eyes.

'Oh Tom, last night was terrible,' she said. 'I think Bootle got the brunt of it. The docks were destroyed right along to the South End, but it's the houses, Tom. Streets and streets of little houses. Thank God a lot of people were sleeping at Maghull, but when you think of what they'll come back to.'

She spoke in a low voice, then went past Tom to bend over a makeshift bed in the little office. 'Are you all right, sweetheart?' Tom heard her say. 'Try to go to sleep like Shirley.' He realised that two little girls were in bed in the tiny office.

Nothing that Tom had seen on his way to the hospital, the devastation, the fire engines from areas miles away from Liverpool, the soldiers drafted in, brought home to him the horror of the bombing more than Roz's appearance.

Usually immaculately neat, now her white apron was crumpled and bloodstained, her face was grimy and her dishevelled hair escaped from a crumpled cap.

'I'll have to go, Tom,' she said. 'I'm needed here. I had to turn to and help, they're so shorthanded. A lot of the girls have been killed or injured.'

He went back to Gwen and she told him that she was all right. 'Rosie nips in to see me when she can,' she said. 'You go and keep your mam company. That's what you came home for.'

On the way back Tom helped to manhandle a piano from a hole in the ground. It was covered in rubble and had protected an elderly woman who lay beneath it but she was amazingly cheerful.

'I've never played a note on that thing,' she said, 'but it come in useful after all.'

When he arrived back at the café he was told

621

that his mother had gone to see Jean.

'I think she's lost her baby,' the woman whispered, and he found that she was right when he reached Jean's house.

'They were looking forward so much to this baby,' his mother told him, 'but she's being very brave.'

The three boys were pleased to see Tom but very subdued. He spoke to Jean later and found her resigned to the loss of the baby.

'Perhaps it's not a good time to bring a child into the world, anyway,' she said. It was now May 8th and everyone braced themselves for another onslaught from the bombers but all was peaceful and the same thing happened on following nights. It was clear that the Lüftwaffe had moved their attention elsewhere.

Tom had only been given three days' leave but he managed to see Roz several times and under less fraught conditions. He also had a long talk with his mother. She told him that she had decided to close the café. It was still being used as a rest centre but neither she nor Jean were able to run the café anyway at present. She told him that she was worried about Gwen.

'The homeless people are sleeping in church halls and places like that, and rooms and empty houses are being commandeered for them. Winnie and Cathy are in my third bedroom at present but they'll soon fix up their flat. If Gwen wants to come here until she gets something suitable she'll be very welcome.'

Tom hugged his mother. 'Roz'll be made up to hear that,' he said. 'She's dead worried about going back, not knowing what'll happen to her Nin.'

It was soon arranged and the two women spent happy hours planning the wedding.

Harry returned to camp a few days later after Tom and told him that his father had been moved to Winwick Hospital.

'I thought that was a lunatic asylum,' Tom said.

'It was, but patients like Dad are there. They think he might be paralysed,' Harry said.

'But they're not sure?' Tom said.

'No, we'll just have to hope for the best,' said Harry.

He said his mother and sister had been only slightly injured as they had been in a shelter, and the house though damaged could be repaired.

Tom found that the rumours that the battalion was moving were unfounded but immediately after his return a group including Tom went on night exercises. By the time he returned Roz had come back from Liverpool and had been sent to a hospital forty miles away to complete her training.

Although they were unable to meet they wrote to each other every day, and went ahead with their plans for a wedding in early September.

Tom had heard nothing from the third publisher but he was feeling the itch to write again. Harry now had a WAAF girlfriend, so Tom could refuse to go to the Saturday dance and other social occasions with an easy conscience, on the pretext of writing letters.

Sometimes as he wrote in the quiet hut he

became so immersed in memories of the past that it was difficult for him to come back to reality when the other men returned.

'Love's young dream,' one of the men joked. 'He goes into a trance when he writes to his girl,' but the jokes were good natured.

When Tom and Roz were both sure of their leave the wedding was fixed for the first week in September and the honeymoon was to be a week on a farm in Shropshire. Gwen was now staying with Nellie, as Winnie and Cathy were back in their flat, and the arrangement seemed to be working well.

Tom arrived first at Lime Street and waited for Roz and they travelled together to his home. They sat close together on the tramcar, Tom's arm round her, unaware of the other passengers looking indulgently at them.

'I can't believe this time has really come,' Roz whispered, snuggling into his arm, and Tom pressed her closer, giving her a quick kiss.

Nellie and Gwen were waiting with the table set for tea, but first Nellie gave Tom a letter with a London postmark.

'This came last week, son,' she said, 'but I thought it might miss you if I sent it on.'

Tom scarcely heard her. He was looking unbelievingly at the letter then he gave a loud shout of, 'Whoopee!' and picked up his mother and swung her round.

'He's taken it. He wants to see me,' he shouted, seizing Roz and kissing her. He waved the letter. 'He says it's "eminently publishable".'

There was an excited chorus of congratulations

from the women, and Roz looked at the letter. 'I think you should go to London, Tom,' she said. 'We've got three days before the wedding.' She stopped, putting her fingers to her mouth. 'Oh, I'm sorry,' she said to Nellie. 'You'll want him here for those three days.'

'No, I think he should go,' Nellie said.

It was quickly decided that Tom would telephone the publisher and arrange to see him. Roz went with him to the station and they bought the wedding ring on the way and she said firmly that she would deal with everything else.

The publisher was an urbane portly man, too sophisticated to show his surprise at Tom's youth and the fact that he was in uniform. He took him to lunch and Tom mentally thanked Miss Helsby for the training which made him able to feel at ease among the wealthy club men, and to speak with confidence.

The publisher probed gently. 'Where do you hail from originally, my boy?' he asked.

Tom found that he was offended by the patronising 'my boy' and he said crisply, 'I was born and brought up in Bootle, which is close to Liverpool.'

'But you were sent away to school?'

'No,' Tom said. 'I had excellent teachers,' and one of them was my mother, he thought, who knows how to keep her own counsel, so you can stop digging, mate.

Aloud he said with a smile, 'I take it that this is your club?'

The publisher accepted the warning signal and

chatted about the war until coffee was brought when he told Tom that he was very impressed by the book.

'A study in depth of the mind of an adolescent boy,' he said. 'And an almost lyrical quality in the prose.'

He offered a two-hundred-pound advance against royalties and said that he would have the contract drawn up and sent to Tom for his signature.

Tom hastily revised his opinion of the man and all the way home on the train the wheels seemed to be beating out the phrase, 'An almost lyrical quality in the prose,' with the thought of two hundred pounds' advance as a backdrop.

Nellie and Gwen were excited and incredulous when he told them the offer, but Roz understood that his pleasure in the fact of publication and the phrases the publisher had used outweighed even the money.

Tom explained that the two hundred pounds was an advance against royalties, which were ten per cent of the price of the book. 'So I won't get any more until the book has earned more than two thousand pounds,' he said with a blasé air.

'Good God,' Nellie said faintly, and Roz asked what the publisher was like.

'A bit pompous and patronising I thought until he made the offer, then I thought he was smashing,' Tom said, laughing.

He felt as though he was moving through a happy dream as they made the final preparations for the wedding, with the thought of his book always in his mind.

Roz was staying with Jean for the few days before the wedding, and Bob got a seventy-two-hour pass to act as best man for Tom. Winnie was Roz's bridesmaid.

The wedding day was bright and sunny and Roz looked radiant in a white silk wedding dress with a small train which her grandmother had made. Nellie's heart was full as she looked at her son's soldierly bearing as he stood beside his pretty little bride. And he's as good as he's smart and handsome, she thought, remembering the fortune teller's words that her son would cleave to her.

And he has. He's been a good son, but it's time now for him to cleave to Roz, she thought, but I'll never lose him completely. We've been through too much together.

Nellie and Gwen made a wedding breakfast in the big front room which had been the café and after it Gwen drew Tom aside.

'Listen, Tom, I'm no limpet, you know. Your mum was very good to take me in but I've had a breathing space now and I'm looking for somewhere to live.'

'But you and Mum get on so well,' Tom protested.

'Yes, and I want it to stay that way,' Gwen said firmly. 'I've talked to a counsellor and he said they help people who are bombed out to get a few things round them when they find somewhere to live. I'm not bothered about anything posh. It's only for myself so it's only necessities.'

'But Mum enjoys having you here, honestly,'

627

Tom said. 'And Roz and I like to think you're together.'

'Your mum's a heart of gold but I'm not taking advantage of her,' Gwen said. 'You see, lad, it'll all come right.'

Tom hurriedly told his mother when they were alone together but she only said calmly, 'Gwen's very independent, Tom, and I can understand that. It'll probably be a while before she can find anything, but don't worry, lad. We'll always be good friends, me and Gwen. You and Roz just go off and enjoy yourselves. Don't worry about us.'

He told Roz when they were in the train to Shropshire where they were spending their honeymoon, and she agreed with his mother. Tom felt like an experienced married man as he thought, women! They've got their own ways. Might as well let them get on with it.

They spent a blissful week in a secluded farmhouse near Wem, munching apples or pears from the trees as they wandered through the leafy lanes filled with the scent of honeysuckle.

Then back to a farmhouse tea of thick slices of ham and eggs, and homemade bread and butter, and quiet evenings just sitting talking beside the wood fire in the cosy little sitting room.

To bed in the scented darkness of the little room with its uneven floor and ceiling and the plump feather mattress and eiderdown smelling of lavender.

They came together naturally and happily, both ready and eager to be one. On the first night a feather worked through the pillow to cause Tom a tremendous fit of sneezing but they laughed about it as they laughed about so many things during that week.

In later years Roz would often say, 'Remember how we laughed that week?'

Tom would always say, 'I suppose it was because we were so happy, love.'

Just once Tom was touched with sadness as he thought of his mother and father. Had they known happiness like this? he wondered. Of course not as much. He thought no one had ever been as happy as he and Roz were, but happy. How hard it must have been to be parted.

He said something of this to Roz but she said sturdily, 'Your dad will come back some day, Tom. I'm sure.'

'He's been gone a long time,' Tom said doubtfully.

'Your mum believes he'll come back,' Roz said. 'And not just because of that fortune teller. I think she feels it instinctively.'

'Well, at least the hope keeps her happy,' Tom said.

The week went too quickly. The farmer and his wife had made much of them, always piling their plates and urging them to eat, and to take what fruit they wanted.

On the day that they left the farmer's wife gave them a bag of apples and pears then took Roz into the barn. 'Just a few eggs for mister's breakfast,' she whispered then produced a parcel sewn into a piece of tarpaulin.

'Not to let anyone see,' she said. She was a

plump Welshwoman from over the border and Roz found it hard to stifle a giggle as she said in her sing-song voice, 'Not allowed to kill a sheep, are we, but this poor little lamb. Fell under a tractor, poor little thing.'

Roz managed to restrain herself until they were away from the farm, but when she told Tom the tale of the mysterious parcel they were both helpless with laughter, rolling from side to side of the lane as they repeated, 'Fell under a tractor.'

It became a family catchphrase used during the war whenever a packet of cigarettes was produced from 'under the counter' for Tom, or Roz queued for scented soap, and in later years for any small self-indulgence. The phrase could always provoke a laugh and happy memories for Tom and Roz.

They had only one night left to spend at home but they came back to exciting news. Winnie had joined her sister Cathy working in the Royal Ordnance factory and both girls were engaged. Cathy's fiancé, who worked with her, shared a house with his married sister who was now moving permanently to Scotland.

They had decided to marry immediately and Winnie's soldier fiancé was coming home on embarkation leave so there would be a double wedding.

'They say one wedding makes another and there's proof,' Gwen announced.

The couples were to share the house in Litherland, leaving the flat free. They had suggested that Gwen might like it, but she said that she had the promise of a room over a chemist shop which would suit her perfectly, and she thought Roz and Tom should have the flat.

'It could be here for you when you come on leave,' Nellie said, 'If you want it. But you know you're welcome here if you don't.'

'It'll be great, Mum,' Tom exclaimed. 'It'll be our own place yet we'll be here with you.'

Roz was just as enthusiastic and later Winnie took them up to look round the flat.

'We'll be gone by the time you are home again,' she said.

Tom was almost as excited about the large envelope waiting for him, containing the contract for him to sign.

'The note says I'm to sign both copies, send one back and keep the other for my files. My files! That'll be the day.'

'That day will come, son, you see,' Nellie said. 'Didn't Prudence say there would be money and success for you?'

'I thought that was for you with the café?' Tom said, but Nellie said firmly that it was for him.

'That fortune teller has been a great comfort to Mum,' Tom said laughingly to Roz later. 'She looks at that bit of paper and twists it to fit everything that happens.'

'Well, I think she's right that your dad will come back,' Roz said. 'And *that's* been a comfort for your mum.'

'If only,' Tom sighed. 'It would make everything perfect.'

CHAPTER 33

The Canadian Fall was at its most beautiful as Sam and Chancer wandered along enjoying the crisp air and the brilliant colours of the leaves.

'Might as well make the most of it,' Chancer said, 'and stay put when the weather breaks.'

'I think you really meant that about the rocking chair,' Sam said with a grin.

They did odd jobs to provide food and a bed if they needed it, but at a large sawmill they worked for a week to accumulate some dollars.

'Looks like we're getting near a town,' Chancer said. 'Better have a stake until we find something there.'

They rarely explained any action, content to drift along in complete accord, taking each day as it came, but without realising it their outlook had changed and they were each unconsciously making plans.

They always carried soap and towels and there was no shortage of pools in which to bathe and wash their clothes. They cut each other's hair in a rough and ready fashion but when they reached the small township they found a barber's shop on the edge of town, and decided to have a haircut and shave before looking for work and a bed.

'You look a bit like the Wild Man from

632

Borneo, Sam,' Chancer said.

The barber joked. 'Sheep shearing's over, Bud,' when he saw Sam's mass of thick dark curly hair.

The barber worked alone except for a lather boy and there were no other customers, but Chancer sat near Sam talking as he waited his turn.

'He's got ears under that. Be careful,' he joked.

The barber, who told them his name was Gus, said, 'I know. I've just found one. I didn't put that nick in it either. I reckon you were born with that, Bud.'

'I think I was,' Sam said. 'It's always been there far as I can remember.'

'Now *that*,' Gus said, pointing at Chancer's scar. 'I reckon you got that with one of these.'

He pointed to an open cut-throat razor and Chancer said, 'You're right. A fella was running amok with it and I got in the way.'

'I can always tell,' Gus said proudly. 'You show me a scar and I can tell you what it was done with.'

He finished Sam's haircut and said he would cut Chancer's hair next then the lad could lather them for a shave. As he cut Chancer's hair he commented again on the scar.

'You could get that fixed, you know,' he said. 'We've got a clever young doctor in town. It was badly stitched but he could just make a little cut here and put one or two stitches in. Wouldn't get rid of the scar but it'd stop it pulling your eye down like that.'

Sam thought Chancer might resent the comments on his scar, but he only said, 'I might consult him some time.'

It was only after they had both been shaved and were ready to go, when the barber said, 'Now, gents, you both look better than when you came in,' that Chancer said sarcastically, 'We feel better too. Less aware of our disfigurements.'

'That's good,' Gus said cheerfully. 'Now, if you're looking for jobs, see that baker's shop down there? He's looking for help and he lets rooms over the shop. I happen to know they're empty. And if you carry on down there there's a corn chandler wanting help and a repair shop further on.'

As they walked away they looked at each other and laughed.

'He should have a notice up,' Sam said. ' "If you can't get insulted here go where you can." '

'He was only trying to help, I suppose,' Chancer said. 'It's handy to know about the jobs and the rooms.'

Sam had never mentioned the scar but now he said, 'He must have a professional interest in scars, because that one of yours isn't noticeable now. It was when I first met you, but I suppose it was new.'

Chancer agreed. 'Yes, I got it when the Prof got the bullet. Fella was going for him with a razor and I tried to grab the fella's arm. He'd already cut two others, so the cops came in with guns blazing and the wrong man got the bullet.'

'Hard luck,' was all Sam said, but he knew how bitter Chancer felt about the episode.

They decided that Chancer, who had worked in a bakery for a spell, would try for the baker's job and Sam would try the repair shop.

Gus had told them that the baker was a widower with one daughter, and his wife had been a Dutch woman. Only the girl was in the shop when they went in, a large blonde girl, unmistakably Dutch in appearance.

Chancer told her that the barber had told them there was a job going, and before she could answer a small dark man came through from the back.

'Any experience?' he asked.

'I worked in a bakery in Toronto for a spell,' Chancer said. 'Just bread, nothing else.'

'That's what I want,' the man said, and Chancer asked about rooms. 'We travel light. We've been wandering but we're clean and honest,' he said.

He pulled out some money, but the man said, 'Go and see the rooms first. Trudie'll take you. I'm Henry Dinsdale. This is my daughter Gertrude, Trudie for short.'

'I'm William Westwood Talbot, and this is my friend Samuel Meadows,' Chancer said formally. They all shook hands and Chancer said, 'We aim to stay here for the winter if we can find jobs and rooms.'

The girl took them upstairs. The rooms were plainly furnished but spotlessly clean and a glance between Sam and Chancer was enough.

'We'll take them,' Chancer said and put his hand in his pocket.

'Leave it to the end of the week,' the baker said easily.

Chancer went out with Sam to walk down to the repair shop, and as they walked Sam said curiously, 'You gave your real name there. You don't often do that.'

Chancer shrugged. 'He seemed a straight sort of fellow,' he said. 'Trusted us too. I liked that.'

Sam liked working with anything mechanical and he was taken on immediately at the repair shop.

'Mostly farm machinery, but we mend anything,' the owner said. He held out his hand. 'Joe Eddy,' he said.

'Sam Meadows and this is William Talbot,' Sam said.

'I've just got a job at the bakery,' Chancer said. 'And we've taken the rooms over it.'

'Henk's?' Joe said. 'That's what his wife called him. Died a few years ago but Trudie's a good help to him. Fella who worked there, had the rooms, cleared off a few weeks ago. Henk'll be glad to have you.'

Sam had wandered over to a broken machine and was studying it, and when they left he said, 'I'll enjoy that job, but by God they can all talk, can't they?'

'I'm not backward in that myself,' Chancer said with a laugh. 'It's just new faces, I suppose.'

They soon settled down in the little town,

which they discovered was called Petersfield. They both liked their jobs and their employers, and were very comfortable in the rooms over the bakery.

'I'd never get tired of the smell of bread baking, and the bakery keeps these rooms warm,' Chancer said. They did their own cooking and cleaning, but gradually Trudie took over these tasks.

At first she went to the weekly cinema with both of them, but when Sam realised how things were between her and Chancer he made the excuse of urgent work to go back to the shop.

On the road no one ever asked about a man's past, and Henk showed the same reticence but after returning from the cinema one night Chancer asked to talk to him. He told him that he and Trudie wanted to marry, and admitted that he had little to offer but he would always ensure that Trudie had a comfortable life.

He produced a few documents wrapped in oil silk, his birth certificate, a few character references from many years ago and the address of his father's solicitors. He had already told Henk that he and Sam had met in a reformatory, so that they had known each other a long time. 'He was there for stealing a pot of jam,' he said. 'And I was there because my father didn't want me.'

Now he said that he had no wish to get in touch with his father but he would write to the solicitors to ask them to confirm that there was no insanity in the family or anything else that Henk should know.

Henk told him that Trudie had already told him how she felt about Bill, as she called him.

'I haven't liked any of the young fellows who've hung around her these last few years,' Henk said frankly. 'And I'm not worried about you having nothing behind you. I've got a good business here that'll go to my girl, but only one thing worries me. You've wandered all these years. Can you settle?'

'Don't worry about that,' Chancer said. 'Sam and I—we decided we'd come to the end of the wandering.'

'It's a good enough life for a man, but not for a woman,' Henk said. 'I wouldn't tolerate it for my girl.'

It was Sam who convinced him. They were having a drink together late one night while Chancer worked in the bakery and Trudie kept him company and Sam said that he planned to return to England soon.

'I've got a wife there,' he said. 'She's with someone else but I just want to see her again. See she's all right. Me and Chancer had a talk before we came into town. We've reached the end of the wandering. It suited us and we suited each other but you know how it is. You just get to it. One part of your life's finished.'

'I'll be sorry to see you go, Sam, and Joe Eddy'll be more than sorry, but I've got to say you've eased my mind. Trudie's like her mother. Easy and placid, but by God if she jibs you might as well give up. There was no changing her mother's mind and there's no changing hers, and she intends to marry Bill. While you were still around I'd worry about him taking off again and breaking her heart.'

'No need to worry,' Sam said. 'He's mad about her and I tell you. He's as straight as a die.'

Joe Eddy was as sorry as Henk had predicted when Sam told him that he intended to return to England.

'You're the best man I've ever had,' he declared. 'You've got a feeling for machinery and I'll tell you now, you've mended many a thing I'd given up on.' To Sam's surprise Joe said he was born in Hull and had deserted from a ship many years ago. 'I've still got relations there though,' he said. 'I can give you a few addresses.'

'Thanks all the same,' Sam said. 'But I think I might make for London. I'll work my passage home but then I'm giving up the sea. You've paid me well and I haven't spent much, so I'll have a bit behind me.'

He decided to wait until Chancer and Trudie were married but before that Chancer went to the doctor that the barber had told him about. The doctor not only altered the scar so that the eye was not distorted but he also rearranged the bones in Chancer's broken nose.

He was able to afford the operation because the lawyer's letter not only made it clear that there was no hereditary taint, but informed him that his father died intestate two years ago.

They had been trying to trace Chancer as his father had left the sum of three thousand one hundred pounds, five shillings and threepence, and a house which was worth upwards of twenty thousand pounds.

'I'm glad you didn't miss out on the five and threepence,' Sam grinned.

Chancer was inclined to repudiate anything that had belonged to his father, but Trudie dealt firmly with his scruples.

It was now the spring of 1939, and after the wedding Sam set off with a light heart to make his way to Montreal. It was a wrench to leave the friend with whom he had spent so many years and who had been a true friend through their many adventures, but he left him very happily settled. They promised to keep in touch, and Chancer said quietly to him, 'Go with an open mind to see Ellie, Sam. What you heard was only hearsay. Best of luck, mate.'

Sam managed to sign on a ship that docked at Cardiff and from there he made his way towards London. War had been declared a fortnight after the ship docked and the blackout and chaotic travelling arrangements made him almost sorry he left Canada.

Now that it was possible to go and see Nellie Sam found excuses to put it off. He had managed to preserve most of his savings but he told himself that he must get some money together before travelling to Liverpool. What if Tommy needed new boots or a gansey, he thought. He would want to be able to buy them for him, then he realised with a shock that Tommy would now be a man of twenty years.

Nevertheless, he was determined to have a good sum of money by him before he went to

Liverpool. The real reason, that the faint hope he still had of a reconciliation would be lost if he found her with someone else, he pushed to the back of his mind.

He had found work without difficulty in a booming repair business not far from Reading and he was amazed at the amount he was able to earn. He felt that there he was less likely to meet any of his old seafaring friends.

It was doubtful if any of them would have recognised him. He was still very deeply tanned and his dark hair which he wore cut very short was sprinkled with grey hairs. His speech had not altered when he was first in America as he and Chancer talked more to each other than to anyone else, but gradually he had picked up some transatlantic expressions. His sailor's roll, once so marked, had been replaced by the long easy stride of a man who walked many miles in a day.

He had found rooms in a small clean boarding house near the works, where the food was sparing but he could have a meal in a local café to supplement it. He thought of going to Liverpool at Christmas but put it off again, and it was March when he finally set off.

'Is your journey really necessary?' a poster in the station demanded. It is to me, Sam thought grimly.

He had heard of Nellie's café quite by chance from a lorry driver from Liverpool. They met in the café where Sam often went for a meal, and after commenting on the food the man spoke of Nellie's beefsteak pies.

'I always time me run so I'm there when she's open,' he said. 'I've never tasted nothing like them. They melt in yer mouth, and tasty! I can taste them yet. Always get a couple to bring with me, but they're better hot.'

'I had a relation named Nellie,' Sam said. 'Used to be good at beefsteak pies. Was this a little woman, used to live in Johnson Street?'

'I don't know, mate,' the man said. 'She's a little woman. Fairish. Sort of brown hair, blue eyes. I took more notice to the other woman. Someone said she was a widow. Nice looking, thin dark woman, named Jean.'

Sam tried to find out more about Nellie but the man only wanted to talk about the food.

'No wonder the place is always packed out,' he declared. 'A proper little goldmine but I don't know how they'll go on when the rationing gets going.'

'Where is it exactly?' Sam asked.

'Near Worcester Road. I don't know the name of the street. It's on a corner. Big old house really. I think her and her family live over the café. Jean lives in a little house round the corner. If you're thinking of going anybody'd tell you where it is,' the man said.

He had finished his meal and taken out his cigarettes and Sam felt that he was looking curiously at him.

'Too far to go for a beefsteak pie,' he joked. 'But I remember how good they were. Quiet little woman though. I'm surprised to hear she's running a café. Her husband's fell on his feet.'

'Not half,' the man said. 'Mind you, for all she's quiet she can soon put a fella in his place if he talks out of turn.' He stood up. 'Ta-ra, then.'

Sam longed to detain him to ask about Tommy but he could only say, 'Ta-ra,' and hope to meet the man again. He could see that the man already thought he was asking too many questions, yet he had not asked the ones he really needed to ask.

Now as he sat in the train bearing him to Liverpool he went over all the man had told him. He was convinced that the Nellie of the café was his Ellie and the fact that the man had distinguished the other woman as being a widow implied that Nellie was married.

And he had not disputed that her husband had fallen on his feet. She must have decided I was dead by this time, Sam thought, and married the fella who moved in after I'd gone. Still, it's all just talk, like Chancer said, so I'll see for myself.

It was still the time of the 'phoney war' when shortages had begun to affect Britain, but before Dunkirk and the Blitz had brought home the reality of war. Liverpool looked little different to Sam. A woman on the tram was in tears and being comforted by two other women and one of them told the conductor that the weeping woman's husband had been lost at sea.

Sam's clothes and his accent had marked him as a stranger so no one spoke of the heavy shipping losses which were bringing such grief to the wives and families of the Liverpool crews, and Sam felt like an outcast in his hometown.

He went first to Johnson Street, drawn there by his memories, but careful to approach it from the bottom way so that his own house was the first one he came to.

The side door opened and a small boy erupted into the passage, closely followed by a bigger boy, both yelling. They looked dirty and neglected and a woman was screaming after them, 'D'youse want to get 'vacuated again? Knock it off.'

Sam jumped back. Nellie was not there, it was clear, and he walked quickly up the entry behind the houses. As he emerged into the street at the top he saw a stout old woman surrounded by several small children and realised with a shock that she was Bella Edwards. She looks like a liner with tugs, he thought, hastily averting his face, but Bella was too engrossed in scolding the children to notice him.

Sam made his way to Worcester Road and found the café without difficulty. As it was Sunday it was closed but he dawdled along on the opposite side of the road looking across at the big shabby house and the large windows showing the empty tables and chairs.

He darted into a shop doorway when the house door opened and Nellie stepped out with a tall man with grey hair and a young boy. They were all smartly dressed. Nellie was wearing a brown wool dress and a short fur jacket with a small hat covered with iridescent feathers on her short curling hair, and brown shoes, handbag and gloves.

The man wore a suit and the boy, of about ten years of age, wore a grey flannel suit with short trousers. Sam was able to feast his eyes on Nellie as she stopped to speak to a woman who was passing, and in the Sunday quiet of the street he could clearly hear the conversation.

'You look smart, Nell,' the woman said. 'Are you off out somewhere?'

'To Jean's for tea,' Nellie said laughing. 'I thought I'd get dressed up. I don't often have the chance.'

Sam listened in amazement. Even her voice was different, he thought, and she looked so changed, relaxed and assured yet unmistakably Nellie.

'That's a lovely jacket,' the woman said.

Nellie replied, 'Yes. Our Tom bought it for me for Christmas. I think Jean helped him to choose it.'

'Eh, you've got a good son, Nellie,' the woman said. 'How does he like the army?'

'He's settled down, I think,' Nellie said. 'How's your Cyril?'

'Having the time of his life be all accounts,' the woman said. 'Plenty of friends to drink with.'

'Tom's with the lad he joined up with,' Nellie said. 'And he likes the other fellows in his hut.'

'I'll tell you, Nell, we miss them more than they miss us,' the woman said and Nellie laughed.

'Well, as long as they're happy,' she said.

The man had gone back into the house and

come out again carrying a parcel, and Nellie said goodbye to the woman and turned away with him. 'David,' she called and the boy ran back to her.

He must be hers, thought Sam, and looking at the red-haired freckled boy thought that he was the image of Nellie's brother Bobby. In the tall grey-haired man he failed to see any resemblance to Bobby as he remembered him, and thought bitterly that the man must be the brandy drinker from the Volunteer he had been told about.

None of them looked across the road and as soon as they were out of sight Sam walked slowly away. He was stunned by the change in Nellie. In his thoughts of her she had still been the timid girl in a black shawl with her hair long and worn in a bun.

Her smart appearance and easy confident manner as she chatted to the woman had taken him by surprise. Evidently she had forgotten all about him and made a good life for herself, he thought, and the best thing he could do was to keep out of it.

I didn't expect her to forgive and forget, like, he thought. I just wanted to see she was all right, her and Tommy, and leave them some money.

In his heart though Sam knew that there had always been a small unquenchable hope that some day he and Ellie and Tommy would be a family again.

Sick at heart, he went directly to Lime Street Station. It was only when he was sitting in the train that he began to feel angry.

Why am I thinking about Ellie forgiving me? he thought. What about me? It was me finding out she'd tricked me that started all the trouble. His anger only lasted for a short time then softer feelings prevailed.

Hadn't he decided long ago that Ellie had been tricked too in some way? It was that wicked old bitch Janey, he thought. She was at the bottom of it all.

At some point in his journey he realised that he felt weak with hunger and managed to get a mug of tea and some sandwiches, but by the time he reached his room he was exhausted.

In spite of that he sat down and wrote to Chancer of what he had seen. 'So that's that,' he wrote. 'Now I know that Ellie has made a new life for herself and it's up to me to do the same.'

He slept heavily and woke determined to make a success of his life. If I ever see her again she'll see I can do well for myself too, he promised himself.

Sam threw himself into his work, and worked long hours. Overtime was readily available and Sam took as much as he could. He still lived frugally, rarely going for a drink and still staying in the cheap boarding house, but amassing money for his private dream.

At supper one night in the boarding house the talk had turned to a local successful businessman, who had died leaving a fortune.

'I'll tell you one thing,' one of the boarders said. 'It's a true saying, no man ever made a fortune working for another man.'

The remark stayed in Sam's mind and fuelled his ambition. Although the factory was booming now he looked ahead to the end of the war when it would probably have to dismiss many of the workers.

If he could start his own business he could prepare for the day when war contracts were finished but repair work was still needed.

A man he worked with, an excellent mechanic, often complained about the inefficiency of the works.

'If I ran this place I'd have none of this,' he told Sam. 'None of the scamping jobs and skiving in the toilets that goes on here. I'd have a good job done in fairness to the lads who'll use this stuff. I've got a lad overseas myself and it makes me mad to see what's passed here.'

Stan Riley was married, but his wife was on war work too and their son overseas was the only one, so Sam thought he must have a tidy nest egg like himself. He considered suggesting that they started up together but first he went to ask the advice of his bank manager.

I'm thinking that Ellie's changed, but I must've changed myself, he thought as he was ushered into the manager's office, and sat down feeling quite at ease.

The manager sent for Sam's account and after studying it approved of Sam's idea of starting up on his own or in partnership with Riley.

'I think a partnership might be wiser,' he said. His eyelids had flickered when Sam mentioned Riley and Sam felt sure that he knew his financial state although he was discreetly silent about it.

Sam asked Riley out for a drink and put the idea to him and the other man was enthusiastic. They decided that after Riley had talked it over with his wife he and Sam would go together to see the bank manager.

It was a fruitful meeting. The bank manager told them he had made some enquiries and that there was more war work than could be handled so there was room for another workshop.

'The Ministry of Supply handles all that,' he said. 'I'll give you the name of a man who can advise you how to approach the department about sub-contract work.'

'My wife's brother drives for him,' Stan Riley exclaimed when he heard the name.

'Very useful,' the manager said dryly.

The manager advised them to see a solicitor and have a contract drawn up. 'I know you are both men of integrity,' he said, 'but snags arise and a contract is very useful.' He also gave them the name of a solicitor.

'And I suppose the solicitor gives his clients the name of a good bank manager,' Sam said with a grin after they left.

Stan Riley invited him to come back with him and meet his wife. 'She's as keen on the idea as I am,' he said. 'So I think she should meet my partner.'

Mrs Riley was still wearing the overall and turban she wore for work when they arrived at the house, but she welcomed Sam warmly.

'I've just got in,' she said. 'I'll just wash then

we'll have a bit of dinner and you can tell me how you got on.'

'Famous,' Stan said. 'There'll be no stopping us now, will there, Sam?'

Mrs Riley produced a savoury hotpot and insisted that Sam joined them for the meal, and memories of Nellie's hotpots flooded back to Sam. He said little at first but Mrs Riley talked so much that his silence was not noticed.

When she heard the name of the man the bank manager advised them to approach she exclaimed immediately, 'Our Henry's been his chauffeur for years. He'll fix it up.'

It was general knowledge that Sam had travelled widely in America and Canada and because of this he found that people expected him to be more knowledgeable and sophisticated than he felt himself to be. Nevertheless the fact that he was treated with respect gave him confidence and he was surprised to find how easily he could grasp the intricacies of setting up a business.

Good job they don't know I was only a hobo, he often thought to himself, but he said nothing. He was surprised at how easily all the details fell into place, and he suspected that many strings were being pulled, after he and Riley had met Riley's brother-in-law's employer.

Premises were found and fitted up, contracts obtained and Sam approached several men from the works who agreed to work for them.

'You can say they're hand picked,' Sam said to Riley.

They were all older men, who took a pride in their work, and were disgusted by the sloppy attitude of the managers and workforce in the big factory.

The new venture was a success from the start and was the best antidote Sam could have found for his bitter memories. He rarely had time to think about the past.

Stan Riley was highly skilled and ready to shoulder his share of the problems, and he and Sam worked well together, but Riley often said he had no head for business. He particularly disliked dealing with the civil servants from the Ministry of Supply.

Sam found that managing the paperwork connected with the business came easily to him, and gradually he took over the business side, while Stan organised the work on the shop floor.

Sam also made frequent trips to London to arrange with civil servants about contracts, and soon became more self-assured on these occasions.

Always, no matter how hard he worked, some small thing could bring memories surging back to Sam. A tune once heard on an outing with Nellie and Tom, a smell of cooking, the sight of a small boy trotting beside his father, would be like the opening of a wound inside him.

If only he had realised how much he loved Ellie, he often thought. If only he could turn back the clock, but with bitter self-reproach he knew it was impossible. Other women had shown interest in Sam but he never responded. No other woman could take Ellie's place in his heart, even though she seemed to have forgotten him.

CHAPTER 34

Nellie's broken arm slowly healed, and she recovered from the deep wound in her temple, but it took longer for Jean to recover from her miscarriage.

'I seem to have no strength,' she told Nellie. 'People tell me I'll feel better when I start another baby, but I don't really want to yet. I feel too tired.'

'Take your time,' Nellie advised. 'Wait until you feel strong again. You've got your hands full at present with the three boys and Bob not there to help you.'

Neither of them felt physically ready to reopen the café immediately and they decided to wait for a while.

'Perhaps when we feel better,' Jean said. 'Because what will you live on without it? You haven't even got Tom's allotment now he's married, and what we've made from the café won't last for ever.'

'Don't worry about me, Jean,' Nellie said. 'I've still got my little nest egg, as you say, and when that's gone I'll get a job. One where someone else does the worrying,' she added with a smile.

'Will it upset you to close it after working so hard to build it up from scratch?' Jean asked.

'I *was* proud of it,' Nellie admitted. 'Proud that I proved that I could do it, although it's been such a worry lately.'

'You proved that all right, and it was a real success,' Jean said warmly. 'It's a shame that the war spoiled it all.'

'Yes, but with all that's happened, Jean, doesn't it make you realise what's important and what isn't?' Nellie said. 'And the café isn't.'

She was quite happy, pottering about her house and visiting or being visited by her friends, and working for the Women's Voluntary Service. Katy had been rehoused in a council house in Huyton after most of Johnson Street had been demolished by a landmine during the May blitz, fortunately while most of the residents had been in shelters or sleeping at Maghull.

She often came to see Nellie and told her that she was very unhappy in Huyton, and her mother Bella who was with her was even more unhappy.

'It's a lovely convenient house with hot water and a bath and gardens,' she said, 'and the kids love it, but it's the noise we can't stand.'

'The noise?' Nellie echoed. 'I thought it was like the country out there.'

'That's the trouble,' said Katy. 'The time those birds start up in the morning and the noise of them. We can't get a wink of sleep from before it's light. Mam's dwindling away.'

Nellie sympathised with Katy but she thought

653

to herself that she must write and tell Tom this conversation. It was the sort of thing he enjoyed.

Jean and the boys and Winnie and Cathy often came to see Nellie, and she spent much of her time with Gwen.

Nellie often went up to the flat to dust and air the rooms ready for when Roz and Tom came on leave and sometimes Gwen helped her.

'I can't wait to see my girl at home living here,' she sighed as she cleaned windows. 'This makes her seem a bit closer somehow.'

Tom had been moved to Wellington Barracks in London, and had been able to see his publisher on two occasions. The book was due to be published in the spring but before that happened Roz and Tom both had Christmas leave.

They spent an idyllic seven days in the little flat planning for their future and recalling happily all that had happened since the night that they met at the concert.

Tom took Roz to meet Miss Helsby and there was an immediate rapport between them.

'Tom wouldn't have had the confidence to write a book if it wasn't for you, Miss Helsby,' Roz said. 'Would you, Tom?'

'No, and I certainly wouldn't have been able to deal with the publisher,' Tom said with a grin. 'Did I tell you he thought I'd been to a boarding school?'

'You told me in your letter, and I was very pleased to hear it, Thomas,' Miss Helsby said. 'I have never approved of the way society is set in rigid layers and my ambition has been to break that mould.'

She turned to Roz. 'I wanted to train my boys so that they could speak and behave in a way that would make it possible for them to move at any level of society. To give them the confidence to move in places that were otherwise denied to them, no matter how able.'

'That's how people are judged,' Roz agreed. 'By their accents and table manners and so forth.'

'I don't envy the rich,' Tom said. 'And I've no desire to move in society, but I want to be able to outface anyone who thinks they can despise me. It annoys me though when God is brought in to it.'

'What do you mean, Thomas?' asked Miss Helsby.

'I mean the idea that some men are born to wear out their lives in long hours of heavy labour in atrocious conditions, and other men are born to live luxurious lives on the fruit of that labour and *God* ordains it. "The rich man in his castle, the poor man at his gate, God made them high or lowly and ordered their estate",' Tom quoted grimly.

'Exactly,' said Miss Helsby, 'I agree with you, Thomas, and in my small way I have tried to alter that state of affairs, but with little success, I'm afraid. You were the only one who was prepared to work to improve yourself, and a young boy I have now for whom I have great hopes.'

'This war will make a difference,' Tom declared and Roz agreed with him.

'People are mixing now who would never have met before the war,' she said. 'Not just the Forces but the Home Guard and ARP and the women in nursing and WVS and all sorts of organisations.'

Miss Helsby smiled at them affectionately. 'The idealism of youth,' she said with a sigh. 'I hope you're right but I'm very much afraid that everything will revert to the old ways after the war.'

The conversation turned to other topics but when they were walking home Tom told Roz that he thought Miss Helsby was wrong.

'Things won't go back to the old ways,' he declared. 'We won't let them. The fellows won't let them get away with it like they did after the first war.'

'I wouldn't want to change *everything*,' Roz said. 'I had a happy childhood although we were so hard up.'

'So did I,' said Tom. 'I was lucky being in Miss Helsby's class and having the chance of extra training, and luckier still that Mum let me go for it and gave me money for the baths and toothpaste and so forth.'

'They must both be glad they did, Miss Helsby and your mum, and very proud of you,' Roz said.

'I'm very proud of *them*,' said Tom. 'Especially Mum, and my dad too. He did so much to encourage me and told me tales about his voyages. I must have been a pest but they never brushed me off. I was damn lucky and now I've got you.'

He drew her close and kissed her before they went into the house.

Roz told Nellie how much she liked Miss Helsby. 'I thought at first she was very stiff, you know, the formal way she talks, but she's different underneath. You'd think a woman of her class would like things to stay as they are but she really wants change, doesn't she, Tom?'

Tom agreed. 'I hope she lives to see it,' he said. Nellie told them that Miss Helsby had retired but had returned to teaching for the duration of the war.

'She's worked so hard for her boys. I'm glad our Tom has been such a success, for her sake,' she declared, looking fondly at him.

'Hey, don't count your chickens before they're hatched, Mum,' Tom protested, smiling self-consciously. 'The book might be a flop.' But none of them expected that it would.

Later, as Tom and Roz lay talking after lovemaking, he said reflectively, 'Remember what we were talking about—that although we were poor as kids we were happy? I hope I've been able to bring that out in my book, Roz.'

'I'm sure you have, love,' she comforted him.

'People of, well, a higher social class, they lump all our sort of people together as The Poor. As if we were all the same, living a sort of animal life, but we know it's not like that. People in Johnson Street—they were all different and there *were* grades.'

657

'I know,' said Roz laughing. 'People at one end of the street looking down on people from the other end because they were common.'

'And for all the poverty and the hunger and the awful verminous houses people still managed to get a laugh out of things, and they were good to each other in trouble.'

'Kids enjoyed themselves,' Roz said. 'I suppose because we didn't know anything different. I know I used to love all the street games, all the girls did, and the lads. We could always find a way of making a few coppers too and we enjoyed ourselves.'

'I've tried to show that in my book,' Tom said. 'But you know, Roz, I've had my eyes opened since I've been in the army. When I start writing again I'll see a lot of things differently.'

'How do you mean?' Roz asked, snuggling closer into his arms.

'The officers,' Tom said. 'Looking at their lives from here, we think they have a great time. All that money and comfort and being able to do what they like, but it's not really like that. Those young Guards officers. They're mostly out of the top drawer but when you know more about their lives you'd feel sorry for them.'

'I don't think I would,' Roz declared.

'But a fellow who was batman to one of them told me he was talking one night when he was drunk. He said he was sent off to school when he was *four*. Imagine that. On his own in a strange place when he was four. I remember my dad taking me on the Overhead Railway when I was four and the way he looked after me.'

'Poor little lad,' Roz exclaimed.

'Then it was another prep school when he was seven, then public school, then Oxford and straight into the army. He was only at home for holidays from when he was four, and half the time his parents were away then anyway.'

'They must be unnatural parents,' Roz said, but Tom disagreed.

'Not by their standards,' he said. 'The same thing happened to them. None of them know the security and affection we take for granted. We're the lucky ones, Roz.'

'Well, our children will have the best of both worlds,' Roz declared.

'I hope so, love,' Tom said kissing her tenderly before making love again.

Afterwards as Roz slept, Tom watched her with love and pride, marvelling that they were in accord in every way.

Tom and Roz were due to leave on the day after Boxing Day, and on Christmas Eve Gwen came to stay with Nellie until they left. Gwen was convinced that the war would soon be over.

'I know we were a bit optimistic thinking it'd be over by Christmas 1940,' she said, 'but I'll bet it'll be over by the summer of 1943. Look how Montgomery has battered them Huns at El Alamein, and Hitler's bitten off more than he can chew with the Russians. This'll be the last wartime Christmas, you see.'

They all hoped she was right but were

unconvinced, but in spite of that everyone agreed that it was the happiest Christmas they had known. If only Sam was here, Nellie thought, although she said nothing, but she knew Tom was thinking of him too.

When the time came for Tom and Roz to leave, Gwen told them that their visit had made her feel ten years younger.

'You feel the same, don't you, Nell?' she said. 'It's done us both the world of good to see you both so happy.'

Nellie was fighting back tears as she hugged and kissed them. 'Please God it won't be long before you're both home for good,' she said. 'Your gran's right, Roz. It does us good to see you so happy. You were made for each other.'

Roz too was tearful as they left. 'I hate leaving them, Tom,' she said. 'Oh God, if only it was peacetime and we could please ourselves.'

'Never mind, love,' Tom consoled her. 'It can't last for ever, and just think. By our next leave my book will be published.'

'Yes, we've got that to look forward to,' Roz said trying to smile.

Before publication day there was even more exciting news for Tom when Roz wrote to tell him that she was pregnant and the baby was due in August. Excited letters flew back and forth between Roz, Tom, Nellie and Gwen and then suddenly there was all the excitement of publication day.

Wartime restrictions meant smaller newspapers and the publisher had warned Tom that there would be few if any reviews of his book. Tom was surprised to find that there were several, all praising the book.

A launch party had been planned but Tom told the publisher that he would be unable to spare any leave to attend it. He was determined that all his leave would be spent at home with Roz.

'Leave it with me, my boy,' Charles Mandred, the publisher, said smoothly. As though by magic a forty-eight-hour pass became available to Tom without prejudice to his leave and he accepted it gratefully.

The launch party went well but Tom was surprised by the comments of the guests, all of whom seemed to see more in his book than he intended, just as the reviewers had done.

'I don't understand,' he told the publisher later. 'I thought I was writing about what it means to be born into one lifestyle and then to be trained for a different one. To be what an old friend called "neither fish, fowl nor good red herring". It didn't actually happen to me. Miss Helsby widened my horizons but circumstances kept me close to my roots.'

'But you took your experience and imagined how it *could* be,' Charles Mandred said. 'As someone once said, "Fiction is fact transformed by imagination".'

'But these reviews,' said Tom. 'I'm delighted with them of course, but they all seem to think I was writing about my relationship with my father. Listen to this. "A poignant account of a young boy's love and admiration for his father, and his feelings of guilt and rejection when he is abandoned by his father." I'm sure I didn't feel that, much less write about it.'

The publisher leaned back in his chair smiling. 'That is what gives the book its unique quality, Tom. You went deep into your subconscious for these feelings, feelings of which even you were unaware. That sort of total recall in depth is very rare. What you really felt has come through in your writing.'

Tom was not convinced but the publisher took a folded paper from his pocket. 'Read this. It's the reader's report which led me to read your manuscript and write to you.'

Tom read, flushing with pleasure. ' "A poignant exploration of the mind of an adolescent boy. His dreams and sorrows, his joy in childhood memories and his grief and guilt at the abrupt ending of his idyll. The deep love for his parents shines through the lyrical prose. Eminently publishable." He seems to be a bit lyrical himself,' Tom said, adding hastily, 'but I'm very grateful to him.'

'A most unusual report from any publisher's reader and particularly from this one,' Mr Mandred said smiling. 'He's not given to enthusiastic reports, so you should be very pleased.'

'I am,' Tom said, but secretly he was worried about the reviews. He thought that his mother might read them and be hurt, but fortunately Nellie read only the report in the local paper which stressed that he was a local boy who had left elementary school at fourteen years old, and made no mention of Sam.

Tom was invited to a dinner party on the evening of the launch and Charles Mandred advised him to accept.

'Some very useful contacts,' he said. 'You'll meet some interesting people.'

Tom was not impressed by the people at the dinner party and felt that they patronised him.

He was glad to return to his hotel room where he wrote to Roz. 'This seems an awful waste of a forty-eight-hour pass. Perhaps you'll be out of nursing if I get another one, and able to come down here. Incidentally I know how this was worked. Mr Mandred told me my commanding officer was his fag at Eton. Wheels within wheels!'

The following lunchtime Tom was interviewed on the wireless as the 'celebrity in town'. He spoke with sincerity and passion about his childhood in Bootle and the debt he owed to his parents and to Miss Helsby.

The interviewer skilfully drew him out to talk about the help Miss Helsby had given him, and his mother's unfailing support and encouragement, then he said smoothly, 'And how old were you when you were deserted by your father?'

Tom's anger flared. 'We were not deserted,' he said forcefully. 'When I was ten my father was on a ship trading on the Ivory Coast. He was ill and put ashore to a hospital. When he finally came home he was still a sick man and that was the cause of what happened.'

'I beg your pardon,' the interviewer said. 'But reviewers have spoken of a sense of guilt and rejection evident in your book.'

'Guilt, yes,' Tom said shortly. 'I blamed myself, as children do. My mother and I still hope that my father will recover and return home.'

'I see. What do you think influenced you to become a writer? An unusual choice for a boy with your background, I would say.'

'Miss Helsby widened my horizons. Gave me a love of books and my mother supplied whatever I needed and encouraged me. I think my father was the chief influence. His stories of his voyages stimulated my imagination and he was endlessly patient in answering my questions,' Tom said.

He knew that the man was sneering at him but he was determined to say what he felt. Prissy little squirt, he thought. Some of our NCOs'd soon straighten *him* out.

'A most unusual attitude for modern times,' the man said. 'Very few young people show such extreme respect for the older generation nowadays.'

'In the circles you move in perhaps,' Tom said brusquely. 'Not in mine.'

He thought of Harry's grief for his father now permanently crippled by the shrapnel in his spine, and his own community at Bootle where the 'ould wans' ruled while they had their strength, and were carefully tended when strength failed.

He was recalled by the man asking about his second book.

'I've started it,' Tom said. 'But it'll have to

wait until the war's over. As you can see, I'm in the army.'

The interviewer was obviously angry, with a red spot burning on each cheekbone, but he brought the interview smoothly to a close. Tom felt that he had made an enemy but was unconcerned.

I want my books to stand or fall by their own merits, he thought. Not on the word of a pipsqueak like that. He had refused an invitation to a dinner party, saying that he had to be back in barracks, although he was not due to return until the following morning, and he never ceased to be thankful that he had told the white lie.

He decided to stroll round London before darkness fell and have a meal in a cheap café. Almost of their own volition, it seemed, his feet took him to Foyle's bookshop, where copies of his books and his photograph were displayed in the window.

CHAPTER 35

Sam was due to visit an official of the Ministry of Supply on the day after the launch party for Tom's book, and as usual he left early for London.

He bought a newspaper to read on the train and when he opened it the name Meadows seemed to leap up from the page. There was a blurred photograph of a young soldier wearing a cap with a Grenadier Guards badge, and underneath it details of Tom's life and the sensation caused by his first novel.

There was also a brief account of the launch party and the information that Tom would be the celebrity interviewed on the wireless in the 'In Town' programme.

Sam sat in a state of shock reading the words again and again and trying to see in the blurred photograph any resemblance to the small boy who had been 'the core of his heart'. The photograph was too blurred to give any clue, but the details given showed that this was indeed his son.

The train had reached London and Sam had stumbled on to the platform before he remembered that Tom was not his son, but his joy at finding him and his pride were undiminished.

He was determined to hear the wireless broadcast, even if it meant missing his appointment. There was a wireless set in a small café he often used when in London and he went there and told the proprietress he would be back later for the broadcast.

'He's the son of a woman I know,' he explained.

'How exciting,' he said. 'You must listen to it in my sitting room. The customers talk loudly sometimes and mine is a better set than this.'

Sam thanked her and went to walk around until it was time for the broadcast. He felt unable to concentrate on the papers he had brought for the civil servant at the Ministry.

The proprietress of the café tactfully left Sam alone when she could see how moved he was by the sound of Tom's voice and his opening words about his childhood in Bootle.

Sam scarcely noticed that she had gone. When the interviewer spoke of Tom being deserted by his father and Tom indignantly denied it, tears began to stream down Sam's face. When Tom spoke of his father's illness and the fact that he and his mother hoped for his return it seemed to strike Sam to the heart.

By the time Tom was speaking of his father's influence in telling him stories of his voyages Sam had covered his face with his handkerchief and his body was shaken by sobs. When the interviewer closed he tried to compose himself before returning to the café and thanking the proprietress. He felt weak and drained by emotion.

'Not at all,' the woman said, eyeing him curiously and offering tea.

Sam went to the café toilet and sluiced water over his face and head. A long time since I've done that, he thought, and never to hide traces of crying.

He left the café, his mind in turmoil. Ellie and Tommy wanted him back. Thought he'd been ill that time. But what about the other fellow? Tommy might still think of him but Ellie had made her own life.

He remembered her as he had seen her on his visit to Liverpool, well dressed and confident. Then unbidden an older memory arose, of Nellie shrinking away from him in fear, her face damaged by him. He groaned aloud but the hurrying crowds ignored him.

How could she ever forgive him? She might have put the best side out for the lad, Sam thought, and Tommy believed her but Sam felt that the truth was different. He walked all day oblivious to the people around him as his mind ranged back and forth over the interview and all his memories of his wife and son.

At one stage he found himself outside Foyle's bookshop where copies of Tom's book and his photograph were displayed in the window. He stared hungrily at the photograph trying to see traces of the child he had cherished.

He was impeding passersby and finally turned away and went into a cabman's refuge for coffee and sandwiches. It was time for him to return home but he decided that he must have a last look at the photograph of his son and he returned to the bookshop.

As he stood by the window a tall soldier paused beside him also staring in the window. They turned away at the same time and came face to face.

Tom's eyes widened and he leaned forward to look into Sam's face then croaked, '*Dad.*'

'Tommy,' Sam gasped, gripping Tom's arm, 'Tommy lad.'

'I thought you were in America,' Tom exclaimed.

Sam seemed unable to speak except to say, 'Tommy,' over and over again, still gripping his son's arms.

He was unable to take his eyes from his son's

face. In the flesh he was so like his mother that Sam was doubly affected. The same blue eyes and brown hair and even his mother's features in a masculine mould.

Tom too was staring at Sam. He saw a man, as tall but thinner than the father he remembered, with touches of grey in his dark curly hair. His skin was still weatherbeaten from his years of wandering although he had spent so much of recent years indoors, and in the set of his lips and in his dark eyes his years of mental suffering clearly showed.

Tom was first to recover. 'Come on, Dad. Let's go somewhere and talk,' he said. 'I know, we'll go back to my hotel. It's not far from here.'

Back in his room Tom produced a bottle of brandy and poured drinks for each of them, then they began to talk. They were still talking when they realised it was midnight. Tom urged Sam to have his bed but neither of them wanted to waste time sleeping. There was still so much each wanted to know about the lost years.

Sam had made a brief reference to his years of wandering and his return to England and Tom had spoken of his life since Sam left but both were chiefly interested in the events of the time of Sam's departure and immediately afterwards.

'It was strange. I knew you right away,' Tom said. 'Although it's been so long. About twelve years. Why Dad? Why did you go?'

Sam hesitated, trying to find words to explain. 'I was drunk, lad, drunk and muddled. I wasn't thinking straight. That fella McGregor and his tart. I got tricked into going to Southampton.'

'And you were still sick, Dad, weren't you?' Tom said eagerly. 'From that voyage.'

'I'd had a facer, right enough,' Sam said. 'Knocked me sideways. I was a bloody fool, lad.'

'Why didn't you come back from Southampton when you sobered up?' Tom asked.

'She told me I'd broke up the place and Bob and your mam's new fella had put me out. Said I'd battered her. The other fella had moved in. You never answered my letter. I just got sick of it and backed off in New York.'

'The flaming liar!' Tom exclaimed. 'We never got a letter. And what other fellow?' He told Sam of the long sad wait for his return and of the boy coming for his seabag while Nellie lay in a drugged sleep. 'He said he had to take it to the Seaman's.'

'I was never near the Seaman's,' Sam exclaimed. 'But I got me bag. I see it all now.' He bent his head and Tom poured another brandy for him.

Gradually as they talked and compared different versions of events Sam realised how wrong he had been.

'I don't understand how you could believe that about Mum,' Tom said indignantly.

'I was a bloody fool,' Sam mumbled again. 'I had me reasons and I wasn't thinking straight, like.'

He told Tom of meeting the man who sometimes drank in the Volunteer and being told about the man from the end house who was drinking the proceeds of Janey's hidden fortune.

'They were the people who moved in when we left,' Tom said. 'They found some money behind a brick, so of course it had to be a fortune according to the gossip.'

'But the fella said they spoke about you. Said you should've had the scholarship instead of some girl that got it.'

Tom laughed. 'That crowd in the Volley. They think women are only good for waiting on them and being a punchbag on Saturday nights, not for educating.'

Sam's face twisted in pain as he recalled Ellie as he had last seen her, and Tom said quickly, 'The girl was Amy Rimmer. She's a cypher clerk in the Wrens now. Mum cut herself off from her old friends but she's in touch with them again now.'

Sam drank more brandy then said quietly, 'Don't think I'm doubting your word, Tommy. It must be something else I've got wrong. I didn't expect to walk back into your lives, like. Just to see if you were all right.'

'But you changed your mind?' Tom said.

'No, I went to the café right enough, skulking round on the other side of the road. It was a Sunday and I saw your mam come out of the door with a grey-haired fellow and a young lad, the model of Bob.'

'But that would be Bob and his son,' Tom said. 'They lived with us until he married again. Bob is prematurely grey.'

Sam dropped his head and put his hands over his face. 'God, I seem to have put two and two together and made five all along the line,' he groaned. 'I thought she'd reckoned me dead and married again, and I didn't blame her. God knows she deserved better than what she got off me.'

'You're wrong, Dad,' Tom said. He told Sam of the fortune teller and how strongly his mother believed that one day Sam would come back.

'But I can't expect her to take me back, properly, I mean,' Sam said. 'Not after the way I left you both. I thought you were getting looked after so I didn't worry about sending money, but going off with that tart like that. She must be bitter.' He stopped, looking embarrassed. 'I shouldn't be talking like this to you, Tommy,' he said.

Tom laughed. 'Don't worry, Dad. I'm a big boy now,' he said. He had said nothing about Roz but now it all poured out. How beautiful and how special Roz was, and their joy in their expected baby.

'And now you'll be back when it's born in August and we'll be a complete family again.'

Sam had interrupted him several times to say 'Great' or 'Congratulations' or 'I'm made up for you, lad,' and now he protested.

'Hold on, lad. That's up to your mam. She might have put a good face on things for you but that's not saying she can just forgive and forget. I don't expect it, although God knows I want to see her again.'

'Don't worry, Dad. That'll be all right,'

Tom said confidently. 'When can you come to Liverpool?'

'Any time,' Sam said. 'I can fix it with Stan Riley. I haven't had a day off in years.'

'I'm due leave in about three weeks,' Tom said, 'and by that time Roz will be home. Finished with the nursing because of the baby and the lifting and that. I'll tell her and she can sort of prepare Mum. We can travel up together.'

Suddenly Sam was overcome with emotion. He covered his face while his body shook with sobs and Tom dropped to his knees beside him.

'OK, OK, Dad,' he said putting his arms around his father while his own eyes filled with tears. He swallowed and said gently, 'This is a shock, Dad, but God, I'm so made up. I haven't half missed you.'

'And I've missed you, lad,' Sam said in a choked voice. 'You know, that old woman was right. You were the core of me heart. I'm so proud of you too, lad.'

He could say no more and Tom said gruffly, 'I've never stopped thinking about you and neither has Mum. I tried to find you, you know, even up to a couple of years ago.'

Sam put his hand on Tom's shoulder. 'I don't deserve you, son, you or your mum,' he said humbly. 'I hope she'll let me try and make it up to her.'

'She will,' said Tom. He stood up. 'Isn't it smashing the way we can just talk to each other, Dad, as if you'd never been away?' He picked up the empty brandy bottle. 'Mind you, I think this helped.'

'Aye, I haven't seen one of them for a while,' Sam said.

'A gift from the publisher,' said Tom. 'Came in handy, didn't it?'

Even with all the hours of talking there was still much they wanted to discuss, but dawn was breaking and soon Tom would have to return to Wellington Barracks and Sam to try for a rearranged meeting with the civil servant.

They shaved and freshened up, each using Tom's razor, then Tom packed up and they went down to leave his key. He was puzzled by the manager's frosty attitude but too happy to care. His breakfast was provided at the hotel, but time with his father was too precious to waste and they went together to a small café for breakfast.

'Not a patch on Mum's place,' Tom said looking round.

During the night he had brought Sam up to date about the affairs at the café and been amazed to learn that his father knew nothing of the May blitz on Liverpool.

'They just said a north-west town on the news,' Sam said. 'Could have been anywhere.'

Tom said it was as well he had not known at the time. Most of Buck Madden's family had been killed, although Buck was at sea at the time. Sam asked about George and Tom told him that his old mate had left the sea and was working ashore. His youngest son had been badly crippled by infantile paralysis.

Now when they left the café Tom said that he was going to say nothing to the publisher about finding his father as they wanted to avoid fuss and Sam agreed.

He said suddenly, 'Listen, son. I'm going to Liverpool. I've wasted enough time. I'll go and see how I stand with your mam.'

'But wouldn't it be better if I came with you?' Tom protested.

'No, this is between me and her, son,' Sam said. 'We'll say what we've got to say face to face. No more guessing and getting things wrong.'

'When will you go?' asked Tom, recognising his father's determination.

'As soon as I've seen this fellow about the contracts and been back to fix things up with Stan Riley,' Sam said. 'I've never had a day off in years so I'm due some time off. You'll have time to write to your mam and tell her you've met me and I want to see her.'

'I'll write to Roz as well,' Tom said, 'and if she gets home before you she can talk to Mum too.'

Meanwhile Nellie and Gwen were happily preparing the flat for the arrival of Roz.

'This is the last time we'll be doing this, Nell,' Gwen said. 'Once our Rosie's home living here I won't interfere.'

'Neither will I,' Nellie said. 'But I want it nice for her coming home. After this she'll make her own preparations for Tom coming home.'

Roz arrived the next day but before leaving

the hospital she had received Tom's letter, and had been astounded to learn that he had met his long-lost father. He also said that Sam intended to come to Liverpool to see Nellie and asked Roz to prepare her for the shock.

Roz broke the news as carefully and gently as she could but Nellie immediately burst into tears. 'I knew it,' she wept. 'I *knew* Sam would come back one day. Not because of the fortune telling, Roz. I just knew it in my heart.'

She was trembling and Roz slipped her arms around her. 'I know, I know,' she soothed her. 'You always said so.'

'And he's coming here? Oh, Roz, I'm frightened. I'm not like he remembers me. We'll be like strangers.'

'No you won't,' Roz said. 'Tom said his dad is nervous too. Afraid you won't want to see him. He's probably changed outwardly but you're the same people underneath. Why don't you think of when he looked after you when you were kids and take it from there?'

'Oh, Roz, you're such a comfort to me, girl,' Nellie sighed. 'But it's been such a long time.'

'Tom reckons he could talk to his dad as though he'd seen him yesterday and I'm sure it'll be the same for you,' Roz consoled her. 'You'll make him welcome, won't you?'

'Of course,' Nellie said. She looked round the large well-furnished living room, at the lofty ceiling and ornate marble fireplace. 'This is very different to Johnson Street,' she said.

'There's still a bright fire and a comfy chair

like Tom says you always had for his dad,' Roz said.

Nellie began to build up the fire and sweep the hearth. 'I'll have it ready just in case,' she said, and Roz was pleased to see that it had taken her mind from her worry about the meeting.

Without saying anything to Nellie, Roz slipped out and came back with a packet of ten Woodbines and a box of matches.

'How did you get them?' Nellie said in amazement, knowing that cigarettes were now 'under the counter' for favourite customers.

'I called in a debt,' Roz said laughing.

Nellie kissed her impulsively. 'Thanks, love. I was just wishing I could get them. Eh, our Tom's a lucky lad,' she said.

They said nothing to Gwen about Nellie's expected visitor when she came, in case nothing happened. Later Roz walked home with her grandmother and Nellie was sitting knitting when there was a tentative knock at the door.

It was after eight o'clock and the black-out was so complete that when Nellie opened the door she could see no more than a tall shape. She said quietly, 'Sam?'

'Ellie,' he said, and she stepped back into the dark hall.

'Come in. I'll have to shut the door before I switch the light on,' she said.

He stepped in and she turned on the dim light in the hall.

'I'm sorry I'm so late,' Sam said awkwardly. 'The trains—'

677

His voice trailed away and suddenly Nellie felt in command of the situation.

The night was cold and wet and she said briskly, 'Take your overcoat off, Sam, and come to the fire.'

She led the way into the living room, hastily snatching up the Woodbines and matches and hiding them in her pocket. We've got a lot of talking to do before we reach that stage, she thought.

She invited Sam to sit in the chair by the fire while she went into the kitchen to make tea, giving Sam time to adjust to his surroundings. They covertly studied each other as Nellie poured tea, and she was struck as Tom had been by the marks of suffering on Sam's face.

The cup rattled in the saucer as she handed it to him but she was not sure whether it was herself or Sam who was trembling. 'Tom wrote to me,' she said. 'He told me he met you in London and you stayed up all night talking.'

'We had a lot to catch up on,' Sam said with the ghost of a smile. 'We straightened a few things out.'

He put his cup and saucer down and leaned forward towards Nellie who was now sitting opposite him.

'I got a lot of things wrong, Ellie,' he said. 'I'm sorry I left you to struggle on your own to bring him up. No money or nothing from me. You did a good job. He's a fine lad.'

'The money was the least of my worries as things turned out,' Nellie said crisply.

She refrained from asking why he had left, as

Tom had done, but Sam said in a low voice, 'I'm ashamed, girl. I should have known you better than to believe the tales I was told. You were well rid of me, Ellie, but I never stopped thinking about you.'

Nellie was near to tears but she said quickly, 'What do you mean, Sam? What tales were you told?'

Sam was leaning forward, his hands between his knees, and he bent his head, looking shamefaced. 'I got told all sorts,' he said vaguely.

'But tell me, Sam,' Nellie insisted. 'What were the tales exactly?'

'Oh, that you were on the game and you had a fancy man,' Sam mumbled. 'I must've been out of my mind to listen to them.'

'That's what it was, Sam,' Nellie said. 'You were sick in mind as well as in body and they took advantage of you.'

Sam shook his head. 'I can't make that excuse, Ellie. I was better by then but I got told something that knocked me sideways, but I shouldn't have believed those tales, I should've known you better than that. I was just drunk and muddled and I let that tart trick me into going to Southampton.'

Gradually they told each other their stories of those fateful days. During it Roz came home unheard by either of them, and hearing their voices through the closed door she crept silently up to her flat.

They had been talking for hours, their chairs by this time close together and Sam holding

Nellie's hand when she said suddenly, 'There's something I've got to tell you, Sam, about when we got married. If you walk out that door I won't blame you. I should have told you years ago and saved all this.'

Her story poured out, about her rape by Leadbetter, her return to Johnson Street and Janey's remedies, and Janey's scheming to marry her to Sam.

'She only wanted your allotment coming in because my dad's had stopped. Maggie Nolan told me,' Nellie said.

Sam clenched his fists. 'Why didn't you tell me, Ellie? I'd have bloody killed that dirty old swine.'

'That's one of the reasons I didn't tell you,' Nellie said, 'I was made up when I knew I was expecting, until Janey started hinting it might be Leadbetter's child. When Tom was born early I didn't know what to think. She was saying he could be Leadbetter's born late, nine months and three weeks, but the minute I held Tom in my arms I knew he was yours, Sam.'

Sam was filled with anguish, knowing that she must be mistaken and wondering whether to tell her or leave her in blissful ignorance of what he had been told.

Nellie went on. 'I know Janey must've said something to Charlie West and he told that lot in the Volley. That's why they said things to you, Sam, and that's why you were jealous too. I should've told you but I could never find the right time and I was afraid.'

'That mate in Canada—he said Tommy was

really my child whether there was a blood tie or not because I helped to rear him,' Sam said.

Nellie's head jerked up. 'So you don't believe Tom is really your son, Sam? He is, honest. He was born early, that's why he was so small.'

Sam hesitated, wondering again whether he should tell her about his sterility, and Nellie chose that moment to ask what he had been told on that voyage.

I'll tell her, Sam decided. I want everything out in the open between us anyhow. The colour drained away from Nellie's face when he told her.

'It's not true, Sam. It can't be true,' she cried. 'Tom can't be that fellow's child.'

She was so distressed that Sam crouched down beside her chair trying to comfort her. 'It doesn't matter, Ellie. Chancer was right. Tom's my son because of the way we are with each other,' but she refused to be comforted.

'I don't believe it. That doctor was wrong,' she said. 'He's your son by blood. He's got that much of you in him. The things he does and the way he's looked after me, just the way you did when we were kids. Doctors don't know everything.'

Sam put his arms round her and she wept, clinging to him with her head on his shoulders. When she was calmer she still said emphatically that the doctor must be wrong.

'I wish I could think they were,' Sam said. 'But they were clever men, Ellie. The old one backed the young one up although I think he was mad he had told me.'

'I don't care,' Nellie said stubbornly. 'If our Tom hasn't come from you he's come from me being raped by that beast, and that I *won't* believe. Not our Tom. He might have my colouring, but he's like you in every other way.'

Whatever response to his story Sam had expected it was not this and he could only hold Nellie and soothe her, feeling amazed and delighted at her reaction. Could it be possible that she was right? He hoped so but he was not convinced that the doctors were mistaken.

Eventually Nellie sat up and wiped her eyes. She looked up at the clock. 'We've still got a lot to talk about but we'd better leave it until tomorrow, Sam. You can stay here, can't you?'

'I haven't booked in anywhere,' Sam said, taking his cue from her matter-of-fact tone.

'It's late for Roz,' Nellie said. 'She wouldn't stay with Gwen without letting me know.' She went out into the hall, coming back looking relieved but embarrassed. 'She's in. The door's locked. She must have heard us talking and gone right up.' She blushed. 'The spare room's ready,' she said. 'I'll show you where it is then you can come down for some supper.'

Sam had brought a small case and she took him up to the bedroom and showed him the bathroom.

'Bit different to Johnson Street,' he whispered.

'I suppose you've got used to better too,' she said quietly.

She slipped downstairs and Sam followed her.

Until now he had followed Nellie's lead but now as she stood by the table he turned her to face him.

'I'm glad to be able to stay now, Ellie,' he said. 'But don't think I expect to walk back into your life. You don't seem bitter against me but I know I can't expect you to forget how I treated you. It'd be asking a lot to ask you to forgive me and I know it.'

'There were faults on both sides, Sam,' Nellie said quietly. 'We both made mistakes, but I don't forget the good things too. I think the best thing we can do is put it behind us. We both understand a lot now that we didn't before.'

Suddenly she was in his arms and all the reasoned arguments were forgotten. Passion swept away all the misunderstanding and sorrows and they clung together kissing as though they could never stop.

'Oh Sam,' Nellie gasped when at last they released each other. 'I was afraid I'd be too shy to talk to you and now look at us.'

'Should I still go in the spare room?' Sam whispered.

'But Roz—' Nellie said doubtfully.

'I'll rumple the sheets,' Sam said and suddenly they were both helpless with laughter.

Supper was forgotten as they slipped quietly upstairs and into Nellie's bedroom. Sam took her in his arms again, kissing her passionately.

'We've got a lot of time to make up, Ellie,' he murmured.

Strangely, as they slipped into bed and into each other's arms, neither of them gave a thought to the last dreadful night when they shared a bed. After they had made love passionately Nellie began to laugh.

'Remember, Sam, how I used to be afraid to let myself go in case you thought I was a loose woman?' she said and Sam laughed too.

'I think you've got over that, love,' he said, drawing her close again.

In the morning before he went into the other room they made love again and Nellie whispered, 'Now, are you convinced that the doctor was wrong?'

Sam grinned. 'He didn't say I couldn't do it, love. Only that I couldn't get results.'

'Rubbish,' Nellie said firmly, and he laughed and kissed her again.

'You haven't changed, Ellie. You've just added to what you were before,' he said.

'I hope you like the result,' Nellie murmured.

'Just perfect,' he assured her, before slipping away to the other room.

Why couldn't it always have been like this? Nellie thought. The closeness, the easy loving, the laughter. Perhaps we needed this separation to grow away from what our lives so far had made us. For me to get away from Janey's scheming and Sam from the things that were worrying him and making him jealous. Most of all to have time to think and to realise how much we loved each other.

She moved over in the bed and pressed her face into the pillow where Sam's head had lain. We've got the rest of our lives together now, she thought, smiling as she drifted into sleep.

CHAPTER 36

The next morning Roz tactfully stayed in her flat until Nellie went up to tell her that Sam had arrived and stayed the night. She blushed as she said it but Roz appeared to notice nothing.

'I saw his overcoat last night so I came right up,' she said. 'It was a bit late for introductions.'

'Come on down now and meet him,' Nellie said. 'Have breakfast with us,' but Roz declined the breakfast.

'I'm a bit queasy in the mornings,' she said, but she accompanied Nellie downstairs and was introduced to Sam.

'I feel I know you already,' she said. 'I've heard so much about you from Tom.'

Sam reddened with pleasure and told her Tom had talked a lot about her to him.

Nellie and Sam were stiff and self-conscious with each other but Roz asked eagerly about Sam's meeting with Tom and soon they were all talking freely.

'Wasn't it wonderful that Tom went to Foyle's window just when you were there?' Roz said. 'The small things that can alter a person's whole life!'

'I reckon all these things are meant to be,' Nellie said. 'Otherwise how could people like Prudence Gilligan see into the future?'

'I wish I could have got my discharge just a bit sooner,' Roz said wistfully, 'then I could have been in London with Tom for the book launch.'

'If you had he mightn't have met his dad,' Nellie said. 'He wouldn't have been walking round on his own.'

'And we couldn't have sat up all night talking,' Sam said with a grin.

'So you're right, Mum. These things are meant to be,' Roz said. 'Have you made any plans?'

Nellie and Sam looked at each other.

'Not really,' Sam said. 'We were too busy just sorting things out. I've got a week off from the works.'

'Then you've got plenty of time to plan,' Roz said cheerfully. She stood up. 'I'll go up to Gran's right away, Mum.'

'Bring her back for your tea tonight,' Nellie said and Roz promised that she would.

After she left Nellie and Sam sat close together planning their future. Both took it for granted that they would spend it together, but at one stage Sam said diffidently, 'Are you sure that this is what you really want, Ellie? I don't want to rush you, girl.'

'Don't worry, Sam,' Nellie said. 'This is what I've been waiting for for a long time.'

Sam drew her close and kissed her. 'It's what I've always hoped for,' he murmured.

'Anyway we can't part now, Sam. Not after last night,' Nellie said, and suddenly they were overcome with laughter again.

'If Roz only knew,' Nellie said. 'The way we were sitting there so prim and proper this morning.'

'I don't care who knows,' Sam declared. 'We're married, aren't we?'

Their practical plans were less easy to arrange, although Sam was in the mood to sweep away any difficulties.

'It'll all work out,' he kept saying.

They were unwilling to be parted again and they decided that Nellie would travel back to Reading with Sam and they would stay at a hotel until they could find a house or flat.

'The works is just outside Reading, a place called Cunliffe,' Sam said, 'but I can travel in each day.'

'I'll be the talk of the place,' Nellie said nervously, but Sam told her not to worry.

'It's different to here,' he said. 'People don't bother so much about each other. You'll like Mrs Riley. She's from Bolton.'

'I won't worry about leaving Gwen now that Roz is here,' Nellie said. 'In fact she'll probably be glad to have Roz to herself. She might even stay in the house until the baby's born.'

They decided that Sam would arrange more time off and they would return for Tom's leave.

'I wouldn't want to leave Liverpool altogether,' Nellie said, but Sam reassured her.

'I'll sort something out, don't worry. I can get a job here until I start my own place. What I've done there I can do in Liverpool. I know how to go about it now and I've got the contacts and I'll have some capital.'

'But what about your partner?' Nellie asked.

'I won't let him down, but I've been thinking. You know I told you Stan's son has been injured and discharged from the army? He's getting round fine on that artificial foot, and he was just out of his time in a drawing office when he went into the army. He can take over what I do and it might solve a problem for them too. He was a sergeant in the army so he'll know how to handle the men too.'

The weather was again cold and wet, but all they wanted to do was talk. Sam built up the fire and Nellie brewed a pot of tea and they talked, catching up on all that had happened to them since they parted.

Nellie was pleased to be able to tell Sam that Harriet was not her mother.

'Although, mind you, she was Bob's, Janey told me. I never said anything to him though,' Nellie said. 'Least said soonest mended.'

'You wouldn't want to tell him he was only your half-brother,' Sam agreed. 'What made his hair go grey?'

'I don't know. He had a lot of trouble with Meg being sick then dying, poor girl, but I didn't think he was the kind to be worried enough to turn his hair grey. You never know with people though, do you?'

'Could be a family thing like some men in a family all go bald early,' Sam said.

'We'll never know about *that*,' Nellie said grimly. 'Seeing how Janey nearly left it too late to tell me anything.'

'What a turn-up about your ma though,' Sam said. 'And that wicked old bitch kept it to herself all those years.'

'She told me all sorts of things about the neighbours that I didn't want to know when she was dying, and not enough of what I really wanted to know,' Nellie said.

She had decided that she would say nothing to Sam about what Janey had said about his family, although they decided that everything must be open between them. The old woman could have been wrong, although when Sam spoke of his mother's constant harping on bad women in ports Nellie wondered whether Janey might not have been right. There was no point in telling Sam.

He was not affected, being born before his father's illness, and he would only be hurt by the knowledge. Nellie felt protective towards Sam, realising how vulnerable he was under his tough exterior.

Roz came back in the late afternoon with her grandmother, and Gwen and Sam took to each other at once. He appreciated her common sense and her forthright comments and realised that she was a good friend for Nellie to have.

She asked him what he thought of the war news and he said. 'It's bad. No two ways about it. This German General Rommel seems to be having it all his own way in North Africa, and Singapore! How could they let that happen? The Japs just walking in and the guns all facing out to sea. And losing the two battleships.'

'That was the worst of all,' Nellie said. 'So

many local lads were on the *Prince of Wales* and some on the *Repulse*. I know two families where the sons have gone down on the *Prince of Wales* and Gwen knows more, don't you Gwen?'

'Yes. The only good news is the air raids on Germany. Giving the buggers some of their own medicine. Anyhow, as they say, we always lose every battle but the last one. We'll win in the end.'

'Of course,' Nellie said, and Sam smiled to himself at their confident tone.

We *will* win too, he thought, just because people believe it. His only worry was of what would happen to Tom before then, but he said nothing of this.

Gwen approved of all their plans and like Sam swept aside any difficulties. 'You'd be fools to part again,' she declared.

Sam had expected to find that Nellie was still part of a tightly knit community, and he was amazed when she told him how her old neighbours were now scattered.

'Katy Rimmer and her family and her mother Bella are living out at Huyton. Poor Bella lost a son and his wife and two children in the May blitz, but most of the people had gone out to Maghull to sleep when Johnson Street was hit.'

'What about Maggie Nolan?' Sam asked.

'Johnny died, y'know. Maggie's living with her married daughter. I see her now and again but it's not the same.'

Later when they went out for a walk Sam could see why the community was scattered.

He was horrified by the devastation. 'I never realised,' he kept saying.

The only person he met from the old days was Katy when she came back to shop in Great Homer Street and called to see Nellie. There was a moment's embarrassment but then she and Sam talked easily and as she left, Katy said quietly to Nellie, 'You done right to take him back, girl. That all seems far away now, doesn't it? You've got to take any happiness you can. God bless.'

They hugged each other and Nellie went back to Sam looking tearful.

'Katy wishes us well,' she said.

Sam had written to Stan Riley to suggest that young Peter might take his place in the partnership when he was ready and to tell him of the plan for Nellie to return with him. Stan wrote back almost by return, enthusiastic about the idea and saying that his wife would find a furnished house or flat. Stan and his wife met them at the station when they returned.

Mrs Riley told Nellie that she thought one of the flats was the most suitable and suggested that they went to see it the following morning.

'No use bringing furniture down from Liverpool if you won't be here very long,' she said. 'The furnishings aren't swanky in this flat but it's spotlessly clean.'

'That's all I want,' Nellie declared.

The flat was suitable and they moved in a few days later. Nellie found that Sam had been right about the lack of interest in her. So many couples were parted at this time that no one found the sudden appearance of Sam's wife at all strange.

Sam had expected difficulty in leaving his war work but when it was established that he intended to start a branch in Liverpool no obstacles were placed in his way. He was helped by Mrs Riley's eagerness to have her son in Sam's place in the works, and her brother, the chauffeur, complained to Sam that she never gave him a minute's peace.

'She thinks I can work miracles,' he said. 'God help me if I drove for Winston Churchill.'

'More ways than one of cutting through red tape,' Sam said to Nellie with a grin.

They returned to Liverpool briefly a few days before Tom's leave was due. Nellie immediately started an orgy of cleaning and Sam went to look at the rundown engineering works he was interested in.

He found the foreman a doleful individual and the works dirty and neglected. 'What's the use of it all?' the foreman said as they began to look round. 'This country's finished.'

Sam said nothing. He was looking at the grimy walls, the piles of rubbish in corners and the workbenches strewn with oily cotton waste. None of the machines seemed well maintained. He was glad when the foreman left him on the pretext of an urgent phone call and handed him over to a young chargehand he introduced as Bernie Alton.

The chargehand was a stocky young man with a round rosy face and he looked scornfully after the foreman as he trailed slowly away. 'It's being so cheerful keeps him going,' he said.

'Doesn't seem very happy,' Sam commented.

'I suppose he's got some reason,' the chargehand said. 'His two sons were lost at sea early on and his wife was injured when the house was bombed. She died three months after. I suppose he's lost heart here too.'

'Aye, I can see the place has gone down,' Sam said. 'What I want to know is why.'

'Several reasons, I suppose,' Bernie Alton said, 'chiefly that nobody's interested.'

'Including you?' Sam asked.

The young man grew red and said truculently, 'No. Not including me, but I was pushing a stone uphill on me own. I got fed up. Why should I get myself disliked trying to get things done when the foreman doesn't care and the owner's saving his skin on a Welsh farm? "Plenty of butter and eggs look you",' he added in a falsetto voice.

'I see,' Sam said thoughtfully. 'What about all this muck?' He indicated the rubbish in the corners.

The chargehand said quickly, 'That can soon be cleared up. Are you thinking of taking over?'

'Depends,' Sam said cautiously. He went round the machines with Alton finding that there was a nucleus of good machinery and that the men were discouraged rather than bad workmen. Sam was noncommittal but later to Nellie he said enthusiastically that it was just what he wanted.

Tom came home the next day and there was

a joyful reunion of all the family. Nellie was anxious not to intrude on the young couple but Tom wanted to see more of his father and Roz was willing to share him with his family, so they all spent a lot of time together.

Nellie and Sam had wondered whether Tom had a right to know about the doubts about his parentage.

'Not that I think there *is* any doubt,' Nellie declared. 'But perhaps we should tell them.'

'Sometime,' Sam said, 'but not now. They've got enough to think about now.'

Nellie agreed, but a few days later Roz was talking about the joy of waiting for her baby and Nellie said impulsively, 'I wish it had been like that for me.'

Roz looked surprised. 'Didn't you want Tom, then?' she asked.

'Oh *yes,*' Nellie said. She hesitated, then with her cheeks red and her face averted she told Roz about her worries before Tom's birth.

'The swine,' Roz said indignantly. 'And did he just get away with it? Raping an innocent little girl?'

'I was afraid to tell anyone. He said I'd get put in gaol and then I was afraid to tell Sam in case he tackled him and got into trouble.'

'I think that's terrible,' Roz declared. 'Is he still alive? Couldn't something be done now?'

'It's not important any more,' Nellie said. 'Now that Sam knows. I mean, Sam knows and he didn't go to see him because I asked him not to.'

She felt that she was floundering in deceit,

694

but Roz said brightly, 'And Tom turned out to be Sam's baby anyway,' and Nellie thankfully agreed.

Sam was right, she thought. Why burden these young people with old worries at this time in their lives? Let Roz look forward to her baby secure that there was no doubt about his family.

She said nothing about Sam being told that he was sterile. She was determined to believe that the doctors were wrong although she knew that Sam only pretended to agree with her. To him a doctor's word was law, but he believed that Chancer was right. Tom was his son because of their closeness in his early years and the strong love between them.

Nellie told Sam later that she had told Roz about the attack on her by Leadbetter. 'It just came out when we were talking about looking forward to her own baby. I didn't say anything about what those doctors told you though because I'm still sure they're wrong.'

Sam shrugged and smiled. 'What did Roz say?' he asked.

'She was all for riding out with a posse,' Nellie said laughing. She put her hand to her mouth. 'Oh Sam, I never thought I'd be able to laugh about that,' she said.

'Good thing you can, girl,' Sam said, kissing her tenderly.

I wish he could believe that those doctors were wrong, Nellie thought. I know he doesn't although he pretends to, and I know he says he feels Tom is his son because he helped to rear him. But to be sure that Tom was his son by blood would make him really happy, she thought.

There was something which Sam had not told Nellie which convinced him that he was sterile. Before leaving Canada for England he had been for a medical check and when he went back for the result he had said to the doctor, 'Am I still sterile?'

'Afraid so,' the man said. 'I didn't know whether you were aware of it.'

'Yes. I was told a long time ago,' Sam said. He said nothing about his illness on the voyage after his marriage, when Tom had already been conceived, because he was unaware that the illness had been mumps and that in a man it could cause sterility but not impotence.

Now Nellie said gently, 'It's easy to talk to Roz about anything like this. She's so matter of fact. I suppose it's with being a nurse.'

'Or being Gwen's granddaughter,' Sam said with a grin. 'She doesn't care what she says, does she? Our Tom's a lucky lad all the same.'

Sam had not wasted any time since he signed the papers for the works. He had persuaded the foreman to retire by making him a lump payment and promising to include him in the pension scheme he intended to set up. He made Bernie Alton foreman in his place.

The day before Tom was due to go back off leave he went with Sam to see the works.

'I've got the men working with me,' Sam said as they walked down. 'I've promised a bonus scheme and a pension scheme so the men will share in the profits—when I make them. Even Bernie's on my side and he's a bit of a Commie, I realise now.'

'That's a respectable thing to be now Russia's on our side,' Tom said. 'Even Mum's supporting them.'

Nellie shopped at the Co-operative Stores and she told Tom that there was a special dividend number for the Aid to Russia Fund. 'You just give that number instead of your own and your divi goes to the Fund. I always do it,' she said.

The works had been transformed in the short time since Sam's first visit. The rubbish had been swept up and the workbenches cleaned and all the machines had been cleaned down. There was a new air of efficiency about the place and Bernie was bustling about happily.

He scowled when he saw Tom and said aggressively, 'I suppose you think I'm skiving here. Ready to give me a white feather or something.'

Sam was ready to be annoyed but Tom laughed.

'You're a bit out of date, mate,' he said, 'that was old women in the first war. You might think *I'm* skiving. I've never been out of England.'

Bernie stopped scowling but he said defensively, 'My da was killed at the end of that war. Ma got no pension and she had to struggle to keep me and my sister while she was a sick woman herself. She died of malnutrition in 1921. *Malnutrition,* when my dad had given his life for this country. My sister died of TB when she was four.'

'So you reckon you don't owe the country anything,' Sam said. 'Fair enough, but it's me you're working for and don't forget it. I want a fair day's work for a fair day's pay.'

'You'll get it, Mr Meadows,' Bernie said. He suddenly grinned. 'I just had to get that off me chest.'

'There's hope for that lad yet,' Sam said as they walked away. 'At least he can laugh at himself.'

Nellie and Sam tried to leave Tom and Roz to themselves as much as possible for the last day of Tom's leave and when he had gone they returned to Reading. Gwen moved into Nellie's spare bedroom to be near Roz until they came back as it was now only two months before the baby was expected.

Sam found Peter Riley well in command of all his paperwork and having also been in contact with the official from the Ministry of Supply. 'I reckon another couple of weeks and you'll manage on your own, Peter,' Sam said.

'There's just a few things I'm not clear about,' Peter said, 'but you've left everything very straight for me, Sam. How are things in Liverpool?'

'Great. The works are looking better already but I could do with being there as soon as possible,' Sam said.

Nellie was also answering questions from Mrs Riley, and telling her how much they had enjoyed Tom's leave.

'We've got a lovely daughter-in-law,' Nellie said. 'A real good girl. Didn't mind us butting in on their time together at all.'

'I should think not,' Mrs Riley said. 'I'd like to see the girl who'd keep our Peter away from *me*!' Nellie said nothing and Mrs Riley went on. 'Are things going well for the works? You'll be anxious to get back well before the baby arrives, won't you?'

Later Nellie said to Sam, 'I could nearly feel her hand in my back pushing me. I was thinking of saying we'd changed our minds just to see her face.'

'She can sleep easy,' Sam said. 'I had a talk with Stan and Peter and we reckon I could be away in another couple of weeks.'

Less than three weeks later they were on their way home to Liverpool, happy in the thought that they would never leave it again. Nellie had written to Roz and Gwen and there was a good meal and a warm welcome awaiting them when they arrived.

Roz had booked into the Liverpool Maternity Hospital in Oxford Street to have her baby. It was very active and Roz swore that it would be a footballer. 'He must be,' she said, 'he never stops kicking,' but Gwen disagreed.

'The way you're carrying it'll be a girl, you see,' she said positively, but Roz only laughed and said that they would soon know.

On the first of August labour began for Roz and on the second she was delivered of an eight-pound baby boy. As a nurse she was given a small private room. Tom wangled a short pass and he and Gwen went in first to see Roz then a little later Nellie and Sam joined them.

Roz was sitting up in bed, her cheeks pink with excitement, and Tom sitting beside her holding her hand and gazing at her lovingly.

'Will you look at her, Nellie?' Gwen said. 'As if she's been on a holiday. When you think the way we were.'

'You're only mad because you guessed wrong about the baby, Nin,' Roz laughed.

'Where *is* the baby?' asked Nellie.

'He'll be back in a minute,' Roz said, and a moment later a nurse came in with the baby in a blue blanket. She laid him on the bed and opened the blanket. 'Look at him. The shoulders on him. Trust me to get one this shape.'

'Nurse Hopkins delivered him,' Roz explained, but the grandparents were craning to see the baby. He was almost square with broad shoulders and a mop of dark curls.

'I said he'd be a footballer. Look at his legs,' Roz said delightedly.

'More likely a boxer,' Tom said. 'Look at his fists.'

The nurse wrapped the blanket around the baby and lifted him up. 'Now who's he like?' she said, glancing round them. She leaned over to the bed to look at Sam and gave an exultant cry. She pointed to Sam's ear. 'Look at that, Roz.' She turned back the blanket from the baby's head and put her finger under his tiny ear. 'Now look at that.'

There on the little shell-like ear was the exact

replica of the nick in Sam's ear.

Sam turned and looked at Nellie and she looked back at him with shining eyes. He held out his arms and the nurse placed the baby in them.

'There you are, Dad,' Tom said. 'Your first grandchild.'

Sam lifted his head and looked proudly round at his family.

'Yes. Thank God,' he said. 'My own first grandchild.'

This Large Print Book for the Partially sighted, who cannot read normal print, is published under the auspices of

THE ULVERSCROFT FOUNDATION